Some Strange Music Draws Me In

ALSO BY GRIFFIN HANSBURY
(WRITING AS JEREMIAH MOSS)

Vanishing New York:
How a Great City Lost Its Soul

Feral City:
Finding Liberation in Lockdown New York

Some Strange Music Draws Me In

A Novel

GRIFFIN HANSBURY

W. W. NORTON & COMPANY
Independent Publishers Since 1923

This is a work of fiction. Names, characters, places, and incidents are the product of the author's imagination or are used fictitiously. Any resemblance to actual events, locales, or persons, living or dead, is entirely coincidental.

Printed in the United States of America
First Edition

For information about permission to reproduce selections from this book, write to Permissions, W. W. Norton & Company, Inc., 500 Fifth Avenue, New York, NY 10110

For information about special discounts for bulk purchases, please contact W. W. Norton Special Sales at specialsales@wwnorton.com or 800-233-4830

Manufacturing by Lake Book Manufacturing
Book design by Chris Welch
Production manager: Lauren Abbate

ISBN: 978-1-324-05079-7

W. W. Norton & Company, Inc.
500 Fifth Avenue, New York, N.Y. 10110
www.wwnorton.com

W. W. Norton & Company Ltd.
15 Carlisle Street, London W1D 3BS

1 2 3 4 5 6 7 8 9 0

part one

1984

It happened that green and crazy summer when I was thirteen years old. A stolen first line, slightly altered, because I'm not much of a writer, but I have been something of a thief. And a liar. I might as well admit that up front. It was a lie and a theft that made everything go haywire that summer.

I cribbed the line from Carson McCullers' *The Member of the Wedding.* At the moment when it happened, or at least when it began to happen, that paperback was jammed in the back pocket of my denim cut-offs as I sat on the dirty, carpeted floor of the Swaffham Towne Drug, reading teen magazines. Syrupy tang of blue Slush Puppie on my tongue. Mosquito bites stippling my legs. I want to remember myself as I was then, a girl that is difficult to grasp. What did she look like? My prize article of clothing was a pair of Nike high-tops, kept hospital white with a bottle of foamy polish. Nikes weren't cheap and I had to make them last. Everything else I wore was off-brand or hand-me-down: my wayward older sister's Lee dungarees cut into shorts, a Michael Jackson baseball tee from Bradlees discount department store, a trucker hat with Pac-Man on the front clapped over my unruly mess of hair. I wasn't good at hair, didn't know what to do with it, how other girls achieved feathered wings and lift. But I had good skin. Everyone said so. "You have good skin," they'd say, admiring what one woman at the Jordan Marsh cosmetics counter called "peaches and cream." I was a winter, dark haired with light skin that didn't tan, but only burned and peeled back to paper white. I blushed so intensely, people would laugh and tell me I was bright red, making me blaze with deeper embarrassment. As for my body, it was an unknowable zone, an overlarge assemblage of limb and belly that felt like a thing of its own making, mostly disappointing, incapable of climbing fences or playing baseball, incompetent at dancing, too heavy in its steps. Heaviness had always been with me. When skipping rope in first grade gym class, the teacher scolded me to be light on my feet. By junior high, my mother prayed that I would stop growing: "So you don't turn into a glump like your big aunt Beverly." My aunt Shirley, the smaller, told me I walked like a truck driver. I didn't mean to. That was just the way my body propelled itself through space. My shape, that enigmatic packaging, had its own design and cared nothing about anyone's objections, including my own. However the message came, the world confirmed what I felt, that my body was off in its most essential calibrations. But even with all its klutzing about, it held deep coils of feeling yet unnamed, and that summer I could sense it getting ready for something new, a quiver of arrows looking for a target.

It was 1984, still fresh in the month of June, and soon I would turn fourteen. Come September, spared the indignities of Swaffham High, I'd be off to Catholic school, an all-girls academy in a town far enough away I'd have to go by carpool. No more riding my ten-speed to the crummy public school. No more jeans and T-shirts. At Sacred Heart I'd wear a uniform, equalized in an ocean of plaid polyester. In that sameness, even with my big bones and heavy feet, I hoped to fail less obviously at girlhood. Something to look forward to. But there would also be no more Jules, my best friend, who could not bear the thought of going boyless in her teen years and opted to stay local. Our impending separation held me in a state of ambivalent attachment, either clinging or pushing away. I believed Jules was too gifted to stay behind. She excelled at science and could play any instrument you put in her hands. On the phone, she could pick out tunes on the push buttons. "Mary Had a Little Lamb." "Twinkle, Twinkle Little Star." Pink Floyd's "Another Brick in the Wall."

No matter how much I pleaded, Jules was going one way and I was going another. It felt like a breakup, like my parents splitting after my sister, Donna, left town in a blaze of shame and anger, pregnant at nineteen by a guy who knocked out dents at Mike's Gas-N-Go and gave her two black eyes before taking her to live in Texas, where she named their kid Stetson because she favored the drugstore cologne and it seemed like the sort of name people get in Texas. My mother told Donna, "Don't come back," and Donna didn't. The house was peaceful, for a little while, without the violent storms between my mother and sister. I lied to myself that I didn't miss Donna, didn't go to her bedroom to feel close to her, but only to pilfer from the records and magazines she left behind. If my mother didn't want Donna back, why didn't she turn the room into the "study" she claimed to need? Though I'd never seen my mother study anything in her life. By then she'd quit waitressing and enjoyed the luxury of a sit-down job, working as a teller in a bank. She spent her nights in bowling alleys and discos, searching for a new man, while my father, resigned to divorced life, moldered in our upstairs in-law apartment, sleeping through daylight and drinking beer until his night shift at the high school, where he mopped floors and it didn't matter if he smelled of Miller High Life. It had been years since I'd seen him in one of his bad drunks, breaking dishes and threatening murder. His resignation came as relief, but I still avoided him. Like an old fighting dog neutered into passivity, he remained in possession of a body muscled with the capacity for violence. Now and then, my parents would pass each other in the driveway, my mother dressed to the nines and smelling of Ambush for a night out, my father slouching off to his mop. It wasn't a house I wanted to spend much time in.

We had twelve weeks until high school took us into its unforeseeable alterations, and Jules and I planned to make the most of it, roaming the town's four square miles of nothing much. We'd spend whole afternoons watching cable TV at her empty house, trying to glean the workings of sex from R-rated movies like *Risky Business*. On Jules' bed we'd lie side by side in the scent of strawberry candles and girl musk, listening to the song that Tom Cruise and Rebecca De Mornay do it to in the movie, that steamy scene on the train, and Jules would insist that the word *come* had a sexual meaning, that when Phil Collins sang, "I can feel it comin' in the air tonight," it meant something different than the utilitarian word we knew. I'd try to connect *come* to the idea of sex, but nothing clicked. Come where? Jules would rewind the tape and we'd listen again, as if to a riddle we could solve with enough repetition, trying to imagine how such a simple word could hold another, more profound and secret meaning. We said the word to each other as much as possible. Over the phone it was, "When are you *coming* over?" "When do you want me to *come*?" "*Come* now." "Okay, I'm *coming*." If our mothers heard, we were certain they would not recognize our attempts to conjure carnal knowledge through the incantation of a common verb that meant only to arrive.

Our days often began in the town square, the center of our little nothing place in the world with its fire/police station, barber shop and pizza shop, a single-screen movie theater with a wilted marquee, Red Mike's Package Store ("the packie," Massachusetts vernacular for liquor store), and the Towne Drug, where the only reading material for miles could be purchased. That's where I was when it happened, sitting at the magazine rack looking through *Tiger Beat* and waiting for Jules. I was in communion with a glossy pinup of Michael Jackson in his shimmering blue jacket with the gold epaulets, arms full of Grammy Awards, when I first heard the voice of the woman who would turn my life in a new direction.

The voice was deep and movie-star dramatic, like Lauren Bacall, both the young black-and-white Bacall and the older one who did those commercials for decaf coffee because "caffeine sometimes makes me tense." I looked up, expecting an old-fashioned starlet. She wasn't, but I could see she was different. In a world of outdated Farrah Fawcett flips, lumpy corduroys, and Dr. Scholl's, she looked like Joan Jett. Shag haircut, tight black jeans and tank top with spaghetti straps, black cowboy boots traced in purple thread. Tall and lean like the rock stars in *Creem*, her arms were strong—from playing guitar, I thought, or maybe the drums. From her leather fringe purse hung a pair of feathered roach clips. She was chewing gum, snapping it in her mouth as she chatted with the pharmacist, calling him "hon," while he filled a paper bag with pill bottles. He looked irritated. The woman must have intimidated him because of what she was. I could see it in every part of her, a special electricity. She was a city person, confident and strange, a blast of cool in that incurably uncool place.

She felt me staring and looked over her shoulder, giving me that glare perfected by people who attract stares. It was the "what are you looking at" glare, the one that says, "Take a picture, it'll last longer." She sized me up and smirked in a way I took to mean I wasn't worth the effort, reducing me to the small-town kid I was, in my stupid Pac-Man hat, my too-white Nikes, copy of *Tiger Beat* on my lap. I felt my skin blush but didn't know why, except that I felt exposed, like she'd seen something true about me, something I had yet to see myself. When she completed her business, she walked out, shaking the bag of pills like maracas. "Cha, cha, cha," she said, door slamming behind her with a tinkling bell. I stood to watch her swing into a beat-up black Trans Am, golden firebird spreading its wings across the hood, and as she roared away, the stereo blasted some strange music I'd never heard, making me wish I could follow.

"Freak," the pharmacist muttered.

I didn't know what he was saying about the woman, except that she was different and maybe had provoked in him something of what she'd provoked in me, a feeling of being mediocre. We were amateurs, but she had power. I thought of "Super Freak," the song we requested from the DJ whenever our Girl Scout troop went skating at Riverdale Roller World.

"She's a very kinky girl," we'd sing as we sailed around in the disco lights, holding hands, two by two. "The kind you don't take home to mother."

•

When Jules finally rolled up to the drugstore on her Schwinn, I was standing outside in the hot sun. Atop the fire/police station, the noon whistle was going *woomp-woomp*, the warning sound of an air-raid siren they tested every day at twelve, keeping it ready for a fire, a storm, a nuclear bomb. The woman was gone. I'd probably never see her again and wanted to commit every detail to memory. Just by existing, she materialized an obscure part of myself I did not yet know but struggled toward, advancing in a way so private, my movement went unseen even by my own awareness.

Jules stood straddling her bike. Led Zeppelin T-shirt, cut-off shorts, a pair of grungy Keds with a hole in the toe. With her dirty-blonde hair tucked behind her ears, she looked like her usual self, plus the recent additions of black eyeliner, silver crucifix dangling from an infected earlobe, and gauntlets of black rubber bracelets ringing her wrists. Jules had been fourteen for months already and was well on her way to mastering its more mature contours. Born in late summer, I was the youngest in my class. My smarts kept me ahead until the changes of middle school left me struggling to comprehend concepts other kids seemed to know, as if they had access to a textbook written in another language that explained all the things that happened at basement parties and in the woods behind the baseball field. I lost Pauline Grasso, my childhood best friend, to that book. Set adrift on the choppy waters of junior high, I gravitated to Jules Cobb because she was the other odd one of our bunch and no one invited her into the woods. We were the same. And then we weren't.

"What are you doing?" she asked.

"Nothing. Just waiting."

"No good magazines?"

"Nah," I said. "Same old stuff. I already looked. For like an hour. What took you?"

It hadn't been an hour, but I was in one of those moods when I wanted to push Jules away.

"I had to wash my hair," she shrugged.

She had shoulder-length, stick-straight hair the color of wet straw and always said she was washing it when she was late. I made a face. I could see her hair was oily, untouched by White Rain, the discount shampoo our mothers bought at Stop & Shop.

She asked, "Did you get a Slush Puppie already?"

I showed her my blue tongue.

"What do you want to do now?"

We walked our bikes to the Greek's for slices of pizza and cans of orangeade in the air-cooled inside. I thought about telling Jules about the woman in the Trans Am, but she felt like something I wanted to keep to myself. If I told her about the woman's cowboy boots, her unusual air, Jules might say, "That doesn't sound cool," and I'd have to reevaluate. In her advanced maturity, Jules better understood the differences between cool and uncool, and I would've ceded to her authority, letting the woman crumble. I didn't want to lose the feeling I had. Besides, I didn't think I could explain it, how I recognized something of myself in the woman, an element I could not name because it came from the future and had not yet formed.

"Whidigat's wridigong widigith yidigou?"

Gibberish, like the word *come*, was part of our secret communications. We didn't use it much anymore, but for two years it had held us together in a world where we felt apart from most people. I don't know how we learned it, only that it came to us through the ether of girltalk, like the hundredth monkey figuring out how to wash potatoes and then transmitting that knowledge across a body of water, from one island to another, through the mystery of animal telepathy. Like those primate sisters, the feral intelligence of teenage girls is sometimes capable of collective witchcraft.

"Nothing's wrong," I said, not wanting to play along. Gibberish, I told myself, was for babies.

"Say it right."

I could feel Jules wanting to close the distance between us.

"Nidigothidiging. Okay?"

To give myself cover, I said I was really in pain over Michael Jackson, I had seen photos of him with Brooke Shields in *Tiger Beat*, and while I knew they were just friends, it reminded me that I would never be loved by him because we came from "two vastly different worlds."

"How do you think I feel," Jules said, letting the orange grease from her slice drip onto her paper plate. "The love of my life is dead."

"True. At least with Michael I have a chance."

I believed that. When I wrote my love letters to him in purple glitter pen, I believed my words would reach him and he would pick me, out of the millions, and take me to his mansion in Encino, California, with Muscles the boa constrictor and Bubbles the chimp. There were other kids—the lucky ones, I thought in the innocence of that time—who were chosen, but I would not be one of them.

"He *came* again last night," Jules said.

She meant the ghost of Dennis Wilson. Jules had a thing for dead drummers: Keith Moon, John Bonham, and now Dennis Wilson, the Beach Boy who drowned in the sea. Drummers, she liked to say, were underappreciated, and loving them felt like doing something important for the world, like saving the whales. Shaggy, druggy Dennis Wilson had first visited her a week before, emerging from the poster over her bed, the one where he sat shirtless, in dirty blue jeans, on the hood of a '55 Chevy. Dead and gone, in his suntan and windswept hair, he had stepped from the poster and lain on top of Jules, pressing his weight onto her sleeping body. And now he had done it again.

"What did he do?"

"Nothing," she said. "And everything. He was wicked heavy, and then he got heavier. I could feel him breathing. And other things."

"What other things?"

She whispered, "I could feel his bulge."

"Did he *do* anything with it?"

"He just. You know. *Pressed*."

I tried to picture it. The blue jeans, the leather belt with its chunky buckle.

"Did he come?" I asked.

"I don't think so."

"Did *you*?"

"I don't know. I felt wicked weird. Like strange."

"When you're strange," I quoted from a Doors song, "faces come out of the rain."

Jules gave a solemn nod to the profound truth of that lyric. While she loved dead drummers above all, her heart held space for other departed idols—Jim Morrison, James Dean, John Lennon—their tragic ends sweetening the impossibility of her desire.

"Maybe you were high," I suggested. *High* was something that happened, not from taking drugs, but from your mind altering itself naturally, because you were a weirdo. When you were high, your head went bubbly, your skin tingled, and you felt things that weren't there. This was part of girlcraft, the power to set your body on fire without a match, and later, to *come* without being touched. When Jules and I were really high, we were in the Twilight Zone, where everything became bright with meaning. A phone that rings twice and then stops. Seeing the time 11:11 on a digital clock. Then seeing it again. Coincidences. Déjà vu. We could also get high from green M&M's, a delicacy we hoarded in our jewelry boxes because we'd heard they produced a psychedelic effect with aphrodisiac qualities.

"Did you take any greens before bed?" I asked, handing over my pizza crust, her favorite part.

"I wasn't high," she said. "It was Dennis. He's trying to tell me something."

"Yeah, he's trying to tell you he wants to get in your pants."

In these discussions, I never stopped to ask why Dennis Wilson, a famous heartthrob who could have any of the sexiest women in Malibu or Hollywood, or anywhere on the planet, would choose to spend his erotic afterlife in the boondocks of Massachusetts to press himself against an average girl still figuring out how to manage a pimply T-zone. Such a question would not only have been cruel, it would have ruined the fun. Also, I believed the ghost story was true. Dennis Wilson chose Jules Cobb the way Michael Jackson, if he'd ever received my letters, would have chosen me, Mel Pulaski.

After pizza, we went to Jules' house, where the television got all the cable stations. Most of the houses in that depressed town were the same, plain Folk Victorians with peeling paint, crabgrass front yards, and cracked driveways veined with green. Lopsided garages hung with netless basketball hoops. Chain-link fences and American flags. "Reagan-Bush '84" bumper stickers on beaters yet to die in the annual Fourth of July demolition derby. But Jules' house was different. It was underground, a cinderblock box buried in the earth. You could see the upper part sticking out, with its asphalt-shingled roof and basement-style window wells dug in the dirt. If you had long legs, as I did, you could walk right over and sit on it.

We dropped our bikes in the scruffy grass, wheels spinning, and descended a set of concrete steps to the subterranean gloom. The place felt like a bunker, spiked with the odor of earth and iron. It was the brainchild of Jules' father, Ray Cobb, a bearded, blustery man who smoked pot and worried about nuclear war with the Russians, his paranoia shifting with the evening news, bending always toward a fear of penetration. He wore a knife in a leather sheath on his belt and stayed close to guns, working a forge at the Smith & Wesson factory, like Hephaestus, Greek god of metal and fire. He had a habit of pocketing the irregular discards, so you might find a six-chambered cylinder wedged between the couch cushions or a snub-nosed barrel sitting in the soap dish on the bathroom sink, as startling as a severed finger.

Jules plopped on the couch, its wheezing Naugahyde patched with duct tape, and pressed buttons on the TV clicker while I foraged in the kitchen. Cases of Tab soda stood stacked by the fridge, off-limits by order of Jules' mother, who'd been stockpiling cans of old Tab since she heard the manufacturers were changing the formula, replacing saccharin with NutraSweet. Ginny Cobb was a Tab fiend, and she did not want to lose the metallic tang of her favorite chemical sweetener, even if it did give bladder cancer to rats. In the mornings, instead of coffee, she heated Tab in a microwave oven and drank it from a mug decorated with a *Ziggy* cartoon: "Hang in there. Today won't last forever." This summed up Ginny's philosophy of life, in which each day was to be endured until its hotly anticipated end. Maybe it was all the saccharin that made her hair limp and her skin gray, pulled tight over the bones of her face, a pair of drop-temple eyeglasses that looked like butterfly wings alighted on the bridge of her flinty nose. Maybe it was just the meanness that dwelled inside her like an incurable condition. Ray scared me, but Ginny terrified. I didn't like being around either of them, but during the day, the Cobbs went to work, including Jules' older brother, Dale, just graduated from Swaffham High, and the house was ours. I found half a pizza in the fridge and we ate it cold, sitting in the air conditioner's chill, watching *Jaws 3* in 3D, except 3D didn't work on the television, so it just looked extra fake when the shark smashed through an underwater window at SeaWorld and started eating the park employees.

"My dad's such an asshole," Jules said.

"Yeah," I agreed, though I didn't know why, in that moment, Ray was an asshole, only that Jules always said so, spurred by some dark thought running on a track in her head. I mostly encountered Ray on Saturdays, when he was on the couch, smoking pot in front of Channel 5's *Candlepin Bowling*, and if we tried to hang around, Ginny would come storming into Jules' room, screaming at us to shut the hell up and go outside, because "Your father is trying to rest goddammit!" Ginny was always kicking us out, and on those lazy summer weekdays in the underground house, I knew it was best to get on my bike by 5:45 so I could be gone before she came home and said, "Melanie, it's time for *you* to *leave*." No one ever called me Melanie. People knew to call me Mel, the way Jules never went by Julie-Anne. But Ginny had a cold-blooded way of kicking me out, and I never resisted. She gave me the sense there was something unlikeable about me, and it generated a bad feeling inside, like my stomach agreed I was rotten at the core.

After hours of television, I said goodbye to Jules and set off. The early evening tasted sweet with settling heat on mown grass and honeysuckle, and I didn't feel like going home. I rode my bike the long way, down the farm roads where the Strawberry Festival had come and gone, and a barn full of cows made milk that got churned into ice cream at the Lazy Meadows Creamery. A bunch of kids clamored at the window, grabbing cones in their grubby hands, and I thought to stop for one but kept going. I worried about my weight. Lately, walking my body through the world felt effortful, my legs grown longer and thicker, but being on the bike made it easy, the way a whale might feel while swimming, unbound by gravity. I had worked up a good head of steam and my body felt smooth and powerful. The sun came in low across the treetops, intensifying the green of their summer-fat leaves, and the sight of that throbbing light, saturated thick with gold, urged me to stick my arms out like airplane wings.

Unbidden, the woman at the drugstore returned. I imagined her Trans Am coming down the road. She would recognize me, pull over, and I'd rest my palm against the sun-warmed metal of the car. She'd have one hand on the wheel and the other out the window, a cigarette between her long fingers clustered in silver rings, bright with lozenges of turquoise. She'd be listening to that music, a song I'd never heard, and she'd tell me the name of the band, opening up a new sonic pathway. She'd offer me a Marlboro, and though I'd never tried before, I'd know exactly what to do. The smoke would go down smooth and warm, tasting of the most delicious thing, an adult flavor, toasted and nutty, spiced with the equine fervor of cowboys herding cattle in snowy mountains. Flavor Country. And then? I could not conjure what came next. Only me standing astride my ten-speed, nodding along to the music, a breeze coming up off the strawberry fields, making the air smell of simmered sugar. Only me leaning down to see the woman's face dusted with warmth from the falling summer light. That's when it came to me, gliding with arms outstretched along that quiet road, flanked by sugar maples and pin oaks in full green, that what I had been struck by that afternoon at the drugstore was a crush and the reason I didn't recognize it was because it was a crush on a woman, the sort of thing that was not supposed to happen. Not to me. And not in Swaffham. I squeezed the brakes and stopped. I had crossed the town line, something I'd never done by myself, and hadn't even noticed.

I looked back at the sign that marked the border. "Entering Swaffham," it read, "EST. 1646," the year of witch hysteria in New England. Nearby stood a sign for Crime Watch Community. "We are watching," it read above an all-seeing eye. "We report all suspicious persons to our police department." Did my new crush make me a suspicious person? I had not asked for this. For some of us, there comes a moment when we realize that the object of our desire lies outside our known world, beyond our towns and families. Out there, we understand, there is another way to want, to have, to be. Sometimes, even when we do not venture out to find it, when we try to want only what we are given, the object comes to us. And the world, without our consent, breaks open and expands.

I took my hands off the brakes and kept going. The sky was turning violet, but I didn't want to go home. There was nothing there for me except the vapor of my mother's perfume, a lonely supper of hot dogs and baked beans, my father upstairs with his six-pack, and television, television.

2019

If you're like most people, you probably don't want to hear about how angry I am. Nobody wants to hear about my anger. There's too much of it. I got the double whammy. First the rage of living as a girl, told to be good, be quiet, be still, followed by the rage of being a transsexual man, unseen and un-understood, alone, erased, and more recently, told, again, be good and quiet. In one body or the other, girl or man, I am getting it wrong. But I'm not supposed to let my anger show. The open-minded still want their transsexuals to come with hat in hand, full of humble gratitude—*thank you for permitting me to exist*—to come with easy stories and reassurances, and to never be critical or bitter or, god help us, angry. So what else is new?

When I was a kid, adults were always telling me to smile. My face wasn't doing what it was supposed to, and it made people uncomfortable. People like Larry, my mother's hairdresser, who never gave me the kind of cut I wanted. A big, bearded, swinging 1970s type, Larry wore unbuttoned shirts, a gold medallion on his hairy chest, and half-tinted sunglasses through which you could sort of see his eyes but not quite. Once he had me in his chair, he would tease me for my downbeat disposition, calling me "Smiley" because I never smiled, and the more he cajoled, the more defiant I became, squeezing myself into a tight snarl of fury. Just once, I retaliated. "Oh, yeah?" I said. "Well, you're fat." Then I smiled, washed in the sweet relief of talking back, but when my mother slapped the smile off my face, I understood something about how power worked. Some people were allowed to dish it out while others had to take it.

It's June again. The middle of the year in the middle of my life. If I live to be ninety-six. An undesirable goal, if you ask me. There are people who want to live forever, but I am not one of them. My knees hurt when I walk down stairs, I've lost a few decibels in my right ear, and my eyes struggle to focus when shifting from far to near. Like the past, the distant is easier to see. It's the close-up things that muddle into slush, so forgive me if I sometimes lack the requisite amount of self-reflection. I'm just trying to get through the present. I am in my mother's garden, pulling weeds. Putting my anger into it, grabbing fistfuls of mugwort, dandelion, clover, whole networks of quack grass creeping rhizomatically through the soil. There's a certain satisfaction in all this ripping out. It's been a difficult year. My mother died in January and I have felt unmoored by her absence, as if something inside me that I cannot name has come loose, a tether snapped. I visited her bedside in the final days, being good, telling her she was forgiven. I had her body cremated and then, in spring, scattered her ashes in this garden, peppering the purple irises, probably the last living things my mother conceived.

Soon after her death, before I could get my footing, the scandal at school knocked me back down. The whole thing could have fizzled out, just another local drama, but then the *Boston Globe* had to do that article, stirring up a Twitter shitstorm, and I collapsed. I would not call what I had a nervous breakdown. It was more like a nervous deflation, a leaking of air that flattened me. I'm on probation, taking the summer to work on my cultural sensitivity so I can (hopefully) return to my job at the Ampleforth Country Day School as a more trustworthy teacher of English and all-around nontoxic person. Let's say, for now, that I said the wrong thing and, again, had to be slapped.

My own house is not a long drive away, but I am in hiding. Sheltering in another place and time. Tending my mother's garden, cleaning out her cluttered rooms, I feel unspooled, cast back through the years, as if I'm still glued to this world, still a kid pushing through the molasses of frustrated hours. Young time is slow time, every season a marathon, and then it sprints. People warn you about that, but it's a surprise when you feel the jolt. I'm not sure I can bear going back to the classroom. I wouldn't mind a sluggish summer. Even in Swaffham.

Much has changed about the town, but mainly at its margins. Developers ripped out the forests and installed asphalt oceans for big-box stores and restaurant chains. They paved the strawberry fields and dairy farms for a gated community with "Swaffington Farms" carved in gold letters, a made-up name meant to convey the exclusivity of a posh bucolic life. In between the new construction, the old town rots. Walmart killed the drugstore. Home Depot destroyed Satterwhite's Hardware. The sun-faded "For Rent" signs drooping in the windows give off a contagious despair that infects the surrounding houses. Gutters sag and screen doors hang limp. The town is covered in litter. Along the roadsides appear the same two items over and over: failed lottery tickets and empty mini liquor bottles, detritus of the white working-class sliding into "deaths of despair"—drug overdoses, suicides, and alcoholic liver disease. Few young people remain and the elderly are dropping fast, leaving houses to successors who can't pay the property taxes.

In the mornings, it's an accomplishment if I get out of bed before ten, stretch, and make a pot of coffee in my mother's sputtering Proctor Silex. To call it vintage would be too kind. Like me, it has merely endured. In the kitchen that hasn't changed since 1970-something, relentless in its avocado-green-and-harvest-gold persistence, I drink the coffee while grudgingly looking through the books assigned by my sensitivity trainer. I don't read in the sun anymore, not since I had a melanoma removed from my leg, and there's no shade protecting the backyard. Over the years, all my mother's trees were cut down due to some blight or another. She never bothered to plant replacements, no green leaves for carbon-scrubbing the future. A staunch denier of climate change, she'd call me up every time it snowed and say, *What global warming?* On one of the last days we spoke, it was seventy degrees when it should have been thirty. "What a wonderfully warm winter we're having, don't you think?" I couldn't stop myself from mentioning the end of human life on earth. "Oh, for crying out loud," she said, "the climate has changed a million times over the eons, what's one more change?" *Easy for you to say,* I thought. *You're leaving.*

I weed in the late afternoon, when the sun is low, and then drink a beer on the deck that juts into the yard, listing on its rotten legs. Now and then, a flock of wild turkeys wanders by. Thanks to overly successful conservation efforts, they've become an aggressive nuisance across suburban Massachusetts. In the birthplace of Thanksgiving, they get their revenge by strolling around in gangs, attacking people in driveways and breaking into houses. I admire their fuck-you attitude and like to see them strutting with their tails snapped open like fans tipped with sunlight. They are the only life around here.

In the blue house next door, the family has moved out, both parents dead. On the other side, the yellow house sits festering in foreclosure, lost by a woman my mother liked to complain about. "She's not neighborly," she told me. "You never see her come out of that house, not once." But the woman's greatest crime was to leave her lawn untended. "When her backyard turned into a jungle, Mr. Spackman mowed it for her. And the poor bastard has lung cancer. Do you think she said thank you? Not once." When the grass grew back, my mother went over and said, "You should take care of this before someone calls the town and they give you a fine." But the woman did nothing and now the yard looks like a jungle again and my mother is dead so there's no one to complain.

My long-lost sister, Donna, keeps texting to say she's coming to help with the house. She can't wait to sell it off to Jerry Logue, of Logue Brothers, Inc., a construction company that's been in town since before I was born. They own half of Swaffham and did a lot of the damage, bulldozing the forests and putting up those developments. When Jerry's letter arrived, the mailman told me he's been buying up properties, waiting for people to die so he can knock down their houses and prep the sites for a big deal. He's already bought the blue house and the one behind that, and my mother's property would round out an extra-large parcel in a commercially zoned area. Donna is hoping for a Dunkin' Donuts because she loves their coffee, but the mailman heard that Logue wants to bring in an Amazon fulfillment center, one of those vast, windowless hangars where the robot overlords have been known to puncture cans of bear repellant, unwittingly scorching human workers with pepper spray, and employees tell stories about urinating in water bottles because bathroom breaks slow productivity at the world's largest retailer. Donna says we're sitting on a goldmine, but the whole thing leaves a bad taste in my mouth. This house is where my anger was born and nurtured. I have little fondness for the place, but don't want to see it fall. There are too many memories I haven't yet fit together into a story that makes sense. Too many weeds I still have to pull.

1984

Days passed the way they do in summer when you're young in a small town, sluggish and dull, swollen with potential and no way to realize it. Without a license and a car to drive, you're shipwrecked, stranded on an empty beach you can't enjoy because you're too busy being lost. I'd sleep until noon, drink a glass of orange juice mixed from a frozen can-shaped lump, and drag a lounge chair to the backyard to lay basted in baby oil, willing the sun to bake my skin the shade and shimmer of buttered toast. It didn't. My skin boiled pink, backs of my thighs blotched as I lay belly down in a faded one-piece Stars 'n' Stripes bathing suit, chin resting on the webbing of the lounger, a paperback open in the grass below. Breathing in the smell of warm plastic. Flicking ants off the pages of that summer's reading list: *Lord of the Flies*, *The Crucible*, *The Scarlet Letter.* I could not wait for high school to take me into its dark and mature agitations.

Was that true? When I look back at that girl today, she is the citizen of another country. Her language and customs are not mine and it's sometimes hard to remember who I was then. Once the self expands, it cannot be brought back to its original shape. That girl is gone. And yet, as I watch her turn on her chaise longue, before she'd ever heard the term *chaise longue*, I know the feeling of turning in the small-town sun, adjusting the elastic of a bathing suit. I know the green abundance of the tall maple, how the leaves shuffled to white in a good wind. That tree has since collapsed, but ghosts remain, as the present also haunts the past. So when I say I could not wait for high school to take me, I say it from the point of having long ago been taken. I know where the story goes. The girl does not. Would she want to go where I have traveled? I never asked. I only went.

After cooking myself, I'd change into shorts and T-shirt, get on my bike, and go find Jules. We'd meet in the sun-scorched Square or I'd ride to her house, Walkman loud in my ears, "Don't Stop 'Til You Get Enough," my tall, heavy legs slowing as I climbed the hill of Pine Street, and then coasted down the other side. Every day was the same, summer's first weeks uncoiling, idle and endless. But on one of those long and constant afternoons, my life veered once again in the direction on which it was fixed. It started, as those days did, with a lot of nothing much.

Jules and I had wandered to the dead-end at the top of her street, where the asphalt crumbled to the woods in rubble, beer cans, and broken glass, where older teenagers parked cars at night and tossed condoms on the ground. We didn't know the word *condom*, but Jules in her wisdom called them "rubbers." *Rubbahs.* Some were dry and brittle, like snakeskins, and others were soft and glutinous. We stepped on them and watched them squish, expelling gooey interiors like crushed gypsy moth caterpillars.

"They're probably full of VD," Jules said. "Or AIDS."

I didn't want VD or AIDS, but you could only get that one if you were like my mother's most recent hairdresser, Lance, a slight young man with a golden fleece of curls. He had to close his salon because he was "sick," and everyone stopped going to him because of his scissors, his hands in their hair, because we were all ignorant and afraid.

"I bet this one's my stupid brother's," Jules said as she picked up a stick and snatched a fresh rubber, holding it to the light so it glistened yellowy white, making me wonder how Dale did it with his girlfriend, Tammy, in his shitty Mercury Cougar that smelled of rotten eggs because of something called the catalytic converter. Dale was the boy version of Jules, long and willowy, with an oily head of dirty blonde hair. I had some sort of feeling for Dale, a tangled desire—sometimes I wanted him and sometimes I wanted to be him, to inhabit his body like a hungry soul taking possession. What did it feel like to move through the world in a boy's body, shirtless and unafraid, taking stairs two at a time? To have and to be. Two desires intertwined. I wanted to ask Jules if she ever felt that way, but something told me not to.

I watched her wiggle the rubber like a fish on a line. The milky stuff had come from inside Dale, and I tried to imagine the internal mechanism of his body, slippery ducts we'd learned in biology. (Vas Deferens, Jules had noted, would make a wicked pissah name for a heavy metal band.) Dale with his greasy hair, Levi's cords and flannel shirts, dirty sailor's knot braided around his wrist. He smelled of unwashed clothes and Irish Spring. Boy smell. Jules flicked the rubber at my face and I jumped.

"Don't!"

She grinned, taking pleasure in watching me flinch, flexing the streak of meanness that ran through all the Cobbs. I called her a jerk. She flipped the rubber into a pool of green water where clusters of frog's eggs floated on the surface like tapioca pearls. Still bristling with wickedness, she poked them with her stick.

"Don't," I said again.

"You're so boring." *Boring* was her new word and it was just about the worst thing you could be. To prove I was not the boss of her, she whipped the eggs, killing the pollywogs nestled in their jelly. The queasy sight made me recall a time, maybe a year before, when she and I had watched while Ray destroyed a nest of rats in the stone wall behind their house. He poured gasoline over the rocks, lit a match, and laughed with pleasure when the animals came running out, bodies on fire, racing in horrible circles. Lately, more and more, Jules could wear her father's cruelty as easily as she wore his flannel shirts. I felt it coursing through her like a fever.

"Hey, *Ray*," I said. "What's got into you?"

"Don't start," she said.

"You're the one who's starting."

"Don't call me Ray."

"Then don't act like him."

She chucked the stick into the trees and strode back to the road where she climbed onto a boulder spray-painted with *SWAFFHAM SUKS*, sat down, and started anxiously picking at the pimples on her forehead. It was a difficult time for both of us, but I could not see that. All I knew is that I was angry at Jules for making me walk into the future without her, and I loved her more than anyone. I didn't know how to say all the cluttered emotions, so I took a seat and pressed my shoulder into hers. She stopped picking and hugged her shins, pressing mouth to knees, to the skin that smelled of vanilla lotion and unbaked bread.

"Sorry," she said.

"S'okay."

"I hate him."

"I know," I said, understanding she meant her father, that she didn't want to be like him, regretting the way he could overtake her, like the devil entering the body of a Salem girl. We relaxed, sinking into each other, and our closeness set off an unsettling throb inside my body, one I had not felt before and guessed had been put there, through some enigmatic transmission, by the woman in the Trans Am. Maybe she was a witch. I felt the commotion she aroused in me spreading, a virus in my cells, like a spell that I, too, might transmit. I smelled

Jules' hair, smog of teenage greasiness and sandalwood incense, and willed her to touch me. Like magic, she turned to the sunburn peeling on my neck and shoulders, around the straps of my tank top, and I closed my eyes, enjoying the sensation of her fingers working the itchy edges of the burn, lifting papery skin. This was how we bonded, one primate grooming the other. This was how we touched, pretending sex had nothing to do with it when it was woven into every fiber.

A blue jay cried from the white pine and, in the depths of the trees, a woodpecker drilled. Our civilized world was surrounded by nature's relentless press, tall green grass reaching for our bare legs, music of crickets in the dry yellow weeds, smell of soil and wildflowers, pine resin percolating deep in the skins of the trees. We were animals, too, trying hard to be people.

"Hey," Jules said.

"Hay is for horses, better for cows. Pigs would eat it, but they don't know how."

"I'm serious," she said and slapped my shoulder.

"That hurt."

"Listen." She sat back and looked at me. "Have you seen the tranny?"

"The what?"

"Don't you know what a tranny is?" Her tone highlighted the distance between her almost-fifteen and my still-thirteen, a distinction she fully exploited. "It's a man who thinks he's a woman, so he wears dresses and wigs. Then he goes to a doctor to have his dick cut off." She made scissors with her fingers to show how it was done. "His balls, too. The whole package."

I tried to imagine it, but could only picture my Michael Jackson doll naked, his pelvis a shield of plastic muscle, smooth and unsexed.

"So," Jules said, "did you see it?"

"What?"

"The *tranny.* My dad saw it up the packie and my mom saw it at Cumbie's. What's a tranny doing at Cumberland Farms?"

"I don't know. Buying cigarettes?"

Jules rolled her eyes.

I asked, "Why are you calling him an 'it'?"

"What would *you* call it?"

I didn't know which pronoun was right. *Him* or *her*?

"Hidige, hidiger," Jules said in gibberish. "Idigit."

"It feels mean to say *it*."

"*It feels mean*," Jules mocked. "You're so queer."

"I am not."

"You love Michael Jackson, and everybody knows he's a fag."

"Don't say that. Remember what happened to the last person who said that?"

The last person was Dougie Nesbitt, a kid in our science class who liked to taunt me by repeating, "I pledge allegiance to the flag, Michael Jackson is a fag." We were melting sugar into carbon and I was holding a test tube with a pair of tongs over a Bunsen burner when I told him to stop and he wouldn't, so I jammed the hot end of the tube into the back of his hand. It was worth a week's detention to shut him up.

"Pyromaniac," Jules said with admiration. "Let's burn something." She took a Bic lighter out of her pocket and flicked it into flame.

"Why do you have that? Are you smoking pot? You're gonna turn into a druggie."

"God," Jules huffed. "You are so boring!"

She hopped off the rock and marched toward the house. I followed. This is how it went that summer. We were bored and boring and all we could do to spark to life was to hurt each other in little ways, to abandon and follow, push and pull. I grabbed my bike from the yard and announced I was going home.

"Don't go," Jules whined, looking sad and young.

"You're being a jerk."

"I won't be a jerk anymore. I'll stop. I swear."

"You swear?"

"Cross my heart and hope to die."

As I followed Jules into the gloom of the underground house, I tried to picture the person she called "the tranny"—a man in a dress and lopsided wig, unrolling pantyhose over a pair of hairy legs. What did I know? I had never imagined such a person, but now that the idea had been introduced, I felt it taking hold, whisking through me like a tonic. I felt unsealed, open to whatever would come next, so when Jules suggested we get high, actually high, I didn't say no. She rummaged through the innards of the coffee table, through the clutter of magazines, empty Tab cans, and motorcycle parts, until she came up with one of her father's pot pipes, a brass contraption that looked like a hunk of plumbing.

"He never remembers all of them," she said. "There's stuff in here."

My big sister smoked pot, in her psychedelic bedroom with boys who came in through the window on nights our parents went out, and the smell of it always conjured Donna, skunky pine and black-light posters, a teenager going nowhere good. I'd never tried it, afraid one puff would turn me into my sister.

"This is a peace pipe," Jules said, "and we need some peace."

"I don't know." I was willing but had to be cajoled.

"Please don't be boring. Please, Melly? Just do this with me? Please."

Jules looked so sad, kneeling on the dirty carpet, lacework of acne across her forehead and black eyeliner crumbling under her pretty blue eyes, a girl trying to forge a whole self out of bits and pieces, scraps of dungaree and flannel, glued together with Aqua Net and spit. How could I refuse? I took the pipe and put it between my lips.

"You inhale," she said. "Like this." She sucked air, clamped her mouth, and exhaled. "Hold it as long as you can. Like holding your breath underwater. Ready?"

I nodded. Jules lit the Bic over the bowl.

"You're not inhaling. Try again."

I tried again.

"You're wasting it," she said, taking the pipe. I watched her suck, hold, and blow a lavender plume of smoke. She'd done this before, I understood. She had another life, private hours kept secret and separate. What else did she do without me?

"Are you feeling it?"

"Yes," I lied. "I feel it."

"Awesome. Now we can party hardy."

She went to her father's cabinet and pulled out a bottle of Wild Turkey, which seemed like a bad idea. She clapped the bottle on the coffee table with two shot glasses and knelt down. I watched her push a greasy hank of hair behind her ear and crack her knuckles, like a cartoon piano player, before she unscrewed the bottle and filled the glasses, amber liquor sloshing over the side.

"Shit," she said, wiping the drops from the dirty table with her fingers and sucking them.

"Ray's gonna kill you."

"I do this all the time. I just put a little water in the bottle. He's too stoned and stupid to know the difference."

She took one of the shot glasses and held it up to catch the weak light coming in through a high window where weeds waved in the earth above. Sometimes, in the underground house, I felt like I was at the bottom of a grave.

"Over the teeth and past the gums," Jules said. She swallowed in one gulp and slammed the glass to the table like people did in cowboy movies. "Your turn."

The whiskey tasted like dirt and kerosene.

"Don't sip it," she ordered. "Swallow."

I tipped the whole glass and the liquor scorched my throat. I fell to the floor, coughing while Jules laughed and called me a spaz. She went to the kitchen and came back with a pair of McDonald's collectible glasses full of Pepsi and ice—as always, I was Grimace and she was the Hamburglar. We'd heard the painted decorations on those glasses contained dangerous levels of lead and they should have been destroyed, but no one listened to the Massachusetts Public Health commissioner. We worried about getting AIDS from our hairdressers, not about being poisoned by Ronald McDonald. Into each glass Jules added a generous pour of Wild Turkey.

"It goes down easier this way," she said. "Take another hit."

She gave me the pipe again and this time I managed to hold in the smoke. I lay on the carpet, a dirty yellow wall-to-wall sculpted like scrambled eggs, and felt my head buzz. Being really high didn't feel anything like the Twilight Zone or green M&Ms. I looked up at the water-stained ceiling and the window where the sun-bright grass juddered in a breeze.

"I'm floating," I said.

"Me too."

Jules lay close enough so I could feel her breathing, and sang the lyrics to a song I didn't recognize. Something about wanting a kiss. Was she singing to me? I tried to imagine her kissing the boys from school, the ones she liked who never liked her back. On the inside flaps of her book covers, fashioned from brown paper Stop & Shop bags, she wrote the names of boys who lived in nice houses with in-ground pools, boys with money for Members Only jackets and Bugle Boy parachute pants that made their legs whisper when they walked. They wanted nothing romantic from Jules and me. We were not the right sort of girl. But while I was still trying to figure out what sort of girl I was, Jules was nailing her version down. She took the bus to school and sat in back, mixing with boys in grungy jean jackets and long hair, the sort who hung out in the woods behind school and came in stoned. They wore "ADIDAS" T-shirts because the letters stood for "All Day I Dream About Sex," and Jules let them grope her in the soggy school-bus stink of body odor and bagged lunches.

"Have you ever kissed a guy?" I asked. "In real life. Not dreams and not posters."

Jules kissed a poster of Dennis Wilson every night, so fervently that his lips had eroded to a pulp of white paper. I kissed pictures of Michael, too, but never with enough passion to disfigure him.

"I kiss my pillow," she said.

"You do?" I sat up, excited to discover that I was not abnormal, ignorant to the fact that every girl on earth kissed her pillow. "I do, too. Oh god, it's so queer."

"It's practice," she said. She grabbed a pillow off the couch and pulled it to her face. "I start slow," she said, kissing with little pecks. "And then," she opened her mouth and dragged her bottom lip along the fabric, moaning as she rolled onto her stomach, hips rocking back and forth. "Usually, I use my tongue, but this pillow's kind of grody."

"You lick it?"

"No der. You lick the guy's lips and he licks yours. Then, when I'm all hot and bothered, I hump the bed."

I watched her grind into the carpet, making out with the pillow's paisley swirls. They looked like the paramecium we'd seen that year through microscopes. *Cytoplasm*, I thought. *Micronucleus. Buccal Overture.* Another great name for a rock band. *Buccal*, related to the mouth. *Overture*, an introduction to something bigger.

"Do it," she said.

I had never kissed my pillow the way Jules kissed hers, and I had never humped my bed, but now that I knew these were things a person could do, I grabbed a pillow from the couch and got onto my stomach. My skin flushed as I listened to Jules' moans and felt her rocking into the carpet. Her bare foot touched mine. When I didn't move away, she slid her leg on top of mine and left it there, the shock of an electric eel, cool and slippery and full of spark. My whole body frizzed. I looked at Jules, but she was in her own world, and her leg on my leg had nothing to do with me. I was like the pillow.

A substitute for the real thing. My thoughts turned away and then, once more, to the woman in the drugstore. We were on the hood of her Trans Am, the bird's wings fanning out from my back, and the woman was—where? The image wasn't clear. Who was the man and who was the woman? I had no other way to picture this alternative pairing. It had not appeared in movies or television. It didn't show itself in teen magazines. It was nowhere. And yet it struggled to materialize inside me, a mass of fuzzy pixels.

With a groan, Jules rolled onto her back and flipped the pillow across the room. "I need more pot." She crawled to the coffee table, grabbed the pipe, and asked, "Did you come?"

"I don't think so."

"Me neither," she said and took a hit. "You have to be careful when you do that with boys. It's called dry humping. My mother told me *it can go through clothes*."

I nodded, not knowing what she meant, and took the pipe, sucking embers of sticky black ash. Jules turned on the television. We put the pillows under our heads, drank our watery cocktails, and watched *Sesame Street*, as if the childhood show could secure us to the place we were leaving behind.

Maybe the pot made me paranoid, maybe it was Jules' leg on my leg, but my mind kept turning to anxious thoughts of Brenda White. A year earlier, she and another girl had gotten in trouble for doing lesbian things. They were younger, in fifth grade, and were caught taking naked Polaroids of each other. Their names appeared in red Magic Marker in the girls' bathroom: "Brenda + Dawn = Lezzies" in a heart with an arrow dripping blood. The message stood as a warning to the rest of us, in case anyone got similar ideas, and in my diary, as if I could ward off transgression with puritanical outrage, I wrote, "So now we've got druggies, alcoholics, perverts, whores, and lesbians in our school. Jeez! What's this world coming to?!"

And yet, in the aftermath, I gravitated to Brenda. She told me that

Dawn's mother was sending her to a psychiatrist and that got her own mother thinking about shipping Brenda off to a mental hospital. I'd seen *One Flew Over the Cuckoo's Nest* on Channel 38, and I thought mental hospitals were places for crazy people, not lesbians. In a blundering way I still regret, I told Brenda about the movie and what happened to Jack Nicholson. I said I didn't think they gave lobotomies to lezzies, but what did I know? She made a plan to run away, to live in the woods behind our houses, and I took charge of the arrangements. I found a place where two boulders provided a shelter, swept out the spiders and dead leaves with a pine branch, and then gathered supplies: blanket, flashlight, toilet paper, half-eaten box of Nilla Wafers. I filled an army canteen with water and brought it all to Brenda. She looked so small sitting there between the boulders, a ten-year-old girl wrapped in a blanket, clutching a box of cookies. I didn't want to leave her, but it was time for supper. I promised I'd return in the morning and I did, hiding a pair of Pop-Tarts under my shirt, but Brenda was gone. The blanket lay twisted with pine needles, Nilla Wafers besieged by ants. Later, she told me she'd gotten scared in the night and walked home, and then she apologized, as if she had disappointed me, as if I were the one who'd wanted her to run away. Maybe I was. I can't remember if the plan was her idea or mine, only that I wanted it to succeed. Brenda disappeared soon after and I never knew where. Whatever happened, I hope she made it through in one piece. I have since tried to find her on the internet, but her name is a common one and the trail too broken to follow. Time swallows up the worst experiences and makes people forget. But I remember. How small and scared she looked in the woods. How her name, written in red on the bathroom wall, told us what would happen if we stepped out of line.

That afternoon at the Cobbs' house, stoned and paranoid, reverberating with the sensation of Jules' leg on mine, I gorged on junk food, Twizzlers and Sno Balls and more Pepsi, until all of my inexplicable emotions congealed into something simple and physical, an ordinary stomachache. I lay on the floor, moaning in discomfort, until 5:57 when Ginny Cobb arrived home in a foul mood. "Gin" they sometimes called her. Like the drink. Like the card game. From the sound of the door slamming, we could tell she wasn't feeling sunny.

"Gin's on the warpath," Jules whispered, stashing the booze in the cabinet and kicking the pipe under the couch as her mother's footsteps came down the stairs.

"What are you two twats up to?" Ginny said, dropping her pocketbook on the kitchen table. "Melanie, doesn't your mother want you home by now?"

"Mel doesn't feel good."

Ginny looked down at me. "What time does your mother want you home?"

"She doesn't care," I moaned.

She shook her head, taking in the junk food wrappers and dirty glasses sweating puddles onto the coffee table.

"You better not be touching my Tab."

"It's Pepsi," Jules said.

"You twats are gonna eat yourselves sick with this shit. Why don't you have something healthy, like an apple?"

"Ma, you don't buy apples. When was the last time you brought an apple into this house?"

"Don't get smart with me. You want to do the food shopping? You want to clip coupons and push a carriage all over Stop & Shop, buying apples, be my guest."

"I'm not the one who wanted apples."

"Melanie," Ginny said, "can you ride that bike home?"

"My stomach's really upset."

"Alright. Get your shoes on and get in the car. Both'a yiz. And hurry up. I don't have all night."

Jules and I hoisted my bike into the cargo bed of Ginny's battered Chevy El Camino. Brown on the inside and brown on the outside, mottled with patches of Bondo, the car went by the nickname Old Brownie, but Jules called it "the Shitmobile." As a maternal vehicle, it was impractical, of little use for safely hauling children, which suited Ginny just fine. The Shitmobile had no backseat, so we all sat in front, with Jules in the middle and me with an elbow propped in the rolled-down window. I knew not to put my arm out all the way, having heard many times from my mother about kids getting amputated by telephone poles, but an elbow in the open window of that gliding car felt fine. It was still light out, the heavy summer air shifting into sweetness, the way it did in the early evenings, seasoned with the fragrance of so much exuberant life, it made you want to drive all the way to Dairy Queen for a cherry-dipped while listening to a song that made you yearn for a future of driving in cars with the person you'd be kissing in the back seat. Jules turned on the radio, unleashing an electric stream of rock, Zeppelin's "Whole Lotta Love." Ginny snapped it off.

"I have a splitting headache," she said. She always had a splitting headache. When Jules tried again, Ginny told her not to push it.

"Push what?"

"You know what."

"No, really. What am I pushing?"

"Don't start," Ginny said.

But Jules couldn't help herself. She was the type to push it and she'd already started. She tried once more, spiking the volume, and Ginny backhanded her, hitting her hard in the chest. Ginny snapped off the radio and we rode in silence, Jules and me trying not to laugh.

"She got me right in the boob," Jules whispered, giggling.

"Keep it up," Ginny said. "I'll hit you 'til you see stars over your head."

It was not a remarkable ride, and I would have forgotten it if it weren't for what happened next. I have thought about this day many times, how every piece led to the next, like one of those Choose Your Own Adventure books. If I hadn't seen the woman at the drugstore, I would not have been open to feeling what I felt for Jules. Her leg on my leg, in the thrill of kissing pillows, would not have made me drown my guilt in weed, whiskey, and sugar. My stomach wouldn't have been upset, so I wouldn't have been at the Cobbs' when Ginny came home, and I would not have been sitting in the Shitmobile, waiting for the light to turn green at that moment outside the Swaffham Post Office, when we saw what we saw and life took its next turn. With a Choose Your Own Adventure book, if you didn't like the ending, you could start over and make different choices. I sometimes try to imagine writing a better story for everyone involved, but I don't possess the power of time travel, and even if I did, it's hard to let go of the way things happened.

The post office was a little cinderblock building with an American flag, a mailbox, and a rusty fire hydrant still painted in Stars and Stripes from the 1976 bicentennial. I was daydreaming when Ginny announced, "There's the tranny," pointing through the windshield at a woman by the mailbox. I gawked from the open window, straining to see something strange and amazing, but as the woman opened her pocketbook, I saw nothing unusual. She looked like any other woman, in shorts and a T-shirt printed with the slogan "I'm a Pepper." So she liked Dr Pepper. What could be more ordinary? And yet an air of otherworldliness hung about her, a mannered tilt to her posture, attentive and keen. Oddly familiar. It was then I saw the boots on her feet. Cowboy, black, stitched in purple thread. The woman from the drugstore.

I felt myself flush with heat as I watched her open the mailbox and drop in a few envelopes, an ordinary act performed by an ordinary person who was yet utterly uncommon. She looked up, brushed the hair from her eyes, and went on with her business, letting the dumb world get its fill with its dumb cow stare. The light turned green. As Ginny pulled away, she muttered something about how we all have to "keep our eyes on people like that," so I did. I kept my eyes on the woman for as long as I could, watching her recede in the mirror. She hitched her purse on her shoulder and walked down the street behind the post office, which could only mean one thing: She lived there. And if she lived there, I could find her.

part two

2019

In the watery light of dawn, the smell of cigarette smoke wakes me. My mother, I think, half dreaming. For the first eighteen years of life I was awakened by her second-hand smoke, a gray "good morning" leaching under the bedroom door. Is it the past again, my mother at the kitchen table with her Salems, mumbling curses into the *Boston Herald*? When the back door slams, I jump out of bed in shorts and T-shirt, put on my glasses, and hurry to find my sister rummaging through the cabinets. At the table sits a girl, dark-haired and tan, swaddled in the baby fat of puberty, wearing a T-shirt emblazoned with a glittery unicorn.

"You could've told me you were coming today," I say to Donna. "And so early. Is the sun even up?"

"I wanted to beat the traffic. Where's the coffee?"

"Same place it's always been. You scared me."

"Sorry, little brother. Gimme a hug, for chrissake."

She feels thick and solid, big old Donna, smelling of smoke and the artificial cinnamon air freshener from her car. The last time I saw her was at our father's funeral almost ten years ago. She looks older, hair shocked with gray, the dark absence of a missing canine in her smile.

"You look good," she says. "Not sure about the beard though. And you're losing your hair. Do the hormones do that?"

"Yeah, well. Getting old."

"If you're old, I'm fucking Methuselah." She sucks her teeth and sets about making the coffee. "You had such pretty hair, too. Remember how I used to braid it? When you were a little girl?"

"Who's this?" I ask, ducking this uneasy line of conversation and gesturing to the kid, who's doing a good job of ignoring us, nursing a bottle of Coke and staring into the cracked screen of a battered smartphone.

"Dakota," Donna barks. "Say hello to your Uncle Max."

"Hello Uncle Max," the girl mutters, not looking up.

"You had another kid?"

"Kota's my eldest granddaughter. Stetson's girl. She's ten."

"I'm *twelve*," the kid says, eyes on the screen.

I strain to recall a baby photo of someone who might have been this girl, tucked into a long-ago Christmas card, but I can't be sure. "How is Stetson?"

My sister shakes her head and says, "I'm stuck raising this one while he's in jail and his baby-mama's doing god knows what. Probably selling her cooch for dope. She's Mexican. They're all over New Hampshire now. Can't keep 'em out."

I say nothing to this, avoiding conflict, and look at the girl. She doesn't appear to be listening, but kids are always listening. I usher Donna out to the deck where we sit with our coffees and she tells me about Stetson's problems, how they started in Texas and continued in New Hampshire, up in the North Country, where they moved years before to some shit town shittier than the last and the one before that. Most recently, he was arrested in a motel room where he'd been mixing Fentanyl with heroin, chopping it up in a Nutribullet blender that exploded in his hand while he was pressing down the canister.

"Almost took his thumb off," Donna says, lighting another cigarette. "We joined a class action suit against those Nutribullet bastards. They explode all the time. You would not believe how many people get injured. Every single day. Cut-off fingers. Third-degree burns. Just from making smoothies."

"Or mixing Fentanyl with heroin," I add.

"Those blenders aren't supposed to explode on people, are they? Now Stet's doing five years for possession with intent to distribute."

I sip my coffee, stifling an unhelpful impulse to defend the manufacturers of Nutribullet.

"Five years," she repeats. "Dakota will be almost legal when he gets out. She's my problem 'til then. Know anyone who wants to adopt a kid? She's housebroken."

I smile at the joke, or what I assume is a joke. "Is she much trouble?"

"Nah, she's a good kid. Wicked smart. Maybe too smart. I just figured my mothering days were over. Between Stet and his sisters, and all their kids, I haven't had my own life. Since I was nineteen, all I've done is raise babies and bust my hump. I'm tired, Max. I want to go on a Caribbean cruise."

I try to imagine my sister on a cruise ship, floating in a hot tub with a glass of rum punch, paper umbrella stabbed in a pineapple wedge, blue expanse of ocean ruffling past. I know so little about her life, only that it's been hard and mean. I hope she gets her wish.

"Speaking of mothers," she says. "What'd you do with her ashes?"

"I put them in the garden. Her favorite spot."

Donna squints toward the flowers at the edge of the yard. "I would've been here," she says, "but the shit with Stet really hit the fan."

"It's okay," I say, recalling the nights I spent alone with my failing mother, rubbing lotion into her brittle skin and soothing her fears of death. Being good. "I've been weeding the garden, keeping it up."

"Why bother? It's gonna be paved over once Dunkie's moves in. Or Amazon or whatever."

"Donna," I start, but it's too early to argue.

"Me and her never really got along. I was a daddy's girl. And you turned out to be a mama's boy."

It's true. She resembles our father, the way she moves, with a sense of resignation. I see it in the way she stubs out her cigarette, dragging it against the edge of the table and tossing the butt to the yard. *Why bother?* I'm more like my mother, who at least tried for something better. You could say I succeeded, though it was never easy. As my mother liked to put it, I've had a *tough row to hoe.*

When Donna asks me to catch her up, I hesitate, aware of the survivor guilt I feel for overcoming the difficult conditions of this life, if you can call what I have done *overcoming*; for arriving in a better place than my sister, anyway, climbing from one class to another. I give her an abridged account of the past decade or so, hoping my life doesn't sound too easy. After I finished my master's degree in education, "Which I am still paying off," I add, I took a job teaching high school English at Ampleforth Country Day, a feeder to the Ivies. The students are radiant with privilege, like well-groomed horses, sleek and healthy from life-long infusions of organic foods and constant encouragement. I envy them. My brightest seniors know more than I did by the time I finished college. In the full flower of late-stage capitalism, the students behave like demanding consumers, rating every purchase, including teachers. I am a luxury commodity. Tuition is $50,000 a year, and I must perform perfectly. That means I must never frustrate or be too challenging. If I press an idea, I might make my students feel *unsafe*. They want me to be like their parents, a snowplow clearing the road of emotional bumps. To be alive, I tell them, is to be uncomfortable. My exceedingly comfortable students bristle at this. They talk about PTSD like they get shipped off to war zones every June instead of summering in posh Cape Cod houses where they float on clouds of hydrangea. Friends who teach working-class kids at public schools don't encounter this phenomenon—to demand emotional safety, to expect it as an entitlement, requires privilege. Must be nice. Unlike other faculty members, I refuse to walk on eggshells around these kids. I suppose that was my contribution to all the trouble.

"Don't get the wrong impression," I say, though I can't tell from the glazed look on my sister's face what sort of impression she's getting. "I'm not one of those edgelord types who go around pushing people's buttons. I was Teacher of the Year three times. They used to love me."

Donna doesn't nod or indicate any sort of understanding.

"Anyway," I conclude, "it's become a difficult place to work. Much worse since Trump. He's triggered everyone, left, right, and center."

Donna sucks her teeth and says, "My liberal little brother. You haven't changed. You know I'm a proud deplorable, right?"

"Let's not go there."

She shrugs and asks about the trouble at school.

"Just some mess I got into with pronouns and gender stuff," I say, keeping it vague, but it's enough to provoke my sister's outrage. I am also outraged, but mine is the righteous indignation of a middle-aged, third-wave feminist transsexual from the 1990s, bitter about his own community, while Donna's is the fury of an outsider looking in. I shouldn't be talking to her about this, but it's too late. She's already going on about snowflakes and attack helicopters. (If you're not familiar with the transphobic meme "I Sexually Identify as an Attack Helicopter," please google.)

"No one actually identifies as an attack helicopter," I say, feeling protective of my people. "Mermaids and unicorns, maybe, but—look, the kids are expanding gender and it's messy. You can't make something new without breaking shit."

"In California," Donna says, charging full steam ahead, "they're forcing kindergarten teachers to teach kids there's fifteen genders. Fifteen! And if the teachers refuse, they can be put in jail."

I tell her she's been "grossly misinformed" and needs to "develop a critical mindset." It is the wrong response, in the wrong tone of voice. I hear myself sounding coastal and elitist, which, let's face it, is exactly what I have become.

"You don't know what you're talking about," she says, her voice pitching toward a histrionic register I recognize from our mother. The point of no return. "You think you know everything about everything, but you don't. I bet you don't even know who had the most slaves in America."

"Where is this going?"

"Guess!"

"I don't know. Thomas Jefferson?"

"Wrong! You are totally wrong. The guy with the most slaves was a Black man."

"Please tell me you don't believe that crap. Are you *that* stupid?"

At this, my sister gets to her feet and puts her finger in my face.

"*You* don't know shit! Teacher of the Fucking Year. If you're so smart, how'd you manage to screw up your life?" It's a fair question that I cannot answer. Donna goes *hmpf*, like she's won the argument, and snatches her cigarettes from the table, making me flinch. "Teacher of the Fucking Year," she repeats, opening the screen door of the house. "You wanna know something? I might've given Ma a lot of trouble, but at least I wasn't a transgender. She talked to me about it. I bet you didn't know that. She said you broke her heart."

She means to wound me, and she does. When she goes inside and slams the door, I take a breath and look up into the soft blue light of morning. It's going to be a long summer.

1984

The next morning, as soon as I heard my mother's car pull out of the driveway, I jumped out of bed, ate a Pop-Tart, and began my search for the woman the people of Swaffham called "the tranny." On my bike I cruised the streets behind the post office, surveying houses and driveways, searching for any sign—the Trans Am, a pair of cowboy boots left on a porch. I saw only dogs chained in driveways, lonely basketball hoops, and scruffy front yards. I saw old women on slumped porches and cats dozing under pickup trucks. Though I was only a mile from my house, those unfamiliar streets made me feel far from home. My personal radius consisted of a few blocks, a few roads, another few blocks, so my world was even smaller than that town. But now I ventured into unknown territory. As I cruised Woodbine Street and Wedgewood Road, Fowler Terrace and Chickatawbut Lane, names I'd never heard before, I wondered if I'd be branded a "suspicious person," if the police would come and question me. Little kids in bathing suits wet from a sprinkler came running at me, chucking rocks and shouting, "You blew it, sucker!" They could see I was strange.

My search went on all week. When I'd see Jules in the afternoons and she'd ask what I did all morning, I'd tell her I was sunbathing and reading. She believed me, because why wouldn't she? I'd never lied to her in my life. Not yet. I told her I was bored with sitting on her couch, watching cable and eating junk food. I didn't tell her I was afraid of being alone with her, afraid of kissing pillows and what that might inspire. I suggested we go out and see what lay beyond the boundaries. We rode our bikes to the Dairy Queen just over the town line, ordered cherry-dippeds at the take-out window, and ate them boldly in the parking lot by the Hell's Angels on their motorcycles, ponytails snaking down the backs of their leather vests, tongues clicking at us like we were cats. We pushed through a chained fence at the abandoned Swaffham Drive-In and rode our bikes over the asphalt humps that once lifted the front ends of cars toward the broken screen. But the farthest we traveled was to Hooley Park, a destination made more seductive because it was forbidden.

Straddling Swaffham and the neighboring town of Brixton, the park consisted of six hundred acres of public ponds and lakes, deep forests, hiking trails, and winding roads, all built in 1915 by W. F. Hooley, a philanthropist who dedicated the park to the betterment of the local factory workers and their families. Around the late 1960s, the park fell into a slump and never recovered. Parents still took their kids to feed the ducks, and in winter they went sledding down Old Indian Hill, but the crimes piled up. A prostitute choked with a string of rosary beads in the front seat of a Chrysler LeBaron. A woman's body dumped in the lake by the famous Turnpike Killer. Two Boy Scouts raped, stabbed, and set on fire, their field notebook found in a culvert, laced with bloody fingerprints. Earlier that spring, an alligator grabbed a toddler by the ankle and tried to drag her into the duck pond. Someone must have acquired the reptile as a baby, a souvenir from Florida, and set it free after it outgrew the bathtub. It was not the first alligator spotted in the pond at Hooley's and it wouldn't be the last. If the cops weren't hunting alligators, they were hassling the gay men who went to Hooley's to cruise. Each spring, like migrating birds, the men arrived to stroll the wooded pathways, finding a few minutes of consolation in the wild honeysuckle, leaving condoms and "other paraphernalia" by the wayside. That's what the police called it in the *Swaffham Sentinel*, making me wonder what sort of paraphernalia they meant.

"Dildos," Jules said as we sat on a bench by the pond, keeping an eye out for gators. "Rubber dicks."

"Come on."

"I'm serious. Rubber dicks. My brother found one. He hangs up the hill with all those kids and he found a dildo in the woods. He said it was *black*. Not like people black. Like *black* black. I don't get it. If you're gonna get a rubber dick, don't you want it to look like the real thing?"

I shrugged. I had no idea if you'd want your rubber dick to look real or unreal.

"Is Dale up here today?" I asked, imagining him at the hangout where older kids drank beer and blasted car stereos. My sister had once been a queen of that place. There's a photo of Donna standing on the hood of a car, bellbottom jeans as wide as the feathering on a draft horse's legs, her fist to the sky, rock and roll.

"I don't know," Jules said. "I don't keep tabs on my stupid brother. What are you, in love with him?"

"No, gross. But what if he sees us? He'll tell your mother. Then she'll tell my mother. And I'll be dead. Hooley fucking Park?"

"He won't tell. He's an asshole, but he's not a snitch. Look what he gave me."

She reached into the neck of her T-shirt and pulled a joint from her bra.

"Jesus, Jules, there's cops all over the place."

"They don't care about us. They're looking for queers."

Queers like me, I thought.

"Come on," she said. "Let's smoke up."

She took her bike and I followed, through a dirt parking lot to a pile of rocks that jutted into the pond. We climbed out to a flat part where we could sunbathe, the gray stone beneath us warm and spotted with lichen. A flock of ducks came quacking for food.

"Get outta here," Jules yelled, shaking a Bic in her fist. "We got nothing! Go on!" She put the joint between her lips, lit it, and held her breath, saying, "Fucking ducks."

"Fucking ducks," I muttered after a hit, enjoying the strain in my voice, and we both cracked up, smoke coming out of my throat like fiberglass, so I was laughing and coughing at the same time. We lay back and closed our eyes, hiking up T-shirts to expose our bellies to the sun. The fine, golden hairs on Jules' arm touched mine and I dared not move, enjoying the electric charge of proximity, until my brain went soft in a sun-drugged stupor. We lazed awhile, drifting on our rock, one of the many glacial erratics left long ago by a sheet of ice. We lived on a scatterplot of prehistoric rubble, points marking so many scenes on the map of our young lives. When I was among them, they lifted me up, those boulders whose bodies I still recall. In my memory, it's like running a hand over the back of a beloved elephant, knowing every curve of that rough skin. I felt Jules press closer. She made a small animal sound and put her head on my shoulder, nudging into me like a dog getting comfortable.

"Sometimes," she said, dreamily, "I forget you're a girl."

I stayed still, not wanting to scare her away, and felt my heart bang. In the water, the ducks softly splashed. I said, "You know what my mother always says?"

"What?"

" 'Fuck a duck.' "

Jules laughed into my T-shirt, "What does that *mean*?"

"I don't know. 'Fuck a duck.' She says it all the time."

Jules sat up and bellowed, "Fuck a duck!" And then we were both bellowing across the pond, daring the alligators and rapists and killers to come for us. But the only one to show up was Dale, driving his shitty Mercury Cougar that stunk of rotten eggs. He pulled into the dirt lot and got out to take a piss against a tree.

"Quiet," Jules said in a hush. I felt caught, but wasn't sure what for, being at Hooley's or enjoying the charge of Jules' body, her head on my shoulder, the momentary forgetting of my girlness.

"What are you two twats doing here?" Dale zipped his fly and jumped onto our rock in his cut-off shorts and striped tube socks. He had his T-shirt off, tucked and swinging from his belt, and he loomed over us, sending out the smell of Irish Spring, cigarettes, and sweat.

"Don't call us that," Jules snapped.

I shaded my eyes with a hand and looked up at Dale, catching a glimpse inside the leg of his shorts. He wasn't wearing underwear and what I saw looked like a plum, purplish pink. I blushed and turned away.

"Ma calls you twats all the time."

"You're not Ma."

"Are you smoking a joint? Is that mine? You little fucking thief. Gimme."

"Fuck you. You *gave* it to me."

"Like fun I did! Gimme or I'm telling Ma you came up Hooley's on your own."

Jules made a face and handed what was left of the joint to Dale.

"The lighter, too."

He shook the Bic in his fist, lit up, and took a big, greedy hit.

"Alright, come on," he said. "Get outta the park. It's not safe."

"Like you give a shit."

"This place is full of freaks. I saw that tranny up here, cruising around. You think I'm gonna let my little sister get raped by that freak?"

I felt myself turn hot with something like anger.

"Come on," Dale said, kicking Jules with his sneaker. "Quit fucking around."

Jules smacked him in the leg, told him to fuck himself one more time, and stood up. We grabbed our bikes and walked to the road, Dale close behind in his car, tires crunching on the gravel.

"Are you gonna follow us all the way?"

"Maybe," he said from the window. "Maybe I'll swing back around to make sure you're out."

He cranked up the radio—Jethro Tull, "Bungle in the Jungle"—and peeled away. Jules flipped him the bird. We got on our bikes and rode back to town, stopping at Coogan's Superette for sticks of Fla-Vor-Ice to take to the cemetery on the main street, where we could watch the traffic and hope for a "good accident." Part of a busy state route, Central Street was a two-way road divided by a grassy median gone wild with blue chicory flowers. A regular spot for car crashes, it was the one street in town where something might happen. We sat on the graveyard's stone wall and sucked sweetness from the plastic sleeves, waiting to be struck from our boredom. Some guys in a Camaro slowed down to say hey. We ignored them, they called us lezzies and drove off. That happened so often, we hardly noticed, only now the word had achieved an extra tang. What did Jules mean when she said she forgot I was a girl?

I looked to the graves. Under the grass, deep in the seventeenth-century dirt, lay the bones of Aldens and Bradfords, Puritans who would've burned us as witches if they'd had the chance. And why not? Our heads were lousy with impure thoughts. Salem gets all the glory, but Swaffham had its share of accusations, women damned by spectral evidence, found guilty by water test, banished to a wilderness creeping with timber wolves. Two were hanged on Swaffham Green. Sent to hell for being strange.

"Hey," I said.

"Hay is for horses," Jules answered, "better for cows. Pigs would eat it, but they don't know how."

"Nevermind."

I jumped off the wall into the grass and Jules followed. We read the names on the gravestones and wondered how the people had died, feeling extra bad for the babies who never had a chance, imagining our own romantic deaths, another kind of erotic charge, our girl bodies laid vulnerable and bare in some exquisite finale in which anything could be done to us without the trouble of our desire or consent. Jules lay down in front of a headstone and closed her eyes, a plucked hawkweed flower in her folded hands. To die young was to die beautiful, and against the grass and clover, golden-haired Jules was beautiful. I suppressed the urge to lie beside her. One word Dale said kept echoing. *Freak, freak, freak.* I kicked the grass, picked up the brown sphere of an oak gall and peeled open its papery skin. The wasp had flown. Jules lay dead and I felt alone. There was so much I could have said, but I didn't know the words, and this wordlessness tumbled inside me, making so much static, I took a deep breath and let out a scream, the loudest I could make. Jules came to life. We took turns screaming, for the thrill of it, the way girls do, feeling the power of our lungs, our magnificent shrieks echoing off the trees, the stones, the clouds. Someone, surely, would think we were being murdered and call the police, but no one did.

•

That night my mother came home from work and started the Hamburger Helper. I did not move, except to crawl to the TV to give the set a smack, to knock out the snow from *The Brady Bunch.* From the kitchen she called, "Turn it off."

"Why?"

"Don't ask why, just do it. Come help me."

"Yes, Irene."

"Don't call me Irene."

"Yes, Ma."

"And don't call me Ma. You sound like a goat."

I moaned as I got up from the floor and dragged my feet to the stove where my mother was pushing pink piles of ground beef around a sizzling pan. She was still dressed for work, in her tuxedo-ruffled blouse and long denim skirt, the blue boat shoes she'd started wearing with slouchy ankle socks, like she was trying to be young and preppy. She was neither. Irene Pulaski was forty-six years old, a former waitress turned bank teller, and she wasn't getting anywhere near the Newport Regatta.

"Take this," she said, handing me the wooden spoon. "Don't let it burn. I have to do my exercises."

She'd started taking aerobics classes at the YWCA and now she was practicing at home. While I stirred the meat, she changed into a purple leotard with matching legwarmers and played her new *Jane Fonda's Workout* video.

"I thought you hated Jane Fonda," I said, stirring vigorously so the pan clicked against the burner grate, making a racket. "You called her a Communist."

"Don't stir so hard," she said, sitting on a towel on the living-room carpet. She stretched her neck and shoulders, flinging her arms up and over to the side while Jane counted, "One, two, three, and four." As the workout progressed, the extra people on the videotape shouted, "Woo!" My mother copied them, calling out her own "woo" from the towel, a threadbare mustard-yellow rag spotted with bleach stains, miles away from a nice exercise mat like the ones on TV. I considered pointing this out. I also considered pointing out that her legwarmers were unnecessary when it was eighty degrees and the air conditioner was off because it "cost an arm and a leg" and she didn't "work for Edison." I wanted her to feel bad about herself.

"The meat's ready," I called, figuring she'd take over.

She told me to follow the instructions on the box. Then she got on her back and started thrusting her pelvis to the ceiling. I looked away, embarrassed. I didn't want Hamburger Helper Cheeseburger Macaroni and I didn't want to make it myself. I wanted my mother to do it. More than that, I wanted her to cook something real. Before Donna left and my father moved upstairs, she cooked real food, roasting chickens and mashing potatoes, making salads with iceberg lettuce. She used to make me eat vegetables, forcing me to sit alone at the table until the broccoli went cold. Later I understood there was something wrong with mothers who didn't serve vegetables, who fed their kids trashy meals from boxes. Mac 'n' cheese. Shake 'N Bake. My mother no longer cared if I ate vegetables. She didn't seem to care if I ate at all. What she cared about was losing weight and finding a man.

I dumped in the pasta, water, milk, and the contents of the special sauce packet. Then I noisily banged the mixture around in the pan, making it slop over the side.

"Just give me five minutes of peace," my mother called. "Will you please?"

It wasn't five minutes. It was never five minutes. I had to do everything. I set the table and filled the glasses from a jug of a new thing called spring water. According to the label, it came from natural springs up in Maine and was totally foreign. In addition to aerobics classes, my mother had been attending what she called "my self-esteem seminar," and she came home with all kinds of ideas for people who wanted to "get the most out of life," including a set of cassette tapes with titles like *Dare to Dream*, *Wants and Desires*, and *Perceiving Your Life as It Is*. Now she was on a pure-water kick. Even though it cost money we didn't have when water from the sink was free. She said our tap water was "loaded with poison." She was so into spring water that whenever I tried to fill my glass with Hawaiian

Punch, she told me to "dump that shit down the drain" because it was "loaded with poison." I didn't understand how Hamburger Helper was okay, but Hawaiian Punch—which she bought herself—was toxic. Cigarettes were okay, but tap water would kill you. My mother had stopped making sense.

She sat at the table in her leotard and legwarmers, her freckled chest flushed red, the feathered wedge of her out-of-style Dorothy Hamill haircut pushed back by a terrycloth sweatband. Looking back at that scene today, I see a still-young woman, a single mother making little money, trying to revive her life, to regain her figure, to re-enter the world of love. She must have been terrified. But I could not see any of that. I saw only my mother, not doing her job.

"Gail is having a dinner party in a few weeks," she said, poking at her plate, moving the food around without eating it. "She says there will be eligible men there. 'Men of quality,' she said. Doctors and lawyers."

"Who's Gail?"

"That new friend from my self-esteem seminar? You've heard me talk about Gail. She drives a Mercedes and lives in Newcastle-by-the-Sea. Where all the nice houses are."

"Everybody just calls it Newcastle. Nobody says the 'by-the-sea' part."

"Well, Gail does and she lives there, so I guess she knows what's what."

"Is she rich?"

"Her ex-husband is loaded. He's a heart doctor. She got the house and the car, but not much money. I mean, more than we have, but."

"But she still needs a seminar for her shitty self-esteem?"

"Watch your mouth. Gail is a high-quality person. She can introduce me to other high-quality people. Don't you want that for us?"

I'd never heard her use the term "high quality" before. Were we low quality? Gail, my mother went on, was *evolved*. She'd already had her *self-esteem breakthrough.* I figured it must have been Gail who'd advised her to start drinking spring water, even though it cost 1,000 times as much as tap water, a fact I'd read in an anti–spring water op-ed in the *Swaffham Sentinel.*

"If we're going to be high-quality people," I said, "does that mean we get to hire a maid? Because I don't want to have to keep making my own supper."

This was the wrong thing to say, and it set us off on a bad course.

"You're fourteen now, Melanie. You're going to start pulling your weight around here. Learn some responsibility. So you don't end up like your nitwit sister."

The *Melanie* stung.

"I'm still thirteen," I said. "Technically. Or have you forgotten when my birthday is?"

"Don't get smart. When I was your age, do you know what I had to do? Every Saturday, I had to scrub the floors. With a wire brush and hot water. Until my hands burned red. And then I had to feed the chickens. Pick worms off the tobacco leaves. We lived on a farm and my father was a tyrant. You don't know how lucky you are."

"Right. Grandpa tortured you. You were a regular Cinderella."

"You have no idea," she said. She put down her fork and grabbed her cigarette case, made of silver mesh that glinted hard and metallic. She lit a Salem Light 100, took a drag, and exhaled before adding, "You've got it made. Made in the shade. You have no idea. Your life is a cakewalk."

I watched her pick up her spring water and drink it down in loud gulps, loading up on self-esteem. I didn't know what a cakewalk was, but I knew my life wasn't that. It wasn't sweetness and froth. But my mother never noticed this. Nor did she notice the good things I did. In her eyes, I was lazy and selfish and didn't lift a finger.

"I mow the lawn, don't I?" I said. "I take out the trash and clean the barrels. I never get any credit for that."

"Credit? Who gets *credit*?" Her voice spiked to a higher register. "Nobody gets any *credit*. You just *do*. You think I get credit? You think I get a *prize*? A gold fucking *star*? Who do you think buys your food and washes your clothes and scrubs the toilet? It's not little *elves*," she said, pointing her cigarette at me. "You don't see me asking for credit. Oh, no. No, no, no. You're in high school now. Things are gonna change around here. I have a life to live and you're going to *work*."

"I work! I do *all* the heavy stuff Dad used to do. You don't do one thing outside."

"You know what you sound like? A spoiled rotten bitch."

"Fuck you," I said, instantly regretting it.

I saw my mother's eyes turn hard, a deadly look she'd perfected during the raising of my sister, and I knew what came next. I apologized frantically, trying to reel it back, but it was too late. She slapped me, hard, in the face. I ran to my bedroom. My mother followed, unleashing a tirade the likes of which I had not seen since my sister lived at home. With her boys and her drugs, with her *smart mouth*, Donna had always been the target of my mother's anger, providing a shield that kept me mostly unscathed, but Donna was gone and I wasn't a child anymore. I was a teenager, the worst thing a girl could be, full of will and staunch defiance. I would need to be broken.

In a box of old cassette tapes, I have one marked "Mom: Summer 1984." It is a recording from that night, the one that kicked off the difficult years, when any moment could be punctured by my mother's scorching rage. As she screamed her way in and out of my room, pacing back and forth across the house, I pressed Record on my boom box where a blank tape waited, forever poised for the right song to come on the radio. I must have done it to exert some control. My mother was berating me, frightening me into silence, but I would put her on tape. I would have evidence. Proof that I wasn't walking on cake. Once, years later, I played the tape for a therapist so he could tell me, "Yes, that was bad," something I could not tell myself. To transcribe it here feels like betrayal, an unfair exposure of my mother at her worst. Later in life, after we reconciled, she would have been ashamed to hear how she'd sounded. But she's gone now and needs no protecting. My thirteen-year-old self pressed the Record button because she needed this document to be preserved. To be witnessed.

"You don't do one thing around this house unless I ask you," my mother wailed, loud enough so I could feel her voice vibrating inside my bones. "Not one fucking thing. Unless I ask you. You take out the fucking garbage. Big fucking deal. There isn't one fucking thing that anybody does for *me*! Not one fucking thing. But they *take* from me. They take everything from me. *Gimme, gimme, gimme.* And then if I ask you, I get a fucking song and dance, like I'm asking you to do something *way* out of line. I raised a fucking nummy. You're a real numb-nut, you know that? You don't do one fucking thing! What's wrong with you? Huh? When are you gonna start helping *me* and being part of *my* fucking life? Why do I always have to be part of *your* life? What's my life? Shit? Shit! That's what I am. Shit! I've been shit on my whole fucking life. Shit! Your father shit on me, your sister shit on me, you shit on me. Do you know you shit on me? *Do you realize you shit on me?*"

I must have smirked, because she told me to "Go ahead and laugh, you idiot," to which I quietly replied, "I'm not laughing." It is startling to hear my girlhood voice, soft and young, trying and failing to exert itself, simple in its lost accent. *Um not laffin.*

My mother went on, her volume rising and falling as she paced in and out, "I used to do things for my mother to make her life easier. Because I *cared* about my mother. I didn't just care about *myself.* My mother worked hard on the farm. I told my mother I loved her. You don't even fucking say it. You don't even have the fucking decency to say it! I don't get love from you. I don't get understanding from you. Oh, but I get plenty of ridicule, that's what I get. You want to be ridiculed? Live with you! I get no love. You don't even know what the word *love* means. It's been given to you a hundred times over and all you do is reject it. You're a fucking nitwit, you know that? Do you know that? Huh? Do you know you're a fucking nitwit?"

When she walked out of my room again, I stopped the recording, afraid of being caught, but the screaming went on. She stalked the house, walking to the kitchen, the living room, and back to my room. I was ungrateful and selfish. I was spoiled. Rotten to the core. If I didn't love and respect her, she said, maybe I should find another place to live. But I had no place to go, so I stayed, unmoving on the edge of my bed, willing myself not to cry. I focused on making my insides still and cool, the bottom of a stream high in the mountains. Like the place where the spring water came from. I made myself into the mountain on the label, covered with ice, until I felt myself freeze into a position I would practice again and again, one that would take the rest of my life to defrost.

Finally, her voice ragged with exhaustion, my mother told me to clean up the goddamn kitchen while she went outside to get some air. When I finished washing the dishes, I took out the garbage and dragged the barrels down the driveway for morning pickup. I took a moment to breathe as I gazed out over the quiet street, listening to the tinny music of a neighbor's transistor radio, a barking dog, the scissor sound of a sprinkler. It was the golden hour, that time in a summer day when the sun slants low and makes everything more beautiful than it really is.

"Hey, kiddo."

I turned to see my father standing in the front yard, holding a cigarette in one hand and a can of beer in the other. It was a rare sighting. He almost never left his La-Z-Boy except to go to work, and entire weeks could pass without a sign of him other than the grumble of his car leaving for another graveyard shift. Now the sun sparked the grass at his feet and made his beer gleam like a jewel. He looked almost young in that light, not yet ruined by the disappointments of life, and I wanted to climb onto his shoulders, to be held high above it all, but those days were a long time gone.

"Couldn't sleep," he said. "Too much yelling." He walked over and put an arm around my neck, the beer sloshing in its can. He smelled of unwashed clothing and cigarettes, and when he kissed my cheek I felt the sharp bristles of his unshaven face. Under his dingy white T-shirt he was skinny, and I doubted he was eating much.

"She really let you have it. What'd you do?"

"Nothing," I shrugged.

"You remember how tough she was on Donna?"

I remembered. My teenage sister balled in a corner of the living room while my mother battered her with a slipper. Donna smashing a plate on the floor. Slamming the front door. Running barefoot into the street. My mother's face gone savage with rage.

"Hate to break it to you, kiddo, but it's your turn," my father said, confirming what I already knew. "Let me give you a piece of advice."

For a moment I thought he was going to tell me how to stand up to my mother, to defend myself against the onslaught.

"Be a good girl," he said instead. "Keep your head down and do what she says. It'll be easier for everybody."

He meant it'd be easier for him. He was weak, like my mother always said. I tried to pull away, but he held me in a loose headlock, the skunky beer can under my chin.

"Fact of the matter is," he concluded, "life's a shit sandwich and you gotta eat it." He paused to take a drag from his cigarette and contemplate the deep wisdom of this. "I got an idea," he said. "You wanna come upstairs? Watch TV with me?"

I never wanted to go upstairs. His apartment was dark and smelled like wet dog. I couldn't keep him company. Maybe my mother was right and I didn't understand what it meant to love. I didn't feel one ounce of affection for my parents at that time. I only wanted to get away from them.

"I'm gonna ride my bike," I said.

"At night?"

The sun wouldn't set for another hour at least and the sky was still blue behind the black lines of telephone wire.

"She won't care," I said.

"If she asks, tell her you were with me." My father kissed me again and let me go, saying, "See ya later, alligator."

"After awhile, crocodile," I responded, trying not to think about how sad he looked in his saggy jeans and T-shirt, skinny like an unfinished boy.

When I went to get my bike from the backyard, my mother had gone inside. I could see her on the phone at the kitchen window, the long yellow cord coiling from the handset at her ear. She was probably talking to Gail, complaining about what a selfish, rotten bitch I was and getting more guidance on what to wear and what to consume in order to achieve her own self-esteem breakthrough and attract a high-quality man. I rode out to the street, heading for the neighborhood behind the post office. I had never searched at night and figured it was worth one more try.

•

Though it wasn't yet dark, the streetlights glowed, attracting halos of flying insects. I could see into lighted windows—women at kitchen sinks, women on telephones, men walking from one room to another. A few kids still played outside, getting in one last game of catch, the smack of leather ball in glove. I was gliding, enjoying the sensation of swimming in air, only half searching for the woman, when one kid said, "Look!" and pointed to the sky, making the other kids look.

In the decades since, in all the places I have traveled, I have not seen a more stunning sunset than the one I saw that evening on a shitty little backstreet in Swaffham, Massachusetts. Maybe it was the shock of beauty after the shock of my mother's rage. Maybe it was my youth. The brain chemistry of adolescence makes everything more intense, so ice cream tastes sweeter, colors are brighter, and love feels more profound than it ever will again. Once the chemicals fade, we remember that time as more alive than anything that came after, but I know that sunset was really something. It wasn't just the chemicals of youth. Everyone came out to see it. Kids called their parents into the yards and soon we were all standing around, primeval humans emerging from caves to gaze up at our god, slack-jawed below a mountain range of clouds burning red, hot lava searing the sky, lacy edges sizzling gold.

In literature there's an idea about the beautiful and the sublime. The beautiful is merely pleasurable, while the sublime is awe-inspiring. It is grandeur, powerful and frightening. That was the sky I saw that evening. It struck me with an exquisite terror, the sense one has before being raptured into the heavens. The sublime. I didn't know the word. I was only feeling it for the first time, gaping at the ruby ceiling of the world as it churned above my little place on the planet. And then I heard it.

"Isn't it sublime?" she said.

There she was, as if she'd been there all along and I only had to turn my head to see. I thought, in the way that young people think of everything as meaningful, that the sunset had brought her, opening a portal through which we now could meet. I gaped at her the way I'd been gaping at that sunset, face to face with the mythic.

"I've seen you riding your bike around here," she said.

"I was looking for you," the truth spilled out.

"I figured."

I could not then comprehend how she knew, and suspected she might be psychic, but now I understand there was nothing supernatural about it. She simply recognized me for what I was—because I was like her.

"Come on," she said. I watched her walk back to her house, barefoot in shorts and tank top. I looked around. The sunset had faded and the people had all retreated to their homes. I was alone and unwatched. I followed the woman who'd been branded as Other, even though—and partly because—it was a dangerous thing to do. On the crooked porch of a two-story cottage covered in chipped white paint, we sat in a pair of wicker chairs, the caning gone haywire, by a table that held an ashtray and a strange pack of cigarettes. It had a foreign word printed on it: "Djarum." She offered one and I took it, wanting everything she would give me. The cigarette was brown and made my lips taste sweet.

"Cloves," she said. "They punch holes in your lungs."

Through the screen door of the house, a lamp cast an orange glow onto a worn rug. Moths stuck themselves to the screen, dying to get inside. The woman looked at me, really looked, as if she recognized something and was trying to place it. I turned back to the moths on the screen, stuttering their powdered wings.

"What's your name?" the woman asked, giving me the same smile from the drugstore, that time I thought she was dismissing me. Now it felt different.

"Mel," I said. She accepted this and didn't ask if it was short for Melanie or Melissa, like most people did. Then she told me her name. Sylvia Marks. I'd never met anyone named Sylvia and it seemed like the Hollywood name of a starlet from long ago, someone born plain, with an unmusical name like Ethel or Gertrude, but who'd been elevated to the celestial. Sylvia. She picked up an unplugged electric guitar and started a quiet tune, closing her eyes and humming like I wasn't there. Now I could look at her. I am ashamed to admit it now, but I found myself looking for signs of her former sex. With her eyes closed I could gaze openly at her face and neck, her arms and hands, bare feet and legs. I think she wanted this, for my eyes to do what people's eyes always do when they meet a transsexual, frisking the body in search of concealed goods. She wanted me to get it out of the way so we could move on to other things.

Sylvia had a strong and pretty face, pale white oval with dark, deep-set eyes, and a mouth with one upturned corner that always held a smirk, in case she needed it, which she often did. Her jet-black shag haircut hung in her eyes and flicked her shoulders. I didn't see what everyone else in town seemed to. Maybe I still hadn't figured out the differences between men and women, didn't know to look for an Adam's apple, a jawline, a brow ridge. Sylvia looked like Sylvia to me, though I'd be lying if I didn't say there was something. I perceived it more as a feeling than a look. She had a kind of muscularity about her that I'd not felt from other women at the time, but I did not know, and still don't, whether to ascribe that to her sex or simply to the way she was. Sylvia was fully situated in her body. She owned it. She didn't sit nervously within it, like a novice behind the wheel of an unfamiliar car where all the settings are meant for another. Sylvia drove her body like she drove her Trans Am, with *balls behind the wheel*, as I would learn she liked to say. In her face, her limbs, her walk, she dared you to just try and stop her from propelling herself through life.

As she sang "Jesus died for somebody's sins, but not mine," I heard a rasp in her voice that sunk to an unearthly baritone and vibrated like a string set too close to the fret wire. It wasn't pretty, but it was good. It was rock and roll. "People say beware, but I don't care." She stopped and opened her eyes. "You know this one?"

I shook my head.

"It's 'Gloria.' The Patti Smith version. Not Van Morrison and not Jim Morrison. Patti Smith. You know her?"

I shook my head again.

"Oh, man, you don't know Patti? You are missing out. What do you listen to?"

"The Doors," I said, not wanting to admit my love for Michael Jackson, which felt that night, on the porch of Sylvia Marks, like a silly sort of childish love. "Zeppelin. The normal stuff."

"Normal? What's normal?"

"I guess it's just what everyone listens to around here."

"Yeah, I remember," she said. "I grew up here. But I'm a bit older than you, so you probably never knew me. I left home pretty early. I escaped. Like a bird. Flew away to New York City when I was—how old are you?"

"Almost fourteen."

"When I was about your age. Can you imagine?"

I tried to imagine. Sticking out a thumb on I-95, holding a cardboard sign: "New York Or Bust." Sylvia must have done that years ago, but how many? I couldn't tell her age, only that she was older than high school and much younger than my mother, landing her squarely in the big-sister zone, an empty space I was eager to fill. My sister owned a guitar, too, but she couldn't play, never bothered to learn. She had no music to teach me. Sylvia, I knew, would be a different story.

"I lived in the Chelsea Hotel," she continued. "You ever hear of that?" I hadn't. "Stayed with a gentleman friend who looked after me. I was a wide-eyed ingénue and he showed me things. Took me places. Max's. CB's. I was there when everyone was there. Andy, Patti, Debbie. You ever listen to Blondie?"

"I love Blondie," I said, too eagerly, trying to prove I knew something of the world Sylvia described. "She's wicked cool. I have her record on eight-track. 'Rapture' is one of my favorite songs."

"Blondie's the name of the *band*, honey, not the singer, but everyone makes that mistake, it's cool. The singer is Debbie Harry. She's bitchin."

"You met her?"

"I met everybody. You know the song 'Walk on the Wild Side'?"

"Lou Reed," I said.

"Thank God *some* culture trickles into this armpit of America. You know when Lou sings about Holly and Candy and Jackie? I met all of them. Except Candy. She expired too soon. I could have been a Warhol superstar, but I arrived too late to make it into the songs. Or the movies. When history looks back on that time, Sylvia Marks will be absent from the official record. Sad but true. I did manage to get my picture taken by Robert Mapplethorpe, but just Polaroids, little black-and-whites no one'll ever see. I'm destined to live in obscurity. And back in this one-horse town, too. *C'est la vie.* What do you do for fun around here?"

Everything I did for fun paled in comparison to New York City and rock stars, and to the way Sylvia talked, with words I never heard anyone use, with a kind of music in her voice, like she believed what she said mattered. I could not tell her I rode my bike or went to the Dairy Queen, that I hung around with my best friend and watched teen sex movies on cable. So I thought of the most rock-and-roll thing I'd ever done and said that.

"I get high," I said casually, like it was something I did all the time, instead of only a few times, and then not vigorously.

"Right on," she said. And then she invited me inside to listen to Patti Smith.

The interior of the house was stuffed with dark uncomfortable furniture, cheap King Louis knockoffs with faded cushions. The walls were papered in flock-and-foil damask, olive-green on gold, and along them hung a torture gallery of the suffering Christ, half-naked and covered in blood. Whipped. Crucified. Crowned in thorns.

"Isn't it grotesque?" Sylvia asked. "I call it mid-century masochism. Mid-*nineteenth* century, to be specific. I haven't had the chance to redecorate since my mother died. Oh, don't be sad on my account.

She was a sick old woman and not very nice. She stopped speaking to me, but she left me this house, so that's something. For now I'm camping out in the den. The den of iniquity."

A bit homier, the den had a rabbit-eared television, a big console stereo, and a La-Z-Boy recliner under a stuffed bigmouth bass. Sheets and pillows lay on the couch and clothing spilled from a pair of suitcases. On the coffee table sat a mess of car parts leaking grease onto a sheet of newspaper.

"That's for the demolition derby," Sylvia explained. "I'm getting a car ready."

"Not your Trans Am."

"Are you kidding? She's my baby, I keep her safe in the garage. No, man, I got a junker for the demo. A real piece-of-shit jalopy."

"You're gonna drive it yourself?" I'd never heard of a woman competing in the Fourth of July derby.

"Damn right. I used to do it when I was a kid. After New York, I came back here for a bit. I tried to fit in, if you know what I mean. Anyway. It didn't take."

She got to her knees and went shuffling through a milk crate of record albums.

"How'd you try to fit in?"

"How do you think?"

I shrugged.

"You know I'm a tranny, right?"

That word, coming from Sylvia, startled me. I'd never heard anyone claim for themselves the ugly words used against them. Now it sounded different, softer and more playful. In her mouth it was doing something I could not yet identify, a neat trick that felt like a powerful way of grabbing hold of language.

"I worked hard to be a proper boy," she said. "For a little while. I put away my girl things. Put away New York. I smashed cars and broke hearts. Here it is."

She pulled out an album styled in black and white. On the cover stood a person dressed in a rumpled white button-down shirt, black suit jacket tossed over the shoulder, and what looked like a skinny black necktie. I couldn't tell if this person was a man or a woman. Square jaw, direct gaze, dark mess of unbrushed hair. I thought, for a second, it might be Sylvia, but this was Patti Smith. I felt something inside me flicker and throb, a sudden hunger to hear everything she had to say. On the turntable, *Horses* crackled to life.

Jesus died for somebody's sins, but not mine.

Sylvia lit a joint and handed it to me. I took a hit, looking up at dying Jesus and thinking about my sins. Did it count as a sin when I humped the floor with Jules' leg on mine? Did it count right then as I thought of kissing Sylvia, enticed by the softness of her plush lower lip? We sat on the rug and listened while Patti sang about doing it with another woman, a sweet young thing in a pretty red dress, leaning on a parking meter. Her name is *G-L-O-R-I-A*. I knew that girl. She'd been around. She took Van Morrison first. Went into his room around midnight to make him feel alright. Then she visited Jim Morrison. Wrapped her body around his and did it hard and fast. In both versions, the man was seduced, passively following. Not so with Patti. More man than the men, she's bored and proud, moving in her own atmosphere. She sees Gloria and puts a spell on her. "I make her mine," she screams, the words pushed through the woodchipper of her throat, outstripping any boy who sang this song before or would dare to sing it since.

"Play it again," I said, and Sylvia did. And again. The song killed me, in the best way. It wasn't the weed. It wasn't the magic brain chemicals of youth. It was that song. When I listen to it today, it still kills me. At the time, however, it was more than a killer song. It was a blast of dynamite, cracking open stone. Listening to that song and being with Sylvia, I felt like Alice tumbled through the rabbit hole into a new dimension, one in which another life was possible. This is why the leaders of small places are afraid of music and books. And queers. They offer another way. But they don't convert. They awaken. Sending a signal to dormant cells, they rouse what's already there. "It's time," they say. "Wake up."

2019

Donna is a bull in a china shop, muscling through my mother's closets and drawers, tossing things in trash bags before I have a chance to look. When I tell her to slow down, she asks who died and made me boss. I want to say *My mother.* And the whole time she's bickering with Dakota, who can't do a single thing right in my sister's eyes. She's a helpful kid, or maybe she's just bored, digging into boxes and holding up junk like everything's a prize, going, *Look at this, look at this*, until Donna shouts at her to go play with her phone, and then I've got to hear my sister go on about how hard it is, raising a grandchild when she's tired, her back aches, money's tight, and all she wants is a Caribbean cruise. I should do something, take the kid for a walk, be a useful adult, but I'm tired, too. Also, I can't tell if Dakota is someone I want to spend time with. Donna says she's a smart kid, but I don't see any sign of that. She's either buzzing around like a caffeinated puppy or staring mindlessly into the narcotic glow of her phone. It's not her fault. She's been raised by wolves. Today the whole thing gave me a headache so I called it quits, got on my bike, and ended up at my old middle school, which no longer exists.

Without children to fill it, the town closed the school and left it derelict, a hazardous relic of asbestos and lead paint, covered in graffiti. When squatters nearly burned the building down, the town demolished it. Now, in its footprint between the crumbling asphalt playgrounds, there has grown a rogue meadow of high grass and wildflowers. I try to imagine the girl I used to be walking those lost halls, but she is gone, vanished into Queen Anne's lace and blue chicory, daisy fleabane and vetch.

"The girl I used to be." Just one note about that. I can say this about myself, but you can't say it about me. That's how it works. When you say it, you're doing something to me. An act of casual aggression. A verbal depantsing. When I say it, well, it's mine to say. *Girl*, in this context, doesn't mean to me what *girl* means to you. It's a flickering kind of boy-girl, a girl-not-girl that isn't not-girl. (Look at how the word dissolves from meaning the more it repeats.) Anyway, it's mine. And yet I don't feel totally entitled to it, hovering as it does in a hotly contested battle zone.

Each time I say *girl* and *she* I feel a flush of anxiety about what my QUILTBAG students would say. *QUILTBAG*, the latest (and hopefully short-lived) acronym to replace the ever-lengthening LGBTQQIP2SAA+, stands for "queer, undecided, intersex, lesbian, trans, bi, asexual, gay," and sounds like a soft, homespun vessel for carrying your knitting, an object drained of all things sexy. I don't like it, but that doesn't matter because I'm a dinosaur and none of my opinions matter. Maybe I've become one of those "old man yells at cloud" types, but understand that when I was a kid, I was starving for elders, older trans people to show me I could exist and did not have to die young. With the internet, who needs elders? I have aged into something disposable. Worse. I have become that which must be destroyed. Maybe I'm wrong, maybe I don't understand the young queers, but I fear they would have my head for using "girl" to describe my past self. And she/her pronouns? Forget it.

Times change, I know, but I fought hard for my words and that means I get to keep them. I grappled with them, tried to kill them as they tried to kill me, and eventually found a way to recycle them into something (mostly) useful. Now I can employ them in the telling of my story, even as others try to criminalize and lock them up. If I sound bitter on this subject, well, that's because I am.

Before the uproar at Ampleforth, I was the opposite of bitter. From their first arrival on the scene, I embraced they/them pronouns, the non-binary youth with their exuberant cotton-candy hair colors, their new names chosen from concrete nouns like Bucket and Spoon. I admire their boundary smashing and the way they demand respect, something I could never do at their age because I was too busy trying not to be annihilated. But when some started attacking older trans people for the language we use, I became resistant, and it was probably this resistance that led to the trouble at Ampleforth. I might as well get into all that.

Years ago I pioneered the first course at the school on LGBT literature (as we called it then). We read *The Well of Loneliness* and *Giovanni's Room*, but it was *Middlesex* that would torque my fate. "Like Tiresias," Jeffrey Eugenides writes in the voice of the narrator, a man who began life as a girl, "I was first one thing and then the other." There is a before and an after. When referring to the character in the time before, I used *she*, saving *he* for the after. This bothered no one for the first few years; my students were appreciative, and my class was celebrated in the local media as a victory for diversity. After a rocky start at Ampleforth—I was a controversial hire, opposed by a group of concerned (transphobic) parents—the trustees were now proud to have a real, live transgender teacher on the faculty. This was after *Time* declared "the transgender tipping point" and my identity, for many years a source of shame, had cachet. I would not, however, have long to enjoy it. This past winter, while teaching the same class, my pronominal decision riled one of my students, a senior I will call

KT, which are not her initials but which I have chosen because they stand for the mass extinction event that wiped out the dinosaurs at the Cretaceous-Tertiary boundary. KT was my asteroid.

Since positioning is important these days, allow me to position KT. An affluent, white, Anglo-Saxon, AFAB (assigned female at birth) individual who used she/her pronouns, presented as conventionally feminine, and dated, no kidding, the captain of the boys' lacrosse team, KT took offense to my use of she/her for *Middlesex*'s narrator pre-transition. It was, she said, "problematic," an "erasure of his identity," and "totally transphobic." I asked the class if anyone agreed. No one raised a hand. I pointed out that my approach was the same as the author's, to which KT replied that Eugenides was "a cis-het white man" who should not have written the novel in the first place. He was "perpetrating an act of appropriation" and should "stay in his lane." Implied was the idea that I should also stay in mine. But what lane did she think I occupied? Looking out at the faces of my students, I tried to make light of the situation. That was my fatal mistake.

"I'm a tranny," I said, grinning like an idiot. "So I can't be transphobic."

I was being ironic. Let the record show that I am well aware that trans people can be transphobic, in our own special self-loathing way. My Gen-X irony fell flat. After class, KT launched herself at my desk where I was packing my satchel.

"You can't say the T-word," she said.

"Which word is that?" I asked.

"*T-R-A-N-N-Y*," she spelled, as if to say it aloud would incur the wrath of God.

The T-word. Always complicated, in recent years it has become highly controversial, debated by reality TV stars, trans influencers, trans Twitter. Some insist it should never be uttered, while others argue it can be spoken as long as it's not to denigrate trans people.

Many say only trans women can use the word, while some believe it's available to trans men and anyone else who fucks with gender. Some reclaim it with pride, like *queer,* while others experience it only as a painful slur. Over the years, I've been called a tranny by people who meant something cruel, and I've called myself a tranny, now and then, but it never quite fit. It's not a word I feel especially attached to and I'm not sure why, at that moment in the classroom, it came out of my mouth, except that I felt angry and unseen, bullied by a rich straight girl flexing her privilege. And maybe I wanted to be provocative. I succeeded. KT was provoked.

"Thank you for informing me," I said, using a de-escalation skill I'd learned from colleagues who'd stepped into similar student minefields.

"You made the space feel unsafe," she said.

"Like I often say, there is no such thing as a truly safe space. In life, we're bound to encounter . . ."

"You don't get it."

She was right. I didn't get it. I still don't. When did fragility become desirable? It's a Gen-X cliché to say this, but I'm going to say it anyway: When I was a kid, in that actually unsafe world, all I wanted was to be tough, to rid myself of any vulnerability that would attract more hurt. Today, weakness is a weapon. KT claimed to feel unsafe, but she did not look fragile. With her backpack hitched on a cocked shoulder, fist gripping the strap, she looked defiant, as righteously heroic as a white knight.

"You might not know this," I said carefully, "but I am, in fact, trans."

"Trans men are men," she said. "You have male privilege."

This pressed an exquisitely sensitive nerve. I reminded myself that KT was young, steeped in the splintery logic of social media. She didn't understand the differences between trans men and cis men, didn't see the disparity in our payloads of privilege, and she probably believed, as many otherwise well-meaning people do, that to acknowledge the difference, to say *trans men are men and also more complicated*, hello, *more ontologically fraught*, is to commit an act of transphobia when it's the opposite. It's affirming our complexity. At least in my experience. Which is not every trans man's experience. (I have to say that. If I don't, you might think I'm trying to *represent every trans man* when I am only trying, inelegantly, to represent me.) I managed to say to KT, in a tone not as gentle as I would have liked, "I'm sorry if I offended you."

"If?" she sputtered. "If? That's not a real apology."

Before I could say more, she strode out of the room, straight to the office of the dean of Diversity and Inclusion. Over the next weeks, the situation snowballed. A few more students accused me of being "problematic" as they brought forth other "troubling incidents." One claimed I had touched her shoulder while walking past her desk during an exam (she had a tendency to let her eyes wander to other students' work). Another said I used the wrong pronouns with them (I did, exactly once, for which I apologized and corrected myself). In a letter to the head of school, KT and her crew enumerated my transgressions, including something about how I displayed my "misogynistic androcentrism" every time I referred to mixed-gender groups as "you guys," and argued for me to be stripped of my ability to make a living. How could people who have everything work so hard to take away my only accomplishment? As one student faction tried to have me terminated, another petitioned to keep me, wearing buttons that read "Free Mr. Pulaski" and "#I'mWithHim," which I tried to explain sounded a bit right-wingish, considering the tenor of the times, and thus counterproductive, but they insisted I was too old to understand hashtags. That's when the parents association got involved. The same people who opposed my hiring in the first place, because they did not want a transsexual teaching their children, now called for my dismissal because I was too transphobic. As one mother told the *Boston Globe*, "The T-word might have been acceptable in the '90s, but it is highly offensive when you're paying $50,000 a year in tuition." Before I could finish the spring semester, Ampleforth put me on probation. Between that and the death of my mother, my mental health didn't stand a chance. I spent weeks embedded in my living room couch, binging on Netflix, sucking cannabis gummies, and trying to resist going on my phone to read the latest hate tweets about me.

Recalling all of this is making my blood pressure spike. I need to catch my breath, come back to the present and practice my mindfulness-based stress-reduction techniques. I am standing at the edge of a meadow. I hear birds and buzzing insects. At my feet, wild strawberries reach out with urgent vines. Did their seeds fly here from the lost farms of Swaffham, the bulldozed strawberry fields where millionaires have planted McMansions? Seeds carried in the bodies of birds. In the shit. To keep life going, nature invents brilliant methods of survival. For some of us, shit is the only way we get from there to here. In this place, when it used to be a school, everyone was called faggot and queer, lezzie and dyke, and no one came to anyone's rescue. We fought our own battles. I remember being on roller skates, making circles on the gritty playground during Park and Rec, when a bigger girl attacked me, pulling my hair and wrestling me down. While she grappled me, I looked up to see an adult, someone's mother, watching and doing nothing. I didn't understand until she said, "You gotta fight your own battles." So that's what I did. I punched that bully in the face and made her bleed. Look. I don't mean to do the old "When I was a kid, we had to walk miles in the snow" thing. Life should get better for future generations. I only mean to say that I weathered it, held it in my mouth like a bitter pill I tried not to swallow, and that should count for something.

1984

We must have listened to "Gloria" six or seven times that first night, Sylvia pulling the needle back again and again. The crackle. The piano. And that voice. Hours later, I could not sleep, the song spinning in my head. And Sylvia. I needed a copy of that record.

In the morning, my mother and I were careful around each other. I toasted my Pop-Tarts. She drank her coffee, smoked her Salems, and read her *Boston Herald,* the tabloid that told of Red Sox games, lottery numbers, and race riots. It was her day off and we weren't going to talk about the previous night's fight.

"It's too bad about Michael Jackson," she said.

The board of selectmen in the town of Foxboro had just denied Michael and his brothers a permit to perform at Sullivan Stadium. They worried about "the unknown element." I didn't say a word, just watched my Pop-Tarts tan in the orange glow of the toaster oven. I wasn't going to let my mother connect.

"I have to go to the mall," she said. "I need towels and they're having a sale at Bed 'n Bath." (This was before Beyond.) "You want to come? You can bring Jules."

This was my mother's way of making amends. She wasn't going to apologize for hitting me and calling me an idiot. She never apologized. She just smoothed over.

"Sure," I shrugged. "There's something I need, too."

"What?"

"Just a record."

"A new Michael Jackson?"

"Someone else."

Over in Brixton, the Shawmut Mall was already old, built twenty years earlier, tiled in brown and beige. It wasn't one of the new two-story gallerias going up in other towns, with sunny atriums decked out in real palm trees and upscale shops like Benetton. But it was all we had. We made plans to meet at Woolworth's lunch counter and went our separate ways, my mother to Bed 'n Bath, Jules and I to roam free.

I did not go directly to Strawberries Records & Tapes, betraying my desperation for *Horses*, which I would then have to explain to Jules, and I was not ready to tell her about Sylvia. We poked around the Shirtery, an iron-on shop whose essence remains indelible, fragrant with the toasty smell of heat-transfer vinyl, walls covered with glittery decals: Pink Floyd and Duran Duran, Felix the Cat and Garfield, the 1980s mingling with the 1970s, "Gag Me with a Spoon" next to "Ass, Gas, or Grass: Nobody Rides for Free." There was no Patti Smith on those walls; she was from another galaxy. We wandered into Chess King, where I always put on Michael's "Beat It" jacket, silver zippers in red leather, much nicer than my knock-off vinyl version, only this time I didn't feel like it.

"Are you falling out of love?" Jules asked, a Blow Pop rattling between her teeth.

I said I didn't know, only that it felt childish to go into high school with a crush on Michael Jackson. "It's like he's part of my past," I said.

I was looking in the mirror, trying on a skinny necktie made of stiff black leather. I thought it looked like the one on the cover of *Horses*, but it didn't have the same effect under the popped collar of my off-brand polo shirt.

I turned to Jules and asked, "What do you think of this?"

"It's cool," she shrugged, noncommittal.

I looked at the price tag. "It's on sale."

I had enough money for the tie and the record, so I bought it and wore it out of the store, leaving it loose so the knot hung low and carelessly cool. We went into Caldor's, attacked each other with perfume, and pocketed tubes of Maybelline Cover Stick for our zits. At Spencer Gifts, Jules shoplifted a pack of sandalwood incense and we got our pictures taken in the photo booth. The strip, deposited in the drying rack, smelled of delicious chemicals. I still have my half. In her Def Leppard T-shirt, Jules is making the heavy metal sign, horns up and tongue out, while I look off in the distance. In my polo shirt and leather tie, I look like a boy.

"Let's go to Strawberries," I said at last. "There's nothing else to do." Like I didn't care. Like Strawberries wasn't the one place I wanted to be. Remember the feeling of flipping records in a bin? The thrill of searching the physical world for treasure with all its texture and surprise? I found *Horses* right away, amazed it had made it there, traveling over the endless Siberia between downtown New York and the Shawmut Mall.

"Who's that?" Jules asked as I handed over the last of my cash at the register.

"Patti Smith. I heard it on the radio," I lied, and we went to join my mother at Woolworth's where she was sitting in a booth, reading *People* magazine, some European princess on the cover with her new baby. She made a snide comment about my tie and then treated us to grilled cheese sandwiches and vanilla Cokes. We looked at the magazine. There was an article about Michael Jackson's choreographer, a man who owned 150 pairs of shoes and relaxed by hanging upside-down in "inversion boots." Jules said, "That's *different*," and I agreed, performing disdain, bonding over things we did not understand.

My mother could be fun sometimes, looking like a girl herself with her Dorothy Hamill hair in a pink plastic headband, an item I usually despised because it was too young for her, but that day I didn't mind. I pushed my plate of potato chips toward her, an act that made me feel generous and good. I wanted her to like me again, to prove that I was capable of love and could be the sort of girl she couldn't possibly hate. When I was small, she would bounce me on her knees and recite a poem that went, "There was a little girl who had a little curl, right in the middle of her forehead. And when she was good, she was very, very good. But when she was bad, she was horrid." I knew the poem was about me because I had a curl in the middle of my forehead, a dark upside-down question mark that my mother set with a licked finger. That afternoon at Woolworth's I labored to be good, not horrid, commenting agreeably as my mother turned the pages of *People*, admiring the lives of ordinary Americans who'd overcome adversity, men and women who were called heroes for going to the brink of death, or donating a kidney, or just losing a tremendous amount of weight.

Later, in my room, I tore the cellophane from *Horses* and put the record on. While the music played, I stared at Patti and stroked my leather necktie. On the back of the album cover, it said the photographer was Robert Mapplethorpe. The same man who took Polaroids of Sylvia. I was only two degrees of separation from everything cool. I plugged in my headphones, lay on the floor, and listened again. An album used to tell a story, and you listened from beginning to end because you wanted to get it. I very much wanted to get *Horses*. I can tell you now that I did not. After Gloria, there are funerals and ravens, the end of existence, a misplaced Joan of Arc, and the story of a boy raped or stabbed by another boy, head filling up with horses,

horses, horses. Another sweet young thing, leaning on a parking meter, only now she's a man. Girl transformed into man. I could not wait to see Sylvia again and talk all about it.

•

When I rolled up to her house, Sylvia was in the sun-bright driveway, standing barefoot before a beat-up monster of a station wagon covered in rust and stripped of its wood paneling. All the car's windows were broken out. The headlights and taillights were gone, along with the bumper and radiator grille. On the driveway, a transistor radio played WBCN, the Rock of Boston, silver antenna pointing to the sky.

"Hey, man," Sylvia said, holding out a gallon of paint. "Help me put some color on this behemoth."

This was how Sylvia greeted people, as if they'd already been there. There was no "How's it going" or "What are you up to." She just folded you into whatever she was doing. Right then, she was getting ready to paint the car for the demolition derby.

"Open that can," she said, handing me a screwdriver. I squatted down and levered the lid to reveal hot pink, the color and thickness of Pepto Bismol. "Just slap it on. I'm not competing for Miss America."

I painted while Sylvia tinkered with the engine. The pink went on thick and dripping, the brush snagging in rust pits, but it didn't matter. I was decorating something that would be destroyed. Now and then I'd look up to see Sylvia bent over the hood, legs bright in the sun, reaching her hand back to wipe grease on the butt of her snug cut-offs. The view sent flutters through my stomach while the music on the radio made me feel dreamily cinematic, like I was in a romantic movie, a fantasy interrupted whenever they stopped to play commercials for SPAM, the meat in a can, and a trucking school that promised big money behind the wheel of a big rig. The

DJ announced the weather, "Seventy-eight glorious degrees at Logan Airport," and then, "Here's music for your headsets, your Walkmans, Walkmen, Walkpersons. On the Rock of Boston."

I didn't think about the neighbors watching, the old ladies at the windows who might decide we were suspicious persons doing suspicious things. On those streets, a mile from my house, I was in another country. I might be Sylvia's friend from the city. I might belong to her and not to that town. But in a place like Swaffham, a mile didn't matter. Town was town and everyone could tell who belonged and who didn't.

"Leave the driver's side door," she said, standing beside me, wiping her hands with a rag. "It has to be white. For safety. So the other drivers don't hit it."

"Why'd you pick a station wagon?"

"A wagon is an excellent demo car," she explained. "You hit with your back end, and wagons have more back end. It's like a battering ram. And just look at her. She's a classic. 1958 Ford Country Squire. Think about some wholesome American family taking her out for picnics, the kids with ice-cream cones, teenagers humping away in the back while the Lettermen sing, 'There's a summer place.' Sandra Dee and Troy Donahue! And now? She's a cold-blooded killer."

"A killer in pink?"

"Damn right. I want all those guys to know they're getting their asses whooped by a girl."

She opened another can of paint and started doing the driver's side door in white. It was getting hot, the sun high in the sky, and sweat trickled down my back into my shorts. I could feel my neck getting red.

"You going to the fair?" she asked.

"If my mother'll let me."

The Brixton Fair, home to the demolition derby, happened every year, for a whole week, over the Fourth of July. Organized around a defunct horse track, its midway filled with games, rides, freak shows, and fried-food stands, the fair had been going for a century. Its heyday came during the Great Depression when Lucky Teter and his Hell Drivers flew cars through flames and Hazel Eaton zig-zagged her Indian motorcycle along the Wall of Death. In recent years, like everyplace else, it had fallen from grace. Biker gangs staked territories along the midway. Carnies lured girls into tents. Teenagers got stabbed with switchblades. The year before, on the night of the Fourth, sixty-two people got arrested for disturbing the peace. But the violence usually held off until the end of the night, after the fireworks, so it was safe to go in the early evening and leave after dark.

"When I used to drive the demo as a kid," Sylvia said. "You know, when I came back from New York and did my boy thing? I had balls behind the wheel, man, I'm telling you. Still do. You'll see."

I'd been waiting for an opening to talk about Patti Smith. "I got that record," I said. "*Horses*? I listened to the whole thing. Like a million times."

"Right on."

"I'm not sure I get what it's all about. That one about the boys in the hallway? What's a sperm coffin? And the one with the boy who grows wings and flys away? It's like poetry. It's cool, but I don't get it. It all feels like dream stuff."

"It's totally poetry and dream stuff. Patti's a shamanistic rock god. Like Jim Morrison or David Bowie. Only she's a girl doing it and she's the *only* girl doing it."

Sylvia propped her brush on the white paint can and sat down on the driveway, legs folded, to light a clove cigarette and give me a lesson.

"The song 'Break It Up' is about Jim Morrison," she explained. "I heard her tell the story in New York. She had this dream where she saw a marble slab and Jim was fighting to get out of the stone. He had wings. Patti was telling him, 'Break it up,' until he got free.

In the song, she breaks through, too. It's about transformation. It's a transsexual story, in a way. Know what I mean?"

I did not know what Sylvia meant at all, but I nodded.

"Patti's saying, like, I'm not just gonna be this girl from Jersey. I'm gonna fly. Ascend to the heavens with all the other rock gods. That kind of glory? It's not just for boys, you know?"

The story captivated me, the way Sylvia told it, waving hands in the air, washed in clove smoke and paint fumes. I couldn't wait to tell Jules, but I hadn't yet told her about Sylvia, and I wasn't sure how to do that—or if I wanted to. Sylvia was *different*, that word we used for things we didn't understand, and I didn't know if Jules could handle just how different. I was still figuring it out myself. I found it confusing and fascinating the way Sylvia talked about boys and girls, how she wanted to show the world that a girl was just as tough as a boy, but she'd been a boy. If she wanted to be tough, why become a girl to do it? What little I knew of gender politics had come through the record *Free to Be . . . You and Me*. As a kid, I listened to it obsessively, taking in the lessons about girls who did boy things and boys who did girl things, how they could wear each other's clothes, and none of it really mattered.

"My mother used to try to make me wear dresses to school," I told Sylvia. "But I fought and won every time." I thought she would identify and tell me the opposite story, about putting on her mother's high heels. Instead, she said, "I didn't like dresses either. I was such a tomboy." But tomboys were girls, not boys, and Sylvia was—what? The full story of her identity and body had not been spoken. *Tranny* was the only word we had. A woman could be *trapped in a man's body*, but nothing more complicated had yet to be imagined in that time and place.

As Sylvia talked, I strained to grasp some particle of how she experienced gender and the crossing of it. For her, it wasn't a simple binary proposition. You didn't start at point A and land at point B.

There was no such position as A or B. Or maybe there was, but it was meant to be disrupted. For Sylvia, gender was like those psychedelic drawings at Spencer Gifts, M. C. Escher scenes on blacklight posters. A Möbius strip that twists on itself so you can never tell which side is which. Confronted by such a shape, the mind fills in the blanks and then flips, revising what it sees—or thinks it sees. Violating the laws of Euclidean geometry, these shapes cannot exist in reality. They are known as "impossible objects." I came upon this term only recently, but if I'd had it then, I would have applied it to Sylvia. She was an impossible object, at least in that place and time, and yet she existed in three dimensions. At that moment she existed in her driveway, on a summer day with the insects buzzing and the smell of paint on a hot car that, when finished, looked like a bar of pink Camay soap.

Sylvia walked into the garage and came back with a can of black spray paint. She shook it, rattling the metal pea, and traced the number 88 on the front doors and hood of the wagon. "Lucky number," she said. "Double infinity." She handed the can to me and asked, "What do you want to write?"

"What do people usually write?"

"Most guys put their girlfriends' names on there. Or their nicknames. Junkyard Dog, that kind of stuff. I don't have a nickname. Or a girlfriend. Put whatever you want."

"Maybe something from Patti?"

"Sperm Coffin!" Sylvia said, laughing.

I aimed the can.

"No, don't," she said. "They'll put me in jail. But yeah, do something from Patti."

I thought a moment and then I knew, a phrase that seemed to say something true about Sylvia. And maybe me, too. "How about 'Misplaced Joan of Arc'?"

"That's totally bitchin. Put it right there," she pointed to the long flank of the car. I took my time forming the letters. It came out a little crooked, but alright.

"Hold out your hands," she said. I did and she slapped them with a brushful of white paint. "Make your mark."

I pressed my hands to the car and left a pair of ghostly prints. Sylvia led me to the hose by the side of the house and squeezed the trigger nozzle while I rinsed my hands. I felt happy. She tilted the hose to the sky to make rain and I ran through, cooling off, whooping with giddiness. Next door, beyond a low chain-link fence, kids splashed in an above-ground pool while their mother, pulling weeds, glared at us. I probably should have cared, but as I said, those streets were another country and I felt like a stranger, unknowable, beyond reach. I went on leaping and whooping in the spray.

The neighbor woman called out, "You're wasting water."

Sylvia released the trigger on the hose.

"What?"

"You're wasting water," the woman repeated, standing up with a handful of grass in her fist and an edge to her voice that seemed to be about something besides water conservation.

Sylvia ignored her and went on making rain, but the good feeling had gone out of it, and she soon dropped the hose and turned off the spigot. I grabbed the bottom of my T-shirt and wrung it out, pulled it up and down through the neck, creating a low-cut crop top, the way I'd seen other girls do, showing off their bellies to each other and whatever boys might be around. I figured Sylvia was one of those, or both—she'd said *girlfriend*, she didn't have a *girlfriend*, the word my mother used for friends who were girls, but Sylvia meant it the other way. I wanted her to look at me. She carried the cans of paint into the garage while the neighbor woman went on eyeing us.

The garage smelled like musty beach towels and gasoline, the metallic tang of the Trans Am where it lay, protected and hidden from view. On the hood, the golden firebird spread its wings, like the boy trapped in stone, trying to break out. I leaned against the car, feeling its power, and tried to flirt, hands in pockets, not knowing how to stand or what to do. Sylvia went on not looking at me. I undid the crop top and tugged my T-shirt down over my belly. The mood of the afternoon had shifted.

"Take me for a ride?"

"Another time," she said, banging around with the paint cans on a shelf full of junk. I gave up, went back to the driveway, and paced, watching the neighbor watching me from her garden. *Rip, rip, rip* went the noise of her fists in the weeds. It seemed like maybe I should get going. I pushed my wet feet into sneakers, picked up my bike, and told Sylvia I was headed out.

"Okay," she said, not looking up from her business in the shadows of the garage. Sylvia wasn't good with hellos, but she was even worse with goodbyes.

"See you at the fair maybe?"

"Yeah," she said. "See you."

I started down the driveway, feeling unsure. Had I done something wrong?

"Wait," Sylvia called, jogging out from the garage, bare feet slapping puddles. "Take this." She handed me a cassette. On a strip of masking tape, written in Magic Marker, it read: "Patti Smith bootleg + interviews DO NOT ERASE."

"Make a copy," she said. "I want that back."

•

At home, while my mother donkey-kicked on the living room floor with Jane Fonda, I shut myself in my room and listened to Sylvia's tape, eyes closed, ears sealed in the foamy cush of headphones. A mix of live songs with stage patter, interviews, and poems, the voice of Patti Smith sounded scratchy and faded, like she'd been copied a hundred times, passed from tape to tape, her voice bouncing around New York, from the Chelsea Hotel and up to Boston in a dashboard cassette deck dusted with lint and cigarette ash, and now, as if by magic, to my middle-of-nowhere place in the world.

Later that night, I talked to Jules on the phone extension in my room. I did not have my own number, but I did have my own phone, a novelty molded in the shape of Garfield the cat, his sleepy eyes popping open when you lifted the receiver. I held it to the boom-box speaker so Jules could hear Patti tell the story of her Jim Morrison dream, the marble slab, the Florida grass, long and waving like hair. We were fascinated by dreams and I thought Jules would think it was cool.

"Who's Patti Smith anyway?"

"She's a singer in New York. She's a shamanistic rock god."

"Where'd you get the tape?"

"This girl," I said, trying to sound casual. "Sylvia. She let me borrow it."

"Who?"

"Just this girl. She's older."

"Like from the high school?"

"What do you think of the song? It's bitchin, right?"

Bitchin was Sylvia's word. I never said *bitchin*. Jules knew it and, in the strained seconds of silence that followed, I knew she knew it. Outside the open windows, crickets and katydids trilled in the leaves of the lilac bushes. I could hear the mumbling of the television in the living room where my mother sat sipping a glass of beer.

"Well? What do you think?"

"It's *different*," she said.

That was the last thing I wanted to hear. Jules and I were supposed to be different together, not different from each other. Maybe if she heard more, she would like it.

"I'll make you a copy."

"That's okay."

"All you ever listen to are dead people," I said, louder than I'd meant to. "Why don't you try someone alive for once in your life?"

"Why are you being a jerk?"

"I'm not," I snapped. "I'm being honest. You say I'm boring, but you know what's boring? You and your obsession with death, that's what."

"There's really no such thing as death," she said. "Just change."

I heard the phone click as my mother picked up the kitchen extension.

"Ma," I said. "Hang up."

"Get off the phone. It's after eleven o'clock."

"Ma. Hang up."

"Jules, does your mother let you stay up this late to gab on the phone?"

"We were just talking about the Brixton Fair," Jules started.

"Jules," I said, but she kept going.

"Mrs. Pulaski, would it be alright if Mel came with us? My mom and dad are taking me and my brother." That was a lie. If we did go, it'd be in the Cougar with Dale and Tammy.

"The fair is dangerous," my mother said. "A girl got her finger bitten off by a monkey at the petting zoo. Last year, there were seven rapes. Seven. In one week."

"Ma!"

"That's one rape every night."

"You always let Donna go," I said.

"And look what happened."

"What happened?" I asked, but I knew what happened. My sister happened, the train wreck of her life, knocked up and knocked around, as if a few summer nights at the Brixton Fair could send your life to hell.

"My dad'll be with us the whole time," Jules pressed, "and he's not gonna let anything bad happen. You know my dad."

My mother considered this. She did know Ray Cobb. He wasn't what anyone would call a family man, but he had a reputation for being violently protective of the people who belonged to him. Like the time a local weed dealer roughed up Dale for not paying, so Ray went to the dealer's house with a pistol in the waistband of his Levi's. This was Ray Cobb, god of fire, Hephaestus of the gun forge. Nobody fucked with him. My mother, born to toughness, approved of Ray's bodyguard brutality, no matter how much she strove to be a "high-quality person," and maybe, as she weighed the question of the Brixton Fair, she imagined him, big and burly, fending off the men who would try to spirit us away to the carny tents behind the Tilt-A-Whirl. Or maybe she was remembering her own days at the fair, back when the nights were safe and daredevil girls dived into pools of water on the backs of horses. Whatever my mother was thinking, she said yes.

2019

Out in the living room, Donna is shouting into her phone. Every few days, she makes the rounds of people who have wronged her: Stetson's lawyer, the Nutribullet people, a clerk at the Traffic Violations Bureau of the DMV, a financial counselor at the hospital where she owes money for the placement of a stent, and a customer service representative in India with an accent that sends my sister into a state of apoplexy. Now she's on with Jerry Logue, talking about the sale of the house. I don't want to hear it.

I'm in my old bedroom. Though my mother removed my posters and filled the space with her clutter of banker's boxes and paper piles, enough relics of my youth remain to arouse a sense of time dilation. Or maybe *dislocation* is the word. My Garfield phone still sits by the bed. I read an internet story recently about Garfield phones washing up on a beach in France. They arrive in pieces: cartoon cat heads, cords and handsets, the bright-orange wreckage of 1980s novelty. For thirty-five years, no one knew where the parts were coming from. Finally, *le mystère des téléphones Garfield* was solved when environmental activists climbed into a remote sea cave and discovered the source, a rusted shipping container run aground, leaking scraps of our nonbiodegradable past. Similarly, in this house stuffed with memory, the girl comes back, but she does not come whole. Melanie, buried in a remote spot on the other side of an ocean, washes ashore in bits and pieces. It used to be painful to see the photos my mother kept on the walls, my former shape staring back from another dimension. Now, enough time has passed that it feels like looking at someone you knew briefly but intensely, years ago, someone you forgot and then remembered, wondering: *What ever happened to them?*

In a photo album from junior high, between Polaroids of Jules and me at Halloween parties and class trips to Rocky Point amusement park, I find a yellowed news clipping. A woman asks: *My niece informs me, after seeing Michael Jackson's "Thriller" on TV, that Jackson takes female hormone pills to keep his voice pitched high. I feel that God simply blessed him with a good set of vocal cords. Which one of us is right?* The columnist answers: *You are.* It's nothing at first, a random artifact, but I am struck by the fact that, at age twelve, I preserved this transgender question under cellophane. That would have been at least a year before I began to know myself, before I met Sylvia, and this brings up the mystery of knowing, how we can know a thing without thinking it, and how that unthought knowledge leaves traces, fragments of the truth before it's fully born.

I want to think more about this, but it's time for my mandated session with the sensitivity trainer. At my old desk, I open my laptop. Through the stuttering Skype window, young and vigorous Autumn Biddle, endowed by the deans of Ampleforth with the power to judge my fitness for duty, flashes a buoyant smile. She's the sort of woman I envied once, and probably still do, a long and lean Anglo-Saxon with hair like a chestnut horse on a leafy day in New England. She belongs on a bale of hay, dressed in one of those Norwegian fisherman sweaters from L.L.Bean, the kind that only made me look lumpy and wrong. For each of our sessions so far, Autumn has appeared in a different room of her new-construction home. I've seen the vaulted living room, the office, and a reading nook where the books are covered in white paper, spines left blank, as hygienic as a surgeon's smock. Today she is in her kitchen, a glittering expanse that would eat my mother's kitchen for breakfast. Where my mother left plaid wallpaper and chipped Formica countertops, Autumn has installed gleaming subway tiles and white marble slabs. My mother's faded-yellow fridge wheezes and shudders, while Autumn's, sheathed in stainless steel, stands as steady and unobtrusive as a servant. I bet it even makes ice cubes quietly, shitting out each frozen brick in a vaporous hush.

Autumn tucks her hair behind her ears and flashes a rack of genetically superior teeth, eager to school me on the super-diversity of genders. If my sister is overwhelmed by the idea of fifteen genders, she would have a conniption over Autumn's list, which runs into the triple digits and includes *multigender*, *blurgender*, and *cloudgender*, the prefixes multiplying, shifting into *omnigender*, *astrogender*, and *chronogender*, until prefix becomes suffix to make *genderflux*, *genderfuzz*, and *gendermutt*.

"What are your thoughts?" Autumn asks, her smile showing a touch of strain. How did she get this job? She is trying her best, but she is out of her depth, and I take pleasure in neutralizing her. If I have to endure these so-called trainings, I'm at least going to make them interesting. Maybe you're thinking I'm a jerk and I should cut this woman some slack. You might be right, but what about my slack? I've never known the exquisite ease of being an Autumn.

"My thoughts are complicated," I say. "All these words are trying to name the experience of non-binary gender, which of course is valid, I mean, it's been around for thousands of years, but in their limitless profusion, the labels risk devolving to the narcissism of minor differences. It's like, the more gender expands, the more it produces these categories that require policing. Who belongs and who doesn't?

While these categories attempt to provide more space, they actually collapse it. Don't you think?"

Autumn frowns. This is not the answer she is looking for.

"I just worry about a community that's more invested in hyper-individualism than, you know, community," I say.

"People are individuals, Max. Everyone's unique."

"Are they though?"

"I'm very unique."

"Uh-huh," I say, doubting Autumn's assertion of singularity. I don't tell her that *unique* is an absolute adjective and should not be modified. I'm a high school English teacher, I can't help it, but I do keep the thought to myself. Give me some credit.

"People have a right to define themselves however they want," she says.

"Yes, of course. That's not what I'm saying. Look. It's a problem of late-stage capitalism. This micro-slicing of differences, asserting all this uniqueness, it's good for consumerism, you know, a different shampoo for every special head of hair, but it can lead to scapegoating, demonizing people for not being, whatever, the right sort of person. That's where political correctness goes awry. When the radical goes too far, it comes round the bend and turns conservative. There's probably a Venn diagram for that."

"You're mansplaining," Autumn says, tapping a note into her laptop, no doubt a demerit for her report to the dean of Diversity and Inclusion.

"I'm a trans man," I say. "If anything, I'm transplaining."

"Trans men are men," she insists.

Autumn cannot permit the differences between trans men and cis men. Like KT and the people on Twitter who repeat this well-intentioned slogan, she thinks if she sees me as trans, different from cis, she will undo my manhood. How did the expansion of gender lead us right back into the binary? Autumn cannot see me. She might see the man I am, but she cannot see the rest. It isn't easy to explain, there's no good language for it, how a person can be one thing and also its apparent opposite without undoing the other. Most people don't have the capacity to imagine more than one gender in a single body. They can't juggle the cognitive dissonance. When they imagine my past, they either force me into being a "real" girl, or they rewrite it, conjuring a boyhood that never happened, keeping my story coherent for themselves—and splitting me in the process. For them, there was Mel and now there's Max, as if we aren't the same continuous person. Early in transition, I welcomed such revisionist history as affirmation, but at this point, the revision hits me as erasure. To be Max, Mel had to go away for awhile, but it's one thing when I make that split and another when others do it to me. My dissonance isn't yours to fix. I would present it in one hand if I could, but I have to speak of myself in two parts to be legible. Otherwise, I dematerialize into blurgender, cloudgender, whatever—cryptogender. (Is that a thing? It's probably a thing.) I want all my parts to exist without one unraveling the other. Trans men are men, yes, but we're also something more.

"You sound like one of those angry white guys on Fox News," Autumn goes on, "complaining about political correctness."

Her comment stings. When my scandal spread beyond Ampleforth, right-wing media tried to weaponize me in their fight against political correctness. It happened around the same time that a high school teacher in Iowa lost his job for staunchly refusing to use a trans student's pronouns. He was the third teacher to get fired for that offense and it stimulated an anxiety in America that Fox could not resist. The teacher went on TV and cited religious freedom. His lawyer said, "This is a prime example of the tyranny of the transgender agenda. We just want tolerance to be a two-way street." The Fox commentator called the misconduct a "thoughtcrime," invoking Orwell, while at the bottom of the screen, the chyron read "TRANS

PRONOUN CRACKDOWN." When news of my situation spread, Fox invited me on. What could be better for their cause than a transgender teacher tyrannized by what they called "the PC trans cult"? I refused. My protest is not their protest, and the last thing this world needs is a trans man going on Fox to rail against political correctness. I didn't want to be misrepresented as a right-wing transfundamentalist, the reactionary type that trans Tumblr calls "truscum," and I didn't want the Twitter death threats that would come with it. I stayed home with my cannabis gummies. The threats came anyway, thanks to that piece in the *Globe*, and I was devastated to see them come almost entirely from trans people. The Trump administration was taking away our right to exist, but somehow they found time to write hate tweets to me. *Why don't you go kill yourself*, they wrote, with their unicorn and rainbow emojis. *Why don't you put a noose around your neck and just do it already?*

Autumn freezes onscreen, her face distorted. I probably look distorted, too, on her side of the bad connection. The symbolism of this technological glitch is not lost on me. I wait to unfreeze, but we lose each other and cannot reconnect. I've had enough sensitivity for the day anyway. I close the laptop and look up to see Dakota loitering by my open door. Has she been listening? When I invite her in, she wanders the room, poking at my mother's piles of junk, until she lands on my photo album. She waits for my nod and opens it, yellowed cellophane crackling over Polaroids of Jules and Mel.

"Is this you, Uncle Max?"

"That's me."

She looks at Mel—at me—and I get a flash of that old queer anxiety, like I'm corrupting a child, showing her something she shouldn't see. Did Donna tell her about me? Or am I too difficult to explain, a secret that I, once again, have to keep?

"Cool," Dakota says with a shrug. "One of my friends at school is trans."

I'm not expecting this and my internal map of the world tilts. Of course there are trans kids in the dismal American hinterlands, walking around, right out in the open. Dakota lives in the present, not the past. Still, I am stunned and delighted, the way I am whenever I find other trans people simply existing—casually riding the T, getting a coffee at Dunkin' Donuts, picking out produce at Star Market. We're everywhere. You'd think I'd be used to it, but it affects me every time I rediscover that I'm not the only one. And now, here in my own hinterland, where I had to be invisible, there's a chance to be seen? I take the photo album and sit on the edge of the bed, motioning for Dakota to sit with me. Together, side by side, we begin to turn the pages.

1984

Inside the entrance of the Brixton Fair, Dale left us, saying, "Be back at the car by nine thirty. Or else." We watched him and Tammy walk off into the cotton-candy air, his wiry arms splashed golden by the early evening sun, her frosted mane of hair tinted pink and blue by the stuttering lights of the Himalaya, a rock-and-roll ride that swirled screaming teenagers to Quiet Riot's "Cum on Feel the Noize." We were free.

Dressed in our best T-shirts and tightest, whitest, special-occasion Gloria Vanderbilt jeans, Jules and I smelled of Avon Skin So Soft and Aqua Net, a hint of bubblegum from the gloss that greased our lips. Jules had washed her hair so it looked soft and fluffy blonde, winging back from her face with the help of a curling iron. Her infected earlobe had healed and she'd replaced the crucifix with a dangling pentagram. Satan worship. Heavy metal. She looked pretty, I thought, as I looped my arm in hers and we plunged into the crowd, the lights, the exhilarating aroma of sugar and fry-o-lator. Jules suggested we start with candy apples because "Boys like to see girls eating candy apples," she said. "It reminds them of sex." I followed her lead. The apple was rock-hard and hurt my teeth.

"Don't bite it," Jules said. "Lick it."

I watched her demonstrate, closing her eyes as she expertly dragged her tongue over the candied sphere, licking sweetness from her lips. Jules excelled at many of the girl things at which I failed. She was made that way. In those tight jeans she was skinny enough to show off a visible gap between her upper thighs where the light shined through. Boys praised that sliver of nothingness, evidence of absence, an empty wedge of air that made a girl more desirable. In school they'd poke it with wooden rulers. But I had no such gap. In the same skin-tight jeans, no light shined through my legs. I was not made that way.

The demolition derby wouldn't start for a while, so we visited the aggie barns and looked at the fancy show birds, the cows with their soulful eyes, and a horse that snuffled our candy-sweet hands with velvety lips. We rode the flying cages and played a few games. I tried the Cat Rack, throwing a baseball to knock down dolls ringed in fluff, and won a rabbit's foot keychain, dyed purple, a color I chose to match the Vanderbilt swan embroidered on the front pocket of my jeans. I hung it from a belt loop at my hip and all night I kept stroking it, hoping for luck.

Outside the Congress of Live Freaks, Jules and I gazed at the wall of colorful banners and their promise of living human wonders like the World's Smallest Woman and the World's Fattest Man, along with a collection of Strange Girls: "Can they marry like other girls? Have children? Be happy as they are? Why were they born?" There was the Headless Girl and the Armless Girl, the Gator Girl and the Snake Girl, a girl who was Tortured Alive, and another known as Boy Changed Into Girl, a half-man/half-woman. I had always longed to go inside the freak tent. My mother never let me, saying it was not for children, but she wasn't here now.

Inside, most of what the banners hyped was missing from the show or displayed only as photographs or props, like the Five-Legged Squirrel stuffed in a cage, looking dusty and deflated. We were too thrilled to be disappointed by the rip-off and gladly paid another quarter to go into a second tent to see Little Gloria, the World's Smallest Woman. She wasn't a miniaturized person, like the painting on the banner, but a regular woman with dwarfism who sat on a child-sized La-Z-Boy, drinking a tallboy of Budweiser and watching a rerun of *Knight Rider* on a black-and-white television. She did not look at us, a skill developed from a life lived in an unusual body, the kind that invites punishment from average people who hate seeing a shape they are afraid of becoming. I felt uncomfortable gawking at Little Gloria, but Jules didn't mind. She asked the woman how she went to the toilet, a tone in her voice that reminded me of the way she poked at vulnerable things, like the frog's eggs in the swamp. Little Gloria narrowed her eyes, focusing on the television, and didn't answer. I wanted to apologize for my friend, who could sometimes be a jerk, but I only took Jules by the arm and pulled her along, hoping the World's Smallest Woman didn't think I was a jerk, too.

For more quarters, we saw the World's Fattest Man and a snake charmer named Goldie, and then Jules was done with the freaks. She was saving the rest of her money for the rides, but I desperately wanted to see the half-man/half-woman. Kids under eighteen could only go in with an adult escort, so I hitched a ride with a guy in a Van Halen T-shirt, tattoos on his knuckles that spelled out *LONE WOLF*. He put an arm around me, called me "honey," and paid my way, which made me feel special and pretty, like a normal girl. We had to wait awhile. This tent only allowed one person or couple at a time. Lone Wolf kept his arm around me, and I could tell he'd been drinking. He smelled like my dad. When he spotted the rabbit's foot on my belt loop, he took hold of it and stroked the purple fur with his thumb.

"This for good luck, honey?"

I nodded, feeling my body bloom with heat, and looked down at the man's thumb, large and thickly knuckled, with a nail turned black and blue. When the guy in front of us went inside, Lone Wolf pulled me forward on the line. We were next. I tried peeking through the tent flaps.

"You excited to see the freak?"

I nodded.

"You know what it looks like?"

I shook my head. Lone Wolf put his lips to my ear, so I could feel the yeasty steam of his breath. "It's a chick," he whispered, "with a dick."

His tongue, wet and pulpy, mashed my ear and then he pulled me forward again, into the tent and the glittering presence of the Half-and-Half. She was the most elegant of all the freaks I'd seen that night and ever since, sitting on a red velvet throne, dressed in a low-cut sequined sheath dress, breasts pushed up high and plumped, revealing pink semicircles of areolae. Her hair was like the cotton candy they sold on the midway, a flossy confection in white gold.

"*You* can see what I look like," the Half-and-Half said to my escort, "but *she's* gotta stay out here. It's a dollar, sweetie, and for that you get plenty of uninterrupted lookie-loo."

Lone Wolf handed over two bucks, buying an autographed picture for me, signed Robert-Roberta, along with a leaflet that explained her unusual situation. He told me to wait while he went behind a velvet curtain. I looked at the leaflet. It featured a diagram of body parts, a pelvis with a dark internal corridor marked "Undeveloped Vagina" and a penis-looking structure marked "Overdeveloped Clitoris." This only confused me more. Looking back, I suspect the leaflet had nothing to do with Robert-Roberta, and it was just something sensational, clipped out of a medical textbook, to earn a few extra quarters from the hicks. She was probably a regular crossdresser, maybe a trans woman on hormones, and had shown my escort nothing more than an ordinary penis. But what do I know? I have since learned that bodies come with surprising architectures and any one of them could have been situated between the legs of the Brixton Fair Half-and-Half.

I stared at the velvet curtain, trying to hear what was happening on the other side, to understand what it all meant, but I knew none of my questions would be answered there. I folded the handbills into my back pocket and walked out to find Jules waiting by the Five-Legged Squirrel.

"That pervert groped me," I told her giddily, grabbing her by the arm and pulling her out to the midway. Late for the demolition derby, we started to run.

In the crowded grandstand, we found two seats, balancing paper plates loaded with fried dough on our laps, trying not to get the powdered sugar everywhere. Down below, in the dirt center of the grass-ringed racetrack, rows of cars lined up for the second heat of the derby. I found Sylvia at the edge, her Pepto-pink wagon blushing in the setting sun. Number 88. Misplaced Joan of Arc. I felt my heart flop behind my ribs and stifled the urge to call her name.

"*Who* groped you?" Jules asked once we'd settled in. "The Half-and-Half?"

"She didn't touch me."

"You said 'that pervert.'"

"The *guy*," I said. "He practically molested me."

"Sounds like fun."

I smacked her arm and called her a nympho. Out on the track, a girl waved a flag, signaling the start. The drivers backed into each other, barely touching bumpers—"That's what you call the gentleman's tap," said a man behind us to his wife—and they went roaring in all directions, kicking up plumes of dirt as they spun and collided, making the crowd moan and whoop with every crash and near miss. I kept my eyes on Sylvia. She was doing well. Other cars stalled or limped along after a few hits, but she kept running, reverse slamming into her opponents until the wagon's back end accordioned. She went on, driving hard, until she was only one of three left alive in a litter of dead cars.

"Is that a girl in Number 88?" said the woman behind us. "She's kicking ass."

I felt proud to know Sylvia, the ass-kicking girl in the pink jalopy, and wanted to say something to show I was connected to her, but I didn't want to give away my secret in front of Jules. She sat licking powdered sugar from her fingers, looking bored, while the three survivors circled the track, jousting and missing. Then Sylvia got into a jam. The two others stalked her, weaving between the islands of wreckage, a pair of sharks teamed up against a single prey. Flanking her from both sides, the cars screeched across the track and hit Sylvia hard, sandwiching her front end between them, crumpling the white driver's side door that was supposed to be off-limits. The gruesome crunch made the crowd groan and cheer. I clenched the armrests of my seat. As the other cars backed away, flames flickered under Sylvia's hood. One second. Two. Fire burst along her undercarriage, tracing a puddle of gasoline, and blossomed into a bright orange explosion. I got to my feet. The crowd let out a long, delirious *Ohhh!* People threw their fists in the air, euphoric in the presence of combustion, the primal joy of fire. Sylvia, struggling to get out of the car, wrestled with her seatbelt. She was trapped.

"Sylviaaaa," I shouted, hands cupped to my mouth.

Another second. Two. Three. Firefighters appeared, dragging a hose. And then Sylvia's silver helmet emerged as she dove headfirst from the window, rolled, and got to her feet, running across the dirt with her fist held high. The crowd cheered, clapping and whooping for this daredevil, this misplaced Joan of Arc, escaped from the flames. Invincible. She would not be burned at the stake. Not that day.

I sat down shaking, hands at my mouth, while the firefighters doused the car with their hose, working to stifle the dark tower of smoke that rose to the sky.

"You dropped your fried dough," Jules said.

I looked down at the greasy mess at my feet.

"So," she said. "That's the mysterious Sylvia."

She held out her plate so I could tear off a piece. I crammed it in my mouth, spilling sugar dust onto my shirt, and said nothing. Together we walked down through the crowd of people holding stuffed animals and cups of beer. Maybe, I hoped, Jules wouldn't recognize Sylvia. After all, she'd only seen her that one time, from the distance of her mother's car, outside the post office. And that was two weeks ago. By the track, demo drivers hung around the gate, dirt on their faces, helmets at their feet. Sylvia stood apart, holding her helmet in one hand, trophy in the other. She'd won the prize for Most Aggressive Driver. When I called her name, she turned and gave me a "Hey, man," with a carelessness that felt like indifference, but was just Sylvia, cool Sylvia smiling in the last ribbon of amber light as the sun dropped behind the grandstand.

Before I could reach her, two drivers stepped between us and slapped Sylvia on the back, the way they did with each other, but harder, a gesture pricked with a barbed message. I hung back. The men wore grimy jeans and T-shirts. One had the sketchy growth of a boyish beard and the other wore a cap with a patch of the Confederate flag. "Hey, S—," that one said, calling Sylvia by a man's name, what I figured must have been her birth name. I won't say it. Today, this is known as *deadnaming*, and it is considered at best a microaggression, at worst an act of violence. We did not know that then, but when I heard the name, it jolted me, throwing me into cognitive dissonance, the clash of seeing Sylvia wrong. I wanted to look away, as if from someone suddenly stripped of clothing. But Sylvia, as always, did not flinch.

"Hey, Jimmy," she said. "Pete, how ya been?"

Pete, the one with the sketchy beard, said, "Doing awright. I'm on the tit, working for the state doing road work, highway maintenance. Can't complain."

"Hey, S—," Jimmy repeated, not letting it go. "What's up, *man*? Nice driving, *man*." He grabbed Sylvia's trophy and hefted its weight. "Most Aggressive Driver. I guess you still got balls behind the wheel. Do you, S—? You still got balls?"

I looked at Sylvia, expecting hurt to break across her face, but she grinned and said, "I've got balls bigger than yours and Pete's put together."

That took the piss out of the men and they laughed a genuine laugh that confused me. It sounded almost like friendship, or at least familiarity.

"We're just fucking with you," Jimmy said, giving back the trophy.

"Yeah, well, you assholes almost killed me with that crunch out there."

"Next time we'll try harder," Jimmy said, maybe joking, maybe not. He grabbed Pete by the shoulder to go, but Pete hesitated. In a tone of apology, he told Sylvia, "Just because you are the way you are, I mean, no kid gloves, right? You can't expect special treatment."

"I wouldn't dream of it, sweetheart," Sylvia replied, pitching her voice high and batting her eyes, throwing the men off balance as they headed back to the boisterous group of drivers down the track. She had scored the last word.

"Assholes," she muttered, and then, "Did you see me out there? Did you see that fire? It was bitchin." She handed me her trophy and helmet to hold so she could light a cigarette. The trophy wasn't as heavy as I'd imagined, but still impressive, a green column topped with a model of a muscle car, all chromed plastic, gleaming fake gold. "Who's your friend?"

I'd forgotten about Jules. Standing beside me, trying to look unbothered by it all, she ran a hand through her feathery yellow hair, looking off in the distance like anything else could be worth watching. She had a chunk of that hair in her mouth, bitten between her teeth, so I knew she felt uncomfortable.

"This is Jules. My best friend."

"Hey, Jules."

"Hey."

"You guys want to hang out?" Sylvia asked.

"We don't have time," Jules said. "My brother's waiting and he'll have a fit if we're late."

"But Dale said nine thirty and it's only quarter of."

"I wanted to ride the rides," Jules complained.

"It's cool," Sylvia said. "I was just gonna grab a beer. Maybe smoke some grass."

That changed things for Jules, who never said no to substances. The three of us walked to the edge of the midway where a cinderblock snack bar advertised "Beer & Wine" on a faded Pepsi sign. While Sylvia procured three plastic cups of Budweiser, Jules and I found a patch of grass, away from the busy picnic tables and pulsing lights, under a tree where the fireflies had come out, blinking green phosphorescence.

As soon as we were out of earshot, Jules said, "Is that who I think it is?"

"Who do you think it is?"

"Lola," Jules started singing, the Kinks song about someone who walks like a woman and talks like a man. "*L-O-L-A*, Lola."

"Quiet."

"He can't hear me."

"She. And her name is Sylvia. Don't be a jerk."

"Why didn't you tell me?"

"Maybe I was afraid you'd act like this."

Jules rolled her eyes and plopped to the ground, sitting cross-legged and smirking, which was better than talking. I placed Sylvia's helmet and trophy against the tree and sat, too, stretching out my long legs and leaning back on my hands, looking to the snack bar where Sylvia stood in the buggy fluorescent light, counting out bills. I watched as she walked toward us, balancing the three foamy cups in her hands, trying not to spill. Jules tugged at the grass, picking out strands until she found one to prop between her thumbs. She blew into it, making a sound like a balloon farting wet air.

"Knock it off," I said.

She looked at me, eyes wide, and blew three more defiant farts before tossing the blade of grass over her shoulder. I was not the boss of her. Sylvia handed out the cups. The beer tasted like a cold penny and cooled my insides as I gulped it down. Sylvia lit a joint and it was good just to be there, at the shadowy outskirts, the noise of the fair like an ocean, its mechanical roar spiked by whoops of pleasure over the throb of rock music, all symphonizing in summer air that smelled of earth and popcorn. The sky had turned deep violet, not yet dark enough for fireworks. The fireflies would have to do. I said, "You know in Patti's song 'Birdland,' that part where she says it was like someone spread butter on the stars?"

Sylvia nodded.

"Look at the fireflies. It's like that. Like someone spread butter on them. See? How the light sort of smears? Squint your eyes."

"You're stoned," Sylvia said, squinting at the green flickers. "*Buttered fireflies*."

Jules didn't say anything. I saw her looking at Sylvia in that way people do, and I could tell she was trying to see it, the residue of a shucked-off sex. I worried she might ask stupid, mean questions, like she did with the World's Smallest Woman, and I wanted to cover Sylvia with a blanket, but I didn't have a blanket.

I asked her, "Are you staying for the fireworks?"

"Nah. I want to get out of here in one piece."

"That's smart," said Jules, chiming in. "Last year? I heard there were seven rapes at the fair. That's one rape every night."

"Oh, really? Where'd you hear that?" I asked, knowing exactly where.

"Everybody knows," she said, "it's not safe here for *girls*." She looked at Sylvia, iciness in her eyes. "Mel got groped tonight at the freak show," she went on. "It was the Half-and-Half."

"No, it wasn't," I said. "I told you it was the guy. With the tattoos on his fingers. Lone Wolf."

"Never trust anyone with tattooed fingers," Sylvia said, not taking whatever bait Jules was dangling. "I read that in a fortune cookie."

"My dad has tattooed fingers," Jules said. "*LOVE* on one hand and *HATE* on the other."

"That's a classic," Sylvia said. "From *Night of the Hunter.* Robert Mitchum plays a preacher who's a serial killer. Do you trust him? Your dad, I mean."

Jules shrugged and starting tugging again at the grass, caught off-guard. I knew the answer to the question was no. She'd been trying to get the better of Sylvia and then it flipped on her. I almost felt sorry.

"Her dad's a real asshole," I said.

Sylvia nodded, "Mine was too. He used to whup me. Whenever I did something he didn't like, which was all the time, he'd say, 'Go git me a switch!' He was from Georgia, a real cracker, and that's how they do it down there. They make the kid choose the implement of torture. 'Go git me a switch,' he'd say and I'd have to go out to our peach tree and cut a branch. If I didn't pick the thinnest, meanest branch, he'd send me back for another. I hated that tree. It never produced any good peaches, either. They were full of worms."

Sylvia sipped her beer, wiping her mouth with the pad of her thumb. She had the ability to tell a story that shocked you into silence, and then she'd sit there, as if she hadn't said anything. Jules and I didn't speak. Our parents hit us, of course. That was normal. Our mothers slapped our faces and called us *twats* and *cunts*. Our fathers smacked us in the backs of our heads and punched our arms, telling us to *smarten up* but *don't get wise*. Once, just once, my father grabbed me by the throat and lifted me off my feet, choking me until my vision went fuzzy. But our parents only used their hands, never switches or belts, and we told ourselves we weren't really hurt. Sylvia's story felt like a step over some invisible line. We got hit, but she'd been whupped.

I said, "You said *was*. Your dad *was* an asshole."

"Yeah, well, you use the past tense for people who are dead. Don't feel bad, though, I was glad when he died. Before that, it was like, even when I was in New York, I could feel him. Like you're in the woods and you know there's a wolf out there, tracking you, waiting to attack. And then, poof, the wolf's gone. You feel that, too. The relief of absence. From miles away."

Jules nodded like she got what Sylvia was saying. Like she understood in a deep and personal way. She often talked about wishing her father was dead. Her mother, too, but mostly it was Ray Cobb she wanted buried and gone.

"How'd he die?" Jules asked.

"Shot himself. Went down the basement with his Baby Nambu, a pistol he took off a Korean soldier during the war, and blammo. Sounds adorable, doesn't it? Baby Nambu? He used to take me back in the woods and make me shoot bottles with it. All that 'make you a man' crap. I wasn't there when he did it. I'd run off to New York by then, but my mother? It totally fucked her up. I think it killed her, too."

"Your mother and father are both dead?" Jules said, savoring the idea of it.

Sylvia shrugged and tucked her hair behind her ears, hair as black and shiny as raven feathers. She was an orphan, I thought, and it was this that made Jules admire Sylvia in that moment. Not her demolition driving, nor her daring escape from the burning car. Not her taste in music, nor her generosity with beer and weed. Jules was most enamored with Sylvia's status as a young person with dead parents.

"Hey, kids," Sylvia said, looking at her watch. "It's after nine thirty. Didn't you say you had to be somewhere?"

Jules jumped to her feet. "Dale is gonna freak."

We took off running, through the crowds, until we got to the parking lot, panting and bent over with cramps. It was nearly 10:00. Dale and Tammy stood by the car, looking pissed. Tammy grinned, enjoying the deep shit we were in, and Dale lunged.

"Get in the car!"

He grabbed Jules, jerking her hard so her T-shirt made a ripping sound as it lifted, exposing her belly. He whipped her around, her feet turning beneath her as she struggled.

"Stop it!" I yelled, smacking and scratching Dale in the arm. I wasn't one to fight back, but the feeling of the men bullying Sylvia was still with me and I sensed something uncoil, some rage I didn't know was there. I kept smacking Dale until he swung his fist into my stomach, knocking the wind out of me.

"Get in the fucking car!"

"Get the fuck off me! Get off me!" Jules screamed, her voice going high and reedy, windmilling her fists at Dale as he flung her into the open door of the backseat.

"You, too!" He pointed at me and I obeyed, still gasping and clutching my stomach, slipping in before Dale could slam the door on my leg. He started the ignition and tore out of the space without looking back, nearly hitting a group of teenagers walking behind. A couple of them pounded their fists on the trunk, saying, "Watch out." When Dale saw they were Black, he shouted, "Get away from the fuckin' car!"

"What's your problem, man?" said one of the guys at the open window. He wore a red tracksuit with white stripes down the sleeves and legs, matching Adidas sneakers, his hair sculpted into a high flat-top. Under his arm he carried a pink teddy bear.

"*You're* my fuckin' problem, spook."

"Dale, for chrissake," Tammy hissed. "Just go. They probably have guns."

"What the fuck did you call me?" the guy said, leaning in the window, his friends gathering behind him. Tammy screamed in what sounded like real terror and Dale hit the gas, making the guy step back. Jules and I turned to see the teddy bear on the ground and a cup flying straight at us. It smashed across the back window, exploding piña colada, white and gooey. Dale jumped the curb and ran a red light, gunning for home, as the smell of rotten egg filled the car.

"I hate my life," Jules mumbled.

Dale's eyes flashed in the rearview mirror. "Did you see what you did?"

"I didn't do *shit*," Jules said, arms folded, pressing herself back into the seat as far as she could go.

"You almost got us killed by those spooks. Ma and Dad would've loved that."

"Eat me."

"Watch that trash mouth," Tammy added. "You girls are so immature. All you ever think about is yourselves. It's boring already."

"Shut up, Tammy," Jules snapped. "Nobody asked you."

"Don't talk to her like that!"

"Then tell her to mind her own fucking business! She's not family. She's just your slut!"

Dale's arm shot back and flailed for Jules, grabbing and smacking at her legs as she kicked furiously at the front seat, screaming "fuck you" over and over, her voice croaking and fierce, a cornered wildcat fighting for its life. The car weaved and jerked across the four-lane road, lurching toward the double yellow. I put my fingers in my ears and turned to look out the back window, through the sticky scrim of piña colada splash. In the distance, over the trees and gas station signs, the fireworks of the fair gushed into the black sky, cascading in blossoms of golden willow and blood-red peony, a garden of sparks. I felt sorry to miss them. I felt sorry, too, about the kid with the pink teddy bear. He was probably carrying it home to someone, his girlfriend or little sister, and now it would be dirty from the parking lot and from the ugly word Dale used, a word that made me feel dirty, too, as if I'd said it with my own mouth. I wanted to apologize to the kid the way I wanted to apologize to the World's Smallest Woman. *I am not these people.*

I got home in one piece, lucky to have survived the Brixton Fair. I hadn't been murdered or raped. I didn't lose a finger to a caged animal. I was not decapitated in a car wreck. The lie I told my mother about going with Ray and Ginny Cobb would never be revealed, even after Dale roared up to my house, radio blasting. When I went inside, the house was empty, the lights and television left on to discourage burglars. My mother, out looking for a man, wasn't there.

In my room, I took off my clothes and slipped on a Kliban cat nightshirt, the tabby in red sneakers that matched my bedsheets. Tossed on the floor, my white jeans had dirt marks on the backside from sitting in the grass and the leaflets from the Half-and-Half were still in the pocket. I took them out and looked at Robert-Roberta, the diagrams marked "Undeveloped Vagina" and "Overdeveloped Clitoris." They made me feel ashamed and criminal. I ripped them into small pieces, took them to the kitchen, and buried them at the bottom of the trash, under the coffee grounds and eggshells, where my mother would never find them. Back in my room, I sat on the bed, holding the rabbit's foot. I thought of the man at the freak show, how he stroked the fur with his thumb. I thought of many things, my brain full of beer and weed, and the violent stimulations of the night. I thought of candy apples and LONE WOLF. The Half-and-Half showing her mystery behind the velvet curtain. Strange

Girls, headless and armless. Fireflies sliding across the dark, brushed with butter. Dale's rage and the swollen plum inside his shorts. Sylvia beaten with a peach tree switch. Gasoline bursting into flame, a bright orange chrysanthemum. The horse's soft lips in my hand. The man's tongue in my ear like a slug, a leech, the neck of a clam. And horses, horses, horses.

I put on my Phil Collins tape, rewound to the start of "In the Air Tonight," and lay atop the sheets in the dark. Holding the rabbit's foot, I stroked the fur with my thumb and used the other hand to touch myself for the first time. Playing a dirty movie in my head, was I myself or Lone Wolf? Did I inhabit the body of a girl or a man? I did not know, exactly, what had turned me on, other than the whole sweaty, stinking mess, its jagged rupture of my existence. Jules kissing a pillow, her leg on my leg. Sylvia in the spray of a garden hose, water splashing asphalt and dirt, churning up the sweet summer smell of rain hitting earth—*petrichor*, the loamy scent of microbial decay. Sylvia barefoot in the puddles. Sylvia smelling of clove cigarettes and motor oil.

When it was done, my heart hammered in my chest and I prayed to God that I was not about to die.

•

"I came," I told Jules the next day.

It was the Fourth of July and we were standing on Central Street in a sparse group of onlookers, waiting for the town parade to begin. Next to us, a few old ladies dressed in red, white, and blue sat in folding beach chairs, nylon slats straining under their weight. A young mother held a toddler in her arms, his mouth ringed with melted popsicle. Like every year, Red Mike Fitzgerald led the procession dressed as Uncle Sam waving a drum major's mace. He was popular in town, the owner of Red Mike's Package Store, but more importantly, he was tall, with a white beard that had once been red, hence the nickname, and he fit the Uncle Sam suit. Behind him, a fleet of girls in ponytails twirled batons while the Swaffham High marching band played "Eye of the Tiger."

"Did you jerk off?"

"First time," I said. "I thought I was having a heart attack. You have to try it."

I felt proud to be the knowing one, the mature one, the guide. Finally. I had something I could introduce to Jules. "Actually," she said, "I didn't tell you, but I've been doing it, too. For like the past year."

This sent me into a tailspin. I could handle the fact that she'd started drinking and smoking pot without me, but this? We were best friends. We were supposed to tell each other everything. I felt like a child, embarrassed by my assumption that I'd arrived first.

"Why didn't you tell me? A whole year?"

"Well, maybe two. Or three."

"*Three* years? Since *fifth* grade?" Fifth grade, when we were going to Park and Rec to play Zimm Zamm and make lanyards out of gimp? That fifth grade? When we were still *children*? "What's wrong with you? Are you some kind of nympho?"

Jules tucked a hank of yellow hair in her mouth and sucked, that nervous habit. I know well that adolescence is a time of exquisite self-absorption, but I wish I could've been kinder to my friend, who was struggling, too. I wish I had understood that she might have felt ashamed, coming out as an early adopter of solo sexual activity, or that she could have wanted something secret, just for herself. But I couldn't see any of that. I only felt betrayed. We stood in silence and watched the Little League teams go by, the Cub Scouts and Brownies in their uniforms, the old vets in their garrison caps. *Piss cutters*, my dad called those hats, because they supposedly looked like vaginas. Was everything about sex?

"You never tell me anything," I said. "Drinking whiskey. Smoking pot. And now jerking off."

"Quiet," Jules hissed. The ladies in the beach chairs glared. I didn't care. I was mad, so much I felt like crying. A decorated flat-bed truck rolled past, hauling girls in sequin tops and leotards from Miss Nancy's Pizazz! Dance Studio. Instead of dancing, the girls sat on bales of hay, idly talking, as if they were in someone's living room and not a parade. An antique couple went by in an antique car, waving flags from the windows, and in the rumble seat sat the VFW Poppy Princess in her crown and sash, waving like the queen of England. She was an ordinary pretty girl with a cheerful smile and long, straight golden hair. The sort of girl who got along just fine in the world. Loved by her parents, later by a husband and children, on and on, the good life unrolling before her like a red carpet. The sort of girl I knew I could never be. I felt my eyes burn with tears, not knowing why I was so upset, except for my unnamed frustrations, which seemed mystifying and unbeatable, afflictions I felt sure would haunt me for the rest of my life, while the goddamn Poppy Princess went about her breezy way.

Jules and I followed the parade to the VFW parking lot, into the fumes of charcoal briquettes and yellow mustard, where we drank wet cans of Pepsi and ate sweaty hot dogs.

"Why didn't you tell me?" I said.

"Why didn't you tell me about the tranny?"

I didn't say that I was afraid Jules would judge me, that she'd see how I felt about Sylvia and know I was some sort of pervert, afraid she'd expose me to the Neighborhood Watchers, cast me into the wilderness, hang me as a witch on Swaffham Green. I wish I could have trusted my best friend, but I'd learned early that even the people who are supposed to love you can turn on you.

"Her name is Sylvia," I said.

"It's cool." Jules shrugged. "I don't care."

There was an edge in her voice that made it hard to know what she really meant.

She said, "I can tell you *like her* like her."

"I don't," I snapped. "Not like that."

"I don't care," she said again.

"What are you, jealous?"

"I'm not jealous."

"Fine."

I clutched the rabbit's foot on the belt loop of my cut-offs and rubbed its purple fur, same color as the bruises on Jules' forearm, Dale's fingerprints, the size of nickels. *We shouldn't fight*, I told myself. We were all we had in that mean little world. I grabbed her hand and squeezed. Her return squeeze was brief, but I didn't let her go and she didn't pull away.

"I'm not going to do anything," I said, not knowing what I meant.

From the VFW we walked to Jules' house. My mother was at her friend Gail's, enjoying a cookout with high-quality people in Newcastle-by-the-Sea, and we were both happy to be away from each other. At the Cobbs', motorcycles and pickup trucks parked cockeyed across the driveway, spilling onto the grass. Over the squat roof of the underground house we could see the backyard full of people, the low-quality sort, sitting on lawn chairs, barefoot, drinking cans of Miller High Life and smoking pot. They had Jules' old Slip 'N Slide hooked up to the hose and a bunch of little kids were hurling themselves onto it, tumbling around in their underpants. Someone's dog ran in circles, hunting for food scraps and sniffing crotches. The radio played WBCN, the Rock of Boston, making me wish Sylvia was there, but only in my dreams would that scenario not go terribly wrong.

"Hey, hey," Ray called from the grill when he saw us walk over. "If it isn't her royal highnesses, finally decided to join us."

I hadn't seen Jules' dad in awhile. He looked bigger and more intimidating than ever, with his Grizzly Adams beard and barrel chest, *LOVE* and *HATE* scrawled on his knuckles. Jules ignored him and headed for the cooler by the picnic table.

"Looking good Julie," said a stringy guy in a Mickey Mouse T-shirt with skull tattoos on his arms. He whacked Jules on the ass as she bent to the cooler and she swatted his hand. "Hey, Ray," the guy called out. "Your little girl's all grown up. You better keep an eye on this one."

"Knock it off," Jules said, grabbing two cans of beer and handing one to me.

"Yeah, Bud," said a lean and leathery woman sucking severely on a Marlboro. She was the guy's wife, his *old lady*. "Knock it the fuck off."

Jules lingered for a moment in the man's atmosphere, taking a stance of aloof defiance, letting him get his fill as she pulled back her hair on one side, pressed the cold can of beer to her neck, and went *mmm*.

"Put that on your jugular," she told me. "It cools your whole bloodstream."

The can felt good against my skin, but my blood didn't feel any less hot, and I didn't go *mmm*. For the next part of her performance, Jules took the can and tapped its top with her knuckle before popping it open and sucking at the foam that squirted out. I'd never seen her do the tapping thing, but she did it like she'd done it a hundred times, so I copied her, not knowing what it was for, but wanting to look the way she looked, practiced and smooth. Not that anyone noticed me.

"*Damn*, girl," the guy called Bud went on, gaping at Jules. "Drinking beer, too. Ray, didja hear what I said? You keeping an eye on this one?"

"She's in high school now," Ray called back, flipping bloody lumps of burger on the grill. "Beer's legal, far as I'm concerned. It's not liquor or nothing."

"Welp," Bud said quietly, "if there's grass on the field."

As we walked across the yard to the shade near Dale and Tammy, Bud kept his eyes on Jules. He didn't look at me, and I felt both relieved and sorely neglected to be exempted from his obscene attentions. I was no Poppy Princess and never would be. We sat in the scratchy grass with our beers and talked with Dale and Tammy about the parade like nothing had happened the night before, like Jules' arm wasn't spotted with bruises from Dale's hand, like I couldn't still feel his fist in my gut.

"It sounds boring," Tammy said about the parade, and I wondered if that's where Jules got that word. *Boring.* I wondered if she weren't hanging out with those two more than she let on. Whatever. I watched the kids plunging down the Slip 'N Slide on their bellies and remembered how it used to feel, to be so small and light that nothing hurt.

Bud was still stealing glances in our direction when Ginny came over and thrust paper plates with burgers into our hands. The meat was dry and gristly from sitting out too long in the sun and Ginny had doused them in ketchup, the watery Stop & Shop brand, so it ran down my hands and smeared across my face when I took a bite. I got up to get some napkins from the picnic table.

"Hey, girlie," Bud said, turning privately to me as I approached.

In his attention, I felt a thrill that shames me now, so desperate was I to be treated like a normal pretty girl.

"Check it out," he said.

I looked to see him open his mouth and, with his tongue, unhitch a pair of false front teeth attached to a gummy pink flipper. He waggled the teeth back and forth, slow at first, and then faster. I was mesmerized, unable to look away from the grotesque.

"Bud," said his wife, "put your flipper away. No one wants to see that."

"She digs it," he said, lisping with the flipper still on his tongue. "She's blushing."

Was this flirtation? I knew the gesture was sexual in some way, but I didn't understand if it meant I was a normal pretty girl or something else. I returned to Jules and didn't touch the burger, just lay back in the grass, looking up at the trees in their swirl of thick summer leaves, and held my rabbit's foot. I closed my eyes, listening to insects sawing in the green. I could smell myself, a light stink of sweat and ketchup, and thought about going home to take a cool shower. What was Sylvia doing? She'd mentioned a cookout and invited me to stop by. I felt stuck. The adults grew louder, drunker, and more stoned. The party was headed nowhere good.

By the toolshed sat a cardboard box full of illegal fireworks someone had brought up from South Carolina. Irresistibly eye-catching with colorful packages of roman candles, bottle rockets, and firecrackers, it made the men impatient and itchy, like children at a pile of Christmas presents. Unable to wait until dark, they lit sparklers and Magic Black Snakes for the kids before moving on to heavier artillery. Ray opened a brick of Black Cat firecrackers and handed them out. The women sat back and watched while the men lit fuses with smoldering punks and stood too close because too close felt like flirting with death, hooting and hollering as the firecrackers popped in smoky fusillades, littering the grass with sprays of paper. Someone placed a cinderblock in the middle of the yard and put a beer bottle on it, filling it with pink-stemmed rockets that went hissing into the trees. The air smelled of charred meat and gunpowder, spiced with the tang of male bodies getting rowdy. As usual, when the men got bored with each other, they turned on us.

Dale lit a firecracker and tossed it at Tammy, who ran squealing across the yard.

"Dale!" Ginny shouted from her chair. "Do not start with that shit."

But it had already started and Ginny, for all her ferocity, could do nothing to stop it. When Ray came out of the house holding his half-empty, watered-down bottle of Wild Turkey, Jules kicked me, worried he'd figure out she'd been drinking his stash, but Ray was distracted. With a whoop of sadistic glee, he put down the bottle and joined in the assholery, lighting a firecracker and tossing it close to Ginny's feet. She jumped from the chair, spilling her Southern Comfort and Tab in her lap, which really pissed her off. She ran at Ray, slapping wild while he laughed his big, god-of-fire laugh and grabbed both of her wrists in one hand. He twisted her arms and wrestled her over to the Slip 'N Slide while everyone watched, the men grinning like jackals and the women shouting at him to stop as he and Ginny slipped and fell onto the rubber sheet. Glasses knocked sideways, she got to her feet and fell again, landing hard on Ray, giving him an elbow in the gut for good measure. Now almost everyone except Ginny was laughing, the Marlboro woman wailing in hysterics about how she was going to piss her pants if they didn't stop. That's when I saw Dale aiming a bottle rocket at Jules. I told her to duck. The rocket frizzled past, hitting me in the chest with a sharp sting. I grabbed the tail and flung it, quick enough so it exploded near Dale's feet.

"Fuck you," he barked.

I stared at him, pulse pounding in my head, and made a decision. "I'm leaving."

"I'm going with you," Jules said, marching to her bike in the front yard.

Ginny shouted about it being too late and where the hell was Jules going off to just before supper, but we made our escape. She stood on the pedals and I sat behind, holding her hips as she pistoned, sailing us away into the light of almost evening.

I directed Jules to the streets behind the post office, to Chickatawbut Lane and Sylvia's house. When we rolled up, there were two guys on the front porch, sipping iced drinks and smoking cigarettes. They looked like twins with matching mustaches and denim cut-offs, striped tube socks, high-top Converse All Stars. They were shirtless and tan, eyes behind mirrored sunglasses. One wore red suspenders and one wore blue. Beyond that, I couldn't tell them apart.

"Howdy," said Blue Suspenders, like a cowboy.

I asked for Sylvia and he pointed us inside. We passed the den, where people sat around the stereo smoking from a bong and playing a Velvet Underground record, the one with the banana on the cover. From the speakers, "Venus in Furs" cranked out its jangly, hypnotic sound, Lou Reed singing of boots and shiny leather. In the kitchen we found Sylvia hacking into a plastic bag of ice with a screwdriver.

"Take over for me," she said, skipping hello.

I took the screwdriver and started stabbing while Sylvia knelt on the floor to dig around in the cabinets. She wore her Levi's cut-offs, black tank top with spaghetti straps, and no shoes. I could see the downy cleft of her ass, the dirty soles of her feet. The sight made me want to get on my knees, too, and—I didn't know what. Something.

"I'm making Harvey Wallbangers. It's the official cocktail for today," she said, half inside the cabinet as she pushed around pots and pans until she came up with an ice bucket. "It's a classic. You ever have one?"

Within minutes, Jules and I each had a large drink in our hands, cold and golden and tasting like strong booze with licorice. Sylvia carried a tray of them, tinkling, to the backyard. A small group, sitting in an odd circle of high-backed indoor dining chairs, applauded the arrival of the Wallbangers. How can I describe those people? They were not unusual in any dramatic way. They weren't glaringly punk or beatnik, not like the caricatures I'd seen in movies with mohawks and bongo drums. If you put them on the streets of the city, they would have turned no heads. But in Swaffham, they were utterly different. One girl had short hair, bleached platinum blonde and styled straight up like the bristles of a horse brush. Another wore combat boots and a checkerboard painter's cap pinned with a button that said "DON'T DIE WONDERING." Two guys, talking softly and only to each other, wore tank tops and gym shorts and looked basically average, except they had an air about them, a dignified poise. They were all white, except for one guy, who was Black, and that alone made him different in my all-white town. He dressed in a French sailor shirt, blue and white stripes with a boat neck that bared his collarbones, and at his throat he'd knotted a yellow silk scarf. "Bang, bang," he said approvingly after sipping his Wallbanger. "Mary, you have outdone yourself."

"Don't call me Mary," Sylvia told him. "I don't like that camp shit. And you know my name."

"Maybe if it didn't keep changing," he replied, "I could keep it straight. So to speak. Last month wasn't it Stella? Or Scarlett?"

"I like *Sylvia*," said Platinum Blonde. "I think you should stick with it."

"It's very poetic," Combat Boots agreed. "Like Sylvia Plath. 'Every woman adores a Fascist, the boot in the face, the brute brute heart of a brute like you.' Just don't end up with your head in the oven."

Jules and I sat awkwardly and sipped our Wallbangers. Sylvia's friends were welcoming, but not especially interested in us, and we receded into the background of their lively chatter. I didn't get the references, but I was happy to be there. I could tell that Sailor Shirt was gay, and I watched him, drinking in all I could. Maybe they were all gay. Their styles didn't go together, they didn't wear the same shoes or haircuts, but something bonded them into this motley tribe. Of course, it was Sylvia. A collector of odd items and lost souls, she drew them to her, much like she drew me, gathering them from different places to her place, a domain beyond geography that moved with Sylvia, wherever she went, a place that Sailor Shirt dubbed "The Island of Misfit Toys." One came from a socialist bookstore in Cambridge and another from a New Age café on Boston's Newbury Street. This one was collected from a rock club in Kenmore

Square. That one from the small-town gay bar I did not know existed just a fifteen-minute drive from my house, tucked down a dirt road behind a Holiday Inn. They came from all over, but most lived in and around Boston, in small apartments with no backyards, so when Sylvia invited them to Swaffham for the Fourth, they just had to come.

"Nature," said Sailor Shirt, pronouncing it *nay-chuh* and spreading his arms as if to exalt the sullen grandeur of the slouching trees, the patchy crabgrass, the blue neon bug zapper hanging off the garage.

"It's so *real* out here," said Combat Boots. "So visceral. So America."

"And, you have to admit, a little scary," said Platinum Blonde.

"Oh, totally," Boots jumped in, excited. "This is totally where a slasher movie would happen. Like *Halloween*. All that suburban menace. The creeping normality. And what's under the surface, right? *Psycho* meets *The Stepford Wives*. The dead mother in the basement, stinking up the place, while all the little conformists go on mowing their lawns. It's the banality of evil, American style."

"I don't know how you can stand it, Syl," the blonde continued. "Do you feel safe?"

"This is my hometown," Sylvia answered. "The motherland to which I was born. What're they gonna do to me?"

It had never occurred to me to be afraid of Swaffham. Not really. Our town had its problems, but we were made to understand that those were caused by outsiders, criminals who came from other places to make trouble. Men passing through in white vans. Suspicious characters. The only suburban menace we worried about was stranger danger. I am still dumbfounded, to this day, to look back and see how much real danger we were in all the time, and not from strangers, but from the people most familiar to us. Boys from school. Family friends. Brothers. Our own mothers with their quick, hard hands. And that one time, just once, as I've said, my father's hand on my throat, lifting me against the wall, my feet dangling. I say "just once" to say "it wasn't so bad" and "other people had it worse," but that kind of thing doesn't leave you. All those hands. They alter the fibers of your membrane, knocking holes in the boundaries of your body. You become so accustomed to getting interrupted by other people's hands, you don't notice it half the time. I see now that Jules and I were always targets, and yet we could not fathom that truth. It was our normal. Was that what Combat Boots meant by the "banality of evil"? I didn't understand. I believed I was safe from real harm. Jules was safe. Sylvia was safe. What could be safer than small-town Swaffham?

I let the Wallbanger relax my mind and helped myself to corn chips dipped in something delicious and green called guacamole, which I'd never heard of before. Jules refused to try it. I scooped some onto a chip and held it up to her, but she made a face. "More for me," I said, stuffing the chip in my mouth. She whispered, "Can we go? This party is so boring," but I knew she was wrong; that party was the opposite of boring. Besides, I liked watching Sylvia with her friends. She didn't act as tough as she usually did. She stepped out of her suit of armor, and while she claimed not to like "that camp shit," she camped it up a bit, joking and rolling her eyes, letting her hands flutter, releasing a joyful, deep, and throaty laugh that unmasked the voice she otherwise worked to cover. She was unconstrained, and I could see that this was what feeling safe really looked like. Among those people, I felt a new feeling. I felt at home. It was odd to notice I'd never felt that before, even though all I'd ever been was, literally, at home.

"Hey over there," a man called from the other side of the chain-link fence. He was holding a bottle of beer and standing next to the woman I'd seen before, the one who told us we were wasting water that day we painted the car. "Hey, you."

Sylvia turned in her chair to look.

"We got kids over here," the man said, gesturing to a pair of boys in wiffle haircuts who were taking turns hitting a Tonka truck with a brick. "You people need to watch your language."

"And what language would that be?" Sylvia asked.

"You know what language," the man said.

Sylvia looked around the circle, eyebrows raised. *Did anyone know what language?* They all shrugged. They'd been joking about Ronald Reagan and his jet-black hair, the obvious dye job, mocking him with the line from an old Miss Clairol commercial. *Does she . . . or doesn't she? Only her hairdresser knows for sure.* Did calling the president "she" qualify as bad language? They said "fuck" a bunch, too, but didn't everyone?

"Just keep it down," the man said. "I don't wanna call the cops."

"And *there* is your banality of evil," Sailor Shirt said, swishing a hand through the air. "Rearing its ugly head."

"What did you say?" the man said, moving closer to the fence.

"We'll do our best," Sylvia called and everyone went back to talking, whispering now, struggling to contain their laughter. Jules looked stricken, a fish out of water. Back at Ray and Ginny's cookout, she'd been fearless and adult. Now she looked like a kid. I fixed my attention on the conversation. I wanted those people to think I was intelligent and mature for my age. Jules wandered back into the house, saying she needed the bathroom. After awhile, when she didn't return, I went looking.

I found her in a bedroom that must have been Sylvia's from the time before. It was a boy's room. Baseball trophies and rock posters. An unmade twin bed in sheets printed with cowboys. The funk of faded adolescence. Jules stood staring slack-jawed at the wall. Next to a team photo of the 1971 Boston Red Sox hung a poster for an art show. "CENSORED," it read in large capital letters, "Robert Mapplethorpe." I recognized the name as the photographer who took Polaroids of Sylvia. And Patti Smith. He appeared on the poster, a skinny white man dressed like a biker in leather chaps and vest, holding a long, black tail snaking from the base of his spine. The tail of a devil. But that wasn't right. The man wasn't holding a tail. He was holding a bullwhip, the braided leather handle buried in the dark, hairy thicket of his asshole.

"Are you seeing this?" Jules asked.

It was 1984 and we didn't know Mapplethorpe. We didn't know that in a few years, after his death from AIDS, everyone, even our mothers, would know his name. His photographs—including this one, what Senator Jesse Helms would call "the homosexual with the bullwhip protruding from his rear end"—would spark a national battle between censorship and creative expression. Just looking at the images, authorities said, would twist our minds and corrupt our souls. They were not entirely wrong. Standing before *Self Portrait with Whip*, I felt my mind torque and my soul swivel. I had never seen such an image. Not in the decks of dirty playing cards I shoplifted from Spencer's at the mall. Not in the raunchy magazines Jules pilfered from her brother's stash. Not even in the flourishing creativity of my own nocturnal mind. That photograph broke the seal on receptors I didn't know I had. Desire is a murky business. For those of us whose desires go beyond the usual, it is difficult to know what you want until it's represented. Looking at that photo, I felt my hands go numb.

"It looks painful," Jules said, gaping at Mapplethorpe. I squeezed my hands into fists and wiggled my fingers to shake out the pins and needles. Jules turned to me. "What are we doing here? What are *you* doing?"

"I'm not doing anything," I said.

"I can see it," she said, pointing at me. "You're changing."

I felt caught, transparent, her finger jabbing some tender part of me, a gray and gummy shape I could not identify.

"So what? People change. And why do you care? You're leaving in September."

"I'm not going anywhere. You're the one who's leaving."

She was right. She wasn't leaving me. It was worse. She was letting me go.

"Come with me," I said, feeling like I might cry.

"It's just high school," she said. "We live here and we're gonna live here forever. We'll get married and have kids, and our kids are gonna play together. Remember? You'll get an in-ground pool and I'll have horses."

"Don't be stupid," I snapped, struck by the pitifulness of our old shared dream. "That's not how it works. Every idiot knows that."

Jules crossed her arms and looked at the floor. When her chin started to crumple, she turned to the window to hide her face. I watched her shoulders tremble as she cried, but I felt steely and remote. I could hear the party, loud and laughing, down in the backyard. I wanted to be with them.

"Those people aren't your friends," Jules said. She turned and looked at me, her blue eyes gone fierce, and I braced. "They're freaks," she said, cutting the ugly word in her teeth. She did not say "like you," but I felt the sting of it just the same. She pushed past me and hurried down the stairs.

I looked around the room. What *was* I doing? On the dresser, I spotted a shoebox and opened the lid. Inside was a collection of mementos: buttons for rock bands and to "Impeach Nixon," ticket stubs, matchbooks. At the bottom, wrapped in a rubber band, I found a stack of black-and-white Polaroids. The Mapplethorpe photos Sylvia had told me about. In each shot, she was young and boy-girlish, long-haired and shirtless in beaded necklaces, holding a cigarette, sitting by a radiator, lying on a bare mattress in a room with an unswept wooden floor and cracked plaster walls. The last photo showed her reclining nude by a marble fireplace stained with soot. She looked sooty, too, slim-hipped with dirty knees tucked up, concealing the shadow between her thighs. Rings on her fingers. Necklaces encircling breasts just starting to soften. The room looked like New York, or how I imagined New York, monochromatic and unwashed in its own grit. Maybe it was that Chelsea Hotel. Outside the windows, taxis honked and muggers mugged. Inside, Sylvia gazed seductively into the camera's lens. How did she know how to make herself into the object of desire?

I heard footsteps coming up the stairs and slipped the Polaroid in my back pocket, burying the rest where I'd found them.

"The neighbors called the cops," Sylvia said, sounding tired. "You better go."

"Where's Jules?"

"She must've left. Come on. You can sneak out the front."

She walked me to the door. The house was empty, most of her guests gone, but the Velvets still played softly from the stereo speakers. With my hand on the doorknob, I looked at Sylvia, into her eyes, willing her to gaze at me the way she gazed into Mapplethorpe's camera. But she refused to be my object of desire.

"Are they going to arrest you?" I asked.

"No," she said. "It's just more small-town bullshit. I can't wait to sell this house and be done with it. Get back where I belong."

It took me a second to register what she was saying.

"You're leaving?"

Until that moment, I hadn't understood that she'd never planned to stay, that she'd been trying to sell her mother's broken-down house for months, and all she wanted was to get back to the city. The news stuck in my ribs like a dart. How could she leave me alone in that place? But before I could form the question, Sylvia turned away.

2019

Jerry Logue is the sort of man who makes me butch it up. This code switching happens without thought. I straighten my shoulders, thrust out a hand for a firm shake, and deepen my voice, dropping back into my native accent, the one I got rid of so I could pass for middle class. "Thanks f'comin' ovah, Jerry, how ya doin' awright?" He tells me he can't complain. He's maybe seventy, tall and buzzcut, with a hand like a chapped leather mitt. He sits at the kitchen table, drinking Donna's coffee, and does the thing men do, talking to me and not my sister, even though she's the one who arranged this meeting to discuss selling the house. This is an example of the male privilege I'm supposed to enjoy, but I don't enjoy it. Being a man is often boring. In early transition, I had to remind myself not to let my voice lift with emotion, to keep my body still and slow, like a cold-blooded animal. So much shuts down with that shift. So much never opens up again.

As Jerry talks about his plans, detailing numbers and square footage, I drift off. My mother's house is getting emptier, but there's so much clutter, you wouldn't know it. Yesterday we went through Donna's old closet. I didn't think she felt sentimental, but when she discovered her old magazines and records, she cried for the first time. "Ma kept my things," she said, wiping her face with a fist. I put a hand on her shoulder while she shook with the knowledge that our mother did not completely discard her. I didn't mention the fact that Irene Pulaski never threw anything away, so those keepsakes might not mean what Donna wanted them to mean. But what do I know about the untold secrets of our mother's heart? I let my sister grieve. Donna who was kicked out, pregnant with two black eyes. Donna who didn't stand a chance. She came into that world tuned to its hard music, while I came out off-pitch, and that dissonance can make all the difference. People don't say this often, but queerness can save your life. It forces you outside, where you have no choice but to find other resources. When you come from a rough place, queerness can set you free. It's the regular kids who stay stuck.

Donna keeps nodding, saying *yeah*, *uh-huh*, and *that sounds good Jerry*. She's eager to sell to the highest bidder. I can't blame her. She spent her life working factories and farms, a slaughterhouse where she ripped out viscera, and for this she got little better than minimum wage and herniated disc pain that qualifies her for disability. She needs the money more than I do, assuming I still have a job, but this was our house, our mother's ashes are in the garden, and I'm not ready to watch it get bulldozed. The more Jerry talks about the declining value of land and lack of infrastructure, trying to convince us that nobody else will buy this property, the more irritated I get. So when Dakota comes in and leans against Donna, whining, and Donna pushes her away, saying, "Gramma's talking, go play with your phone," I seize my chance.

"Let's take a ride," I say to the kid, getting up to go.

"Max," Jerry says. "This is a good deal I'm offering."

When I step outside it's like getting out of jail, a familiar feeling. Am I almost fifty or still fifteen? I get my bike and give the helmet to Dakota. She sits sideways on the crossbar as I pedal down to Walmart, where I tell her to pick out any bike she wants. Delirious with glee, she goes for a lemon-yellow Schwinn and we ride to Hooley Park, to a bike path paved between the trees along the water. Dakota breaks out ahead and I race to keep up. "You're so fast," I tell her when we stop at the big pond. She does a victory dance that involves a move called "dabbing" and we sit on a bench to watch the ducks. The park is cleaner than it used to be and a pair of swans has moved in, giving old Hooley's a touch of elegance. A mother and toddler toss in bits of bread. They are dark-haired and tan, like Dakota, and the mother says something to the boy in Spanish.

"I wish I knew Spanish," Dakota says.

"Your mom didn't teach you?"

She shrugs. She doesn't have much to say about her Mexican mother. The woman played a minor role, in and out of Dakota's life, and then completely disappeared last year, "took off," as Donna put it. When I asked my sister if she might have been taken by ICE, Donna said, "God willing," and when I asked what God had to do with children in cages, forced to drink water from toilets, she told me not to start. I don't say any of this to Dakota.

"Did you know," I say, "there used to be alligators in this pond?"

"No way."

"Way."

I point out the rock where Jules and I used to sun and we head over, climbing onto that glacial erratic, where I go into Teacher Mode, telling Dakota about glaciers, how they carved this park, but she already knows about glaciers. She's smarter than I thought. She knows that 75 percent of the Earth's fresh water is frozen in glaciers and the deep scratches in the rock are called *striations*. She tells me the planet's ice is melting because of global warming, but "Gramma says global warming is bullcrap."

"Well, Gramma's wrong," I tell her. "She's wrong about a lot of things. My sister watches too much Fox News."

Dakota rolls her eyes and says, "She watches it, like, twenty-four seven. It's super boring."

I ask about life in New Hampshire and Dakota says it's also super boring, she's not allowed to do anything fun. Like driving a snowmobile. Other twelve-year-olds are allowed but she's not. She makes a face of displeasure that evaporates when the swans glide over, white chests pushing the water into silvery waves that spread out in fans.

"They're so beautiful," Dakota croons. "Did you know swans mate for life? When one of them dies, the other one dies, too. From a broken heart. It's super sad."

I remember a story about a pair of swans in a Russian zoo. The female was killed when a visitor fed her a sewing needle hidden in a piece of bread. Without his mate, the male swan fell into depression, refused to eat, and died of starvation. *Humans*, I think. *We deserve what's coming to us.*

"It's hard to tell which one's male and which one's female," Dakota says. "That's how you know they're monogamous. Or maybe they're non-binary."

Before I can ask what she knows about non-binary, she hurries on. "I'm obsessed with nature stuff. I want to be a marine biologist," she says, telling me how she wants to save the lives of sea animals, suffering because of all the plastic in the ocean, and did I know that turtles think plastic bags are jellyfish, so they eat them and choke, but plastic straws are the worst, and she never, ever gets a straw for her Coke, and have I heard about the Great Pacific Garbage Patch, a floating island of trash that's twice the size of Texas? And what about all the whales washing up dead, stomachs stuffed with plastic bottles, but the absolute worst was when a pregnant female washed up on a beach with her baby inside, dead in a belly full of trash. "It's really bad," Dakota says.

I agree it's really bad. They say we've got twelve years to save the world from climate catastrophe or humans will be done by 2050. I'll be eighty, close to death, and it makes me glad I never had children, but with Dakota I feel an unexpected twinge. What if I'd had a child? What kind of parent would I be?

Unable to sit still, Dakota jumps up and starts dancing, jerking her arms and stomping her feet on the rock, ponytail flipping. She sometimes seems younger than her age. I don't know much about today's twelve-year-olds—at Ampleforth, the Lower School is distant from the Upper—but the ones I've encountered in my world tend to radiate the cool detachment of teenagers. Cultivated children of the affluent and educated, they are miles ahead of kids like Dakota—and kids like me when I was that age, when my friends and I self-identified as hicks who said "ain't" and didn't know a single person who'd gone to college. I used to secretly read the dictionary, letter by letter, harboring a wish for escape. Does Dakota also hold private reservoirs of self, waiting to unfurl? For now, she is awkward and immature, a goofy kid vibrating with unbridled energy, and I admit it's fun to be around her. I'm entertained by her dance. The swans, however, are not. "Oh my god," Dakota gasps as they turn and swim away, "I scared them." She shrugs, brushes the hair from her face, and plops back down. Was my body ever that bouncy? At twelve, I was slouched and withdrawn, crushed by puberty. That's when my friends shifted course and I attached myself to Jules, who brought me back out. Two years. Maybe three. That's all our best-friendship lasted. And yet it scored itself deep inside. People my age sit around and marvel at the way time accelerates, as if it's something stunning. And we are stunned. That summer with Jules? Three months was a lifetime. Even now, when I look back, the past maintains its slow shape, a long braid of rope, coiled in circles.

1984

The morning after the Fourth, I woke to find the house empty. My mother had not slept in her bed, and I figured she'd spent the night at Gail's. I was alone.

"She can't talk," Ginny said when I called Jules. "She's on punishment."

"What for?"

"You know what for."

A hot flash of fear burned through me. Had Jules told her about the bullwhip photo? Had she blown the whistle on my friendship with Sylvia?

"I have two words for you," Ginny said. "*Wild Turkey*."

"Oh, that."

"Yes, that. Did you idiots really think we wouldn't notice half the bottle missing? Put your mother on the phone, I want to speak with her."

"She's not here."

"Don't lie to me, Melanie."

"I swear. She's not here."

Ginny considered this. I could hear her sucking on a cigarette, exhaling the smoke. "When she gets home," she said, "you tell her to call me. And don't bother coming around. Jules isn't allowed on the phone or out of the house."

"For how long?"

I heard a click and Ginny was gone.

An unexpected sensation of relief filled my chest. Jules was grounded. I was alone and free. I went to my bedroom, took the photo of Sylvia from the back pocket of my cutoffs, and kissed it in the delicate way I used to kiss a certain Michael Jackson poster, his lips still full, not yet sanded away by surgeons. Kissing Sylvia's photo was more exciting because she was a real person in my life, an actual possibility, and I kissed her again, wiped the Polaroid on my nightshirt, and slipped it between the pages of a book on the care and feeding of gerbils. All my childhood rodents were long dead and buried. No one would ever open *Know Your Gerbils*.

I decided to make some changes. I removed most of my Michael Jackson posters and went hunting through Donna's room to find something new, more adult, in her stacks of *Creem* and *Rolling Stone*. Her room still smelled vaguely Donna-ish, a residue of baby powder, weed, and Jean Naté. I told myself I didn't miss her. What I felt about Donna's absence was complicated, having more to do with the loss of potential. I missed the sister she was not. What pained me was the empty space where some other sister should have been. I picked up her guitar, with its missing strings and a crack down the middle, and plucked a sour note, wishing she had learned enough to teach me, but she never even figured out how to get the thing in tune.

I took a pile of magazines, along with one of Donna's left-behind white T-shirts, to my room where I tore out pages and taped them, intentionally crooked, to my walls. Satisfied with my new décor, I cut the sleeves off the T-shirt and stuck a few safety pins in the shoulders. I put on my leather necktie, leaving it loose, and brushed out my hair, hanging my head upside down for maximum volume. Then I creamed back the sides with foaming mousse. From my mother's makeup stash, I painted my lips fuschsia and outlined my eyes with black pencil. In one ear I hung a purple lightning bolt to match my rabbit's foot. I thought I looked older, like high school, maybe even college, and walked around the house pretending to be at a *sophisticated* party in the *sophisticated* city, Boston or New York, talking to people who made witty jokes about the world beyond Swaffham. The people from Sylvia's party were all there. Combat Boots, Platinum Blonde, Sailor Shirt. Mapplethorpe and Patti Smith, too. In my white high-tops I minced from one to the other, holding an invisible Harvey Wallbanger between thumb and forefinger, my other hand loose at the wrist, swirling the air. I tried out a new laugh, tossing back my head, my mouth going ha-ha-ha. "But of course," I said to the living room mirror, in a British accent. "That's absolutely *hilarious*!"

When I heard my mother's car pull into the driveway, I ran out the back, grabbed my bike, and escaped along the far side of the yard. I didn't want her to break my spell. I headed for Hooley Park. It was one of those sweet summer afternoons when the heat and humidity subsides, July kicking off its muggy blankets to let in a freshness that feels almost like the coming of fall, a new year, blank notebooks in which anything might be written. I locked my bike to the rack by a cinderblock hut that held a pair of public restrooms and headed down a paved footpath between the trees, a wooded section identified by the *Swaffham Sentinel* as a cruising spot for gay men.

It is difficult to explain what drew me to that place. Maybe it was Sylvia's party. Maybe it was Mapplethorpe with his bullwhip. More and more, I suspected I had something in common with the men in those woods. The experience I would later call queerness was still one big singularity in my mind, hyper-compressed, not yet fragmented into a million identificatory bits. No narcissism of small differences. We were one. I was one. I went to the woods to find myself, to live deliberately.

The quiet path, spattered in sunlight and shadow, wound around itself, leading me deeper into the wooded ramble. I strained to see men hidden between the trees, but found only dark shapes that resolved into rocks. At each rustling, I turned to see nothing but squirrels digging for acorns. I didn't feel scared so much as keyed up, electrified by the possibility of peril and connection. What was I expecting? I was out on the edge, mingling with murderers and perverts. Like Jules said, I was changing. The image of the bullwhip accompanied me. Is that what gay men did? In the bushes, dressed in black leather, were they all dragging bullwhips behind them like devil tails?

I sat on a bench and waited. Now and then, a man strolled by, looking me up and down before walking on. Sometimes, the same man would come round again, going in circles. None carried bullwhips. They were ordinary small-town men who looked like fathers and husbands in button-down shirts and beer bellies. Maybe I was in the wrong place. I was about to leave when one of the circlers approached. He was gray-haired and ordinary, older than my father, in scuffed penny loafers and a digital watch with a band that dug into his plump wrist. I watched him loiter, tugging his nose and glancing my way. After some deliberation, he sat beside me.

"Are you in drag?" he asked, his voice hushed and thirsty.

I didn't understand.

"Are you a boy in drag?"

The question corkscrewed inside me. I was often taken for a boy, but even now, in so much makeup and mousse? I sat bewildered in my strange and formless shape and tried to think of an answer. What was I? Necktie and lipstick. Flat chest, broad shoulders, and something else. The way I sat, long legs sprawled and hands in pockets. The way I walked, like a truck driver. I had another substance moving inside me and this man could see it. Maybe that's all I wanted from those woods. To be seen.

"I like boys in lipstick," the man said, deciding my shape for me. To be a boy in lipstick felt sexy, like rock and roll, Patti Smith and David Bowie, "Rebel Rebel," a beautiful mess, but when the man took my necktie in a gentle, hungry hand that smelled of Old Spice and cigarettes, I looked at his bulldog face and felt heavy with guilt. I was not what he wanted. He was not what I wanted. But I could not say this. I could only disappoint him as I pulled away and hurried back to the parking lot, my bike, and the pond where the dirty water cloaked a secret nest of alligators just below the surface.

•

My mother hadn't come home on the night of the Fourth because she'd met a "high-quality" man at Gail's and went to his place, a nice house on a large piece of property with its own goldfish pond surrounded by a green haze of fern. My mother had always coveted a goldfish pond, a sign of wealth and elegance, and this must have been like hitting the jackpot. They'd seen each other a few times since, my mother dousing herself in Ambush before each date, filling the house with a perfume fog that made my eyes water. The man's name was Richard, not Ricky or Richie like the guys we knew. Richard. He treated her to lobsters and white-wine spritzers. He gave her an ankle bracelet with a dangling heart that struck me as childish, a trinket any boy could buy at the Shawmut Mall, engraved in script by a salesgirl with good penmanship. I told my mother this when she asked what I thought, raising her ankle high in the air, the heart winking in the light of the living room lamp. Richard was a *chiropractor*, she informed me. I'd heard of those. My father had refused to see one when his back went out. He said they weren't real doctors, but "quacks" and "snake-oil salesmen." The whole affair made me feel sorry for my mother, so desperate for a man's attention.

"Richard gave me a good adjustment," she told me over supper one night. "If you know what I mean."

She said this with the same raunchy tone she used whenever we watched *Magnum P.I.* and the sight of Tom Selleck in his mustache and unbuttoned Hawaiian shirt, his dark coils of chest hair, provoked her to say, "He can put his shoes under my bed anytime."

"That's gross," I said, letting a forkful of gluey macaroni and cheese drop to my plate. "I don't need to hear that."

"Well, you're going to be hearing it a lot more. I know things are moving fast, but Richard and I are really getting to know each other. I'd like to have him over sometime. You'd like him."

"Doubtful," I said.

"Don't be a bitch."

I felt my cheeks redden and got up to clear my plate, scraping the sticky orange noodles into the trash.

"You're wasting food," my mother said, not turning around.

"I cooked it."

"You cooked it, but you didn't pay for it."

I gripped my plate and stared at the back of her head, her stupid, outdated Dorothy Hamill haircut, her pale neck and shoulders freckled with sun damage and middle age, the skin starting to crease. I hated her.

"You're fourteen now," she said, rounding up my age, like she couldn't bear for me to be a kid one more minute. Looking back, I think she was done being a mother. She'd been at it for almost a quarter century and was eager for the next phase of life, for a second go-round at love and sex, to savor the waning vitality of her body before it collapsed in a heap. She didn't want me getting in the way of her forward momentum.

"You're going to be learning about adult things. Like sexual pleasure between a man and a woman."

"Mom, please."

"After you were born, your father and I stopped having sex, but in the beginning, it was out of this world. He was a magnificent lover. We used to do it right here on the kitchen floor."

"Mom, stop!"

"Don't be such a prude. Someday, you'll discover there's nothing like a good fuck with a dick up your cunt."

I froze in shock, my mind reeling with sudden pornography. My mother habitually used all three of those four-letter words, but never in such vivid and startling succession, and never to mean what they really meant. A person could be a dick or a cunt, and people could go fuck themselves, but this sentence assembled the parts to conjure real flesh, solid and slick. My face burned as if she'd slapped me. I looked at the plate still in my hand; somehow, I hadn't dropped it.

"You like boys, don't you?" she went on, poking at her mac and cheese, taking small, birdlike bites. I could hear the noodles mashing inside her mouth, making a wet and clammy sound I didn't want to hear while discussing this topic. I looked out the window over the sink, into the waning blue of evening. Did I like boys? I felt caught. "You're not a baby anymore," she went on. "It's time you started acting like a young lady. Put on a skirt once in awhile. You're old enough for makeup. I don't want Richard thinking I raised some kind of ragamuffin."

I tossed the plate into the sink, harder than I'd meant to, and stomped to my room.

She shouted after me, "It's time for you to grow the hell up. You hear me?"

I shut the door, turned on the radio, and dove onto my bed. I missed Jules. It had been a week and I was done being alone and free. I would forgive the things she said at Sylvia's party. She was my best friend. I needed to call her and complain about my mother, my crazy bitch of a mother, and Jules would tell me about her own crazy, bitchy mother, and we would plot their demise, have a good laugh, and grasp toward the future when we'd be free together, in our own houses with in-ground pools and stables full of horses. But I couldn't call Jules. I had to wait until her punishment was over, whenever that would be. I had no one. I pulled *Know Your Gerbils* off the shelf and opened to the Polaroid of Sylvia. I kissed my fingers and touched them to her face.

Later that night, when my mother was settled into the couch with her cigarettes and television, I crept down the hall to the bathroom and helped myself to her Queen Helene Mint Julep Masque, a formula that promised to shrink pores, remove blackheads, and make anyone into a real woman. I pushed my hair back in a headband and painted my face the color of pistachio ice cream. I liked the way the masque tightened, pulling me together, setting my face and all its fragmented feelings into alignment. *This is something girls do*, I thought. Back in my room, I stared at my Garfield phone, itching to talk to someone. Anyone. I started dialing random numbers, like I used to do in sixth grade with my former best friend, Pauline. We would dial until we hooked someone, and if they were good, we'd add them to our list of regulars. We referred to these as "crank calls," but they weren't really. We never had pizzas delivered or asked if the refrigerator was running. We just wanted to be other people with more interesting lives.

Pauline hooked one guy named Robbie who worked at a tuxedo shop. He'd answer, "Marty's Tuxedo Warehouse," and we'd say hello in husky voices, calling ourselves Chatty Cathy and Betty Beavsey. I was Betty, a raven-haired beauty, fascinated by Robbie's talk about the day-to-day business of tuxedo rentals, singing to him along with Olivia Newton-John on the boom box, "Let's get physical." We called another guy whose number passed from girl to girl, written inside a paperback of Judy Blume's *Forever.* We called him Mr. Zucchini because that's all he talked about—"D'you like zucchini? D'you like to *do it* with zucchini?" He also talked about his "jism," a strange word that sounded to me like *chasm.* It tasted like pineapple, he said, and I tried to imagine it, his pineapple chasm, and where such a cleft might be found on a man's body.

While men were the easiest marks, we had one girl on our list. For her, we pretended to be boys. Danny and Scott. We lived in the next town over, we said, and met at her school's Halloween party. Didn't she remember? The girl played along, imagining a night she spent bobbing for apples with Danny and Scott. We pitched our voices low and talked about nothing. Pauline got bored, but I never did. I loved being Danny. Sometimes I'd call the girl by myself. I'd be Danny for long stretches of time, talking about my adventurous life as a boy, and the girl listened, the way girls do when boys talk. I can still feel him today, the boy I constructed, in his dungaree jacket, Levi's corduroys with a blue ink stain on the back pocket, so cool, Danny from the next town over, who walked bow-legged in yellow work boots and rode a dirtbike. Good old Dan.

Now I was at it again, dialing random numbers, Mint Julep Masque cracking on my face. When a woman or a kid answered, I hung up. Those calls never went anywhere. If I got a guy, I'd say, "Hey, what's up," acting like I knew him. In those days the telephone was an unregulated playspace where a caller's identity remained untraceable. There was no caller ID and no star 69. We had party lines and crank calls, heavy breathers and men who claimed to be college students conducting surveys on human sexuality and could we please spare five minutes to answer a few questions for research. At the mall, pay phones were forever ringing, inviting us into otherworlds of smut.

"Who's this?"

"You *know,*" I said. "Don't you recognize my voice?"

"Oh . . . is this Jill?" the man said, hooked.

"Yeah. What're you up to tonight?"

On it went. I was Jill. Or Linda. Or Barb. I used my old Betty

Beavsey voice, low-slung and sultry. I tried out the name Sylvia, inhabiting her cool. *Don't you remember me? We met at that disco. Yeah, that's the one.* This new guy wanted to meet, but I refused. Let him beg. I was the amazing, untouchable Sylvia. What kind of music do you like? What's your favorite color? What are you wearing? Do you like to do it? Where do you like to do it? *In the backyard,* I said. *In a treehouse.* He called me "the adventurous type." I was trimming my toenails, letting the clippings drop to the carpet where I mashed them into the fibers with my feet. *In my goldfish pond,* I said, *surrounded by ferns.* I bet you have big boobs. *Oh yeah, they're, like, totally enormous.* I was Sylvia and the guy was saying her name over and over, crooning like that French skunk in the Bugs Bunny cartoons. *Sylvia, oh Sylvia.*

"Who are you talking to?"

It was my mother on the extension. I hung up.

"Who is this?" she was saying out in the kitchen. I held my breath. "Hello? Who is this?" I heard the phone clatter into its cradle and my mother's feet thumping down the hall. I went on cutting at a hangnail on my big toe, pretending like nothing had happened. She opened the door.

"Don't you knock?"

"Who were you talking to?"

"No one. Some guy. It was a wrong number."

"It didn't sound like a wrong number. Who's Sylvia?"

I shrugged and went on hacking at my toe, making it bleed. My mother looked around my room, eyes roving over the walls, past the few remaining Michael Jackson posters, my corkboard thumbtacked with messy ephemera—tickets from school dances, fortune-cookie fortunes, stickers from Wacky Packages. She leaned in close to a collage I'd made, a mishmash of words cut from magazines: *Escape, Depression, Love, Sin.*

"What does this mean?"

"It doesn't mean anything," I said. "It's art."

She went on with her surveillance, past shelves of board games and books, *Know Your Gerbils* where the Polaroid of Sylvia hummed like a beacon. I held my breath.

"We should get rid of this junk," she said. "Operation. Battleship. Do you ever play these anymore? I'm sure some needy kids would love to have them."

I shrugged and picked up an orange stick, pushing back my cuticles, pretending to ignore her while she inspected the items on my bureau. She opened my jewelry box and poked around in the compartments where I kept my baby teeth and a few green M&Ms.

"It's nice to see you taking an interest in your appearance," she said, gently, in the voice she used when she wanted to be friends. "I noticed you helped yourself to my lipstick."

"You're awfully nosy."

"Maybe I have to be."

"Do you want to look in my underwear drawer, too?"

"Should I? Do you have something to hide?"

I pushed hard at my cuticles, the pain keeping my thoughts away from the Polaroid, in case my mother had the power to read my mind. Sometimes I believed she could enter my head, especially when she was following a scent. Fee fi fo fum. She could smell blood. Like a shark turning toward a single drop in the depths of the ocean. Her eyes made another sweep of the room, landing on a pinup of Patti Smith from *Creem* magazine. Covering her breasts with an album, Patti wore nothing but a ring and a bracelet, her dark hair mussed, heavy-lidded eyes looking into the camera. My mother read out loud from the text printed on the page: " 'This is Patti Smith. She is a filthy slut with absolutely no respect for anything.' Oh, Melanie, how nice! Is this what you're about these days? Being a filthy slut with no respect?"

"You're one to talk," I said. "Sleeping with some guy you just met."

"I'm an adult. I'm entitled to a sex life."

"So am I."

"No, you're not," she said, pointing a finger in my face. "Your life hasn't started yet."

"Make up your mind. Am I a baby or a grownup?"

"Mark my words," she said, one of her favorite lines. "Before you know it, life is gonna sneak up and bite you in the ass. Until then, you'll do as I say. And I say cool it with the dirty phone calls. You're too young for that shit. And you're tying up my line. What if Richard's trying to get through?"

I couldn't stand to hear the desperation that slipped into her voice, her need for Richard with his lobsters and ferns. She couldn't bear her own vulnerability either, and I watched as she righted herself, shifting back to the comfort of her cruelty.

"I don't know what's going on with you," she said before heading out the door, "but I liked you better when you were still in love with that Black faggot."

2019

Through the fuzzy FaceTime connection on her iPhone, Autumn Biddle sits behind the wheel of an SUV. From my digital position on her dashboard, I can see the espresso leather interior stretching back into infinity and a good New England town receding past the windows. Autumn's nanny is sick today and can't pick up her kid from day camp, so we'll have our session on the way. She hates pickup, she says, *it's torture*.

I'm in a bad mood. Autumn is lecturing me about gender, using the words *essentialism* and *constructivism* like I wasn't minoring in women's studies the year Judith Butler's *Gender Trouble* dropped. I slouch at my desk and watch her go zipping along a green pasture hemmed in white paddock fencing. I have not been keeping up with her assigned readings. Instead, I went deep into my old closet and dug up a pile of musty paperbacks I once hunted and gathered from bookstores in the city, seeking the way out. *In a Different Voice*. *SCUM Manifesto*. And so much Virginia Woolf—I used to hide in the closet and read her correspondence with Vita Sackville-West like a dirty magazine, all aflutter when Virginia told Vita, "You shall ruffle my hair in May, Honey: it's as short as a partridge's rump"! The book sits beside me now, one corner smashed from the time my mother threw it against my bedroom wall, shouting, "It's all that Virginia Woolf you're reading!" Books, she understood, had the power to take me away from her.

What does Autumn Biddle know about my body and mind, here in Swaffham, in this house? She tells me to read when for years I read in secret, afraid of being caught—admittedly the most thrilling way, making every word more dangerously potent. Autumn doesn't care about my history and I can feel her trying to box me into a present-day shape. I won't let that happen. When she pauses her lecture to turn onto the day camp's campus, I tell her about the transsexual dark ages.

In the early '90s, I explain, after years of searching and not finding trans men, I landed in a support group called the FTM Society, "open to all female-to-male transsexuals (pre-op & post-op)." We met in the basement of a feminist bookstore, a fluorescent-lit, carpeted space that smelled of patchouli oil and cat piss. Trans men made up a small minority, invisible and undesired, marginalized within an already marginalized community, and there were only six of us, mostly working-class guys who used to be working-class butches. We had a carpenter, a welder, and the captain of a fishing boat. I was the only one with a college education, the only one who had not yet started testosterone. I expected that notorious hormone to make the men cocky, but whatever butch swagger they'd once employed had melted into self-loathing. They spoke quietly, looking at the floor, and talked about transition as an alternative to suicide. One guy with a tough South Boston accent kept repeating, like a mantra, "If I hadn't'a buried Rose-Marie, Rose-Marie woulda buried me." Rose-Marie was his birth name, what we now call a dead name, and every time he said it, I'd picture him dumping a girl version of himself into a shallow grave. He was sure that poor old Rose-Marie, with her bad haircut and lumpy hips, would've killed him slowly, hanging on his neck like a millstone. She had to go. That's what we all believed. We had no choice but to bury our girl selves and hope they never came to the surface.

Autumn says *uh-huh* and *wow*. She's waiting in the pickup line, tapping her nails on the steering wheel. *This is torture*, she says, meaning the wait. Through the SUV windows, I can see a gothic stonework building, a Gilded Age castle occupied by overprotected preschoolers, the type easily felled by the proximity of a peanut.

"During that time of early transition," I say, "I had recurring dreams about burying the bodies of women."

This gets Autumn's attention. She fixes her eyes on the screen, squinting in at me. In every dream, I explain, I was digging a hole, shoveling dirt so dark and visceral I could feel the grit on my hands, the sensation lingering for hours after I woke. I had no memory of murdering the women, only burying them. Sometimes the bodies were in pieces. Sometimes they were in suitcases. They threatened to rise to the surface. A rainstorm washed away the topsoil. Police came hunting with cadaver dogs. Each time, I would wake in a panic, flooded with guilt.

"Who was I?" I ask. "The murdered woman or the man holding the shovel?"

I wait, stupidly hoping for understanding.

"Max," Autumn says, giddy and wide-eyed. "You hate women."

"The women in the dreams were *me*," I say. "Their bodies were my body. *If I hadn't'a buried Melanie, Melanie woulda buried me.* Don't you get it?"

She doesn't get it. I have dug my own grave, so to speak. She's going to tell the dean of Diversity and Inclusion that I'm a murderous hater of women. I'll lose my job. I'll have to move back into my mother's house permanently and work at Walmart, stocking shelves, collecting food stamps on the side, weeding the garden until I die.

"These were trans anxiety dreams," I insist.

"Max, we're going to have to pick this up next time."

She should end the call, but instead she retrieves her daughter, leaving the camera on. I watch the girl climb into the back so Autumn can buckle her into a car seat. They look alike, same apple-butter hair and bright smile. The girl carries a magic wand topped by a glittery star streaming ribbons.

"Did you make that at camp today?" Autumn says. "Are you my pretty princess?"

The girl nods and smiles brighter, waving the wand in the air. For her, I imagine, this is a simple question. I consider the possibility that I am wrong about that, but does it matter? From my position, it's all I can see.

1984

Alone, again, I went back to Hooley's, riding my bike by the entrance to the gay cruising spot. This time, I found Sylvia's Trans Am parked in the small dirt lot. The T-top was open but she wasn't in the car. I wondered if she was in the woods. Maybe she found the guy who smelled of Old Spice. I was locking my bike to the rack when she came out of the women's restroom, wiping her wet hands on her jeans.

"What did you do to your hair?" she asked.

"I'm trying out a new style."

"I'm not sure it's working for you, but I dig the leather tie. Where's your buddy?"

"Grounded."

I started telling her how it had been too long and I was missing Jules, when her attention snapped to something behind me. I turned to see a couple with a baby carriage coming down the road toward us. They had ice-cream cones in their hands and were giving us dirty looks.

"Make a comment," Sylvia muttered, eyes on the couple. "Come on."

The husband stopped at the edge of the lot, a few yards away, while the wife stayed with the carriage. He was husky, with a blonde mustache and Red Sox cap.

"I saw you," he said, pointing at Sylvia. "Stay outta the ladies' room. You're not fooling anyone."

"Mind your business," Sylvia said, taking a step forward. She stamped the dirt with her cowboy boot and the man flinched.

"Mike," said the wife. "Let's go."

"Girlie," the man called. He meant me. "You there. Girlie. Is this person interfering with you?"

The word *girlie* bothered me. I felt diminished by it, and by his concern. I was not his property to protect.

"She's my big sister," I answered, wishing it were true.

He gave me an appraising look and then, seeing the formless something that marked me as different, shook his head. I did not belong to him and he knew it. Ice cream melted down the sides of the cone and onto his fist. He stood looking back and forth between Sylvia and me, considering his next move.

"Mike, let's go," the wife called as the baby started fussing. But the man wasn't done. I saw his face turn a darker shade of mean. He'd decided. I tensed as he reared back and launched a white gob of spit. It landed in the dirt, missing Sylvia and me by a good two feet. He walked away, saying, "Get outta the park. Both'a yiz. We're calling the cops."

"Go to hell," Sylvia yelled.

We watched the couple stroll away, licking their cones and pushing their baby toward the duck pond. Who made them the police of everything?

"I can't wait to get out of this fucking town," Sylvia said, reminding me that she had every intention of leaving for good. "Let's drive."

The Trans Am, that glorious chariot, smelled of leather and breath mints, and felt like the coolest music video. We pulled out with the engine roaring, stereo blasting the Runaways' "Cherry Bomb," making me feel tough and real. *Hello world, I'm your wild girl!* Arm out the window, tempting fate, the wind ratting my hair as Sylvia beelined onto the highway where she aimed straight for the city, that far side of the moon. Just thirty minutes away, I had rarely been to the city and then only on field trips to the Children's Museum with its giant milk bottle or to visit Faneuil Hall Marketplace on a "girls' day" with my mother and sister, Donna acting like a sullen spoilsport, refusing to try gourmet jellybeans because they were new and different. The city was otherwise inaccessible, no trains or buses linked it to Swaffham, and the thought of being there with Sylvia thrilled me. As we crested high ground, in the hazy distance I glimpsed the two tallest towers of the Boston skyline. The Hancock and the Pru. They were not New York's Empire State or Chrysler, but they still beckoned with promises of freedom, sky-blue pillars catching the sun of another world. And yet it wasn't Boston proper we headed for. It was Cambridge. Harvard Square. Where the weirdos gathered.

Sylvia parked the car on a run-down street off Mt. Auburn, across from a hulking green triple-decker. On the sagging second-story porch, a man leaned over the rail, smoking. He wore a white undershirt, the kind we used to call a "wife beater," with a black mustache and thinning hair greased back. His tough pose broke open when he saw Sylvia and he waved excitedly, bracelets jingling on both wrists. Vincent's apartment, when he ushered us in, was a jungle of animal prints, tiger and zebra stripes slashing across throw pillows and rugs, leopard spots dotting upholstered chairs and sofas. The head of a wild boar stared from the wall. In his undershirt and black silk pajama pants, gold chains around his neck, Vincent hugged Sylvia and asked, "What brings you to this neck of the woods? Bored of life out in the boondocks?"

"We came for your professional services," Sylvia said. "The kid needs a real haircut."

This was news to me.

"I can see that," Vincent replied, scrutinizing my head. "Mind if I get in there?" He plunged his fingers into my hair, pushing and tugging, gently but with purpose. "It's a bit of a rat's nest, but you've got a nice curl. And so thick, *madonn'* is your hair thick. I wish I had this hair. Lucky kid."

My intractable thicket of dark hair had never made me feel lucky. All I'd ever wanted was a sheet of gold that lay flat and thin, like Jules' obedient strands that feathered and stayed fixed with just the barest spritz of Aqua Net.

"Vincent used to cut at Astor Place," Sylvia said. "In New York. It's famous."

"People line up around the block for those cuts. I did all kinds of styles. The Guido. The Mohawk. The *Spina di Pesce.* That means 'spine of the fish.' It's kinda like a ducktail, but more punk. What are you looking for?"

I shrugged. Vincent stood back and looked at me the way a painter does his subject, one hand cupping his elbow, the other fingering his mustache. I was to be rendered, sculpted into a new shape, but what that shape was, I could not know. I could only submit. He took me to the kitchen and had me hang my head in the sink so he could lather it with shampoo that smelled of green apples. He squeezed my head in a towel, sat me in a chair, and draped a leopard-print smock over me. Then he began to cut. He had no mirror, so I could not watch, and that was fine with me.

Sylvia sat at the table, smoking a clove cigarette and leafing through a magazine. They chatted a bit, making idle gossip about people they knew, while a radio played old music, Frank Sinatra and Peggy Lee. I watched the sun on the dirty kitchen window, trash trees waving their branches from the lot next door, and enjoyed the feeling of Vincent's hands moving my head from side to side, combing through my wet curls, the crisp efficiency of his scissors, transforming me.

"Some asshole tried to kill me the other night," he told Sylvia. "In the Fens. He came at me with a baseball bat, screaming about 'the gay plague' and all that bullshit."

"Stay out of the Fens," Sylvia said, not looking up from her magazine, as if such violence was a minor annoyance.

"He didn't know he was messing with the wrong faggot," Vincent went on. "I'm from East Boston. You don't mess with faggots from East Boston."

"What did you do now?" Sylvia asked.

"I wiped the streets with him, that's what," Vincent said, reaching for a pair of clippers. "He takes one swing at me, I grab the bat out of his hands and start whaling on him. I didn't stop 'til I heard the ribs crack. I did a hell of a job on him."

"Just don't get yourself arrested again," Sylvia said.

"What do you mean *again*? When'd you ever see me get pinched?"

"Weren't you up Walpole?"

"One stint. A million years ago," he said, waving it away with a hand. "I got to meet the Boston Strangler, though. A real bullshit artist."

He turned on the clippers and pressed the humming blade to the side of my head. I leaned away, crewcuts were for scrappy boys and boot-camp marines, but Vincent told me to *hold still* in the same tone my mother used when she'd pry a tick from my scalp, pull a splinter from my foot, pin a hem on a dress, and I held still. When he finished, he took a blowdryer and sculpted what remained of my hair with a rounded brush, mousse, and spray, tugging until it felt frothy and light, a candy-smelling halo.

"*Finito*," he announced. "Bathroom's down the hall. Go take a look."

In the cloudy mirror, I saw a different person, cooler, more sophisticated. The right side of my hair was cut close to my scalp, while the top swept to the left, cascading over my ear in shining wedges of feathery vegetation. Rock and roll. I didn't dare touch it. When

I walked back to the kitchen, Vincent and Sylvia were talking low and I stopped as he lifted his undershirt to reveal a furious cluster of plum-dark spots on his lower back.

"I match my furniture now," he joked. "Leopard print."

"You're gonna be okay," Sylvia said, slipping a few folded bills into his hand.

When he bent to kiss her cheek, he saw me in the doorway.

"How do you like your new 'do?" he called, pulling down his shirt.

I didn't know where to put my eyes or what to say.

"It's okay, kid," Vincent said. "You can't get it from a haircut."

He picked up a broom and started sweeping the cuttings on the floor. I thought of my mother's hairdresser, Lance, the skinny one with the golden fleece who had to close his salon because everyone was afraid. I felt ashamed, but didn't know how to say it, so the feelings sat inside me, crackling and acidic, like Pop Rocks in my stomach.

"That cut is called 'the Asymmetrical,'" Vincent said while he swept. "It's all the rage. Syl, tell her it looks gorgeous."

"It looks gorgeous," Sylvia said, "totally bitchin." She meant it. Her smile, the slender gap between her front teeth, warm and bright. "So? Do you like it or what?"

"I love it," I said, rubbing my fingertips over the bristly patch. I did love it, but I also felt a strain of worry. Not about catching AIDS, but about catching something else, something the eyes back in Swaffham would see. "What's everyone going to think?"

"They'll think you've been to New York. They'll all be jealous," Sylvia said, stabbing her cigarette in an overflowing ashtray. "Come on. We've got places to go."

We said goodbye to Vincent and set off on foot into Harvard Square. I felt buoyant in my new haircut and proud to be walking next to long, tall Sylvia in her climate of cool. A few people stared at us, some with confusion and others with open admiration, but most didn't take notice. In the city, I discovered, so many people had weird looks that it wasn't weird at all. Sylvia strode along in her cowboy boots, moving with the speed of the street. I wasn't used to walking so fast and had to work to keep up while trying to look at everything and everyone, gawking like the hick I was.

We passed hippies handing out free meals under a banner for Food Not Bombs and a group of Harvard students holding signs to "Boycott Apartheid." We dropped coins into the guitar case of a woman singing folk music, a captivating sound, and while I wanted to stay and listen, Sylvia pulled me along. When we passed a group of punks in spiked hair and combat boots, hanging around a subway entrance, Sylvia said, "That's the Pit. And those are Pit rats. They're cool." As we hustled on, past bookshops, record stores, and cafés, I felt cool, too, catching glimpses of my reflection in windows, barely recognizing myself. Asymmetrical.

"Hungry?" Sylvia asked as she led me into a little lunch counter called The Tasty. We sat side by side on stools and ordered grilled cheese sandwiches with vanilla Cokes. At the end of the counter, a skinny guy nodded off over a cup of coffee. The air felt greasy and warm and the open door didn't cool it off.

"We need to get you some new clothes," Sylvia said when the cook brought our plates. "To go with that hair."

"I don't have any money."

"Don't worry about it. I'm your big sister, right?"

I nodded, feeling a warm fizz in my heart. Already, the scene at Hooley's seemed like a million miles away, the man's spit fading into the dirt.

"Does that happen to you a lot?"

"Now and then," she said, mouth full of grilled cheese.

"That's scary."

She shrugged, "I don't scare easy."

"What about Vincent? Why would someone want to hurt him? He's so nice. And he's sick, right? With AIDS?"

There was so much I didn't understand about human cruelty. As a little kid, I was the type who answered ads in the backs of magazines, mailing away dollar bills in exchange for shocking, glossy brochures on seal clubbing and animal vivisection, the eyes of the Draize test rabbits seizing my child heart. I would show the photos to my parents and insist, *We have to do something.* Blood in the snow, spattering the white coats of baby seals. Kittens with their skulls lifted open like sugar bowls, electrodes fixed to their brains. But my parents only shrugged. *That's life.* I sent off more dollar bills, donations of quarters and dimes Scotch-taped to my letters. How could such brutality exist? I did not yet understand that softness can be an irresistible magnet for hate.

"Vincent is dying," Sylvia said, "because the world doesn't give a shit about us. Our lives don't matter. They want us to die. And if they can take us out with their own hands, all the better. When you're queer, and people can see it, this is what happens. But you get tough. Like me. You put on your armor and march out into it. That's what it's like when you're in the life." She wiped her mouth with the back of her hand. "People think it's a choice, but it's not. You don't choose it. It chooses you."

I didn't know what to make of Sylvia's lesson. It was frightening and harsh. Men with baseball bats would go on doing the terrible things they did. You could fight back, but more would keep coming. People would call the cops and the cops would not protect you. That was just the way. I wondered what to look for, to know if someone was in the life. A certain haircut, a way of walking, waves of energy radiating from the body? People could see it, even when you didn't want them to.

"Has it chosen me?" I asked.

"That's for you to figure out."

"But you can tell, can't you?"

"Nobody knows how anybody's gonna turn out. People change and then change again. That's one thing I've learned. I mean, look, do you like girls or boys or both? And what do you want to be? Do you wanna be a girl or a boy or what?"

Both. Or what. There were other options besides one thing or the other?

"All that is for you to figure out," Sylvia said, taking a last bite of her grilled cheese. "And this shit takes time. Like years. You're what, thirteen? You can't possibly know it all right now. Be patient. And eat your lunch."

I had barely touched my sandwich. I took a few bites, trying to figure out how to ask Sylvia what I wanted to ask. I had so many questions.

"How many years did it take you?"

"I don't know," she said. "A few. But I was different. I mean it's different for girls like me. I'm not like you, right? What I mean is, it's different for regular girls. Like you. Whatever you turn out to be, it's not like—it just doesn't work the same, that's all."

She stopped talking and drank her Coke, sucking the straw until she was down to rattling ice. Sylvia, confident about almost everything, struggled to talk about this. I see now that she was still a kid, probably no more than twenty-three years old, self-assured and bold, but also young. And she was alone. Her friends were unusual, queer, but none were queer like her. Maybe she didn't know how to talk about it, either.

"How does it work?" I asked, not entirely understanding what "it" was, but I wanted to get started on figuring it out, especially if it was going to take years. "For someone in my situation."

"I honestly don't know," she said, lighting a cigarette. "If you *are* like me, well, I'm sorry to tell you this, but I've never seen anyone go in the other direction. I don't know if it's even possible. I mean, theoretically, sure, but I've never seen it."

Everything Sylvia said confused me. She spoke in abstraction and I needed clarity. What I got was a vague sense of implausibility, the unlikelihood of my becoming what I did not know I wanted or needed to become. Before I could ask another question, Sylvia paid the check, mashed her cigarette in the cole slaw on her plate, and we were off again, to a thrift shop around the corner where she knew the owner, a German woman named Uta who owed Sylvia money, so I was allowed to pick out whatever I wanted. The clothes smelled of moth balls, dead people's closets, but the place wasn't anything like the Morgie's back home where we brought our old things to donate to people poorer than us. Uta's was decorated with dusty taxidermies, antique suitcases, vintage hats atop a row of styrofoam heads painted pink and silver. It had style. So did Uta. She wore a seafoam green 1950s housewife dress, as sudsy as a pistachio milkshake, topped with a bob haircut bleached to shocking white that matched her eyeshadow. She smoked cigarettes from a long holder and when she spoke, in her Marlene Dietrich voice, her breath smelled of poor dental hygiene.

I knew exactly what I wanted—a man's black suit with a white button-down shirt, so I could look like Patti Smith. Sylvia and Uta approved. But in the mirror I didn't look anything like Patti. She was as skinny as a drainpipe and I had what everyone called "big bones." Her face had angles and edges where mine lacked definition. And my hair, even in its new asymmetrical shape, was just wrong.

"You look like *you*, my dear," Uta said, smiling with lipstick on her teeth. "Very chic. And that suit fits you perfectly." She moved around me, tugging down the jacket and pulling up the pants. "It's absolutely perfect. Now. Stand up straight." With brisk efficiency, Uta arranged my body, squaring my shoulders and adjusting my hips until my posture was right. I did look better. It wasn't Patti in the mirror, but it was someone.

Even though the weather was too warm, I wore the suit out of the store, the way I did as a kid whenever I got new sneakers. Now, on my feet, a pair of battered black cowboy boots clomped when I walked. Sylvia had one last stop she wanted to make. We crossed the Square to a Moroccan coffeehouse, a dazzling place of tile mosaics, grapevines, and hanging lanterns of arabesque filigree, where we sat at an outdoor table to "see and be seen." Sylvia ordered a pot of mint tea with a plate of something called hummus and instructed me to scoop it up with triangles of pita bread. I'd eaten pita once or twice, from our grocery store's ethnic aisle, but never hummus, and the surprising taste of it made the world expand, beyond Massachusetts, across the Atlantic, to other continents. *Casablanca*. I was Bogart, Sylvia was Bergman, and the problems of life didn't amount to a hill of beans in that crazy world. Sylvia, with her shiny black hair falling into her eyes, her skin powdery soft in summer light, a sheen of sweat on her neck where it sloped. I could have kissed her. Instead, I tried not to think about her leaving Swaffham and prayed that her mother's house would never sell. We smoked clove cigarettes, even though they punched holes in our lungs, and as I sat there in my new clothes, my new look, I did not feel formless. My body eased and expanded into the shape of the suit, the boots, my long, strong legs thrust out, ankles crossed, my arm draping the back of a chair, cigarette in hand. Next to a girl like Sylvia. Rubbing the patch of buzzcut on the side of my head. Unfolding from hidden places beneath my skin, I felt a different, more confident body emerge and begin, cell by cell, to fashion itself around my frame.

Sylvia dropped me off in Hooley Park, at the spot where I'd left my bike. I sat in the idling car, clutching the shopping bag full of my old clothes, and tried to think of an eloquent way to express the gratitude I felt, but all I could muster was "Thanks for everything." It didn't feel like enough, but it was all I had, and Sylvia never asked for more. After she drove away, I stood alone in the dusty lot, feeling unprotected, my new look unsuited for that place. The residue of the day's earlier confrontation lingered, the angry man's spit still fizzing inside me. Remembering what Sylvia said about what can happen when people see your queerness, I went into the ladies' room to change back into my everyday shorts and T-shirt. But first, in the graffitied mirror over the sinks, in the greenish light of buzzing fluorescence, I gazed upon my new self. Still looking like the city, I squared my shoulders, put my hands in the trouser pockets, and thought of Humphrey Bogart. Kissing Ingrid Bergman on the rain-wet tarmac. I was lost in reverie when two young women walked in.

One said to the other, "Are we in the men's room?"

"He's in the wrong place," her friend replied.

"Get outta here, perv. This is the ladies."

"I *am* a lady," I insisted, my voice high with panic.

"Oh my god," she laughed. "It's a dyke."

I cannot describe these women as separate individuals. In my memory, they are a single entity, a combined weapon formed against me. The energy in the room tilted. In their stormcloud of high-teased hair and drugstore perfume, they were winning at gender while I was not. As the shame of my failure seeped out, reeking of fear, they smelled it on me and grew bolder. Now I was the soft thing, a baby seal on the ice.

"You sure you're not a guy?" one said, moving closer to inspect my body, her eyes frisking every part of me.

"I'm not," I answered in a small voice. I still cringe to remember this scene, wishing I'd been stronger, like Sylvia, but I'd been trained to retract. Be quiet and good.

"Prove it."

"Yeah," said the other, smirking. "Pull your pants down and show us."

I stepped back against the wet sinks, shopping bag clutched in front of me. I'd been cornered like this before, but always by boys, in the woods, the shallow end of a swimming pool, a dead-end street. *Show me*, they said. *Do it or else.* I got away each time, running for my life. I didn't know I had to worry about women too.

"Prove it," they said. "Show us."

When I did not move, one turned to the other and whispered something, smiling wickedly. "Do it," said the other. One stepped in, close enough so I could smell the rancid spearmint of chewing gum in her mouth. She grabbed my chest and laughed, "It's got tits." With a sudden shiver, my body burst into flight and I bolted past, knocking her back, my boots slipping on the wet floor. Outside, I sprinted across the grass to the trees and ducked into a dark shelter of evergreen. They didn't follow. I hurried into my old clothes, tripping out of the suit pants and shoving everything, littered with pine needles, into the shopping bag. Then I waited, watching the door of the restroom.

A memory emerged. I was maybe ten years old, standing in Pauline Grasso's driveway. We were playing Around the World, tossing a basketball at the net that hung from her garage. Two younger girls played with us. I never knew their real names, only the terrible nicknames bestowed by their terrible mother. Nasty and Stinky. My friends and I might have been working class, but Nasty and Stinky were what we called "piss-poor," covered in dirt and scabs, living above a convenience store in a small apartment so messy you could not see the floor. Their mother would leave her bedroom door open when she had sex with men, and Nasty and Stinky would watch. I have this scene in my mind, their mother's bed with its wicker peacock headboard, sheets rustling over bodies, but I can't remember if I saw it or only imagined seeing it. That day in the driveway, Pauline's mother called her into the house, and I was left alone with the girls. Nasty did a weird thing. She sidled up to me and fiddled with the zipper of my Baracuta jacket, moving her eight-year-old body in a sexy way I'd only seen women do in movies. I froze. "I know what you want," she said, looking into my eyes while Stinky watched with glee. I felt stripped and grabbed. They saw what I was, the thing I could not hide. "I know you like it," Nasty said, touching my chest like a boy's chest, radiating hot waves of sexuality she must have learned from her mother. And her mother's men. "Quit it," I said. "You're being gross." Her smile shifted into something hard and mean. "When Pauline comes back," she warned, "I'm gonna tell her what a dirty freak you are. I'm gonna tell her you tried to touch me." Her accusation cascaded inside me. "I didn't do anything," I said, but maybe I *had* done something. Maybe just the existence of my wrong body had triggered weird tremors in the air. Had I touched her without touching her?

This is the fear inside every queer, that we are a contamination, an overstimulation, making normal people feel what they don't want to feel. Crouching in the trees of Hooley Park, watching the women leave the restroom, I felt closer to Sylvia, understanding more about the danger she faced—because others believed she was a danger to them.

When I got home, my body still tense from the confrontation, my mother sat at the kitchen table, drinking coffee with a man in a baby-blue Izod shirt and khaki shorts. He had wavy salt-and-pepper hair brushed back from his ruddy face and the beginnings of a belly. On his feet, a pair of leather sandals did nothing to conceal his large, yellow toenails. I disliked him instantly. Before I could breeze past them to my room, my mother took one look at me and launched into it.

"What did you do to your hair?"

"Nothing," I mumbled, trying to walk by. She grabbed my arm.

"Nothing? You look like a rooster. A sick rooster. You shaved off half your head! Who did this to you?"

"I did it myself."

"With what? Not my good scissors."

"Jules has clippers at her house," I said, not lying.

"*She* did this to you?"

"I *told* you, I did it myself."

"You look ridiculous."

"I think it looks alright," the man interjected. "That's the style now. It's how they're wearing it."

My mother let the subject drop, not wanting to argue with her guest.

"Richard," she said, "this is my daughter, Melanie."

So this was the chiropractor. Owner of goldfish ponds, consumer of lobsters and white-wine spritzers.

"Hiya, Melanie," he said, showing me the soft, pink palm of his hand.

"People call me Mel."

"Alrighty," he said, winking at my mother. She smiled back, girlishly, like they were in on something together, a couple of teenagers with a secret. I didn't care for this turn of events.

"What's in the bag?" she asked.

"I got some stuff up Morgie's," I lied. "Can I go to my room?"

"*Used* clothing? You paid money for other people's clothing? It probably has bugs."

"What's Morgie's?" Richard asked.

"Morgan Memorial," my mother explained. "The Goodwill. Where poor people shop. And what are you doing riding your bike all the way to Brixton?"

"It doesn't have bugs," I said. "We bring *our* old stuff there. Do *we* have bugs?"

"You're getting awful smart."

"Like you say, I'm in high school now."

My mother waved this away and turned back to sip her coffee.

"Melanie hasn't grown out of her tomboy phase," she said to Richard. "I was just the same when I was a girl, but then I blossomed. We're still waiting for Melanie to blossom."

Richard smiled and leaned back in the chair, lacing his hands behind his head. His shirt stretched over his chest, tight enough so I could see the eraserheads of his nipples. I looked at the table and its box of Entenmann's butter loaf. My mother only put out the Entenmann's for special company. Richard flexed his chest and exhaled with pleasure, making his hip bones audibly crack. People had all sorts of ways of taking up space, throwing their weight around, making other people feel small.

"So, Melanie," he said, "are you going to show us what you bought?"

"Oh, yes," my mother chimed in, grinning artificially, like a maniac. "Show us. Show us what wonderful things you found at the Goodwill."

I wanted to smack her. Instead, I muttered, "I'm going to my room," and stomped away. Down the hall, I could hear the two of them giggling. I tossed the shopping bag in my closet and flopped onto my bed. On the radio, I fiddled with the tuner, looking for something new. At the lowest end of the FM dial, where I never ventured, I found a station that played folk music, like that woman in Harvard Square, a song about being a small, blue thing. I knew the feeling. "That was a demo recording from a new singer on the scene," the DJ announced. "Suzanne Vega plays around Greenwich Village in New York City and her influences, she says, are Lou Reed, Joni Mitchell, and Laura Nyro." I grabbed a scrap of paper and wrote down the names I did not know. Once you started to look for them, the world was full of hidden trails to follow.

2019

Dakota and I are going through my closet. She's supposed to be helping sort and trash, but she's fascinated by my photo albums. She can't believe that's really me, with the baby face and all that hair, a kid around Dakota's age, trying to figure it out. I struggle to recognize myself. I thought I was overweight, but the photos show an average-sized kid. How did I get it so wrong? I'm probably getting it wrong now. Do we ever get to enjoy our bodies while we live in them? At breakfast today, Dakota was talking about bathing suits. She wants a new one, she told Donna, a one-piece, because last summer she had a two-piece and, "Everyone was staring at me. It was like boom-bada-boom-boom." When I asked her to clarify, she said, "I have *boobs*, Uncle Max." Donna made an unkind comment and I felt bad for the kid, having to endure the pains of adolescence under the cloud of my sister's disgruntlement. I wish she had another option, but she'll survive, I tell myself. Like I survived. We all have to fight our own battles.

Dakota plops to the closet floor and tugs at a dresser drawer so crammed with stuff, she has to prop her foot against the frame and wrench it open. When she pulls out my Michael Jackson "Beat It" jacket, red vinyl slashed with silver zippers, she slips it on and dances around, mimicking the moves that have survived three decades, embedded in the DNA of pop, despite the revelations of child abuse. What does Michael's downfall mean to those of us who invested our first experience of erotic love with him? Were we collectively groomed as children? I still listen to his music.

"It's so retro," Dakota says, hugging the jacket to her. "Can I keep it?"

"Put it in the trash."

"But *why*? It's super cool."

I hold open the garbage bag and give it a shake. "He's been canceled," I say.

She huffs and drops the jacket to the floor. I put it in the bag, followed by more devalued memorabilia, buttons and bubblegum cards, the doll I thought would be a collector's item, the one I undressed to see what Michael had underneath, finding only smooth plastic. Love, I think, is inscrutable.

"Who are you into?" I ask Dakota. "Who's cool these days? Justin Bieber?"

"Eeew," she says, "Gross! He's super disgusting."

"You're twelve. There must be someone."

"My favorite YouTuber is Jeffree Star," Dakota says. "Yas, honey!" She raises a hand in the air and snaps her fingers like a drag queen. Jeffree Star, she explains, is a gay YouTube celebrity, famous for applying elaborate contouring makeup to his face. She shows me a video on her cracked phone. I don't care for the contouring trend. It makes everyone look like an avatar, too cartoonish to be human.

"He looks like one of those Kardashian people," I say.

"Oh my god," Dakota gasps. "I hate the Kardashians! You can tell how Kylie's lips are fake and Kim's butt is fake. I don't know which one is worser."

"*Worse*," I say. "*Worser* is incorrect. It's a double comparative."

She ignores my pedantic correction and goes on to talk about drag queens. "Do you watch *RuPaul's Drag Race*?" she asks. "It is the best show on television ever. You really should watch it. Because you're trans and everything."

"I'm not the fabulous kind of trans," I say, shoving a pair of glitter socks into the trash. "I'm the boring kind."

Dakota's love for drag queens and gay boys in makeup makes me curious—is she some kind of queer?—but it's not surprising. Riding the internet, genderqueerness has permeated the nervous heart of the Heartland, going mainstream and sending boondock America into hysteria, panicked about bathrooms and social contagion, while its enlightened children strap on unicorn horns, ditch the binary, and live without shame. There is power in numbers. Before Sylvia, I had only Michael Jackson, whose gender remains a mystery but could have been, now that we have the words, cloudgender, agender, gendermutt. (In a *New York Times* article from 1984, a psychologist said, "His androgyny holds a fascination for adolescents. . . . Unconsciously, it's hard to give up the possibility of being both sexes. This ambivalence is more obvious in the early teens, and goes underground around 15 or so. He embodies someone who seems to live out that ambisexual fantasy.") It is almost impossible to become what you cannot see and cannot name. I grabbed every scrap.

Here's my Michael Jackson glove, decorated with sequins I sewed myself. I wore it to school every day, an act of defiance at a time when the Glove was outlawed. Across the country, teachers confiscated them, claiming they were overstimulating to the student body. They, too, worried about queerness as social contagion. When I toss it in the trash, Dakota gasps. Her fascination with drag queens includes a reverence for sequins and she asks if she can have them. When I say yes, she finds a pair of scissors and carefully snips away each silver disk, collecting them in a pile on the rug. "Yas, honey," she whispers as she cuts, a soothing incantation. I wonder if she, too, has been touched by the unicorn's glitter horn. I ask, "Are you into gender stuff?"

"One of the kids at my school is a non-binary person," she says.

"Is that your trans friend?"

"No, someone else."

"There's more than one?"

She shrugs, like *duh*, and then explains non-binary, as if I might not know. "Sometimes this person can be a girl," she says, "and sometimes they can be a boy. You can't assume someone is female if they have breasts and long hair and stuff. Gender is what's in your head. If I wanted to be non-binary, it wouldn't be because of my body parts, it'd be because of my head."

This is how a twelve-year-old from the hinterlands gives a more astute explanation of the difference between gender and sex than most of the college-educated adults I've known. Certainly, no one in my family ever talked like this. The word *gender* was never uttered. Hearing it now, from family, I find myself struck by a longing for kinship: *Maybe I'm not the only one.* But this is a Mel feeling, a line cast from the deep past where nothing can ever change, and I shake it off.

After lunch, Donna and I tackle the upstairs apartment alone. When my father died, it became another space for my mother's junk—piles of clothing, papers, and defunct appliances, including no less than four blenders and three cake mixers. It's a toxic nightmare of mold and mouse droppings and I wear a dust mask to protect myself. Donna refuses to mask. "I've breathed worse," she says. Sifting through the room where our father drank away the years, under a brown cloud of his tobacco stain on the ceiling, we are archaeologists digging through geologic time, our mother's upper layers giving way to our father's bedrock, a mass of unopened mail from collection agents, half-used tubes of denture cream, a book called *The Science of Getting Rich*, and other lamentable items, including my high school yearbook photo, a battered eight-by-ten of my former face, haloed in a soft-focus lion's mane, smiling uneasily, lips frosted pearly pink.

"You had so much hair," Donna says.

"You know what they say. The higher the hair, the closer to God."

My sister laughs and hands the picture to me. I remember that day, putting on the makeup and dress my mother insisted I wear, posing for the photographer who twisted my body into an awkward position and told me to smile. After the shoot, I drove to my girlfriend's house. She liked my makeup and said I looked pretty. I felt like I was in drag, a boy in lipstick, but didn't argue as she poured shots of Napoleon brandy from her mother's stash, put on an Air Supply record, and took me to bed.

"Keep it," Donna says, and I do.

We go on stuffing our parents' junk into garbage bags and it's only when we can at last see the floor that we take a break. Donna sits in my father's chair, immune to the residue of his death, and lights a cigarette. I stand, though my back is aching, because the only other place to sit is the sofa and it's covered in unidentifiable stains.

"There's something I've been wanting to ask," my sister starts, sounding serious. "You and Dakota have been spending a lot of time together."

It's true. We've been riding our bikes in the evenings, hanging at Hooley's and the cemetery, talking about all kinds of nothing much. I'm enjoying the avuncular feeling that has come over me, but I don't admit this. As a kid, people wanted me to swoon over young children, to play with dolls and then to babysit, practicing for motherhood. I always resisted. Now I shrug and say, "Dakota's alright," as if I don't care.

"I know how you are," my sister says with an edge, like she's heading off an argument. "You don't like to be bothered by people. You're a loner."

"You make me sound like a crazed gunman."

"I'm tired, Max," she sighs. "I've got this herniated disc, and the high blood pressure. The hospital bills never stop and my house is falling apart. I'm gonna have to put on a new roof before winter."

I can't tell where this is going. "Are you asking for money?"

"I don't want your money."

"Then what are you trying to say?"

My sister looks at me and blurts out, "Would you take Dakota?"

"Take her where?"

"Take her. Just for a few years, until she's eighteen or Stet's out of jail, whatever comes first. I know it's a lot, but it'd be a really big deal for me."

It's suddenly hard to breathe. I take off the mask and sit down. When I lower myself onto the ratty sofa, my knees crack. I'm old, I think, too old for something new.

"I don't know, Don," I say. "Raising a kid? I don't even have houseplants."

"You've got a nice house, a good job with a salary."

"Yeah, well, I might not have a job."

"You'll have a job," she says. "People like you always have a job."

People like me. What kind of person am I? A loner who doesn't want to be bothered. An old man with creaky knees and no houseplants. I tell Donna I have a lot going on, my life is full, but that isn't true at all.

1984

The town library had a collection of record albums, but I'd never looked at them before. They were kept in the Adult Reading Room, a dark and forbidden place I'd only visited once or twice when my neighbor, Greg Wozniak, an older boy and the sort of person we might now refer to as neurodivergent, used to practice playing the Wurlitzer organ they had there, producing a breathy, quavering music that was part cathedral and part haunted house, a sound that suited that room with its heavy curtains and dark wood, leather armchairs, newspapers hanging on sticks like folded wings. No children were allowed inside, but I was less and less a child and I entered quietly, the way I entered church, approaching the long bins of records with reverence. Close together in the alphabet, I found Joni Mitchell and Laura Nyro. It felt like a miracle that names I'd only heard the night before, on a radio station far down the FM dial, could appear there, in my nowhere town, where they'd been my entire life, waiting for me.

Here's how it worked. You gave the record to the librarian to play on a turntable behind the desk while you went back to the Adult

Reading Room and plugged a pair of headphones into one of the jacks built in to the arms of the couch and chairs. I was the only listener, sitting alone for hours, sometimes accompanied by a senior citizen who would read the *Globe*, paying no attention to me in my private rapture. Without control over the turntable, I could not replay a song and I could not skip. This was no place for the impatient exertion of will. I had to listen straight through, surrendering to the artist's intention. "California" and "A Case of You." Walking back to the desk, asking the librarian to play the next one. "Lonely Women" and "Stoned Soul Picnic." How had that room been there all along and I'd never discovered it? I wanted to tell Jules. I would not have long to wait.

After a few days, I owned the Adult Reading Room and I no longer tiptoed in and out. I was hurrying one-two-three down the orange shag-carpeted steps to the front desk, holding *Songs of Leonard Cohen*, when I saw Jules standing with a stack of books, looking very much like herself—greasy yellow hair in a ponytail, Led Zeppelin T-shirt, Keds—yet changed in a way I could not name, as if a buttery glaze of nostalgia had been spread upon her, making her fuzzy at the edges.

"Jules!"

I threw an arm around her neck and crushed her to me. We hadn't seen each other in over a week, the longest we'd ever gone, and the angry scene at Sylvia's party felt far away. We jumped up and down until the librarian told us to shush.

"Are you free?" I whispered. "Have you been liberated?"

"One more week. But my mother lets me come here to do summer reading."

"When? Every day? We can meet. They have records. We can listen together."

"What happened to your hair?"

I put a hand to my head, fingertips touching the soft bristles on the shaved side. Jules chose to be kind about it.

"It looks cool," she shrugged. "Sort of like Cyndi Lauper."

"Thanks," I said. "I told my mother I cut it at your house. Okay?"

"Where did you really do it?"

"With Sylvia. We went in town." *Town* was the city. *Where ya going? In town.* "I got these boots, too."

"Pissah," said Jules, not meaning it. I didn't let her lack of enthusiasm bother me. I only wanted her, however she showed up.

I got a second pair of headphones from the librarian and pulled Jules into the Adult Reading Room where we plugged in and sat side by side on the couch. I went back to Joni Mitchell. "Blue" on *Blue*. We couldn't talk and that was good. I didn't have to not tell her about my adventures in the woods at Hooley's, or Harvard Square, or anything. I held my friend's hand and watched her face. When Joni sang, "Acid, booze, and ass, needles, guns, and grass," Jules' grin opened wide, big and beautiful, with the crooked front tooth and a bottom gap that sometimes made her press a finger to her lip to hide the imperfection. Did she know she had a beautiful smile? Poor Jules. And me. We didn't know what magic we had. We didn't know we would never again be so fluid and bright.

Through the remaining days of Jules' punishment, we'd meet at the library, where our friendship existed only in that room, a protected bubble of time and music. We sat on the couch cross-legged, shoes off, face to face, while the music made us close our eyes and nod our heads. Sometimes it made one of us cry and the other would follow, mirroring the way girls mirror. I held her hand, squeezing it tight when the music overtook me. During those wordless hours, an intoxicating feeling unfolded between us, crystalizing in the moment when Jules reached out to pull a thread from the hem of my cutoffs, by my inner thigh, wrapping it around her finger and tugging slowly until it gave. As I watched her roll the thread into a ball, and she watched me watching, I felt a pulse throb between my legs and decided, one day, I would kiss her.

On one of those afternoons, after Jules had gone, I went to the library's card catalog, looking for the story that could explain me. I located the drawer that ranged from *TON* to *TWA*, and in the long stack of typewritten cards between *Tonawanda Band of Seneca Indians* and *Twain, Mark*, I found *Transsexualism*. There was only one card for that subject. One result. Maybe in larger libraries, in cities or universities, there were others. I have since searched the internet, hoping someone took photos of whatever cards were available then—I want to see evidence of the actual artifacts, the courier typeface in fuzzy ink—but found nothing. Googling "library catalog card homosexuality" turns up *A gay bibliography: eight bibliographies on lesbian and male homosexuality*, but in 1984, there was no such thing as a transsexual bibliography. What would go on it? Who would compile it? Years later, I would discover other books, studies written by psychoanalysts and endocrinologists, one memoir by a trans man whose 1977 author photo shows him bearded and smoking a pipe, and a 1946 treatise on "masculine inverts" by another bearded, pipe-smoking trans man, a British physician in the Merchant Navy who exiled himself to India, became a Buddhist, and died of uncertain causes before the age of fifty. But that day, in the Swaffham Public Library, in my only world, in the murky age before the internet made this so much less lonely, I knew nothing about what existed. I found just one card: *Morris, Jan, 1926–. Conundrum: from James to Jan – an extraordinary personal narrative of transsexualism.*

I carried the book, face down and smoldering against my chest, to the farthest corner of the library, to an unpopular spot on the carpeted floor in the history stacks. I sat hunched around the contraband and read a chapter or two at a time, day after day, dog-earing the page to mark my place, always returning it to the shelf where I could find it again. I did not dare check it out. My name would have been stamped forever inside the cover and I wanted no record of that seditious act.

"I present my uncertainty in cryptic terms," Morris wrote, "and I see it still as a mystery. Nobody really knows why some children, boys and girls, discover in themselves the inexpungeable belief that, despite all the physical evidence, they are really of the opposite sex." Boys *and* girls. Was it possible? Sylvia said she'd never seen it, but surely someone had made the opposite journey from female to male. In the library's reference section, I scoured the medical encyclopedias until I found my answer. I can almost see the page. A urological diagram surrounded by small type. What did the entry say? I can only sum up the message I took away: The female anatomy could not be changed and so, I misunderstood, a girl could not become a boy. I was the most impossible object. More, even, than Sylvia. I envied her. She had Lola, who *walked like a woman and talked like a man*, and Holly, who *shaved her legs and then he was a she*. Even poor, old Sweet Loretta Martin, who *thought she was a woman*, as Paul McCartney put it, dressed in *high-heel shoes and a low-neck sweater.* These trans women, though they never spoke for themselves, and their visibility made them vulnerable, danced into our imaginations from radios and record players, telling us they were possible. Nobody sang about trans men. We remained unimagined. I'm not playing Oppression Olympics here. Trans men and women bear burdens both similar and different. I'm just saying that, without others like me, I could not exist. I was a thing not even dreamed.

When her punishment ended, Jules dropped all interest in the library. She was free, in the still-succulent middle of summer, and the last place she wanted to be was indoors. She pulled me back to the streets, roaming without a goal except Slush Puppies and pizza slices, smoking the dried-out scraps of pot she scrounged. On one of those aimless afternoons, we were sitting on the rusted merry-go-round in the kids' playground behind the high school, doing nothing. My life had started to feel splintered into a kind of dual consciousness. There was the part that lived in Swaffham, hanging around with Jules and arguing with my mother, and another part that crackled inside, yearning toward the city, life with Sylvia and her people.

"You still hanging out with the tranny?" Jules asked.

"All the time," I said, though that wasn't true. I didn't see Sylvia as often as I wanted, but I rode past her house whenever I could, and if she was on the porch, she'd invite me in to listen to music and that was more than enough. That was everything. "Don't call her that word. You know her name."

We were blowing bubbles of Bazooka gum, making the merry-go-round's platter groan on its spindle as we lazily paddled our feet against the dirt, drifting in stoned circles.

"I'm worried about you," Jules said. "I hope you're not turning queer."

I thought of the time she put her head on my shoulder, and her leg on my leg, and I said, "You're the one who's a lezzie," the word cutting my mouth like hot pepper.

"I like *boys*," she insisted.

"So don't I."

"I like *real* boys. You don't like anybody. Except *Sylvia*."

"She's not a boy."

"I rest my case."

"What if I did like her like that?" I asked. "I'm not saying I do. But what would that make me?"

Jules and I thought about this. It was not an easy question to answer. We sat there, drifting in the not knowing, when three little boys came running into the playground with their worn-out, crabby mother shuffling behind in flip-flops and a "Foxy Lady" T-shirt.

"Do you like *me* like that?" Jules asked in a low voice.

"I told you," I said, "you're barking up the wrong tree."

"Remember what happened to that girl, Brenda White? They sent her to the loony bin for being a lez."

"I told you," I started to say again.

"Look, Melly, I don't really care what you are. All I'm saying is, be careful, okay? There are people in town who don't like Sylvia."

"What do you mean?"

"People are talking."

"I'm not a lez," I said and fell back onto the sun-warmed surface of the merry-go-round, covering my eyes with an arm. What were people saying about Sylvia? I felt a sharp jab at my ribs. And then another against my leg.

"What the fuck?" I sat up. Rocks pinged off the merry-go-round.

"Hey! Cut it out," Jules yelled at the boys. They stood grinning like jackals, streaks of popsicle dirt striping their bare chests. "It's the Children of the fucking Corn," Jules said. "Little demons possessed by Satan!" Two kids came closer and started mocking us.

"Hey, alligator tits," one of them called.

"You have big butts," said the other.

"And *you're* a boy," said the first one, pointing at me.

There it was again, the seeing, the knowing.

"Shut up, you little demons. She's not a boy," Jules shouted.

As mean as the dogs my neighbor kept tied to a clothesline, the boys kicked dirt at us and chanted "alligator tits, alligator tits, alligator tits." From her bench, their weary mother told them to *knock it off,* but they ignored her and she turned away. We had to fight our own battles. We took off on our bikes, rocks whizzing by our heads. Today, I would not remember those boys if I hadn't written about them in my diary. They were just another scrape. It seemed, back then, that someone was always coming for us. Just because we were girls. I managed to escape, one scrape after another. And then I didn't.

•

My mother took me to a nighttime party at Gail's in Newcastle-by-the-Sea. In my black suit with the boots and leather tie, I put on eyeliner and glossed my lips with bubblegum Kissing Potion. In the car, driving toward the Atlantic Ocean, my mother fumed about my outfit. "People will think I raised a kook," she said. But she was wrong. Gail and her friends were high-quality people and they knew style when they saw it.

"The Annie Hall look! I love it," Gail exclaimed when she met us in the bright, crowded kitchen of her Queen Anne house, a buttery tumble of gables, bay windows, and turrets, an actual mansion I couldn't wait to tell Jules about. I didn't know who Annie Hall was, but it sounded like a compliment, especially coming from the famous Gail, the woman who told my mother to buy spring water, sleep with Richard, and who knows what else. She was far more captivating than I'd imagined and it was obvious why my mother followed her instructions. Gail, who had self-actualized thanks to that self-esteem seminar, was a definite person, rendered in crisp focus. She had honey-colored hair streaked with silver, worn up in a twist held by a pair of lacquered chopsticks, and looked like a retired valkyrie, long and willowy in a way that neither my mother nor I would ever be, dressed in liquid white linen pants and a matching top kept spotless under a "Kiss the Cook" apron. At a deluxe culinary island, she stood blackening the skins of red peppers on a built-in grill. When she kissed our cheeks, holding a pair of tongs in one hand and a cocktail in the other, she smelled of rosemary and ylang-ylang.

I'd never been in the home of a rich person before. When I was little, my mother would take me driving through one upscale town or another so she could look at the houses, stopping at curbs to peer into chandeliered windows. I learned about envy on those drives, and about lack, how to yearn for something that would be forever out of reach. Above Gail's kitchen island, a rack held a glittering collection of hammered copper pots that looked like they'd never been used. On a shelf sat a wire basket of fruit, real fruit, not my mother's Styrofoam apples and pears pinned with colorful beads because real fruit rotted before you could eat it and that was wasteful. Gail had a double sink, plus a third sink, a miniature basin whose purpose was limited to a mysterious specialized task. This was wealth, the ability to possess more than you needed, and then more on top of that. The freedom to let good food go bad.

In the presence of this abundance, my mother straightened her posture and arranged her face into an attitude she must have thought looked sophisticated. Eyebrows raised, lips slightly pinched. I felt embarrassed for her as she scanned the crowd, asking if Richard had arrived, her expression failing to disguise her desperation.

"Not yet, darling, but don't worry. Dickie's always late," Gail said, knowing Richard better than my mother did. "Come. Let's fix you a drink." She ushered us to the bar. "Aperol spritz?"

My mother looked lost. She'd never heard of Aperol. In the awkward gap, I asked, "How about a Harvey Wallbanger?"

My mother shot me a look.

"Listen to this kid," said Gail, impressed by my boldness. "*How about a Harvey Wallbanger.* How old are you? Sixteen?"

"She's thirteen," my mother said, deflating the compliment.

"I'm almost fourteen."

Gail nodded and said, "No Galliano, I'm afraid." She fixed two Aperol spritzes, pouring bright orange liqueur, sparkling wine, and soda into stemmed glasses of ice. "I'll make one light," she added, diluting mine with extra soda. "Your girl is mature, Irene. In France, children learn to drink at a very young age."

My mother accepted Gail's breezy dominance, and while I appreciated the alcohol, I wasn't sure how I felt watching my mother roll over. As we mixed in to the party, holding our drinks and small plates of unfamiliar morsels, it both pained and pleased me to witness my mother straining to belong, making that Hollywood face, laughing a brittle laugh, nodding at conversations like she knew what people were talking about, subjects that slipped her grasp—their houses in Wellfleet, the *dreadful* over-development of Cape Cod, and did you hear that John Hinckley, Jr., was already begging for release from the mental hospital, that lunatic, and something else about the banks and deregulation, all while my mother nodded and went *mmm-hmm* and *oh, yes, of course.*

She kept glancing around, awaiting the arrival of Richard, like his presence at her side would elevate her to a higher status, which it probably did. I wish I could have felt compassion for my mother, but even now it hurts to think of her trying hard to tread water, out of her depth, grinning like mad on the surface while her legs furiously kicked. I knew her as a formidable woman, but when I remember her in that house, she is diminished. Nothing about her fit. In that crowd of beige and white, artfully rumpled cotton and gauzy linen, she stood out in synthetic candy colors. With her polyester dress patterned in a lurid geometry topped with shoulder pads, she looked like a tropical parrot blown off course and dropped, disoriented, into a Ralph Lauren catalog. I didn't fit in either, but my not fitting was deliberate, a different kind of faking that could render a person, if not acceptable, at least interesting.

"Do you use one of those Walkmen radios?"

"What?"

The man asking me this question was an ear, nose, and throat specialist. An *otolaryngologist*, he explained. He spoke so quietly, my mother had to lean in close and stare at his lips.

"What?" I said again.

"She's already gone deaf," he told my mother. "These kids with their Walkmen radios, they are doing long-term damage to their hearing. Do you want to go deaf?"

I looked away, around the parlor, taking mental notes for my sophisticated future. Spotless white couches and real plants without a single dead leaf. Framed posters from museums in New York City. Matisse. Three goldfish in a jar beside a reclining nude. "Masterpieces of Tapestry." A lady holding a mirror to a smiling unicorn's face. It had not occurred to me that a poster could be framed. Posters were cheap things you bought at the mall and hung with thumbtacks. But in Gail's house, ordinary objects took on exalted and unusual forms. Her silverware, for example, endures in memory. Modernist and Scandinavian, it felt strange in my mouth, the spoons and forks flat where they should have been curved, square where they should have been round. Taking a bite from a wedge of quiche with one of those forks, I allowed myself a traitorous thought: What would life be like if I'd been born to Gail and not my mother? I would live in a mansion and be exposed to art and music. I would be a different person, with a better vocabulary and more self-esteem.

A woman advanced on me, wild-haired, dressed in a breezy linen skirt set the color of dusty lilac. She touched my sleeve and told me she loved my "look." She did astrological charts and was a little bit psychic. "I'm getting very interesting vibes from you," she told me. "My guides tell me you're going to do big things. Creative things. Are you an artist or a writer?"

I shrugged. I wasn't anything.

"You will be," she said. "In a past life, you were Janis Joplin."

I started to explain that this was impossible, Janis died just after I was born, but the woman kept going.

"She was bisexual, too," she whispered. "Male and female energy intertwined. Yin and yang. Anima and animus, if you prefer Jung to the Chinese."

She went on about Jung, but I was stuck on *bisexual, too*, my insides clanging. Is that what I was? How did she know? It is embarrassingly obvious to me now, but back then, no matter how many times people saw the queerness in me, I was stunned by their X-ray vision, unable to see that it was broadcasting from every part of me.

"Richard!" my mother called over the shoulder of the ear, nose, and throat specialist, who stepped away, outclassed by handsome, pushy Richard wading through the crowd to kiss my mother's cheek. I saw her eyes soften for a moment, before they narrowed on the half-empty glass in his hand.

"You've already had a drink?"

"My second," he said.

"You've *been* here?"

"I got stuck in the kitchen, talking to Gail and the girls. Is that alright?"

"It's fine," my mother said, strained, forcing a masklike smile and clutching his arm. "I'm just *so glad* to see you."

She was too much. Even then I could see she was too much. She'd been waiting for him, needing him, enduring the monologue of a low-talking monopolizer while Richard let himself get distracted for God knows how long, gabbing with girls and getting tight on bourbon. But Irene Pulaski wasn't in any position to lay down the law. Not with Richard of the goldfish ponds and chiropractic adjustments. She would let him get away with anything. Just like she'd done for years with my father. Until one day, eventually, she'd reach her limit.

"Hello there, Melanie," Richard said, smirking at my black suit and tie. "Where's the funeral?"

I rolled my eyes and turned back to the room, searching for that psychic. She sat on a sofa next to a man holding a copy of the *New York Times*. I wandered over, hoping she'd tell me something more, about how to be the sort of person I was, and what my future held. I perched on an ottoman and the woman nodded, but otherwise gave me nothing. The keen spotlight of her attention had moved on.

"Put the paper away, Philip," she told the man, her husband. "You're at a party."

"I'm not the one who wanted to come," he said. "Did you see this story?"

"I don't want to see it. I'm having fun. At a party."

"A terrible thing happened."

"Terrible things are always happening."

"Right here in New England."

"Not *here*," she exclaimed, clutching her crinkled chest in mock horror. "In New England? The fountainhead of all terrible things? How could it *be*?"

"Listen," the man said. "They murdered a homosexual boy up in Bangor. Tossed him over a bridge into a river. It's not easy these days for homosexuals up in Maine."

"My uncle Lemmy lives in Maine," said a wispy woman seated on the floor, barefoot and hugging her knees. "He's not a homosexual, though. He's a podiatrist."

I looked at the psychic to see if she would give me away as a bisexual, but she paid no attention. That newspaper story, coming up in conversation, struck me as a mystical coincidence. More and more, it seemed like queerness was following me, like a message from the universe, or maybe it was all random. The Baader-Meinhof phenomenon. Synchronicity. The song by the Police started playing in my head.

"They talked to one of the local lesbians," the man read on. "She says, 'The only way we could exist in Bangor is by fitting in, by not looking different. And that was Charlie's problem. He was very open about it. Charlie was so outlandish, swishy and flamboyant.' It says he carried a purse and wore earrings and makeup."

"Sounds like he was looking for trouble," said the ear, nose, and throat specialist, butting in. He spoke loud and clear, and I suspected he used his quiet voice to force women to get close to him, to look at his lips.

"Ted," the psychic said, scolding flirtatiously, "you're a monster."

"I'm not condoning the murder. I'm just saying, when you flaunt it like that, you can't act surprised when things don't go your way."

"No, I suppose not."

"Actions have consequences. It's like I was telling this young lady here, about listening to those Walkmen radios. When you end up going deaf, don't act surprised."

"That's hardly the same thing," the psychic said, giving me a sympathetic look.

"Isn't it though?" Ted went on, making me shift over on the ottoman so he could sit. "Actions have consequences. And this homosexual up in Maine, who's to say he didn't harass the other kids? Come on to them with a sexual advance. That kind of thing happens all the time. And boys that age? They react. It's self defense. Especially today, with AIDS and all the rest. People are scared. That's all I'm saying."

"Did you hear about the needles in the gas pumps?" the wispy barefoot woman interrupted. "I'm deadly serious. Stay away from self-serve gas stations. They're rigging the pump handles with hypodermic needles full of AIDS."

"Good thing I never pump my own gas," Ted said.

"I think you *are* condoning the murder," the psychic told him. "Next thing you'll be saying is that I ought to be attacked because I'm wearing a skirt."

"Well, now that you mention it, you do have great legs. She does! Take a look! Aren't they great?"

He elbowed me in the ribs. I didn't like him and I didn't want to comment on the condition of the psychic's legs.

"Philip never looks at my legs anymore," she said, pushing out her lower lip like a child. "Do you, Philip?"

Her husband turned the page and went on to other news. I felt troubled by the story of the boy in Bangor, killed for carrying a purse. Was Sylvia "flaunting it"? But she wasn't a homosexual, she was a woman. I supposed she could have been a lesbian, but I didn't know if she liked men or women, or both, or how that worked with transsexuals anyway. Did bisexuals get tossed in the river, too? The thought made me shudder and I slipped away, wandering the room, looking again at the poster of the unicorn gazing at its own reflection.

Everywhere I turned, people kept holding up a mirror, showing me slivers of myself, so pleased with their powers of perception. Like that psychic. Or the mean little boys at the playground. I have since learned that many people take pleasure in the unmasking of others. They like to locate tender hidden spots, jab a finger, and announce, *I see it.* As if those spots were theirs to uncover. As if bodies were puzzles for them to solve. Why was the lady in the tapestry holding that mirror? The unicorn was smiling, but maybe he was just being polite. Maybe he didn't want to see his weird horn. Maybe he wanted to pretend it wasn't there, and having people point it out made him feel like an object to conquer, instead of just an ordinary horse going about his business.

"Darling," Gail said, suddenly at my ear, her breath a rich broth of garlic and wine. "There are young people out on the veranda. Why don't you join them?" She put a hand on my shoulder and steered me to the kitchen, pointed me toward a pair of glass doors, and disappeared back into the party. I fixed myself another Aperol spritz, stronger this time, and headed out to the wraparound porch that blossomed into an octagonal gazebo lit by strings of white lights. I'd never seen a gazebo in real life, only in romantic movies and magazine ads for Gunne Sax dresses, frothy with roses and lace, and it made me feel as if I'd stepped into a better, more beautiful reality.

With drink in hand, I felt mature, at least sixteen, but the young people weren't that young. College kids dressed in shades of sherbert, they stood around with their floppy hair and orthodontically enhanced smiles, the guys doing all the talking while the girls nodded along. I lingered, hoping they would invite me in, but they ignored me, going on with their talk about rowing crew, making dirty jokes I didn't understand about something called a coxswain. I refused to be like my mother. Instead of looking needy, I arranged my face into an expression of superior boredom. It worked. One of the girls asked my name. She was sweet and warm, with a bouncy brown flip to her hair, like that girl in the old TV show. Gidget. So normal, so healthy, the sort of girl who curls the phone cord around her toes and jumps into convertibles, forever sunshine and white teeth. Instant crush. Her name captivated me. Hadley. I'd never met a Hadley. She asked about my hair and I told her I had it done in Harvard Square. She said that was "rad." A few of them went to Harvard, she explained, but most of the guys were at Amherst.

"Some of us were at Andover together. Now I go to Mount Holyoke," Hadley said. "I know, it's ridiculous, a girl named Hadley going to Holyoke?"

I shook my head, not getting the reference.

"It's an all-girls school—sorry, *women's college*, I'm still getting used to saying that—one of the Seven Sisters? And it's located in the town of South Hadley. So, yeah, it's pretty ridiculous."

"There are colleges just for girls?"

"Sure, but it's cool, there are plenty of guys nearby, so it's not like you go *hungry* or anything. It makes it easier to focus on your classes when there aren't guys around. And I love men! It's not like I'm a *feminist* or anything. I shave my legs." We talked about life at college, how she was planning to major in English and really getting into Emily Dickinson, who went to Mount Holyoke, too, a hundred *million* years ago.

"You know what I always say," one of the guys interrupted. "Why screw a Smithie when you can mount a Holyoke?"

He looked like all the Ivy League boys in the movies, a little Andrew McCarthy and a little Robert Chambers, the Preppy Killer who would soon strangle a teenage girl behind the Metropolitan Museum of Art in New York City. This guy wore not one but two alligator shirts, lemon yellow layered under pistachio green, the collars popped up. He had dark hair parted on the side, an upturned nose with flared nostrils, and a wolfish grin that said he could devour the whole world and no one would stop him. In fact, they'd reward him for it. He'd probably end up as the president of a multinational bank or taking a seat in Congress, or both.

"Shut up, Brett," Hadley told him, but I could tell she liked him. He put his arm around her. "This guy," she said, laughing, "is an animal. Stay away from him, Mel."

"You're safe," Brett told me. "I'm not into boys."

"She's a *girl*."

"Oh shit, sorry."

"It's okay," I shrugged.

"She called you Mel, so I figured."

"It's okay," I said again, wanting him to stop. The attention of the crowd had turned toward me.

"What's with the suit and tie anyway?" Brett asked. "Going to a funeral?"

He exchanged a glance with the other guys. They grinned at the joke, but I'd heard it already.

"It's vintage," I said, putting on a tough voice. "I got it in Harvard Square."

"I go to Harvard," said one of the guys, a skinny, underdeveloped freshman whose name I can't remember, though he remains indelible. I'll call him Randy because that descriptor suits him well. "Are you one of those Pit rats?"

"Yeah," I lied. "I hang out in the Pit all the time."

"Awesome. Pit rats are wild."

Stamped with that cachet, I was no longer the moneyless small-town nobody, I was a Pit rat, a wild one, maybe a prep-school kid gone bad, one of those feral girls they saw on their way to get croissants at Au Bon Pain on the Square, an object they could never touch because all the rats thought Harvard boys were douchebags. And yet here I was, sucking down Aperol spritzes in Newcastle-by-the-Sea. Within reach.

The four of us split off from the rest of the group and stood talking by the porch rail overlooking the backyard, a grassy expanse that broke over a hill above a cove salted with sailboats. The town was on a jagged peninsula, technically an island tied to the mainland by a causeway, so you were never far from water. Brett handed out cigarettes. I didn't like him. He was an operator, moving us around like pieces in a game. When he made another joke, I must have rolled my eyes because he told me to "relax" and grabbed my shoulders with both hands.

"You're so uptight," he said. "Here. Turn around."

From behind, he squeezed my neck, digging in with his thumbs.

"Do me," Hadley said. I thought she was talking to me, but it was Brett's hands she wanted. He moved on to her and she closed her eyes, his fingers wandering inside the collar of her blouse.

"Hadley," Brett said. "You do Randy. And Randy, you do Mel."

Randy's grip was determined, thumbs and knuckles pressing my neck like the lumps of clay Jules and I used to pull from the ground, squeezing them in our fists. I couldn't wait to tell her about this. She would be so jealous. Randy kept asking, "Is that good?" He wanted me to like it. What did I know about good? I said yeah, hanging in a state of suspension at the front end of our train, the only one with empty hands.

"Got any pot?" Randy asked.

"Nah. My mom found my stash." Another lie, but I was a Pit rat, and Pit rats had stashes.

Brett said he had something in his car. Hadley took my arm in hers and pulled me along. I would follow her anywhere. Down the dark driveway, we passed streamlined European cars, Mercedes, BMW, and then my mother's Chevy Citation, shabby and out of place. "Who drove this shitbox?" That was Brett. I punched the hood, betraying my mother and myself. "Ooh, tough girl." Hadley squeezed my arm tighter and I felt boyish, buoyant and right. When we arrived at Brett's Volvo station wagon, parked on the grass under a chestnut tree, he reached through the open window into the glove compartment and pulled out a small bottle. It had white powder inside and a spoon built into the cap. He scooped out a bump and held it under Hadley's nose. She sniffed. He refilled the spoon and offered it to me. I hesitated.

"Not so tough?"

"It's just coke," Hadley said, giving my arm another squeeze. "A little bump's no big deal. It'll make you feel zippy. Like coffee, only better."

I trusted her. Those warm brown eyes, that Gidget smile. I leaned in and clumsily sniffed, smearing it on my nose.

"She didn't get enough," Hadley said. "Give her another."

"No way," Brett said. "She's wasting good shit. This isn't amateur hour."

I got enough. My nose tingled and I tasted metal, like sucking on a paperclip, the drip trickling down my throat. Brett and Randy each took their bumps with snorts of pleasure. I felt caffeinated. The sky swelled with stars, humming in summer heat. What was next? Maybe music. Maybe dancing. Hadley. I watched Brett take her hand and pull her into the back seat of the car. That wasn't the way it was supposed to go. I thought we were all hanging out together, the four of us. The door slammed, leaving me alone with Randy. Nervous and nineteen, dressed in clothes too big for him. Oxford shirt messily tucked into madras shorts. Chapped lips. Blue eyes with long lashes that made him look soft and pretty. I watched his feet shifting in the grass. Scuffed bucks and no socks. He kept smacking his tongue.

"Cottonmouth," he said. "I am so high. Are you?"

"I guess."

"I was at a party where this guy did so much coke, he burned a hole right through the septum of his nose. He could hang a coat hanger through it. It was awesome." He moved closer. "Do you want to make out?"

"Okay," I shrugged.

He mashed his tongue in my mouth and pressed me against the car. I felt the erection inside his shorts and thought, *This is what a dick feels like.* All those times Jules and I had talked about sex and, finally, I was the first to arrive. I memorized the details so I could tell her about it. Then I remembered what her mother said: *It can go through clothes.* My heart revved. Randy's hands moved over my body, untucking my shirt and slipping his hands inside, over my bra and then under. He grabbed too hard, too fast. When I yelped and jerked away, he clamped a hand over my mouth.

"I'll go slow," he said. "It's okay."

That hand. I froze under its power. Like my father's hands. My mother's hands. Telling me to be good and quiet. And I was. Randy went back to kissing my neck and feeling under my shirt, more gently this time, like he was searching in the dark for something he'd dropped. I turned away, looking through the window of the car to see the shapes of Hadley and Brett. Was he doing the same thing to her? Did she like it? I pictured Brett's hands on Hadley's breasts, and my thoughts flipped to the boy in Bangor, the hands of boys grabbing, tossing him in a river. *Bisexual* the psychic said. That meant both. You can *want* both and you can *be* both. While I might take some strange, unnameable shape, maybe I could also be a girl who liked boys. In this way, I thought, I could be saved.

"Let's go to the barn," Randy said, pulling me over the grass to a place that smelled of hay and manure, puddles of motor oil on the dusty cement floor. I could hear a horse moving in its stall.

"Gail has horses?"

"Take off your shirt."

In the blue-black darkness, I couldn't see the horse, I could only hear and smell it, but it felt like fate. Horses, horses, horses. I was Patti Smith and Randy was kissing me again, his tongue sweeping mine. When he took my necktie in his hand, the gesture sent a pulse between my legs. I became the boy in the song. Boy with boy, I kissed him back, feeling my power. He groaned and held my head in his hands, rubbing a thumb over the buzzcut bristles on one side, gripping the hair on the other. I could see it now, what other people saw. I was the Half-and-Half. The asymmetrical Strange Girl. I could see it all, my freak show banner waving: Melvin/Melanie. Step right up and see an illusion! I was an impossible body. Magnificent and unusual. The unicorn in the tapestry. And so, almost fourteen and filled with my own splendor, I let that boy pull me down into the hay of an empty stall, moonlight trickling through a window laced with the knitting of cobwebs. In that faint glow, over the low wooden wall, I could see the shape of the horse, its head and neck, glittering eyes looking as if it knew me. And then the chime of the boy's belt buckle. My pants tugged down. Too fast.

"Hey," I said. But hay is for horses.

Desire goes sometimes like this. You can want the thing, but not the whole thing. You can want an idea of the thing, but not the thing itself. These distinctions are often inexpressible, especially when it's moving fast. I still don't know what I wanted that night. Maybe it was the suddenness that unsettled me, the speed with which I was turned, against my will, from a unicorn to a horse, just an ordinary beast, un-horned.

"Gimme your hand," he said, gripping my wrist.

His penis was slick with what I thought was sweat. Hard but also soft, the skin moving in a way that surprised me. I thought of a ham shank, oily pink meat on bone. He touched me, too, his fingers blunt. I didn't like it. When he said, "You like it like that," song lyrics cascaded through me: *You're rolled down on your back and you like it like that.* I squeezed my legs shut. He shifted, maneuvered on top, and started to press against the place between my thighs. I clenched tighter. "Wait," I said, grabbing for something solid in the slippery straw. I couldn't find a grip. "Stop." *Suddenly. Johnny. Gets the feeling. He's being surrounded by.* Randy didn't stop until, with a gasp, he did. A gluey spill against my leg that made me think of the swamp, jellied frog's eggs, clammy rubbers. Made me think of the man's spit foaming in the dirt of Hooley Park. I took a fistful of hay and cleaned it off. Wiped my sticky hand on the splintered wall. Pulled up my pants.

"Don't say anything, okay?" he said, buckling his belt. "To Brett. Or Hadley. Just let them think I scored, okay?"

I didn't answer. I was trying to make sense of what he asked. Hadn't he scored? But maybe it didn't count if he didn't get inside. What did I know about anything?

"Come on," he said, before I could respond. "Don't be a bitch about it."

Was I being a bitch? I walked out of the barn feeling fogged and syrupy slow, like I'd awakened from a nap in a strange place, or else in the usual place but it looks strange, when you think you're in another bed, but you're not. The unfamiliarity of the familiar. Hadley was waiting at the side of the house, her Gidget smile dimmed. I had an impulse to embrace her, thinking we might console each other, but held back. She lit a cigarette, took a drag, and handed it to me. I smoked the whole thing, tasting the wax of her freshened lipstick on the filter, while she brushed and plucked every stick of straw from my hair and clothes, removing all evidence of disarray. We walked into the house and drifted in separate directions. I never learned what happened to her in Brett's Volvo or how she felt about that night, if she wished, like I did, that it had gone a different way.

I fixed myself another drink. The Aperol was done, so I poured vodka, straight, with a couple of ice cubes. I wasn't sure how to define what happened in the barn, and still don't, but in that moment, some interior mechanism clicked into position and I decided: It was good. As I solidified around that resolution, every element took on a hyper-real glow. The ice cubes, the silvery booze, all glittered cinematically. Extra. I felt extra. I made myself bigger than I was, and as I wandered from room to room, watching people from an airy distance, I knew they were too blind to see that I had changed, transfigured by the wild incantations of sex. Taller, more aloof, I leaned in a doorway, observing the crowd, noting how dull they all seemed, how old and constricted, while I was young and alive. On the stereo, Carole King sang about feeling like a natural woman and I thought, *Now I know what she means.* This must be what it's like, to feel real and right, properly situated in one's sex, instead of doubtful and misplaced, waiting to be claimed from the lost and found.

I was immersed in this new sensation when my mother's unnatural laugh rang out from across the parlor. She stood next to Richard who was telling a story to a circle of people, spreading his hands to show the impressive size of something, a fish maybe, and my mother acted like it was the most hilarious thing she'd ever heard, even though I knew she didn't give a shit about fishing, that she hated when my father would come home from Lake Tuckernuck stinking of largemouth bass and boastful stories. She was such a phony. Clutching Richard's arm. Hanging on for dear life. Her eyes wild with frivolity. In that instant, my dreamy cloud hardened into a hot climate of hate.

Even now I cannot fully grasp the clash of feelings that gripped me that night. I felt at once cocky and knocked out of joint by what happened in the barn. My life, with a hard bang, lurched toward the brink of making sense, as if some corrective semblance of sex with a boy could fix the problem of me and keep me from getting tossed in a river. Or thrown in a mental hospital. Or being spit on. As if sex with a boy could jam the square peg of me into the right round hole. I thought of Sylvia with sympathy. She couldn't avoid the hate of the world, but maybe I could. Maybe I could find a way to pass right through. Underneath that feeling, however, there coursed a sense of having been betrayed. By Hadley and my mother. Hadley hanging on Brett, my mother on Richard, both doing what girls did, buoying the boy and letting the girl sink.

A year before, on my thirteenth birthday, my mother sat me down and told me about boys. You should wait for sex, she explained, until you really love someone, but boys would try things and I had to be smart. She told me about a time when she was a teenager and went on a date. She made the mistake, as she put it, of getting into the boy's car and letting him drive her to a dark, secluded spot not far from her house. He attacked her and ripped her blouse. She managed to run, into the trees and through the fields where her family raised Connecticut shade tobacco under canopies of cheesecloth, the broad green Havana leaves slapping her face. She had one shoe on and the other lost, her sock slipping in mud. When she got to the house, her father beat her for losing a shoe when shoes were expensive. I sat stunned by the story, imagining my mother fighting and escaping, only to get beaten by my grandfather—hit with the remaining shoe, a loafer with a dime still wedged in its slot for an emergency phone call she never made. But my mother wasn't troubled by it. "These things happen," she said. "If that boy had caught me, it would have been my own fault for being there in the first place." Confused, I told her she had it wrong. It wasn't her fault. But she wouldn't hear it. "I was stupid," she said. "That boy just did what boys do."

I watched Richard put an arm around my mother's waist and pull her to him. She squirmed with delight, happy in a way I only saw when she was in the glow of a man. I vowed never to tell her what happened in the barn. She would say that I was stupid and what did I expect? After all, she had warned me. I took an acid gulp of my drink and bore down, sending rays of hate across the room. My mother was pathetic, I told myself, and I would never be like her.

She started dancing, taking Richard's hands and making him move his feet back and forth. People laughed and shook their heads. Surely, I thought, everyone could see how pathetic she was. And Gail, half-sprawled on the sofa with her Viking hair let down from its chopsticks, her linen top stained with a single drop of red wine, what did she see in my mother? A conversation piece? A dancing monkey? In that hideous tropical dress. And those sad blue boat shoes. And that hairstyle. Nobody wore a Dorothy Hamill anymore. She was doing it all wrong. Surely, everyone could see that, but it was near the end of the night and things had turned sloppy and unfocused.

"The prodigal daughter returns," Richard bellowed when he caught sight of me.

"And with a drink in her hand," my mother said in a chiding way, dancing over to seize my glass in front of everyone. She sipped it coquettishly. "Where've you been all night? Hanging with the college crowd?"

"Yes," I said, clipping my words. I didn't like it when my mother got flirty. "In fact, we were discussing Harvard. And Mount Holyoke. Have you heard of it?"

"I know Hahvahd," my mother said, accentuating the Brahmin accent. "*Every*body knows . . ."

"Mount Holyoke is an excellent women's college," I interrupted, making my voice flinty and cold. "Emily Dickinson went there. Have you heard of her?"

"Of course I've heard of Emily Dickinson," she said, dropping her act, not liking my game. "I'm not an idiot. She's a poet."

"She *was* a poet, Irene. She's been dead a long time."

I glared, waiting for her next move.

"Emily Dickinson," Richard mused, coming in for the rescue. "Wasn't the old girl famous for writing dirty limericks? *There once was a man from Mass.*"

"Oh, I know this one," my mother exclaimed. Richard bowed dramatically, giving her the stage. She took a belt of vodka and recited to the room: "There once was a man from Mass., whose balls were made out of brass, when they clanged together, they played 'Stormy Weather,' and lightning shot out of his ass!"

The crowd cheered. From the sofa, Gail raised her wine glass in salute. Richard planted a kiss on my mother's cheek. She kissed him back on the mouth, making it sexy so the crowd whooped and hollered, *Atta boy Dickie!* She was tipsy, I could tell, but not really drunk. I'd seen her do this performance at parties before. She liked to have a drink or two and then put on a Hollywood act of being bombed. It was her way to have fun while maintaining control. If you watched carefully, she always had a drink in her hand, but never finished it, and her eyes stayed sober and sharp.

Defeated, I flopped down next to Gail. She put an arm around me and squeezed me to her. She sniffed my hair.

"Were you kids in the barn?"

I froze.

"I don't care, darling," she said. "Just tell me you weren't smoking in there. It'll go up like a tinderbox."

"No, no smoking."

She took my hand and patted it. "Did you have a good time with the kids tonight? Aren't they wonderful? And I just love your mother. She's a hot ticket."

I looked at my mother, talking with Richard and that psychic woman, and wondered what qualified her to be a hot ticket. Gail must have read my eyes.

"Give your old mama a break," she said. "She's having fun. It's not easy at our age."

"Yeah, right."

"You'll understand one day. When you're a woman of a certain age and you find a man who makes you feel like Irene feels with Richard, you'll understand." She pulled my head onto her shoulder and played gently with my hair, something my mother used to do when I was little but didn't do anymore.

On the drive home, my mother gave off a frizz of irritation. The night didn't end the way she'd hoped. Richard did not invite her back to his place. If that had been her plan, it was news to me. I told her I didn't want to sleep in some strange guest room anyway, and without my pajamas and toothbrush? What was she thinking? We sat in silence, crossing the causeway that connected Newcastle-by-the-Sea to the mainland. A tied island, its tether consists of a two-lane road on a ribbon of sand. I stared out at the navy-blue velvet of the bay, feeling sleepy, until we rolled onto the route that took us inland along a twisting street that unsettled my stomach.

"You talked to a lot of people," my mother said, her voice tight. A familiar warning that I'd done something wrong.

"I guess so," I said.

"Some strange woman came up to me and said you were poised. That's the word she used. *Poised.* And mature. That's nice. But do you want to know what I think?"

I steeled myself.

"I think you're a snob."

"I'm not," I muttered.

"You think you're better than me?"

"I don't." My stomach didn't feel well and I wasn't up for a fight.

"You're not better than me," she hissed, taking the curves too fast.

"All that Emily Dickinson bullshit. All those books you read. You think you're so goddamn smart."

She turned sharp onto a four-lane road, past houses and mini-marts and gas stations glowing like alien ships. I tried to will myself into another car, to teleport from the rotten atmosphere of my mother's Chevy, growing heavier and darker with her poisonous mood. I'd seen these shifts, mostly when my sister was still at home. With the slightest provocation from Donna, my mother could extrude from her depths a bewildering darkness, an oily cloud that permeated the whole house, sticking everyone in its slick. I have felt this darkness inside my own body, once or twice, in adulthood. It's like a spreading black tar, my dark mother, coming to show me what was happening inside her all those years ago. At the time, however, I only knew what it was to be a small animal trapped in her tar pit. I cracked the window to let in a blast of air and slumped against the car door, sick to my stomach, trying to put as much distance between us as I could. Maybe I muttered "Jesus Christ" or "Gimme a break." Whatever it was, my mother snapped.

"You shit on me!" she shouted, making me flinch. "All night long. You shit on me."

A briny tang of acid climbed up my throat.

"I didn't."

"Oh no? I saw how you looked at me. You shit on me. With your *eyes*."

My gut roiled, sending waves of heat up my spine, and I started to shake.

"Don't think, for one minute, I can't see inside you," my mother went on, her voice dropping to a deeper register. "All the way down, girl. You are *full* of shit."

"You don't know me," I managed to say.

To this my mother replied the way unhappy mothers do when

their daughters challenge the reach of their omniscience: "I know you better than you know yourself."

"Pull over," I cried. "I'm gonna puke."

"Don't mess up my car," she said, jerking the wheel to the right.

I opened the door, the car not fully stopped, and leaned out vomiting onto the sandy shoulder of the road, my insides erupting the fizz of Aperol spritz, vodka, and quiche onto red spangles of broken glass from accidents past. My mother did not break form. She did not put a comforting hand on me. She lit a cigarette, rolled down her window, and blew mouthfuls of hot smoke into the night.

2019

The Swaffham Public Library looks the same and, incredibly, smells the same, of rainy days and old carpet, but they've replaced the wooden card catalog with computer terminals and added a section for teens with LGBTQ books on display. No more hiding in the stacks. Today, a dozen moms and kids have come to see Bernice Sanders, a socialist drag queen in a frothy purple wig and matching cocktail dress. Across the country, Drag Queen Story Hour has been making people crazy. At a library in Texas they arrested a man who showed up with a gun, and in Washington the police came prepared for war, posting snipers on rooftops. Thankfully, Swaffham's event has slipped under the radar. Dakota is disappointed that the anti-trans protesters didn't show—"I was ready for a fight," she says, further endearing herself to me—but she is thrilled to meet a real, live queen. She has made a T-shirt for the occasion, decorated with the upcycled sequins from my Michael Jackson glove. As she settles in with the other kids around the glittering feet of Miss Sanders, I steal away, back to the Adult Reading Room.

The records are gone and their long wooden bin has been converted into a display case for the artwork of Swaffham's high-school students, depressing clay sculptures of everyday objects—a lopsided cheeseburger, a toilet with an open lid. There's a Massachusetts flag on the wall, its oppressed Native American under the conquering sword of Myles Standish, though he may not last much longer now that a commission has formed to redesign the official seal of the commonwealth. It's yet another thing Donna grumbles about, claiming we're "erasing history for political correctness."

Donna. Am I really going to let Dakota stay with her, spending her teenage years steeped in right-wing paranoia and resentment, glued to a screen and eating junk food? No one saved me from that fate and I turned out okay. Mostly. I go back and forth in my mind and Donna's not making it easy, moaning about her chronic pain and money troubles. Ever since we met with Jerry Logue, she's become dead set on seeing our mother's house demolished for Amazon. The place is getting emptier by the day, and it's likely I'll soon be leaving Swaffham forever. I feel an inexplicable urge to hold on to it, a town I never liked, so small it barely exists, omitted from many maps. I survived life in the boondocks and so will Dakota. Was it really so bad? Maybe I've imposed a false narrative on the place. It bothers me that there's no way to go back, to view the past like a videotape. There are only scattered notes and diary entries, a few photos, fragments of story. Searching the reading room for more evidence, I discover copies of the annual *Town Report* dating back six decades. I pull out 1984.

Births, deaths, general statistics. Reports from the Town Nurse, the Fence Viewer, the Sealer of Weights and Measures, the Dog Officer venting his frustration with the problem of unleashed dogs. Wild species removed from homes that year totaled: 2 Raccoons, 2 Skunks, 2 Snakes, 3 Bats, 5 Birds, and 8 Squirrels. The Remover of Carcasses shoveled 218 dead animals from the streets. As for the humans of the town, they contracted a handful of Communicable

Diseases, including 1 case of the Mumps, 4 cases of Gonorrhea, and 1 Hampster [*sic*] Bite, which is neither communicable nor a disease but somehow made the list.

There were several crimes committed in Swaffham in 1984. Among hundreds of larcenies, assaults, and incidents of suspicious activity, the police reported 55 complaints of Operating While Drunk, 162 acts of Vandalism, 4 Arsons, 19 Annoying Phone Calls, and 7 Youths in the Street. What about the things that happened to Sylvia? They must be here among the numbers, anonymous and stripped of particulars. Or did they not count, because they happened to her? And what about the things that happened to me? I made it through unscathed, I tell myself, but that would mean nothing happened in the fields and woods, in the barn with that Harvard boy, in the women's restroom at Hooley's, and later in a parked car, another something I told myself was nothing much. Reading back over my life, through the sharpened lens of today, I see these incidents differently than I did then. Psychoanalysis has words for this. In German it's *Nachträglichkeit*, "afterwardsness," and in French it's *après-coup,* a re-transcription of the past. Something you thought was nothing, you later understand was really something. The soil washes away and the bodies rise to the surface. If I hadn't buried Melanie, would Melanie have buried me?

When I go to collect Dakota, she's in a crowd of busy kids around a craft table where Bernice Sanders has taught them to make seed bombs. Dakota proudly introduces me to the queen, loud enough for everyone to hear, "This is my great-uncle Max. He's trans." I feel a shiver of fear, but remind myself, again, this is not 1984. The mothers smile and the queen tells Dakota, "Lucky you." I am not destroyed. On the walk home, we pass an empty lot, a ruin that used to be a house, foreclosed. Dakota takes a bomb from her paper bag and hands it to me. It's a dumpling made of clay, stuffed with wildflower seeds and potting soil, rolled in glitter—an apt metaphor for queer contagion. She pulls out another and launches it over the fence. "Throw it," she says. I hesitate, law-abiding schoolteacher that I am, but Dakota won't let me chicken out. "Throw it," she insists, and I do. It feels good and, as we walk, we toss the whole bag, one bomb after another, onto front yards and median strips, seeding the town with the possibility of wildflowers and shimmer.

1984

My father had always been in charge of mowing the lawn, but since his exile to upstairs, he'd let the grass grow wild. It wasn't his problem anymore. I was in the backyard, struggling with the mower's pull cord, the motor sputtering out and stinking of gasoline, when he ambled over with his bow-legged cowboy walk. It was Sunday. The whole town buzzed with lawnmowers and transistor radios as summer drifted into its final month of heat. Can of beer in hand, he surveyed the overgrowth of clover and plantain weed and declared it a "fucking jungle." I couldn't remember the last time I'd seen him, beyond a passing hello, and it felt like months instead of weeks. He wore cut-offs and sneakers, no shirt. The hair on his chest, once a blaze of coppery brown, was dusted with silver, like the stubble on his face. Not a lick of suntan. Working the graveyard shift and sleeping through the days, he'd turned into a nightcrawler, as white as the bellies of the fish he pulled from Lake Tuckernuck.

The thought of telling him about my mother and Richard was tempting. After last night's ugly car ride, I wanted to embarrass her, expose her childish behavior at the party, and win my father over. I needed an ally, but there was no winning with the two of them. I'd have to take whatever scraps of kindness I could get, so when my father, tired of watching me struggle, elbowed me aside to show how it was done, I gladly relinquished the lawnmower. With one pull, he yanked the engine into a roar. I took his beer as he set off across the lawn, bending to toss rocks out of the way, his legs spattered with juicy flecks of cut grass.

The beer was warm, but I drank it, trying to ease my first hangover. Sitting on the decaying boards of the porch steps, I watched my father and wondered what he'd been like as a boy, if he ever took girls into dark barns or ripped their clothes in parked cars. What did I know of young men? My father had been handsome once. People said we looked alike with our dark eyes and crooked smiles. We were both tall and broad shouldered, but he was slim where I was thick, hard-muscled where I was soft.

I closed my eyes, breathed in the bright scent of shaven grass, and waited for Jules. First thing that morning, before I rinsed last night's vomit-sour from my mouth, I got on the phone and told her to come over, I had something to tell her. By the time she rolled up on her bike, my father was finishing the lawn.

"So what's the big news?" she said, propping her foot on a step below me and leaning back against the wobbly railing, arms spread so her T-shirt rode up, showing a pale sliver of belly. She was so skinny, her stomach looked concave. "Tell me," she said, but my father was rinsing his hands in the hose and I didn't want him to hear. I kicked Jules with the toe of my boot and she got the message, making a zipping gesture across her lips as my father walked over, wiping his hands on his shorts.

"Hey there, Jules, long time no see."

"Hey, Mr. Pulaski."

"What's cookin'?"

"Nothin' much," she shrugged.

"*Nothin' much*," my father echoed, his eyes flicking to her bared stomach. "Well, you look great. You're so skinny. How come Mel's not skinny like you?"

"I've been exercising," I said defensively. "I ride my bike but nothing happens. I'm not built to be skinny."

"Anyone can be skinny," he insisted, "if they try hard enough. You're not trying hard enough. I bet if you were in a concentration camp you'd be skinny."

I'd seen pictures of concentration camps in my history book. The people were starving skeletons, all rib racks and hollow eyes, shoveled into pits like bags of leaves. I smiled, stupidly, unable to respond. He was probably right. I wasn't trying hard enough. He turned his attention back to Jules.

"You're really growing up," he said to her. "I think the last time I saw you, you were climbing that tree over there. You still climb trees?"

"No," Jules laughed, her throat going blotchy pink. She shoved her hands in the pockets of her shorts and hunched her shoulders. I didn't like the way my father talked to her, like the way he talked to waitresses at the A&W he sometimes took me to for burgers and frosty mugs of root-beer slush, reading the girls' nametags and making a show of calling them *Cheryl, Debbie, Belinda*, inciting them to smile and blush.

"Did I hear you say something about big news?" he asked.

"Just boring kid stuff," I said. "Nothing you need to know." I got up, hooked Jules by the arm, and started walking.

"Hey," my father barked. "Don't you say thank you?"

"For what?"

"For *what*," he said. It had all been playful, and then it wasn't. That's how it went with my father. Light and breezy one minute, royally pissed the next. Easily slighted, he was a minefield of tender spots that flared into rage. Years later, one of my therapists would call them "narcissistic wounds," the way she called my mother "borderline." Back then I thought my parents were just difficult, not diagnosable.

"I didn't have to spend my Sunday mowing *your* fucking lawn," my father shouted, "did I? Huh? Did I?"

"No," I said. Jules hugged my arm tighter.

"I did you a favor."

I hadn't asked for any favors, but I kept my mouth shut.

"So why don't you say thank you?"

"Thank you," I mumbled.

"You're so fucking selfish," he said. "Just like your mother. And your sister. Do you want to be an ungrateful bitch like them? Huh? Next time you don't say thank you, I'll give you a boot in the ass."

He walked back to the hose, noisily winding it onto its hanger. Jules tugged me along, across the yard, through the chainlink fence and across the neighbor's property, past their sad rabbit locked in a hutch, under the crab apple trees, skirting around Snoopy, the latest in a series of short-lived barking mutts they kept tied to a clothesline, until we plunged into the cool, shady woods where I could breathe. Jules knew I felt more peaceful when I stepped into those trees. I'd spent my childhood there, but it had been awhile since I'd visited. The old paths had gotten crowded by knotweed and greenbrier but I knew their shapes. I can still trace them in my mind today. Sometimes they appear in dreams. The little pine grove, its floor a smooth carpet of coppery needles. The rocks where I made a shelter for Brenda White the night she ran away, their notch full of dried leaves. The bog crossed with waterlogged wooden planks. The twin mattress someone had dragged in years before, probably for sex. As a kid, I would sometimes find a pair of underwear tossed beside it, tangled and dirty. Now animals had gotten to the mattress, raiding its stuffing for nests, a sapling pushed up through its rusty springs.

Jules kept pestering me to tell her my news, but I didn't want to say a word about the Harvard boy in the barn until we got to the spot we called "the Waterfall," even though it wasn't any such thing, just a gurgling stream that spilled out of a culvert made from a corrugated steel pipe, good for sitting astride, telling secrets. When we crossed the field where the long grass lay down in humps, I knew we were close, and soon we were stepping across branching rivulets of water, grabbing slender trees, hopping from one mossy island to the next, until we reached the pipe, softly sloshing into a shallow pool. We straddled the warm steel, face to face, feeling the sun through the clearing. I want to remember this perfectly. Everything of that deep and manifold forest is gone now, bulldozed for a housing development. It sometimes stuns me to imagine it erased, but that culvert pipe, more than any of it, remains a permanent notch on my heart. It was there that I told Jules everything—how a boy's tongue feels in your mouth, the grip of his hands, what a penis feels like, soft and hard, and what it means for a boy to *come*. It was there that I enjoyed my moment of surpassing her, an explorer returned with tales of another world she had yet to visit. And it was there, too, that I would take the next step on my passage from one life to another.

Jules told me to hang on. She pulled a tube of bubblegum lip gloss from her pocket, wiped it across her lips, and handed it to me to do the same. Then she lit a dirty roach and we each took a deep hit. So fortified, she gripped my knees and said, "Tell me more." She wanted to know, *How much come was there?* About a teaspoon, I told her, the image of a dainty spoonful of semen making us crack up, joking about mixing it into cups of tea. *Did you taste it?* No. *Did you like it?* Which part? *All of it.* I wasn't sure. I told her how my body felt. The things that happened inside me. And I told her about the horse, how it watched me and I felt transformed. Jules listened with dreamy eyes, her bottom lip bitten between her teeth. She tilted her head and the mood tilted with it, making the air between us thicken with warm incandescence. I'm not sure what made her do what she did next.

Maybe I was safe because I had been with a real boy. Or maybe she wanted a taste of boy while he was still fresh on my body. All I know is that, when she leaned in and kissed me, I kissed her back with a fervency I did not feel in the barn.

Oily taste of bubblegum gloss. Wheaty hint of warm beer. Jules' soft tongue moving with mine. She didn't push or pull. She was just there. My hands in her yellow hair, the knobs of her spine, our shirts pulled up to press skin on skin. How did we know we could do that? After a flurry, our kissing relaxed into leisurely exploration. Neck and earlobes. Mouth again. I found my grip. A part of me clicked and I took her. That was the word that came to mind: *take, taken, took.* My body changed shape, as if my reluctant soul had at last stepped up to stretch out and expand my reach. Jules could feel it, too. With my mouth on her neck, she started rocking gently astride the pipe, the third party in our fling. I followed her lead. No hands. Like flying. Like riding a horse. And didn't the books warn us we could lose our virginity that way? Against the bare back of the metal pipe, the seams inside the crotches of our shorts dug in, pressing while we kissed and touched, until we both came, bucking in each other's arms.

Sweat trickling down my back, heart thumping, I looked over Jules' shoulder to the clear water below and spotted, at the sandy bottom, a *Star Wars* action figure. Lando Calrissian. An odd detail in that moment, in that secret place where no other human, I believed, had ever tread. But there was Lando, the friend who betrayed Han Solo and sealed him in carbon freeze, looking back at me. Was it a warning? Or just the unsettling evidence of others? Wherever I went, someone's eyes were watching. I felt caught, guilty, as if the cops were about to burst through the trees, put me in handcuffs, and drag me away. I looked out at the trees, the rocks, the blackberry brambles. What had I done?

Jules pulled away. I thought, for a moment, she would turn sour. But she only swiveled to lean back into me. I held her gladly, my cheek against her temple, feeling how light she was. That skinny girl, such a force in my life, I never realized there was so little of her. Wrapped around her, my arms and legs felt big, but not in the usual way. Their bigness now made sense of my body. I felt like a boyfriend. Like denim jacket and yellow workboots. Like *Little ditty 'bout Jack and Diane*. Backseats and Dairy Queens. The horsey smell a leather baseball glove leaves on your hand. I felt like that. Like real.

We sat a long while on the pipe, watching the stream flow through the trees. I thought of Sylvia, how I could love her and Jules at the same time, and the thought made me feel expansive and good. I wanted to stay in that place forever, but our backsides ached from sitting on steel and our stomachs grumbled with hunger, the afternoon hurtling by, life moving us on the way it had to. Jules hopped off, sneakers squishing in wet earth. She took my hand and we walked out, through the grassy field, past the spoiled mattress, and over the bog, by the rocks where I sheltered Brenda White. I told Jules how she'd been too scared to stay the night, and how I worried what had become of her, if they really sent her to the mental hospital for kissing a girl.

"We're not like her," Jules said, letting go of my hand. "We're not lezzies."

I didn't have to ask what she meant. I understood. You could *do* a thing or you could *be* a thing, and the two were not the same. We would barely speak of it again and I would only return to the culvert pipe alone, for a connection to what happened there, which began to feel, over time, more like something I had dreamed but did not do.

As we passed out of the woods and into my neighbors' yard, I felt myself contract to my former shape, galumphing in cowboy boots, my legs awkward again. Jules, too, became the usual Jules, bigger and rougher than she'd been in my arms. She picked up a crab apple and chucked it at the dog barking and lunging at us from his clothesline. I told her she was mean. She shrugged and chucked another apple, letting me know that nothing had changed. I still was not the boss of her. Whatever spell we'd woven in the depths of the woods had crumbled. But my soul, once stirred, would not lie down easy.

•

Sylvia's Trans Am sped along the back roads to Walden Pond. I hadn't been there since I was little, when my father would take Donna and me fishing for smallmouth and bluegill, gritty nightcrawlers twisting in our hands. Like everywhere else, Walden in the 1980s was dirty and degraded, but it was a hot day, nearly ninety degrees, one of the hottest that summer, and I looked forward to a swim. We walked down the dirt path, beach towels around our shoulders, shorts over one-piece bathing suits, both of us in cowboy boots. Almost twins, I thought proudly as we passed groups of ordinary people sprawled on the sand, surrounded by beer coolers and radios, the detritus of half-eaten sandwiches and potato chip bags. A few looked askance. We were special. Different. Better.

Kids splashed a few yards from shore and I watched to see if one would go under and not come up. It seemed every year we heard about someone drowning in those literary waters. Now and then, the state police would drag the deep center, looking for the dumped bodies of murder victims. Most famously, they had searched for a college student named Joan Webster who disappeared from Logan Airport on her way back to school after the Thanksgiving holiday. Tips from psychics and anonymous letters sent the police dragging ponds and lakes across Massachusetts, focusing on Walden, but no body turned up. They found the girl's handbag in the marshlands of Saugus with her BayBanks and Star Market cards, her Clinique Honey Raisin Lip-Gloss, but her bones would not be discovered for years and the prime suspect, Lenny "the Quahog" Paradiso, would die in prison, never confessing to the crime.

Because my life at that time revolved, at least in part, around the terrible things that could happen to the body of a young woman in the world, it was Joan Webster I thought about as we spread our towels on a secluded wedge of sand and not Henry David Thoreau, though his cabin site was nearby, marked by a sign with his famous quote about living deliberately. I knew Thoreau, of course. You could not be a public-school student in Massachusetts and not know Thoreau. He was like the Pilgrims and witches, like Lizzie Borden and her axe, part of the state's spiritual landscape. But he was not important to me. I thought more of bodies than of minds.

Sylvia sat on her towel and took off her boots. I watched her push her bare feet in the sand, shoving away twigs and pinecones fallen from the trees that protected our backs from passersby on the path. Like a cat preparing a spot to rest, she massaged the earth with her hands until it was just right, plucking a hunk of broken beer bottle from the sand and chucking it into the bushes. Satisfied, she lay down and, with a groan of pleasure, closed her eyes behind a pair of white Wayfarer-style sunglasses. The sky was a pale and cloudless blue, insistent with August sun, and I wanted to let myself swelter a bit, so the water would feel like a blessed reprieve. I pulled off my boots and shorts, oiled myself with Hawaiian Tropic, and leaned back to watch the pond, lightly waving. It did not escape my notice that Sylvia had opted not to remove her shorts, and this choice to remain concealed provoked in me an urgent curiosity about what she had underneath, the way a fig leaf in a painting makes you more curious than the naked thing itself. Remarkably, this question had not fascinated me before. I hadn't thought much about it. But now, since the barn and the culvert pipe, sex was all I thought about. Bodies and secretions. Internal tremors. The private things people did and what they used to do them.

I thought of the Harvard boy's impatient penis and Dale's plummy testicles, trying to imagine them, a pair of matching separates, on

Sylvia's body. There was something surprisingly sweet about this image and I was struck by the way a masculine configuration of parts could turn soft on a woman's form, tender, like certain bisexual-looking flowers, the calla lily with its petal folded around a pollen-dusted spadix. Or had Sylvia removed those parts and replaced them with a new shape? In *Conundrum*, Jan Morris describes traveling to Casablanca to a surgeon known as Dr. B—, the only one who could "rescue" transsexuals from their "wandering fate," and it is there that she says goodbye to her "maleness," as she puts it. After surgery, she becomes less forceful, explaining, "There was to the presence of the penis something positive, thrusting, and muscular. My body then was made to push and initiate, it is now made to yield and accept." Was that the true measure of a body? Whatever Sylvia had, she had thrust. And me? Even without the right parts, I had thrust, too, on the culvert pipe with Jules. The boyfriend feeling that had filled me while we kissed was a force with its own objective. It wanted to push, not yield. To pitch, not catch. Next to Sylvia, however, that energy swiveled, uncertain of which way to go. If we kissed, I wondered, who would I be? I stared sidelong at her body, her skin rosy in the sun, scooped collar bones, chest sloping to breasts pressed under black bathing suit. A flat belly that I envied. And then. I stole a more focused look at her shorts, to see if they bulged behind their zipper. I couldn't tell. Denim could be difficult. She stirred and I looked away.

"I knew a boy who killed himself at this pond," she said lazily. "Not far from here, I think. He hung himself from the branch of a tree."

I looked over my shoulder at the paper birches and oaks flickering green in the sun. Sylvia, often drawn to talk of death, told me about the boy, who was just sixteen and had no friends because he was odd, though no one knew which variety of odd, and no one would ever know. He'd taken his sister's jump rope to do it, Sylvia said, and the sister blamed herself and was never the same.

"Why'd he do it?"

"Same reason anyone does it," she answered cryptically.

I waited for more, but none came, and I rolled onto my stomach to read *The Ballad of the Sad Café*. It was not on my summer reading list and would not be required until I took a college course on the Southern Gothic, but I wanted more Carson McCullers, even though I'd fallen behind and high school was only a month away. After a few pages, I lay my head on the book and closed my eyes.

When we were good and hot, the sun heavy on our skins, it was time to go in. Sylvia slipped out of her shorts, adjusted the elastic of her bathing suit, and tested the water with her toes. It felt impolite to stare while she waded in, so I looked out across the pond to the distant, khaki beach crowded with people. Ordinary people behaving in ordinary ways on the other side of the world, hollow and dull. But they had what I was sure Sylvia and I never would. Acceptability. Safety. Access to the normal path of life.

Sylvia ducked under and came up with her dark hair slicked back from her face. "Get in!" she called. I obeyed, hugging myself as I stepped over rocks that rolled underfoot. The water was cool, as clear and bracing as vodka. I dunked and stayed under, opening my eyes to see schools of minnows, sunbeam, and Sylvia's lower half. In the wavering light, I stared at the V between her legs.

"You can just ask, you know," she said when I came up for air. "You don't have to spy."

"Ask what?"

"You know what. Don't act like you weren't looking."

I pressed my hands to my eyes, pretending they were irritated, and sank to my knees, so the water touched my chin. Ashamed, I felt myself tremble. Had she seen me on the sand, too, my gaze undressing her? If she knew, why didn't she say something? Maybe she needed me to see her, the way I needed her to see me. It occurs to me now that, while we were a decade apart in age, we were the only two people like us in that world. We had no one else to be our mirrors.

"I don't mind it," she said, sinking to her knees, too, so we were two heads bobbing close together on the surface of the pond. "A lot of girls do, but I don't. I have no intention of getting rid of it."

When Sylvia talked about sex and gender, she often spoke of "it," leaving me lost as to which "it" we were talking about. This time I understood. I told her about the Half-and-Half at the Brixton Fair, but it was the wrong thing to say.

"You think I'm a carnival freak?"

"That's not what I meant."

"Having what I have doesn't make me any less real."

"No, yeah, totally," I said.

"Some people think that," she went on. "Some people think you can't be real unless you have the operation."

"I don't. I don't think that at all." But I wasn't sure. The medical encyclopedia at the library said they couldn't make a girl into a man because doctors didn't know how to make a penis out of no-penis, and wasn't that what made you real? I didn't know what I thought. I blurted out, "A girl should have a dick if she wants one."

Sylvia mused for a moment, the glimmer of a smile on her face, and said, "That's very liberated of you. But that's the wrong word, I think. I always thought there should be another word for when it's on a girl. Because it's not the same. What do you think of *Jane*? Like Dick and Jane."

I thought it was clever and told her so, thinking again of the calla lily, how a part could change shape without changing shape, just by being on a different body. I ventured to ask, "What would be the opposite?"

She looked at me like she didn't understand and her confounded expression cast me back into impossibility. If Sylvia could not see me, who could?

"What would be the word," I continued, "for a boy with a you-know-what?"

"No, I *don't* know," Sylvia teased. "What?"

"You *know*," I said. I didn't want to be teased. Not then. Not about that. She wanted me to say the word but it didn't feel right, and neither of us wanted to speak it out loud. I splashed water at her and she ducked under.

"It's not something I've ever imagined," she said when she stood up. "I've known some bulldykes you'd swear had dicks, but a guy with a *you-know-what*? I can't believe you call it that. You're really a kid, aren't you? I probably shouldn't be talking to you about these things. I probably shouldn't be hanging around with you at all. I could get arrested."

"I'm not such a kid," I said. "I've had sex," though I was not sure that what I'd experienced, either in the barn with the Harvard boy or in the woods with Jules, qualified as actual sex. Embarrassed, frustrated, I held my breath, let myself sink, and watched the flashes of fish in the shifting light. Sylvia's white legs like towers of alabaster. I turned away, not wanting to give her the satisfaction of my gaze, and looked out to the murky green darkness in the yawning center of the pond, where the bodies of girls were sunk. Staring into the gloom, I sensed the tortured spirit of the girl they didn't find. It gave me a shiver that sent me crashing to the surface where I saw Sylvia swimming away, cutting foamy laps with her strong limbs. I floated on my back, arms spread, ears muffled with pond water. There were bodies and there were parts, and the two didn't always match. Those bodies and parts interacted with other bodies and parts, and those didn't always match either. To make matters more complicated, there were also souls, or energies, that could be influenced by the changing body, like when Jan Morris went from forceful to yielding. So what was I? And did everyone think about sex this way? It was too much to untangle. Even the mystical waters of Walden could not set it straight.

It is difficult now to recall the feeling of those days. The intensity of first lust in all its urgency and polymorphous appetite felt like the sensation of lift that comes in dreams of flying, dreams once so frequent and pleasurable in adolescence, grievously lost with age. I don't know where those feelings go, I only know I felt them and, that day at Walden Pond, they filled me with a delirious sense of my own power, a build-up of steam that pressed to overflow, so that once we were back on our towels, stretched out glistening with pond water and sun, I rolled over and kissed Sylvia on the mouth. Her lips, still cool from the swim, tasted like rain. Like rainwater on a green summer leaf. She did not kiss me back. From behind her sunglasses she said, not unkindly, "What do you think you're doing?"

"Kissing you."

"You can't do that," she said, matter of fact. "You're a child."

Though she said it without malice, the word cut me. *Child.* I wanted to plead my case, to show her what a mature sexual being I had become in just the past week, but I only fell back on my towel, burning with shame, a cascade of self-reproach. I was a freak and a creep, a predator filled with filthy compulsions. I had made a terrible mistake. She should have slapped me. A slap would have been relief. Just then, a pair of men's voices passed on the path behind the trees. Fear turned into a dark wish: *Let them see us.* We were two queers at the edge of the woods and they were average men with murder in their hearts. Like every average man. Like all the ordinary people who spit and grabbed and called us names. Let them take their pleasure in destroying us. Let them slice us open with their fishing knives and stuff our bellies with rocks, sink us to the middle of the pond, down with the bodies of all the murdered girls, where my shame would be blotted out. But the men did not oblige. They continued on and didn't trouble us.

"No one saw," I said, my voice weak.

"That's not the problem. The problem is that you're a child and . . ."

"Stop."

"You're a child and I'm an adult."

I sat up and glared at her. She remained unmoved behind her sunglasses. I wanted to snatch them from her face and make her look at me. "I had sex," I said again. "With a college boy. He's nineteen."

"I'm a few years older than that," she said. "And nineteen is too old for you, too."

"You lived with a grown man when you were my age. In the Chelsea Hotel."

"It was different for me."

"How?"

She sighed, like this was the most tedious question in the world, and turned to look at me over her shades. "I was a tranny girl alone in New York without a penny to my name. You're a girl who lives with her mother in the suburbs. I had to survive. You get to live."

It sounded like she was saying what adults were always saying, that my life was a cakewalk, when every day felt like marching barefoot on hot coals. I get to live? Couldn't she see I barely existed?

Back in town, Sylvia needed cigarettes. She parked at Red Mike's Package Store and went inside while I waited. I'd been quiet on the ride home from Walden, stewing and withdrawn, trying to make Sylvia sorry. She should have understood me, but she didn't. Alone in the car, I felt like making a scene. On Sylvia's mixtape, Lou Reed was doing another song about another trans woman, Candy, who hates her body and all it requires. Where were the songs about me? I pressed the fast forward button. Patti Smith—singing about She and He, one taking over the other, heading for a spin while "some strange music draws me in." Turn it up. Way up. In the next parking spot, a man loaded cases of beer into his trunk. He turned to look as I stood on the seat, dancing barefoot through the open T-top, making a scene, losing my sense of gravity, a spectacle in my Stars 'n' Stripes bathing suit. To hell with Sylvia. She was going to leave me anyway, sell her house and skip town. She couldn't wait to get away. Let her go. But when she walked out of the packie with a fresh cigarette between her lips, and I saw her stop to light it, cupping her hands around a Bic, I felt my heart flip. Sylvia. I could never be mad at her. I thought of that first time I saw her at the drugstore, how I watched with an unknown longing as she got into her Trans Am and took off, and now I was in that same car, in that strange music. She was with me. I was with her. What could be wrong?

"Hey," she said, getting in and turning down the stereo. "Sit and do some of these scratchies with me. I feel lucky."

She waved a handful of scratch-off tickets in my direction but I stayed standing. She smacked my leg playfully and said, "Come on, Pulaski, get your ass in here." As I watched her dig around the dash for quarters, the man next to us slammed his trunk and walked over. He leaned down to look in the car, at Sylvia, and then straightened up and said to me, "Is this person bothering you?" I'd been asked this before, by the man in Hooley Park, and I understood it meant something about me being a girl and Sylvia being the wrong sort of person, the sort other people worried about, especially around girls like me. I was a thing that required protecting, until I wasn't. I looked down into the man's face, an ordinary Swaffham face, dull and hard at the same time, and said nothing.

"Tell him," Sylvia said, "I'm your big sister," like I'd done before, but still I said nothing. Maybe I wanted to punish her—for recognizing me but not enough. "Recognition," the queer theorist Lauren Berlant once said, "is the misrecognition you can bear." As a thirteen-year-old impossible object, I could not bear even that.

"You okay here?" the man asked.

What did he think? That I was kidnapped? Another girl who'd end up sunk to the bottom of a pond, dumped in a gully, identifiable only from the fillings in my teeth? If he really believed that

Sylvia would be the one to end me, then he didn't know anything about anything, but before I could form the words to tell him, Sylvia turned the key in the ignition. I slid down into my seat and cranked the music, acting like I didn't care. The man stepped back, shaking his head, as we pulled away.

"You can't do that," Sylvia said, accelerating through town.

"Do what?"

"You can't be silent in those situations."

She was right. I was a child, like she said, too stupid to know better. The town rolled by, ugly and dull, broken houses, broken life. I was broken, too, and didn't know how to be a person. "I love this car," I said, instead of saying *I love you*, hoping she would know that I was sorry for everything, for all the bad things that happened and would go on happening. I wanted to rescue her, to be a lucky charm in her life. To make her stay. I picked up a quarter and started scratching the tickets, hoping for a jackpot to prove my worth. They were all duds, but Sylvia didn't care. She liked me, for reasons I still don't fully understand, when all I ever brought her was misfortune.

When she dropped me a block from my house, that distance we both believed was safe, she asked, "Do you know what Trans Am stands for?"

I shook my head.

"Transsexual American."

"No way."

"Way."

Sylvia with her smart-ass grin. Her crooked mouth. Sylvia whose lips tasted like rain. Though she would not kiss me back, and we never touched romantically, my time with her felt as thrilling as a secret affair. We knew we could not be seen together. But we were both young and dumb, the slumberous air of late summer had made us reckless, and we believed we were getting away with everything.

2019

I am back in the closet, literally, continuing to sift through my old books as if they still might have something to tell me. I dig up Carson McCullers' *The Ballad of the Sad Café*, smelling sweetly of crumbling paper, the memory of lying next to Sylvia on the shore of Walden Pond that day I kissed her. That was the moment when a lie, outside my awareness, began to take shape, because I wanted to love but did not know how. Maybe I still don't. I hate to think that my slanted love destroyed Sylvia. That's overblown, but it's true that the lie I told that summer has held me in confinement, a kind of quarantine, protecting others from my toxicity, and I haven't yet learned another way.

Between the pages of the book, a few grains of sand mingle with the petals of a flower, pressed and dried, a small blue thing I must have picked that day. I wonder if it still grows by the pond. Climate change, I read in the *Globe*, is killing Thoreau's wildflowers. The dogwoods and lilies are declining. Rising temperatures are increasing phytoplankton levels, making the once crystalline water cloudy. The algae feeds on the phosphorous and nitrogen in human waste as, every day in summer, hordes of tourists descend on Walden and piss while they swim, making it the most urine-filled body of water in Massachusetts. People are killing the pond by loving it to death.

I teach (or should I say *taught*?) McCullers' book in my class on LGBTQ literature because it's about a big, masculine woman who falls into unrequited love with a hunchbacked man, and that is a queer story, written by an author who has been variously claimed as bisexual, lesbian, transgender. Whatever she was (*they* were?), McCullers wrote about the lover and the beloved, ideas that stuck inside me as a teenager, and I believe they say something about how I would conduct myself in the realm of love for the rest of my life:

> There are the lover and the beloved, but these two come from different countries. Often the beloved is only a stimulus for all the stored-up love which had lain quiet within the lover for a long time hitherto. And somehow every lover knows this. He feels in his soul that his love is a solitary thing. He comes to know a new, strange loneliness and it is this knowledge which makes him suffer.

With Sylvia and Jules, I was the lover and they were the beloveds. My love was a solitary thing, strange and interior. In my memory of that summer, I am freighted with longing, a body pulled taut with unmet want. It is a sensation I would seek for years with every beloved, the experience intermixed with some notion I had about masculinity, and here I do not mean maleness, but rather a deportment I learned from the lovelorn butches of literature, alienated and brooding in their sad cafés and wells of loneliness because that is the condition of female masculinity. At least, it was when I was young.

In the murky early years, I placed ads in the personals section of the *Boston Phoenix*: "Female-to-Male Transsexual Seeks." Women never left messages in my mailbox—that's how it worked, you got a telephone code and called a voice machine—but men did. They thought

I was a trans woman, the only kind of transsexual that existed for most people. No one knew about trans men. We held no fascination. We were nobody's kink. I was a nameless thing, unthinkable and undesired. Only one respondent to my personal ad got close, a man with an attraction to women in male drag. While that did not fit my particular gender, I called him back and he told me about his love and the one strange, solitary way he could express it. As the custodian of a police station he had access to a CPR mannequin named Resuscitation Annie. Late at night, he would go to the basement, under the jail cells, and dress her in his own male clothing, take her in his arms, and dance with her. (If he did anything else with Resuscitation Annie, he did not say.) I found this to be the saddest love I'd ever heard of, sadder than any I'd felt myself, and I was grateful to the man for telling me about it. We never spoke again, but I think of him sometimes, whenever I am feeling at my most unloveable.

There's a poem by Denise Levertov that I teach alongside the McCullers. I first found it sandblasted into the train platform at Davis Square Station in Somerville, a few blocks from my house. In the poem, Levertov starts, "Not to have but to be," and ends with the wish, "To become the beloved." Wanting to have and wanting to be. Sometimes, in love, it's hard to know which is which.

Over the years, I kept trying. To have. To be. There were a few relationships that evolved and collapsed, with lesbians who wanted women and straight women who wanted men, momentary lovers for whom I was not enough of either one and too much of the other. I tried a few men, but they could not see me as anything but a temporary solution to their own ambivalence. Finally, at forty, I resolved to accept my lovelessness. Contrary to the suggestion of a therapist, I am not one of those transsexuals who rejects anyone who would love a transsexual, a variation on the old Groucho Marx joke. I am, however, aware that I sabotage myself. I have forever had a sense that my love is a calamity, like those tourists overwhelming Walden, and it's best kept contained. After all, the first time I let it out, in that summer of 1984, it made a terrible mess.

I keep digging. My childhood closet is deep and wide. I find a collection of boxes that once contained government cheese, orange bricks given to the poor by Ronald Reagan's Department of Agriculture, perfect for my mother's grilled-cheese sandwiches and, later, for holding keepsakes: bubblegum cards, tickets to the Swaffham Drive-In, a note from my old friend Pauline ("Tracy's bum is wiked big. Robert's hair is wiked greesey. Do you have alot of homework?"), a Socialist pamphlet bought for ninety-five cents in 1988 (*The Militant*, "Abortion Is a Woman's Right"), my purple rabbit's foot gone skeletal, its fur thinned to the bones, a token that once promised to bring me luck.

When I was a teenager and my mother felt that I had failed her, she would tell me I did not know how to love. She was partially right. I did not know how to love her. But it is also true, and sad to admit, that she did not know how to love me. I don't blame her. It is difficult to love something you cannot comprehend. And how can you comprehend that which has hardly been imagined? How could I imagine the shape of my own love? Of course it came out slant. But I loved Jules. And Sylvia, too, didn't I? Sometimes I worry that my love for her was just a way to have, to be.

Max doesn't want to be bothered. That's what Donna thinks. When she asked me to take Dakota, she said, "I know how you are," but she has no idea. She does not know that I am afraid to love. She does not know that I believed our parents when they said, as they often did, that I am selfish and cold. What happened to Sylvia only proved them right. My selfish way of loving is a destructive force. Donna wants me to raise this child? What good could I possibly be?

In the last of the boxes, among the souvenirs, I find a cassette tape marked "1984." I put it in my old boom box. Over the static and squeak of the spindles comes the sound of a bird, a long since perished red-breasted robin, and then rain, a summer thunderstorm I recorded from my bedroom window. Behind the storm, I can hear the woomp-woomp of the town's noon whistle, blaring atop the fire station to warn of possible disaster, and my mother in the kitchen, exclaiming, "Oh my god," each time the thunder hits. When the storm subsides, the tape clicks to another lost voice. Jules. She is speaking low, late at night in her bedroom that smelled of musk and strawberry candles. I forgot this. I used to ask her to record herself talking to me, so I could listen while I fell asleep, the sound of her voice a kind of lullaby.

"Hi," she says, husky and tired, exactly like Jules. "I'm in bed. I'm just kinda lyin' here. Not doin' nothin'. I'm waitin' for some movie to come on Home Box. It's called *Foxes*." She takes her time describing the movie, a story of suburban teenage girls. "Oh yeah, and speakin' of foxes," she goes on, telling me about a fox she saw run across her yard that evening. "It was cool-lookin' 'cause it had this weird body, and a wicked pointy snout, and this fuzzy big tail. It was neat." She pauses, asks, "Are you almost asleep? I don't know what you want me to say, 'cause like the tape's gonna run out and it's gonna be dumb." What did I want her to say? It didn't matter. I just wanted something of Jules to take to bed, to hold me while I fell asleep. This must have been before our kissing on the culvert pipe, before she pushed me away. But who's to say we were not, the two of us, in love with each other? She stops to check how much tape is left. "It's almost over," she says. "There's not much left." She waits, the tape twittering on its reels, and then says, "Goodnight. This is your best friend, Jules Cobb, signing off on July 15, 1984. You can listen to me breathe until the tape runs out." She breathes. She breathes. And then she's gone.

A sob catches in my throat. Ghosts of the past hover around me, a scent I catch and quickly lose. I need to hold them. Searching for their music, I shuffle through my albums for *Horses*. Patti with her black suit jacket, the shape that helped to shape me. I put the record on my old stereo and the needle sends up crackling, warm and deep. Then the piano, the voice, the words. I close my eyes, falling through time, because it's late, because the night, because I want to dream among the dead, thunderstorms that came and went, birds gone to dust, bones in the graveyard, the voices of the lost, the girls I loved, the girls I buried—the girl I used to be, fragments of her remains working toward the surface.

1984

"Go get the bundles," my mother said, carrying a brown bag of groceries to the kitchen table where I sat reading a book. She looked tired and irritated. "Stop & Shop was mobbed," she said. "And the traffic was brutal."

Days had passed since my trip with Sylvia to Walden Pond, enough time to make me think I'd gotten away with it, but my mother's irritation unsettled me. Whenever she was in a bad mood, I believed it was because of me. She could see inside me, where my thoughts roamed over kisses, Jules in the woods, Sylvia on the sand, troubling them the way your tongue haunts a broken tooth. To block my mother out, I hummed the Bumblebee Tuna jingle in my head.

"Melanie," she said when I had not moved. "Now."

I closed my book and huffed to the driveway where the trunk of the car gaped. I took three bags at once, feeling strong, and we emptied them, putting bottles of cheap Stop & Shop–brand soda in the fridge and crummy TV dinners in the freezer, along with two pints of Häagen-Dazs gourmet ice cream. It was expensive, but Richard liked it so Richard got it. He was taking up more space. His special health food occupied our cabinets, including a green powder he swore could ward off cancer, his "all-natural" toothpaste and deodorant squatted in our medicine cabinet, and the stink of his Polo cologne lingered in the fabric of our couch.

Out of a bag came frozen orange juice, Steak-umms, two half-gallons of milk in cardboard cartons—because Richard said the plastic of the gallon jug leached into the milk and caused cancer. I held one carton and read the back where a black-and-white photograph of a missing girl stared out. She was my age. White female, brown eyes and hair, last seen in 1981 at the Contoocook Valley Fair in New Hampshire. The milk carton kids were new, another way to tell us that our lives were filled with danger. Serial killers and Satanic ritual sex abusers. Nuclear missiles and AIDS. Cyanide in Tylenol capsules. Razor blades buried in apples on Halloween night. But it was the missing kids that most captivated me. I saw my own face in their photos each morning at breakfast. Sometimes, though I knew where she was, I looked for my sister's face, as if Donna had been snatched against her will. Maybe, in a way, she had.

"I ran into Gladys at Stop & Shop," my mother said, stacking cans in the cabinet.

Gladys was our mailman. Today we would call her our letter carrier, but we called her our mailman. She wore a blue uniform with a little cap, like a police officer, and she loved to gossip.

"She said she saw you up the Square. Sitting in a car outside Red Mike's. Listening to loud music. With a long-haired man. Who was that?"

"We were just riding around," I said. "And that wasn't a man."

"Who was it?"

"You remember Jodi Rizzo?"

There was a Jodi and there was a Rizzo, but Jodi Rizzo only existed as a spontaneous fabrication, enough truth to make her real.

"Vaguely."

"Mom. *Jodi Rizzo.* You don't remember? We were in Girl Scouts together. She came to my tenth birthday? Her mother drove the school bus."

I didn't know where these details were coming from, jumbled bits of different kids from school, but I was grateful for their arrival. Lying had never come easy, but this one flowed out of me. My mother handed me an empty grocery bag to fold, a job I hated. I could never get the creases to bend the right way and the brown paper smelled of damp lettuce. I felt her inspecting me.

"Was Jodi the girl who broke her arm falling off the roof?"

"Yeah, that's her," I said. "It's her big sister's car."

"I didn't know you were spending time with her again. You never mention her."

"We ran into each other up the Square," I shrugged, like that explained everything. I smoothed the folded bag against my chest and added it to the stack under the kitchen sink.

"You said that was her *sister* driving the car?"

She narrowed her eyes at me. I thought the matter had been settled, but this last bit troubled her. It must have been something Gladys said. Gladys, who knew everything that went on in that town. Goddamn Gladys.

"Yeah," I said, meeting her gaze. "Her sister Janine."

I didn't know a single Janine on the face of the Earth.

"Gladys thought it was a man," my mother persisted. "With long hair. Why do I feel like there's something hinky going on?"

"Ma, nothing's hinky."

"You better not be lying to me."

"Janine's a big girl," I said. "She plays basketball."

"Janine Rizzo," my mother said, trying to place the name as she went back to organizing cans. I could feel her gears turning, the puzzle not quite clicking. "I just hope you're not hanging out with nitwits."

"I'm not," I said and grabbed my book, saying I'd forgotten to close the trunk of the car, which was true.

In the trunk's carpeted interior, a stray apple had escaped the bags. I took it, closed the trunk, and went to the front yard. I wanted to slip away, but it was too close to supper to ride off on my bike, so I stuck the apple between my teeth, shoved the book in my pocket, and climbed the catalpa tree, settling onto a familiar branch. Maybe if I stayed there long enough, hidden behind the big leaves, my parents would think I had gone missing and put my picture on a milk carton. I might not have succeeded in running away, but I had learned to lie skillfully to my mother, another kind of departure. It is the stories we tell about ourselves that determine our decisions to stay close to home or hazard the difficult passage out. When I say *home*, I don't just mean a house or a town. I mean all that is familiar and given, all the stuff thrust onto and into a person, the stuff that takes work to shuck away. Most people don't do that work. Maybe they like the role they've been given. It fits. For those of us born in a different shape, however, the stories we tell can take us to safety. That summer evening, in the dappled cover of the catalpa, I told myself I had gotten away with my story, and yet I could not shake the feeling that I was about to be found out.

•

Sitting on the cemetery wall, flipping through Jules' dream dictionary, we were dressed as hippies because we were bored and thought it would be entertaining to walk around town in tie-dyed T-shirts and peace symbol earrings, bandannas and feathered roach clips in our hair. Jules was a perfect hippie with her hair long and straight, all greasy golden, and her skinny flower-child frame like a girl on a soft-focus album cover, sunlight humming through a meadow. I was too lumpy and blunt to pull it off, my hair too curly and asymmetrical.

I compensated by carrying Donna's old guitar, though it was missing two strings, and idly strummed while Jules looked up the secret meanings of our nocturnal transmissions.

"Riding on a train means you're traveling from one phase of life to another," she read. "It also means sex."

"Everything means sex," I said, "according to that book."

It had been days since we'd seen each other, since the culvert pipe, and I was sure Jules had been avoiding me. Now, sitting cross-legged, face-to-face, our knees nearly touching, I wanted to kiss her again, to push my thumb into the hole in her jeans where skin showed through. But we were pretending it never happened. I looked into her blue eyes. Did she know that blue was the rarest color in nature? I told her about the satin bowerbird, how the male attracts a mate by building an arbor out of twigs and decorating it with blue things—flowers, feathers, berries, even bits of trash, plastic forks and bottle caps. It's difficult, I explained, because there isn't a lot of blue out there. It's special, I said, meaning *you're special*, and if I could have won her by building a bower of blue, I would have. But Jules wasn't mine to win. Like Sylvia, she was out of reach.

She turned her gaze to the cemetery. The slate markers stared back at us with skeleton faces and weeping willows, reminding us that someday we would die. She wondered what would take us to the other side. Sickness, accident, murder. How long did we have? She believed she would depart at the age of twenty-seven, just like Jimi Hendrix, Jim Morrison, and Janis Joplin. Her name also started with a *J*, so it was fate. She didn't want to live longer anyway. Who would? In her developing fascination with death, she'd found a copy of Anton LaVay's *The Satanic Bible* in the occult section of Waldenbooks at the mall, and shared passages over the phone that were full of unsettling sexual scenes, including the Black Mass, in which a woman is penetrated on the altar with a loaf of bread and a turnip, both of which we agreed would be uncomfortable. She'd started burning hex candles and sticking herself with common pins. She held out her arm and showed me a daisy wheel of pinpricks on her skin.

"Sometimes I feel like I'm a piece of dust," she said. "Like I don't really exist. Do you ever feel that way?"

I felt a lot of strange ways, but not like a piece of dust. Not like nothing. If anything, I felt like too much, my body a crowded house. I didn't understand what Jules was trying to tell me, that she felt insignificant, maybe worthless. If I could go back, I would ask questions, like why was she sticking pins in herself? I would be a better friend. But you cannot rewrite the past. I shook my head. No, I did not feel like a piece of dust.

"I'm just in a weird mood," she said, brushing it off. "Let's go down the school. Some guys are playing basketball."

"What guys?"

She hopped off the wall and started walking. I followed.

"You know Sue Mooney's big brother Jeff?" she said. "He's been coming up my house a lot. Hanging around with Dale. He's got a dirt bike." Jeff Mooney was a year ahead of us, but two years older because he'd been held back. He was a bad-tempered kid and I wasn't looking forward to seeing him.

When we got there, our old school seemed small and foreign, the low brick building abandoned in the doldrums of August except for the four dirt bikes parked in the lot where Jeff and his friends played two-on-two. We found a strip of shade under the building's overhang, by a sign that said "NO LOITERING," and leaned there, feeling bored. Jules had shifted into a different energy, turned toward the boys and away from me. I didn't want to pretend-play the guitar anymore and the dream book felt childish. Still, I wasn't ready to let go of being hippies. I found some broken chalk on the ground and we covered the wall with peace symbols, *LOVE* with the *O* made into a heart, and Satanic pentagrams.

"I have to tell you something," Jules said, perfecting a five-pointed star, "but you'll probably think I'm stupid or gross."

"What is it?"

"Nevermind."

"Tell me."

She shoved a chunk of hair into her mouth. I braced, expecting her to say she couldn't be friends with a lesbo after all. Instead, she said, "I kinda made out with Jeff."

"You what?" I looked at her. "When?"

"I don't know," she shrugged. "The other day. He came up my house to see Dale, but Dale was out. It just kinda happened."

The thought of Jules kissing Jeff Mooney, or any boy, made my stomach clench.

"Did you do other stuff?"

"Don't be mad, okay?" She gave me a pleading look. Those blue eyes. I would make her a bower if I could, but she didn't want my bower.

"He's not very deep," I said. "He's mean and his friends are jerks. They're so stupid, they make me sick." Jules agreed that his friends were stupid, but Jeff, she insisted, was deeper than he looked. He only acted like a jerk, but really he was filled with profound thoughts. I was not convinced.

"Hey, Jules," Jeff said when he and the boys walked over, shirtless and sweaty. His hair was long, down to his chin, and he'd grown a flimsy mustache since I'd last seen him. He took the chalk from my hand and wrote *FUCK* on the wall. Jules said it was pissah and followed his lead, writing *SUCK IT.* I didn't like where this was going.

"What are you two supposed to be, like hippies or something?" asked a kid named Eddie. The other boys laughed.

"No der," Jules said, cutting Eddie with the *der* of derision, performing toughness for Jeff's benefit. "But I'm a bad hippie. I'm Squeaky Fromme."

"Who's Squeaky Fromme?"

"She was in the Manson Family, der," Jules said. Ever since she'd learned that Dennis Wilson had a relationship with the Family, letting them squat in his house on Sunset Boulevard for druggy jam sessions and orgies, Jules wanted to be a Manson girl. She was over Dennis, but not death. "Haven't you read *Helter Skelter*?"

"Like the Beatles song?"

"No der. They wrote it in blood on the 'frigerator when they killed those people."

"That's cool," Eddie shrugged, indifferent to Jules' fusillade of *ders*. He turned to me. "So what does that make you, a good hippie or a bad hippie?"

"She's a bad hippie, too," Jules answered. "She's Gypsy and I'm Squeaky. We can kill people, so don't fuck with us." She reached into her pocket and pulled out a jackknife, showing off the blade. I didn't know she had a knife.

The boys laughed and said *yeah, alright*, and then Jeff said they were going over to the pits to ride their dirt bikes and did we want to come watch. Boys always wanted girls to watch them do dumb things. I wasn't interested, but Jules climbed onto the back of Jeff's bike, arms around his waist, so I had no choice. I got stuck with Eddie, holding onto his belt with one hand and Donna's guitar with the other as we bolted over the ball fields and into the woods, down an unpaved fire road to a place I'd never been, a grassy bluff looking down into a wide bowl of blonde sand, bright in the sun and shaped into dunes so it looked like another planet, desolate and Saharan. It was part of a plant that made concrete, Jeff explained, pointing into the distance to the rusty tops of crushing towers and conveyor belts. He told Jules and me to "stay," like we were dogs, and we sat in the grass while the boys descended, their bikes turning up and down the waves of sand, whining and blatting like chainsaws.

"It sounds like farts," I said, plucking the sour strings of the guitar.

Jules didn't laugh.

"That Eddie kid is wicked dense," I tried.

"Oh my god," she agreed, "total density. He's, like, the biggest moron on the Earth, I swear."

I nodded, glad to be on the same page, but then Jules drifted. Watching Jeff. It bothered me that she'd chosen him, in particular, but Jules making out with any boy would have bothered me. I didn't understand my own feelings. I'd made out with a boy, too, but it was clear that Jules had a feeling for Jeff—a feeling she did not have for me. I picked up a rock and chucked it into the pit. The bikes went whining up and down the dunes. I chucked another rock. Maybe, if I could make Jules feel what I felt, give her a taste of the jealousy that slithered through my belly, I could pull her back. There was only one thing that might work. When I assembled the words, they formed what seemed at the time like a harmless lie.

I said, "I made out with Sylvia."

Jules gave me a stricken look and I knew I'd made a mistake.

"Are you crazy?"

"I'm serious," I said, doubling down. "We went to Walden Pond and kissed on the beach for hours. With tongues. It was amazing. I think I'm in love."

She looked at me like she didn't recognize me. Like we were in one of those body-snatcher movies and I'd been taken over.

"What *are* you?" she said.

People have their limits and you don't always know where they are until you run smack into them. Jules could kiss a girl like me and she could handle the existence of Sylvia, more or less, but there were other borders she patrolled that I was not permitted to cross. Once I stepped over that line, I became a foreign body.

"Ever since you started hanging around with that person," she said, "it's like I don't know you anymore."

"*You* don't know *me*? What about *you*?" I said. "When did you start carrying a knife? And all that stuff about the Manson Family and those Satanic rituals?"

"I don't do Satanic rituals."

"You stick yourself with pins. You think *I'm* a weirdo? Take a look in the mirror."

"At least I'm not a queer nympho. Like you."

"You made out with me!"

"Shut *up*," she hissed, looking to the boys on their bikes. They couldn't hear a word over the noise of their engines. "That was one time, for god's sake. It practically didn't happen. Besides. I'm not like you."

That statement still quakes inside me. *I'm not like you*. We were different. I was different. That word we used for things outside our comprehension, held at a distance.

"I'm not a lez," she went on, her voice hushed. "Or, like, a bisexual person or whatever you are. I swear, Mel, sometimes I think you're really a guy. You *feel* like a guy. Maybe you're a tranny, too."

"If I *am* a guy," I ventured, "then I can't be a lez for making out with you."

"Shut *up*," she said. "That's not the problem."

"Then what is?"

"You made out with *Sylvia*, for god's sake."

"She's a girl. And you said I'm a guy. Doesn't that make me normal?"

"No," she said. "It makes you a total fucking freak."

I felt my face crumple. Jules wasn't playing. She'd finally said the terrible thing she'd been thinking all summer. A total fucking freak was worse than a nympho or a queer. A total fucking freak was something monstrously other, the abject, barely human. We could not look at each other. She stared into the pit, at the boys, and I sensed a door close between us as I sat frozen, waiting, the cells of my body buzzing like a hornet's nest. Unable to stand it, I jumped to my feet, grabbed the stupid guitar, and stomped off, tracing the dirt road back through the woods. Jules didn't follow.

Insects whirred in the trees and I started to cry, alone, watching myself from outside my body. Why did I tell that stupid lie about kissing Sylvia? Fucking Jeff fucking Mooney and his moron friends. I lifted the guitar and smashed it against a rock. It was a piece of shit and my sister wasn't coming back for it. She'd left it behind, like she'd left me. Fucking Donna. Fuck them all. I kicked the guitar's pieces into the middle of the road for Jules to find. I wanted her to think I'd been abducted and killed, another face on a milk carton. I wanted her to know that I was in pieces and would never be put back together again.

part three

1984

They pulled an alligator from the waters of Hooley Park that August. Animal Control officers waded into the lake with catchpoles and dragged it out thrashing, tied its jaws with duct tape, and brought it to the town of Hockomock, to Mother Goose's Story Land, a scrappy kids' amusement park with a fairy-tale theme. The park had a castle with a muddy moat and a fiberglass alligator that opened its mouth when you pressed a button. Now they had a real one. They surrounded it with a chain-link fence and named it Tick-Tock after the crocodile in *Peter Pan*. It forever troubled me that the alligator would go through the rest of its life being mistaken for a different species.

While the capture of the gator had nothing to do with Operation Safe Park, the recently launched sex sting that local cops liked to call "Operation Bag a Fag," the media tied it to the crackdown, declaring it a triumph for the family-friendly future. Under the headline "Making Hooley Park Unsafe for Predators," the *Swaffham Sentinel* printed the gator's photo next to one of a handcuffed man on a perp walk, like a pair of hunting trophies. "The 1970s are over," the Brixton Chief of Police announced. "This is a family park. We want to clean it up and make it safe, especially for women and children, so they won't be exposed to danger. Whether that means alligators or people who want to engage in some type of despicable behavior." The man in the photo faced charges of "lewd, wanton, and lascivious conduct and annoying a person of the same sex." According to the police report, he was walking on the trail when he "looked at the genital area" of an undercover cop and asked, "How big is it?" To be taken in handcuffs, all you had to do was let your eyes stray and ask the wrong question.

Day after day, the *Sentinel* printed the names of arrested men—first and last with address and phone number, to maximize the potential for humiliation, job loss, and vigilante justice. As I read them, wondering if any belonged to the man who thought I was a boy in drag, it did not occur to me that Sylvia's name might make the list. She was a woman, not a gay man, and had no interest in the wooded trails behind the rest area. So when her name did appear, I almost didn't recognize it. S— Marks, it said, the deadname of the boy who ran to the city and returned in the form of a woman who didn't give a damn what anyone had to say about it. She was brazen, like the boy in Bangor who went over a bridge, and while my town might tolerate a local queer for months, maybe years, once your name appears in the paper, once they call you lewd, wanton, lascivious, and annoying, people will feel compelled to do something.

I spent an hour dialing and redialing her number, letting the phone ring, whispering *pick up, pick up* as I imagined the worst, Sylvia dead, my heart banging inside its cage, *let's go, let's go.* I got on my bike and rode hard to Chickatawbut Lane. What I found was both shocking and banal, so typical in stories like this one, you could almost call it a custom. Across Sylvia's garage door, spray-painted in black letters, it read: *FAGS = PEDOFILES* and *MOVE OR DIE TRANNY FUCK.* My first thought was a trivial one. They say this happens in moments of shock—a woman in a crashing airplane calmly applies lipstick, a drowning man thinks about the library book he failed to return. For me it was the misspelling of *pedophile*. More than the ugly words, this error unsettled me. It showed the havoc of a disorganized mind and I took it as a sign of real danger.

No one answered Sylvia's door. Through the windows, the house looked empty and showed no signs of violence. Sylvia was in jail, I told myself, not murdered. I went back to the garage and stared at the message. Whoever did it must have done so early in the morning, when no one would see, right after the paperboy tossed the *Sentinel* on their doorstep and they saw Sylvia's name and address. I imagined high school boys, maybe Jeff Mooney and his stupid friends on their stupid dirt bikes. The easy way he wrote *FUCK* on the wall of the school, he probably wrote it all the time, an expert of the expletive. I looked around. There was no one except the old man across the street, sitting on his porch in a Red Sox cap, sipping a beer as if the world hadn't just gone twisted.

The sound of Sylvia's telephone jolted from the open kitchen window, startling me. There's a strange desolation to a ringing phone in an empty house. Was it the vandal calling? Maybe he was still there. My imagination filled with killers. Charles Manson, Ted Bundy, John Wayne Gacy. Jules had a book about Charlie Starkweather, who looked like James Dean in his denim jacket and pompadour. What if Jules wrote the ugly words? Hadn't she scrawled *SUCK IT* on the school? I'd been imagining a boy, but in those true-crime stories, there was often a girl at the boy's side. Starkweather had a girlfriend, Caril Ann Fugate, who was just fourteen when she rode shotgun on a murder spree. Now I pictured Jules, playing Caril Ann, or Squeaky Fromme, knife in hand, waiting on the other side of the garage door, ready to rid the world of me for being annoying to her, sexually, like the newspaper said. But when I heaved open the door, there was no one. No Jules, no killers, not even Sylvia's Trans Am. Just the smell of mildew and the scratchy sound of crickets. I grabbed a can of white paint, same one we'd used for the demolition car on a day that felt like forever ago, and got to work.

The paint spread slowly over the words, thick with humidity. I took my time, listening to the splash of the next-door swimming pool, the scissor snip of hedge clippers, a transistor radio telling the news, life going on the way it did, as if nothing rotten had happened. Later, in high school, I would read the poem "Musée des Beaux Arts" by W. H. Auden and a memory of that scene would come to mind, the smell of paint fumes, buzz of insects, and the bitterness in my mouth, a contempt I felt for the people who did nothing but enjoy life while the world shattered. Auden writes about human suffering and how no one pays attention. "It takes place," he says, "while someone else is eating or opening a window or just walking dully along." People witness the tragedy and go about their business. In retrospect, the poem would explain how I felt that day, but at the time I could not name the specific loneliness of being a sole witness. All I felt was the unfairness of life, painting until there was no paint left in the can, until I was splattered, cowboy boots ruined, and no trace of the message remained. Through it all, relentless and piercing, Sylvia's telephone kept ringing like a fire alarm.

•

"I had to take my phone off the hook," Sylvia told me when we met again, days later, at her house. "People are assholes." The cranks kept calling to describe the terrible things they wanted to do to her. She kept an aluminum baseball bat nearby. Someone had started sitting in a parked car across the street, watching, she said. And the vandals had returned. On the garage door, on top of my coats of paint, they'd left a new message, with another misspelling. "Time to move fagot," it read. "30 days."

"I'm not scared," Sylvia insisted, sitting in her kitchen, legs crossed, bouncing a flip-flop on her foot. "And I will not be intimidated by morons who don't know the difference between a faggot and a transsexual." As for moving, she would go when she was ready. While the real estate listing on the house had attracted no buyers, Sylvia remained hopeful. With the money from a sale, she said, she could buy an apartment in Cambridge. Maybe New York. Something cheap. Something not Swaffham.

It was hot and stuffy in the house, and Sylvia's talk of leaving got me tangled up in sadness. I wanted to sit on the porch, get some air, but she said it was too exposed. The strange car might come back. It was best to stay inside. At the table we sipped powdered lemonade from sweating glasses that matched her mother's padded vinyl chairs, decorated in sunflowers. The cushions stuck to our thighs and wheezed as we shifted.

"People are assholes," she said again. "I'm being treated like a criminal and for what?"

For the third time, as if she could not hear herself, she told me what had happened, how she'd stopped in the park to sit by the pond, to commune with nature and sort her thoughts. She used the women's restroom, like she'd done many times, only this time the cops grabbed her on the way out, hands still wet from the sink, yanked behind her back and cuffed. They charged her with indecent exposure and loitering for "the purpose of engaging in a prostitution offense." She did not do these things, but this is how they punish trans women for being trans in public, for peeing where they don't want you to pee.

The town had tolerated Sylvia for as long as it did because she belonged to it. Born at the Deaconess Hospital, where almost everyone in Swaffham entered the world, she attended the local school, performed as an altar boy at St. Andrew's, and played Little League. When she first ran away, neighbors visited with covered dishes and kind words for her mother. When she came back as a not-quite-boy who'd lived as a girl, still with the shimmer of girl upon her, those same neighbors felt relief when she vanished again. Still, Sylvia was one of us. So when she returned this time, even though she'd taken the shape and name of a woman, and even though that shape and name strained their forbearance, the people of Swaffham did not set upon her. They kept their eyes on her—they were a Crime Watch Community, after all—but they did not strike until Sylvia stepped into a territory that trips the wire of hysteria among people who fear trans women, and it set off a chain of explosions, one detonating the next in breakneck succession. After the graffiti, the *Sentinel* published an op-ed about the dangers of transsexuals in public restrooms. "Imagine your wife or daughter using the ladies' room and being violated by a man posing as a woman," the editor wrote. "It makes me sick. What is happening here in our hometown should alarm every American." The editor did not mention Sylvia by name, but everyone knew. The trigger finger of the town itched for its next shot.

"Where am I supposed to take a piss?" Sylvia said. "In the men's room? So I can get the shit kicked out of me? Assholes."

She stubbed her cigarette in the ashtray and lit another. I watched her take a long drag and exhale to the ceiling, holding the cigarette aloft, elbow resting in her other hand as the flip-flop agitated the air between us. For a moment, when she pursed her lips and it seemed she might cry, I saw the young Sylvia, the one in the Polaroid, breakable and small. I didn't know how to help. If I could, I would have taken her pain. If only we could swap bodies, I thought. If only I could be S— and she could be Melanie, maybe she would stay and everything would be okay.

"I'm sorry," I said, the most useless words on earth. I could not find the courage to say "I love you, I'll protect you, I'll follow you to the city, go anywhere, do anything, as long as it's with you." Instead, I told her about the time I used that same restroom, the day we went to Harvard Square, how the women turned on me and I felt monstrous. Sylvia looked at me appraisingly, her eyes moving to my broad shoulders, thick hands and long legs, the way I'd looked at her that first night on the porch, searching her shape for traces of a past sex. Now I felt her tracing my future, the form I would one day take. She was not the only one who could see the secret in my body. Strangers saw and called me names for it. Children saw and threw rocks at it. My mother saw and pretended not to, called it graceless, an awkward phase. When Jules saw it, she wanted its mouth on her mouth, but then pushed it away. Sylvia was the only one who did not recoil or strike. Imagine what that is like, to have just one person in your life who does not behold your truest self with fear or disgust. It's the most wonderful and terrible thing. That person delivers you, brings you into being, as she reveals, at the same time, how alone you really are.

I felt a constriction in my throat and didn't want to cry, so I said I needed air and went out to the porch, to the broken wicker chairs, ashtray filled with rainwater and swollen butts of clove cigarettes. Was it already dusk? Before I could catch my breath, I saw the car. Dale Cobb's shitty Mercury Cougar across the street with Dale in the driver's seat, watching the house like a cop on a stakeout. He waved, like this was an ordinary thing to do, and I strode over barefoot, angry and unafraid.

"What are you doing here?" I said.

"Protecting you."

"I don't need protecting."

From the passenger seat, Jeff Mooney leaned over to bark, "Get in the car."

"Fuck off, Mooney."

"We have to talk to you," Dale said, softening his voice. "Something happened to Jules." He got out and ushered me onto the front seat between him and Jeff, my bare feet perched uneasily on the transmission hump, seatbelt buckles digging into my hips. I can't explain why I got in that car, except that I knew those boys and no one ever told me to be afraid of boys I knew. The car stunk of weed and pine-tree air freshener, peppermint Schnapps on the boys' breath. Dangling from the mirror, instead of fuzzy dice or a St. Christopher medal, there hung a six-chambered cylinder from a revolver, one of Ray's irregular gun parts.

"What happened to Jules?" I asked.

Dale stuck an 8-track tape into the deck, Mike Oldfield's *Tubular Bells,* its opening theme made famous by *The Exorcist*, the story of a girl possessed by a foul-mouthed demon.

"Your mother sucks cocks in Hell," Jeff growled in my ear, imitating the movie monster.

"Cut it out," I said, elbowing him. "Is Jules okay?"

"We were looking for you," Dale said.

The surreal music made me feel strange, not quite inside my body, and it was then, in the instrumental tension between those jittery boys, that I began to worry.

"We know all about it," Jeff said. "We know you're doing it with the tranny."

I heard a strain of violence in his voice and my thoughts flashed to the graffiti. Ugly words. Ugly boys. I knew they did it.

"I am not," I said.

"Don't lie," Dale snapped. "Jules told us everything."

"Jules?" It all felt confused.

"What is she, deaf?" Jeff said. He waved his hands around, mock-signing, "Are you deaf? *We know what you're doing.*"

"I'm not doing anything." The weird mood and its music made the lights inside me go dim. "Is Jules okay?"

"She doesn't get it," Jeff laughed. But I did get it. Dale lied to get me in the car.

"Nothing happened to Jules, did it?"

"Light dawns on Marblehead," Jeff said.

"Did she help you?" I asked, meaning the graffiti.

"Have a drink," Jeff insisted, pushing the bottle of schnapps to my face.

I turned away and, in a weak voice that still shames me, pleaded, "Let me out."

Dale put a cigarette in my hand and punched in the lighter on the dash. "We can fix it for you," he said.

"Fix it," I mumbled, a question that came out wrong, like a request I hadn't made. And then Dale's mouth clamped mine, tongue like brackish water, weed and liquor. Jeff's hand dug into my crotch. I froze. Did they switch places? Hands and tongues moved across my body in ways I couldn't track. I did not fight. Maybe some sorrowful part of me wanted to be fixed, to finish what the boy in the barn could not complete, obliterate what the women in the restroom had rooted out. Maybe these boys, with their rough, plundering tongues, would do the trick. I heard the lighter pop in its socket and remembered the cigarette—pulverized in my fist, the one part of me where anger flared, hot and alive. Then the door yanked open and someone said, "Get out."

Sylvia. She seized Dale by the hair. He swung his fist into her gut, making her yelp. That was the jolt I needed. *Don't hurt her.* I grabbed the lighter from the dash and pressed it to Dale's neck, jamming hot coil into skin. He fell, squealing, to the street, and I scrambled after, Jeff holding my ankle until I kicked his face and broke free, asphalt biting my palms, skinning my knees. I stumbled to my feet and ducked behind Sylvia as she slashed her baseball bat through the air, smashing it against the car. Joan of Arc with her silvery sword.

2019

Cross-legged and face-to-face, Dakota and I sit on the cemetery wall, sucking on Fla-Vor-Ice sticks. This is our routine. We work on the house with Donna, have an early dinner, and take the bikes around town, ending up here in the slanting sunlight of day's end. This is our talking place, the way it was for Jules and me, and like so much this summer, it casts me back. My freeze pop is blue and hideous, the flavor of sugared chalk, but I need a Proustian trigger to help me grasp what it felt like to be a kid sitting on this wall with the trumpet creeper and the grassy hummocks of the dead, skeletons and willow trees carved in stone faded from the passage of another thirty-five years. Across the street, Coogan's Superette is now the Kwik Pik Market, run by a guy named Faruq. Everyone in town calls it "the Iraqi Packie," though Faruq is from Yemen and he doesn't sell liquor.

Dakota is telling me how she prefers the company of older people. "I'm mature for my age," she says. "Someone asked if I'm fourteen. I can look fourteen when I want to be mature, but sometimes I act like a two-year-old."

This week I will turn forty-nine, a birthday gladly uncelebrated, on the dreaded verge of fifty. Sometimes I feel as though I haven't changed since I was Dakota's age. Are we all doomed to be ourselves forever?

"I want a gun," she declares. "So people don't mess with me. I want to be—can I say a swear word?"

"Sure," I say. These days, we should all be swearing. The world is ending and Nazis are on the march. Dakota has active-shooter drills at her school. She hides under a desk while her teacher gets shot by plastic bullets that spill across the classroom floor like pearls from a broken string. Of course she wants a gun.

"I want to be badass," she says, making fists. "Even though I'm not at all. But if you mess with me, my fighting skills will go off the chain and I will wreck you."

"Who messes with you?"

"Kids at school. I had a bully last year. He was so rude. I wanted to wreck his face and punch him in the balls. I'm a fighter. But I'm also a lover. I don't mess with people unless they mess with me first."

"What do people mess with you about?"

"Being Mexican," she shrugs. "And other stuff."

She goes *uggghhh* and falls back on the rock wall, arms splayed, freeze pop spent, empty plastic sleeve a silvery ribbon in her hand. I wonder what the "other stuff" might be. With all her talk of queerness, I've been waiting for her to say more. A yellowjacket buzzes my melting pop. From the trees, a flock of turkeys steps tenderly among the graves, pecking at the grass.

"Turkeys," I whisper. "Look."

Dakota is not impressed. Turkeys are so common, they might as well be sparrows.

Gently, I ask, "So what's the other stuff?"

"I dunno," she sits up and focuses on her knee, picking a scab. "Can I tell you something, Uncle Max? You have to promise not to tell Gramma."

"Of course," I say, ready to hear the words, to have the Big Moment, to give Dakota what I didn't get when I came out.

"Umm," she starts and then stops. "It's kind of terrible. I feel really bad about it."

"You don't have to feel bad."

"It's just," she stops again, digging into the scab. And then she blurts, "I don't miss my dad. Like at all. He's kind of a jerk and sometimes I wish he stays in jail forever, even if living with Gramma kind of sucks. All she does is drink and smoke and yell about everything. It's so boring! I want to be eighteen already."

"That's the terrible thing you wanted to tell me?"

"Yeah."

"It's not so terrible. Everyone your age hates their parents. Is there anything else you want to tell me?"

"Like what?"

"Nothing. I just thought—honestly, I thought you were going to say you're gay or non-binary or something."

"I'm pan," she shrugs, like this is obvious, but I don't know what she means. She clarifies, "Pan*sexual*? Like I like all kinds of people, boys, girls, trans, cis, non-binary, whatever. You won't tell Gramma, right?"

"About being pan?"

"She knows *that*," Dakota says, exasperated. "I mean about how I hate my dad and everything. It would just make her madder and she's mad enough already."

"You came out to her? She knows you're—pan?" The word feels awkward and blunt and makes me think of cookware.

"I *told* her, I guess that's coming out. But she doesn't get what it means. She's pretty old."

I am old, too, slow and dumb, implicated in a general oldness, a soggy blanket draped over my entire generation. Does anyone come out anymore or do they just exist, seamlessly, without ever being *in* in the first place?

"So you're not non-binary?"

"Mmm, I dunno, I'm kind of a demigirl," she says brightly. "Like sometimes I don't feel comfortable in girl clothes, but whenever I put on comfy sweatpants and stuff, Gramma says, *You look like a scrub.* I don't like showing my curves. I want to look like a straight ruler, but my curves are like, *Boom, you're a pineapple.*"

Dakota is light-years ahead of me, wielding all the language I did not have at her age. She has *pansexual, demigirl, non-binary.* She has *cisgender,* the word I didn't have until my forties, naming a concept I could not properly think until my life was half over. Dakota has the language necessary to think herself into being at an age when I had nothing. I hope this means she will have more love than I ever did. But how will her love be shaped in the North Country, where the roads are broken, the woods are cold and deep, and the people are stewed in resentment? In a few weeks, she'll be gone. At the thought of her leaving, I am surprised by a feeling of loss and throw my arms around her. She tells me I am hugging too tight, but I don't let go.

Back at the house, Donna's on the couch with a beer. She's usually at the VFW by now—*down the Post,* as she calls it—boozing with barflies, making me worry about her driving home. I've told her I'll come get her, but she says she's been driving home from bars her whole life, so give her a break. She's gotten extra prickly since she asked me to take Dakota and I still haven't given her an answer. Even now I tell myself the kid doesn't need me. When there are queer friends and books, an internet full of drag queens and gay boys in eyeliner, who needs a Sylvia? I'm not necessary. But then, I think—selfishly—maybe I need a Dakota.

"If it isn't Frick and Frack," Donna says, an expression from our mother. Dakota rolls her eyes and drifts away to her room. I stand staring at the screen, Fox News, mesmerized by the story of a multimillionaire sex criminal who planned to seed the world with his sperm and then cryogenically freeze his penis for future revival.

"Take off your coat and stay awhile," Donna says, though I'm not wearing a coat. It's another of our mother's expressions and I wonder what's next. *They don't have a pot to piss in. Christ on a crutch. I'll beat you to a bloody pulp.*

"I'm alright," I say, looking at the television without committing to it.

"Did you hear?" she says during a commercial for a transvaginal surgical mesh class action suit. "They're renaming the manholes in California. The word is sexist, according to the PC police, so they're getting rid of it. How do you get rid of a word?"

The television says, "Protrusion of the mesh through the vagina. Pelvic pain. Organ perforation. Infection. Bleeding."

"They passed a law," Donna continues. "Now you have to call manholes 'maintenance holes.' Who's gonna say 'maintenance hole'? Number one, it's too long."

I wait for number two, but it never arrives. My sister is trying to get me to join her, to connect in grievance, but I won't. Even though, truth be told, I do think the manhole thing is a bit much. I watch the television where the next commercial sells a diabetes drug with an especially horrible side effect. "Necrotizing fasciitis of the perineum," the voiceover cheerfully explains, is a flesh-eating disease that devours the skin "between your anus and genitals."

"Next thing you know," Donna says, "they won't let us say *menstruation* because it's got the word *men* in it."

I want to say that those are two very different things, that the *man* in *manhole* refers to men, while the *men* in *menstruation* is from the Latin, meaning *month*, also *moon*, but I keep my mouth shut. What's the point? I get a beer from the fridge. At the kitchen window, I search for the moon, a silver disk behind the trees. My real home is like that, miles away, serene and empty. No plants, no pets. I'll be going back soon, to the rooms I keep neat and clean, free of clutter. The perfect quiet of undisturbed space.

1984

When I was little, when the mood struck, my mother would ransack my room. I was permitted to make a mess up to a point, and that point was the end of my mother's rope, a flimsy tether that snapped without warning. I could predict it every time. Walking home from school, I'd get a psychic sense of dread and I'd know: She'd done it again. All my toys, stuffed animals, and books would be piled in a mountain on my bedroom floor. Even the things I'd kept neatly put away would be pulled down from shelves and yanked out of drawers. I had too much, my mother would say as she made me choose what to give away to the needy children of Goodwill. "You don't care about your things, but some other little girl will love them," she'd say, braiding punishment with charity and then lacing it with my inability to love the right way. *My things.* As this lesson repeatedly taught me, nothing was mine—my books and animals, even my body, belonged to her. (Sometimes I wonder if transition was a way to seize ownership of this body, away from my mother.) She liquidated her own possessions, too, purging with a ferocity that I now understand as her way to control life—and to fight her own packrat nature. After I left home, she gave up that fight, letting the house mushroom with clutter. Maybe her surrender was already underway by the summer of 1984. It had been years since she'd attacked my room and I'd mostly forgotten about it until I turned my bike into the driveway and the old dread squeezed my gut.

It was a Saturday and I'd spent the morning at Sylvia's. We'd painted over the garage again, no more graffiti appeared, and Dale's Cougar had not come back, but I worried about her and wanted to stay close. Sylvia was still in an indoor mood, so we hung around in the den, listening to records and leafing through *Vogue* and *Elle*, magazines I cared nothing about, but which Sylvia regarded with an unexpected reverence that didn't jibe with her tomboy swagger. "Look at her," she'd say, holding up a glossy face. Fascinated by the novelty perfume ads, I lifted scent strips, rubbed the paper on my pulse point, and held my wrist out for Sylvia to sniff. "Too much," she'd say after each one. When I rubbed the magazine on my neck I thrilled to the sensation of her nose behind my ear, if only for a second, before she recoiled and said, "*Way* too much." It felt, for a little while, as if nothing terrible were unfolding in the world outside.

Biking home, reeking of Coco and Giorgio, I thought I smelled sophisticated, too good for that town with its banal superettes and package stores, its minor factories, dusty baseball fields, and small-minded people, boys like Dale and Jeff, going nowhere. To hell with them. And Jules, too. I was lost in a fantasy of running off with Sylvia when I rolled into my driveway and felt the sensation of my mother's wrath, like a hot cloud of steam wafting off the house.

"Get over here," I heard my father say. I hadn't noticed him on his hands and knees in the front yard, digging out the flagstone walkway, ripping up years of grass and soil that had swallowed the stones. He ventured into daylight so infrequently, he looked like an apparition, tenuous and pale. "Don't you say hello?"

"Hey, Dad." I dropped my bike and walked over, aware of the house behind me, shingles radiating a current of maternal anger.

"Give your old man a kiss," he said, and when I bent down to peck his scratchy cheek, he told me, "You smell like a brothel." The grass he tore made the sound of ripped threads. "Your mother's on the warpath."

"What now?"

He shrugged, "Just watch your ass."

Inside the house, I didn't see my mother, but I could sense her, waiting like a spider, and I walked into my bedroom tensed for assault. I found all my things heaped on the floor. Clothing and cassette tapes, games and stuffed animals that had survived purges of the past. And books. *Know Your Gerbils* sat arranged in front, set open like a trap. My body surged with alarm. I grabbed the book and shook the pages. No Polaroid.

"Come with me," my mother said in the doorway. I followed her to the kitchen table, where she dropped the photo of Sylvia, young and tender, so exposed, I wanted to cover her, place a paper napkin over her nakedness, protect her from everything that would happen next. My mother told me to sit and I obeyed.

"Ginny Cobb called," she said, standing over me.

"Who?" It was the only word I could muster. My mind had gone dim.

"She told me what you've been up to with that—person."

"Who?"

"*Who. Who.* What are you, an owl? You lied to me. You're a liar!"

"I'm not," I said quietly, but she was right. I had lied about everything. About what Gladys saw outside Red Mike's. About who cut my hair and where I got new clothes. And about making out with Sylvia.

"Don't deny it," my mother said, pointing her finger in my face. "Dale told Ginny everything."

"Dale's an asshole."

"Watch your mouth."

"He's trying to get back at me."

"For what?"

I told her how Dale kissed me and I fought him off, but for reasons I don't understand I didn't tell the whole story, about the two boys and their grabbing hands. Already, that part was disintegrating from memory, so the incident became just: Dale tried to kiss me and I fought him off. Surely, my mother would understand. She was the girl who fought off a boy and escaped across the tobacco fields. Of course she would sympathize, put an arm around me, and say, "Me too." But my calculations were wrong.

"What's so terrible about Dale," she asked. "Is he not good enough for you? Or don't you *want* to kiss a boy? Do you? Do you want to kiss boys?"

My face burned red. I looked down at my fingers and picked at a hangnail. My mother made a knowing sound, like *hm*, a detective confirming a clue, as she went on watching me, seeing inside my head, where there was nothing I could hide from her. She made the sound again, *hm*, and shifted the air in the room. A master at the art of changing atmospheres, she kept you guessing, unprepared for what came next.

"He was arrested," she said, cannily. "Did you know that? Your *friend*." I thought she was talking about Dale, maybe he'd gotten caught for the graffiti, but that's not who she meant. "He was arrested for messing around in the ladies' room. Men with that problem put on skirts and wigs so they can go into ladies' rooms and do bad things. Did you know that? Did you? Oh, sure. You think you know everything, you're so fucking smart. You and your liberal ideas. You and your *books*. You think you're smarter than everybody. But you didn't know *that*, did you?"

"Sylvia doesn't wear skirts or wigs," I said, focused on the blood seeping from my cuticle. My mother snatched the Polaroid from the table and shoved it in my face.

"Is this *Sylvia*? Is that what he calls himself? I know that name. I heard you talking to him on the phone. Talking about sex!"

"I wasn't."

"I *heard* him. An adult man. Trying to act like a woman. And with a young girl!"

"That wasn't her. It was me."

"This is a twisted person. Is that what *you* are, Melanie? Are you twisted?"

"No," I muttered and began, against every effort, to cry.

"I can't even *look* at you," my mother said, flinging the Polaroid at my chest. She went to the sink and stared out the window, through the suncatchers we'd made together years before, sprinkling grains of colored plastic into molds and baking them in the oven to make a ladybug and butterfly. She liked me once, but she didn't like me now. I wiped my eyes and looked at the photo, fallen on the floor. To make my insides still, I thought of ice. The entire Atlantic Ocean turning to ice, all the way down, as cold and sterile as rubbing alcohol, freezing the fish and ocean junk in a frozen blue everything. I imagined ice until I felt a hard chill spreading from the deepest pit of myself, up through my chest, into my throat, and behind my eyes. When my mother came back to the table, I was numbed and ready. But she shifted gears again, putting on a concerned expression as she sat and took my hands in hers, running her thumbs back and forth over my knuckles in a rough gesture meant to be maternal.

"Do you think something might be wrong with you?" she asked, her voice soft and cajoling. "You can tell me. I promise I won't get mad. If there's something wrong with you, if you're mixed up, we can get help. We can fix it before it's too late. We'll do it together. Easy."

There was that phrase again. *We can fix it.* I would like to report that I did not consider the offer, but I was so young and felt so crooked, like something important had gone slant, and if fixing it would be easy, like smacking the television when it went on the fritz, well, I could withstand a hard smack if it meant a life without static.

"It's okay to tell me," my mother said. "Do you like boys or girls?"

I swear I heard an audible crack inside my skull, like breaking ice. Stupidly, I answered, "Both?"

My mother let go of my hands and sat back in her chair. She shook her head, no, no, her bobbed hair shaking with it, and I knew I had made a mistake.

"Both," she echoed coldly. "Do you know what that is? That's being greedy."

I thought being greedy meant you took the bigger half of a cookie or asked for fifty cents instead of a quarter. I didn't see how liking boys and girls could be the same.

"I've read about this," my mother went on. "In *Reader's Digest*. Girls your age are in the danger zone. You can take the wrong path. But I won't let that happen."

She stood and paced, talking to herself about how she let my sister slip away but she wasn't gonna let me, no way, this time she'd find a psychiatrist, a doctor to straighten me out, and it wasn't gonna be cheap, but she'd use her life savings if that's what it took. I saw myself going down the drain, like Brenda White, sent to the loony bin, my brain rearranged. I would disappear with all the lost girls, to the bottom of Walden Pond, to the swamps, to the woods, reduced to a bundle of bones in a culvert pipe.

"We are gonna nip this in the bud," my mother said. She took the Polaroid from the floor. I was afraid she would rip it to pieces, but she folded it in half and used it to point at me. "You are not gonna be some bulldyke," she said. "I'd rather kill you myself than have you be that way."

Something happens to the people in a small town when they feel threatened by an outsider. There is a reservoir of violence that bubbles up in places where community is tightly knit, where the ties must be patrolled in case they come loose. These are the people who fear the gaps in border zones. They need walls topped with razor wire. Sameness, purity, cohesion. Everything else is contamination. While outsiders typically come from outside, they can also be created from within. In the early days of Swaffham, good Christians executed their neighbors. The witches were people who began behaving differently, outside community norms. They became strange. And the small is terrified by the strange.

When my mother said she'd rather kill me than allow my strangeness to flower, she spoke from the fearful place inside a small-town farmer's daughter, a girl who plucked horn worms and grasshoppers from the leaves of tobacco crops, fighting contamination and ruin. A girl who was beaten for losing a shoe. A girl who was informed by her father, when she told him at the age of twelve that she wanted to run away and join the rodeo, "There's only one of two ways you'll get out of this house. In a white dress or a pine box." Married or dead. My mother's two choices. She wanted more for me, a different life, but not too different. In that moment in the kitchen, I became the other, the witch, the worm that spoils the crop. I became destroyable, if only for the duration of my mother's madness, when she fell out of herself and stopped seeing me as her child. This happens sometimes when ordinary people come face-to-face with a person who loosens the gender boundaries of the body. They go crazy, the ground beneath them giving way. If such a fracture could split me from my mother and put the wish for murder in her mouth, what chance did Sylvia have against the hysteria of that town?

•

There must have been days during that time when nothing terrible happened, days of reading books and going to the mall, but I don't remember them. I only remember the blows. After I burned Dale with the lighter and Sylvia smashed his car with her baseball bat, after my mother made me into an Other, Ginny Cobb made wanted posters. She swiped an actual wanted poster from the post office and, with scissors, glue, and the Xerox machine at her job, rearranged it with Sylvia's name above an amateurish drawing of her face. It looked like a bad police sketch of a serial killer, beady-eyed and thin-lipped, with hair like black straw. Underneath, in hand-drawn letters, it read: "Keep Perverts Out of Swaffham." The flyers, printed on red paper like angry Valentines, appeared one morning on the doors to the drugstore and hardware store, the post office and dry cleaners, the beauty parlor and barbershop. When my mother sent me to buy her Salems at Red Mike's packie, I found one Scotch-taped among the pictures of shoplifters and writers of bad checks.

I knew it was Ginny who made the flyers because Sylvia told me. She'd been sitting in her Trans Am outside Coogan's, scraping a quarter across a scratchie, when Ginny leaned in the window. She had a stack of flyers and tossed one in the car, hissing, "Get outta this town, or my husband's gonna rip your head off and shit down your neck," invoking the threat of Ray Cobb, god of fire, the man with the guns. Sylvia told me these words didn't scare her, she'd heard worse, but a friend encouraged her to go to the police. The cop refused to file a report. He took the flyer and said Ginny was "exercising her free speech" and there was nothing they could do because "it's a free country."

Sylvia told all this to me over the phone because my mother had forbidden me to see her, and while I could have snuck away, the eyes of Swaffham were upon me and I didn't want to make things worse—for myself, but mostly for Sylvia. At the time, I believed, in the way young people believe they are more important than they are, that I was the reason for the town turning against her. It wasn't Sylvia in the ladies' room that lit the fuse, it was me. To this day, I can't really know how much my lie about kissing Sylvia contributed to the problems. It is not quantifiable and probably not worth trying to measure, though for many years I have kept myself on the barb of its hook.

•

Since the Cobbs were leading the charge against Sylvia, I tried to get through to Jules. I hadn't talked to her since our fight at the sand pits and I held my breath as the phone rang, hoping she would answer and hear me out, though I was not sure what I would say. Dale picked up. He called me a cunt, hung up, and left the phone off the hook. I knew Ray and Ginny would be at work, so I rode my bike over. The house and yard looked the same as ever. Empty beer cans on the picnic table, spent bottle rockets languishing on the sunken roof, a rubber tire full of rainwater and mosquito eggs. Across the backyard, I spotted a new addition: Propped against a tree stood a wooden board painted with the shape of a human body, gouged by knife scars. Target practice.

When I knocked, Dale opened the door a few inches and squinted into the daylight, a vampire irritated by sunshine. He wore gym shorts and nothing else except his grimy rope bracelet. The smell that wafted from the underground house was rancid with dirty laundry and skunky weed covered over with incense. I'd forgotten what Jules' house smelled like and, while it was rank, the odor comforted me, bringing back memories of being close, nestled in our twinship. I missed that. Dale looked me up and down, and while you'd think

I'd be afraid of him after what happened, all I can say is that I was used to being hurt by people and then going on like it was nothing.

"What do *you* want, lez?"

"Can I talk to Jules?"

"She doesn't want to talk to you."

"Come on, Dale, let me in."

"What, so you can contaminate my house with your lesbian cooties? Go fuck your tranny girlfriend."

"Come on," I pleaded.

"Look what you did," he said, showing me the burn on his neck, red and ringed like a bull's eye. I apologized, immediately wishing I hadn't. I wasn't sorry. But it's what Dale wanted. He looked past me, to the houses through the trees and along the road. Other than a stray dog loping down from the dead end, we were alone.

"Make you a deal," he said, lazily scratching his bare chest. "Spend five minutes in my bedroom, prove you're not a lez, and I'll let you talk to Jules."

I wish I could say that I told him to go fuck himself, but I gave it a thought. If five minutes with Dale could make things better for Sylvia, maybe it was worth it. I recalled the taste of his mouth, the dank swale of weedy breath, and steadied myself. But before I could make my next mistake, Jules emerged from the subterranean gloom, her mussed, yellow hair luminous in the dark, eyes rimmed in smeared mascara. She wore a Mötley Crüe T-shirt over a pair of cut-off short-shorts and her crummy Keds, the backs mashed down so they fit like slippers. Looking like she'd just gotten out of bed, seeming more stoned than ever, she pulled her hair back with a rubber band, said, "Hey," and smacked Dale in the arm, yanking him into the murk of the house. I could hear the resonance of their voices, quarreling their way to an agreement: I could not enter, but Jules would come out to meet me.

We walked to the dead end, by the frog swamp and litter of used rubbers, Jules scuffing her Keds on the gravel. She looked too skinny and pale, her thighs smudged with the purple moons of bruises. I wanted to say I was worried about her, but it didn't feel like my place anymore, so we talked about nothing, the coming of school in a couple of weeks, the end of summer and how much that sucked. Eventually, I got around to it.

"What did you tell everybody about me and Sylvia?"

"I didn't tell *everybody*." She shrugged. "Just Jeff."

"Jesus, Jules. What did you say?"

"I was upset, okay? It was that day at the pits when we had that fight and you walked away. You never came back. I was worried about you."

Isn't that what I'd wanted, for Jules to worry? I looked past her into the woods, to the trees, the wild grapevines, masses of pokeweed heavy with the purple berries we used to smear on our skin, decorating our faces with war paint and lipstick. We had no idea the berries were poisonous. How did we ever survive?

"What exactly did you tell Jeff?"

"Just that you and Sylvia made out. I guess he told Dale. And then, thanks to your stunt with the lighter, Dale told my mother."

"Your mother told my mother."

"Fuck," she said. She shook her head with what might have been remorse, but then shrugged it off, a gesture I took to mean, *Well, what's done is done.*

"Sylvia's in deep shit. And so am I," I said. "Why'd you tell?"

"I was worried about you," she said again.

"Nothing happened."

"You were making mistakes."

"Your mother made wanted posters."

She waved this away. "Gin's on the warpath. It'll blow over."

"They're gonna kill Sylvia."

"They are *not*."

"Your mother said Ray's gonna rip her head off and shit down her neck."

Jules laughed.

"It isn't funny."

"Jesus, Mel, she says that all the time. She said it to Dale last night just for being his usual asshole self. Don't be so sensitive."

I wanted to believe it was bluster, that Ginny didn't mean it. People said terrible things all the time. Didn't my own mother say she wanted to kill me? I looked down at the litter on the ground and wished I could be a stone, a stick, a rusty bottle cap, something guiltless and dumb. The rubbers, with their teeming jelly interiors, no longer held mystery. Once you know a thing, you can't unknow it, and while I tried to connect with my more innocent self, the girl I was at the start of that summer, I couldn't find her. I was already becoming something else.

I heard a door slam and looked down the street to see Dale walking toward the wooden board with the painted figure. He lifted a bowie knife over his shoulder and flung it. The blade stuck with a hard *thunk*. He pulled it out and threw again, making sure I understood this performance was for me, to show me yet another hurt he might inflict.

Jules wandered over to our rock, the one with *SWAFFHAM SUKS* spray-painted on the side, where she once peeled my sunburn, sending shivers of pleasure through me on a day that felt like a lifetime ago. Now she sat hugging her shins with her T-shirt tugged down like a tent, chin propped in the cleft between her knees. A strand of greasy hair fell loose and, as I sat beside her, I wanted to tuck it behind her ear, to show that I loved her, but I kept my hands to myself.

" 'Shout at the Devil,' " I said, reading her shirt. "You're into Mötley Crüe?"

"Tommy Lee's wicked hot."

"He's *alive* anyway," I joked. "That's progress."

She gave a little smile and then dropped it. "You were my best friend," she said. "Until Sylvia came along. Now you're going away to that fancy school."

"It's not fancy," I said. "It's just Catholic school."

"It's better than stupid Swaff High."

She was right.

"You think you're better than everybody around here," she said plainly, without anger. "And maybe you are."

"You're better than me at lots of things," I argued. "You could be a great musician. Or a scientist. Or both."

"How?"

"You can play 'Mary Had a Little Lamb' on the phone and you're wicked good at chemistry."

"That stuff isn't special. You think I'm special, Mel, but I'm just like everybody else."

"That's not true," I said quietly, because I knew it was and didn't want it to be.

Thunk went the sound of Dale's knife hitting the board. Tuned to her brother's temper, Jules pulled the jackknife from her pocket and poked the blade along her sneaker sole where she'd written *SUCK IT* over and over in black ballpoint pen, surrounded by pentagrams. I didn't want to be better than Jules. I wanted Jules to be better than Jules. I wanted her to accompany me into the world, to high school, college, and whatever lay beyond, but she was held back by forces I did not understand. It troubles me, even now, to admit there must have been much about Jules' circumstances I did not know, things that happened that she never shared, wheels turning deep inside that I could not see. Watching the knife in her hand, I asked myself if she was capable of the cruelty necessary to write the hateful words on Sylvia's garage. I considered her moments of meanness, when she whipped the frog's eggs in the swamp or chucked crab apples at my neighbor's dog. Abusing animals, people said, was the hallmark of a serial killer, the latest breed of murderer that the nightly news couldn't stop talking about, the sort that had seized Jules' fascination. Did she really want to be another Squeaky Fromme? Where else could she look for power? Maybe it was better, as a girl in that world, to dream yourself into the killer instead of the killed.

•

The last time I saw Sylvia was on a rainy afternoon. I was at the Mister Donut on the far end of town, sitting alone at a booth, drinking coffee, which felt like a forbidden, grown-up thing to do, and which I felt entitled to now that I was finally fourteen. My birthday had come and gone. There was no party and no cake, but I told myself it didn't matter because I was another year closer to adulthood and escape. I went to Mister Donut to be alone, treating myself to a pink frosted with rainbow sprinkles because it was the closest thing to a birthday cake I could find. I didn't notice Ray Cobb until he got up to pay his bill. I hid behind a copy of the *Globe* someone had left behind and eavesdropped as he stood talking to a pair of cops, all buddy-buddy, while they dunked their donuts.

"Is that a Crown Vic?" Ray asked, eyeing the black-and-white cruiser in the lot.

"Oh yeah," said one of the cops.

"How's it run?"

"Wicked comfortable. Probably the best domestic value you can have."

I imagined they would talk about Sylvia, outlining a plot to get rid of her, but they didn't. My imagination, however, was powerful enough to summon her, or so I believed when her Trans Am pulled into the lot. I felt afraid. But Ray took no notice of her, walking out as she came in, and I understood that he, god of fire, was never the Cobb I had to worry about. My heart pulsed to see Sylvia, but I didn't want to get her in more trouble with the cops, so I stayed behind the paper, watching as she took a seat at the counter, turned away from me. I wished we could sit together and talk. I wanted to tell her the things I was beginning to remember, the forgotten parts of myself that only became available to me because she existed.

In one memory, I would tell her, I am four years old. I know this because I'm at my aunt Shirley's house in Florida and she only lived in that house the year I was four. There are hibiscus flowers and saw palmettos in the yard and I am running barefoot across the rough, scratchy Florida grass, playing a game like tag with my cousin Kenny and the two girls who live next door. When they catch him, the girls cover Kenny in kisses, something they don't do when they catch me. I understand, for the first time, that I am not a boy. I didn't quite know it before and now I do. It is not a happy awakening. I go running to the other side of the house, where I sit on the steps and cry. When my aunt appears in the doorway and asks what's wrong, I know enough to say: *Nothing.* The Nothing stays inside me, accumulating shame, taking the shape of impossible longing. Years go by. I learn how to leave my body. I forget what I know about myself. Now and then, quietly, it makes itself felt.

In the next memory, I'm maybe eight years old. I am in my own backyard with Timothy, the son of friends of my parents, a boy I see infrequently but love because he is gentle and smart, unlike most boys I know. Timothy is maybe ten. He wears a blue sweatshirt, the color of faded denim and, to my mind, dolphins. I inform him that he is a dolphin and I am a fisherman. I stand atop a low stone wall and throw out a line, the other end of my jump rope, while Timothy cavorts in the waves below. I want, desperately, to catch him. His blue sweatshirt, the way it fits snug against his chest, makes him extra boyish in a way that feels ideal, the quintessence of all that is boy. More desperately, I want to be him. *Not to have, but to be.* I want a blue sweatshirt that will fit my body like dolphin skin and total boyness, a perfect merger of Flipper and Sandy from the television show *Flipper,* a semiaquatic hybrid, bare-chesty and streamlined. I want to *have* the dolphin-boy and *be* the dolphin-boy, the two desires braided into a mysterious, proto-erotic gender melancholia, saturated by the knowledge that I will never achieve such perfection. I am neither dolphin nor boy. Nevertheless, I toss out my line, again and again, hoping for a spark of magic, for the boy to catch on and let me reel him in.

I would then explain to Sylvia (if I had the words), that while I'm fourteen now, and it seems as if I'm coming awake, I know only a little more about the Nothing than I did as a child. It has rolled around for so long on the dark bottom of my ocean, accumulating an abundance of shame, anger, and envy, it can no longer be identified for what it is. Like a sea turtle so covered in barnacles and algae, you can't tell it's a turtle. It might be a rock, something not alive and not dead, moving only because the water is moving. It will take years to scrape it clean. It will never be scraped clean.

Though this conversation only happened in my reverie, I remember it as our last talk. In the reality of that gray and drizzly day, Sylvia finished her coffee and donut, dropped a couple bills on the counter, and walked out without knowing I was there. The police did not take notice. Nothing bad happened and maybe, fingers crossed, I could take that to mean that nothing bad was going to happen. From the window of the donut shop, I watched Sylvia swing into her Trans Am, as I'd watched her that first time, on another day in another place, before the whole world opened wide—and then collapsed.

•

The week before Labor Day, my mother took me to a special store that sold uniforms for Catholic schools. We selected one plaid skirt and gray blazer, five white Oxford shirts wrapped in crinkly plastic, five pairs of dark green knee socks, and a little necktie that crossed over and snapped, like I used to wear in Girl Scouts. It was called a *tab*, like the diet soda. According to Sacred Heart's guidelines, their dress code permitted a choice in neckties—girls could wear the tab or the more traditional men's style. At the mirror, I held the men's tie to my collar and tried to conceal my desperate desire. My mother glared and said, "I'm not spending money so you can look like a dyke." I put the tie back on the rack.

Since the day she found the Polaroid of Sylvia, my mother had gone cold, handling matters between us in a clipped and business-like manner. I believed her icy mood had everything to do with me. I did not consider the possibility that she was also going through a difficult time with Richard, a fact I found out years later and might have gleaned, had I been paying the slightest attention. I did not notice they were spending less time together and that my mother was drinking extra glasses of beer in the evening, letting her Jane Fonda workout tape gather dust, letting the tide of clutter rise, giving up.

We were driving home from the uniform store when it happened. My mother sent me in to Coogan's for a pack of Salems and a six of Miller Lite. I was on my way out, paper bag on my arm, when the noon whistle started whooping from atop the fire station. It wasn't noon. I looked to the sky for bad weather, but it was clear and blue. The only blemish I saw was a plume of dark smoke—rising from Sylvia's neighborhood. Did I drop the bag? Did the beer bottles break? Did my mother shout from the car as I ran?

When I got to Sylvia's house, every window overflowed with orange flame, roaring like a summer rainstorm punctuated by gunshot pops. I had never seen such a fire and I stood frozen in the street while the house thundered. It seemed impossible that anyone I loved could be inside that hell, and while I told myself that Sylvia was out, gone to the store for cigarettes, gone for coffee at Mister Donut, whatever, wherever, I whispered *please, please, please*, a useless prayer for the shape of Sylvia to appear at a window, behind a curtain of fire, to reenact her derby stunt, leaping headfirst in a silver helmet to roll across the yard and rise unharmed, fist in the air. But this did not happen.

I knew it was the Cobbs who did it. And Jules? I again recalled the time when Ray burned out the nest of rats, how Jules had smiled at the animals' suffering, her face aglow with what looked like cruel pleasure. I remembered feeling disturbed by that smile, and then writing it off as nothing. But now, looking for guilty parties as I watched the fire, I added the incident to the list of evidence, putting Jules at the scene of the crime, a Cobb among Cobbs, splashing gasoline onto Sylvia's house. Lighting a match.

People had come out of their houses to watch the fire, the way they'd watched the wild sunset that night I first met Sylvia and she uttered the word *sublime*. They stood in the street with arms folded, tugging their T-shirts over their mouths to keep from choking. I recognized most from around the neighborhood, the old man in the Red Sox cap, a barefoot woman in a housedress, kids on bikes. There were others, too. George Duffy, a muckety-muck in town, head of the board of selectmen, sat with his wife, Margie, in a pair of lawn chairs, entranced by the scene, as if they'd come to enjoy fireworks on the Fourth of July. Only later would I think that was strange, like so much about the fire. The way the town's siren stopped whining, but still no trucks appeared. And the sky. I will never forget how it remained relentlessly blue above the black plume, and how that felt like betrayal, like God had forsaken us. If you turned away from the disaster, the world went on. A man watered his garden. A woman hurried past, pulling a toddler in a red wagon. She had somewhere to get to and sailed calmly on.

For awhile as it burned, the house stood, looking like a structure from which a person could emerge, opening the door and walking out; until, with a discordant sequence of groans, the structure caved, like a house of sand, and stopped being the sort of recognizable thing that could hold a life. Part of the roof crumpled. A wall slumped in a shower of sparks. Panes of glass shattered musically like seashells on a wind chime. The fire climbed, devouring the leaves of the oak tree that shaded the yard. It seized the front porch where I first sat with Sylvia to smoke clove cigarettes and listen to her sing. Now its white columns turned into torches, the railing spindles a mouthful of teeth spitting flame. When the trucks finally arrived, the firemen went about their business methodically, you might even say leisurely, fussing with helmets and unrolling hoses, a pair of yellow ribbons that swelled with water. But it was too late. The house was gone. And Sylvia was nowhere.

part four

2019

It's that time of summer when you can smell September in the breeze, a time that always makes me eager for school to begin. Impatient to leave my mother's house, I endure one last sensitivity session with Autumn Biddle in which I keep my mouth shut and let her do the talking. I nod and smile and swallow my anger. I am good and quiet, the way I was taught to be. If I want to keep my job, I have to stop fighting.

Donna keeps harassing me about Dakota. Am I going to take her or what? As if the question is that simple. Turning it in my mind, the place I come back to is this: Since getting to know Dakota I no longer feel alone, in the way I always have in my family, in my queer singularity. I never imagined a child could remedy this loneliness. What Dakota is for me must be what I was for Sylvia, a relation from her native place, and I understand: I didn't just need Sylvia, she also needed me. But this seems like the wrong reason to raise a child. People tell themselves that having children is a selfless act when it is so much about the self. It's not like children are waiting around in some ethereal limbo, begging to be born. Parents want children so they'll fix something for them—loneliness, identity, the past, the future. I don't want to saddle Dakota with the weight of my unmet love.

After the sensitivity session, I find Donna in the living room, in front of the television. It is evening, the sky gone violet, the sun down behind the trees out back, just a few left where there used to be woods. I pour myself a glass of water from the kitchen sink and drink it standing barefoot on the linoleum. Looking out the window, I wonder what the real estate developers did with the rocks in the old woods, the big erratics I used to climb, where I hid Brenda White on the night she almost got away. I feel a peculiar pain, a longing for those rocks, the woods with its paths through greenbrier and fern, swamps and streams, the glowing-green mossy place where I found a cluster of jack-in-the-pulpit, their purple tongues alien and wild. In the woods I could be a boy, a soldier with a gun, a knight with a sword. The old Puritans of Massachusetts were right to fear the forest—it's where witches and other outsiders run free.

Dakota is in her room, immersed in her phone, and I sit down with Donna to watch a sitcom about two older women living together in a beach house. It stars Lily Tomlin and Jane Fonda. Donna laughs out loud, cigarette smoke streaming from her mouth, though I've asked her a hundred times to please smoke outside. She's been drinking more, too, beer cans gathering on the coffee table.

On the television, Jane Fonda fixes a martini. When I look at her, I think of my mother years ago, on this same living room floor, younger than I am now, doing the workout that promised to keep her body from falling apart. She was not fond of Fonda, but she wanted the body that would attract a better life. For her and for me. By the ends of their lives, my parents had come to different conclusions about the controversial actress. In my last phone call with my father, he brought up Hanoi Jane. "Boys died because of her. I'll never forgive her for what she did in Vietnam." My mother, on the other hand, told me, "She was just a kid when she pulled that stunt with the antiaircraft gun. She didn't know what she was doing. We've all done stupid things in life." I took that to mean that my mother had learned to forgive not just the stupid things Jane Fonda did, but the stupid things she had done herself, maybe the stupid things we all do. And what about my own capacity for forgiveness? My mother and father, my sister, and Jules, have I forgiven them for not being the people I needed them to be?

I keep trying to talk to Donna, to get closer to the big sister who used to cartwheel across our backyard, who taught me how to braid hair, and then vanished, leaving me with our mother's rage. She keeps waving me away, offering some mixed platitude like "No use crying about water under the bridge." We don't have much time left in this house and I want to be known by the last living person who remembers what it was like. I want her to understand why I cannot do what she is asking of me.

"Can I say something," I say.

"I'm watching this, Mel," Donna says, looking at the television. *It's Max*, I don't say. Sometimes she slips. It's not what you'd call a microaggression. It's just my sister not knowing who I am, holding an older version of me that she can't release. Maybe that's a kind of love, too.

"It was hard, you know," I say, "when you left home."

She sucks her teeth with impatience and picks up the remote, closes one eye at the buttons, clicks pause, and looks at me. I want to say something about how I needed her, how I missed her, but that isn't true. I needed someone. Someone to buffer me from the afflictions of my parents and tell me how to be a person. I missed someone, but it wasn't Donna. It was the empty space where a big sister should have been. The space that Sylvia filled. For a little while.

"It was hard," I say again.

"You think it wasn't hard for me?"

She can't hear me. She can only hear the howling of her own teenage self, a girl with two black eyes, dragged to Texas and set down on the road that would lead to this place, sitting on her dead mother's sagging couch with a belly full of beer, unpaid hospital bills, a son in prison, and a granddaughter she has no desire to raise. "Let me tell you about hard," she says, but she doesn't, though I wish she would. I would listen.

"You've had it tough," I say, giving up on the possibility of knowing and being known.

"Damn right," she says. "And with no end in sight. I'll be raising kids for the rest of my sorry life. You have no idea how good you've got it."

I hear an accusation, as if I should bear responsibility for her bad decisions, for my mother sending her away, for the rough road that led to Dakota, the object standing between my sister and a Caribbean cruise, rum punch in her hand, paper umbrella fluttering in the ocean breeze. I feel my blood rise and want to say something about how it's not my job to fix her sorry life, but I stop myself.

"No," I say quietly. "I guess I don't."

She gets up with a heavy groan, tugging her T-shirt down over her stomach, and lumbers to the kitchen for her purse and car keys. "I'm going down the Post," she says. "It's Meat Raffle Monday." When I offer to drive her to the VFW, she swats the air and goes out the door, leaving me with the television. It's still frozen on Jane Fonda in a blue Adirondack chair, at the end of her life, finally forgiven. My thoughts turn back to the woods, the rocks, the trees. To the shape of my life, formed by so many rough hands still holding me in their grip.

I turn off the TV and spend a few hours tackling my mother's last piles of clutter, boxes and bags full of nothing worth keeping, nothing that tells me anything I don't already know about her. She was a woman who wanted a certain life and didn't get it. Instead, she ended up with Donna and me, prizes of little consolation. She knew how to want, but no one taught her how to have—or to be. Over the years, her anger simmered down. She accepted and loved me as I am, a feat that I am certain took more effort than I'll ever understand. Through it all, my mother was a woman capable of forgiveness. Maybe that is why she kept the artifact I find next.

From a shoebox full of buttons and bric-a-brac, I unearth the Mapplethorpe Polaroid. It feels like a miracle. Here, again, is Sylvia. In black and white, pale skin and dirty feet, a crease across her middle where my mother folded her in half that day everything went sour. Sylvia who first saw me. I have not seen her face in thirty-five years and the sight of it unknots a tight coil. For years, I worked to snuff her out, dissolving her down to tissue paper, so I would not have to remember what it felt like to love and then lose her, all because my love took the wrong shape. I buried her. But the buried never really stay down.

That day of the fire, I stayed outside Sylvia's house until the smoke softened to cloudy gray and fizzled in the wreck. Firefighters walked through the smoldering remains, poking at blackened beams with pike poles, but the show was over. The Duffys folded up their lawn chairs and everyone went back to their houses.

"Go on home," a fireman shouted at me, like I was a stray dog. I ran all the way, late for supper, where my mother put a pork chop on my plate and we ate in silence. After I cleared the table and got ready to wash the dishes, my mother, in a rough approximation of kindness, took the sponge from my hand and said, "I'll wash. Go take a shower, you smell like smoke."

Under the veil of water, I put my hands over my mouth and sobbed. Though I was alone, I felt self-conscious and slapped my face, once, twice, as hard as I could, telling myself to stop being dramatic. But how could I not be? Everything was my fault. I had stolen the Polaroid. I had lied about the kiss. And while I did not stand on

Swaffham Green and accuse Sylvia of bewitching me, I was no better than the deceitful girls of Salem. In my adolescent logic, I was just as bad as Abigail Williams, touched by imaginary spirits, pointing a finger at Tituba, the dark outsider. I was the afflicted girl who had to be protected, saved from evil's invasion, and the only way was through purification by fire. Sylvia was dead because of me. Because I was greedy, like my mother said. I wanted too much.

After my shower, I stayed in the living room to watch TV, waiting for the local news. My mother sat at the other end of the couch, drinking her third glass of beer. When the story came on, I held my breath. The camera showed Sylvia's house, a pile of scorched timber, firefighters soaking hot spots, and I heard the reporter say, "One man is displaced after his house caught fire in Swaffham earlier today." I could not make sense of the words, and then realized that *man* meant Sylvia and *displaced* meant not dead. "No one was home when the fire started and there were no injuries," the reporter continued. "While the cause of the blaze is still unknown, officials say it appears to have been an accident." A sound came out of me, a strangled *O*, the choke of release. My mother said, "Your friend's okay," and went back to her beer. It was the best she could do.

Sylvia was alive, but she remained lost to me. I had no way to reach her; she had no phone and no address. As far as I knew, she never returned to Swaffham. Like my sister, she was gone, and I was alone again. I spent months waiting for a call or a letter, but nothing came. Maybe my mother intercepted the mail. Maybe Sylvia just wanted to move on, to remove herself from that town and the complications of friendship with a fourteen-year-old kid. I was not nearly as important to her as she was to me. This is simply true. I have since wondered why she even bothered with me. The conclusion I keep coming to is that she bothered because we were the only ones of our kind in that place, two impossible objects drawn together, trying to will each other into existence.

Now I am again gazing into Sylvia's eyes, in black and white, lost in the past, stitching her back into memory. I flinch when my mother's phone rings. It's after midnight. I pick up the receiver, expecting a ghost.

"Hey, little brother," Donna says, "I need a favor. Max? You there?" I'm here, not here, still staring at Sylvia. "I'm up the police station. Can you come get me?"

I let Dakota sleep, get in my car, and drive to the station. When Donna comes out from the back, she looks blurry, squinting under flourescent lights. I pay the $250 with my credit card and watch her fill out paperwork, collect her purse and shoelaces in silence. In the parking lot, she lights a cigarette and breathes the air hungrily, like she just got busted out of solitary on a life sentence. She left her cell phone in the car, she says, and couldn't remember my number, that's why she called the house. "My car's impounded," she adds, like that explains everything.

"Don, what happened?"

"Davey fucking Whittaker, that's what happened. He bagged me. For nothing. For banging a U-ey," she says. "Back in high school I let him feel me up. You'd think he'd owe me one."

"You were arrested for making a U-turn?"

"He followed me from the Post. Made me take a breathalyzer. It's entrapment. I was barely over the limit."

"You were driving drunk? You could go to prison."

"For a first offense? Nah, I'll get a fine, suspended license. Same shit, different day."

"Donna," I start.

"Don't bust my balls," she says. "Not tonight."

I do not bust my sister's balls. I drive her back to the house, where we take a couple of beers out to the porch. Even though I don't smoke anymore, this seems like a good time for a cigarette and I take one from my sister's pack. It gives my head a pleasant buzz. When the beer makes me burp, I hear my mother's burp. No one tells you this will happen, that after your mother dies you will continue to hear her voice in your own burps, an uncelebrated inheritance.

"I can't catch a break," Donna says. "Every time I start to get my shit together, something happens."

You happen, I think, but I listen as my sister goes through her litany, the hospital bills, the car troubles, the whole mess with Stetson, the burden of a grandkid. Her dream of a Caribbean cruise. She repeats herself, going over the same details, how she tries and tries but nothing works. She sounds like the target audience for those TV commercials, the wounded, the unemployed, in need of a personal injury lawyer, a new skill, a magic pill. I listen and nod, until she starts in about Mexicans causing all the problems.

"Did Mexicans get you drunk and put you behind the wheel of your car tonight?" I ask. "Don't blame immigrants for your own mistakes." This feels harsh and I regret it.

"Don't start with your socialist garbage," she tells me. "You're like that nut-job congresswoman, what's her name? She wants to take away hamburgers. She thinks hamburgers cause climate change. She wants to put windmills all over the place. Did you know windmills give you cancer?"

"Windmills do not give you cancer," I say. "I'll tell you what gives you cancer."

"Let's not start. It's been a long night. Let's try and have a nice time."

There is nothing nice about this time. I have just bailed my sister out of jail. The glaciers are melting and fascism is rising. My mother is dead and Amazon is putting a fulfillment center on the garden where her ashes rest, where the weeds have taken over, because I have stopped pulling weeds, because why bother.

"Fulfillment center," I say out loud. "That's a misnomer."

Out in the dark, something trips the motion-sensor lights and the yard floods into murky, surreal green. An animal freezes mid-gallop and stares at us.

"Coyote," Donna says in a hush.

The animal is vividly alive, a shock of the real and wild, eyes glowing like jade.

"What's in its mouth?" I ask and feel queasy when I see it's a dead cat, tail and legs hanging limp. Someone's pet. Donna stomps her foot, shouting *hyah*, and the coyote takes off trotting into the next yard, to the cover of the unmown grassy jungle. I hear the bell on the cat's collar softly jingling. *Nature*, I think, *red in tooth and claw.* Donna and I each take another cigarette and drink our beers, cool and wet in the warm night. For a while we don't talk. It's been a long summer. My sister is right about one thing: I don't know her life. In another circumstance, had I been born straight and regular, it might have been my life, too. Maybe I'm fighting slings and arrows, but I've also dodged a bullet. Earlier tonight I thought: It's not my job to fix my sister's life. But what if it is? What if this is the job of the survivor?

"I'm sorry, Don," I say, breaking the long silence.

She wipes her face with both hands and inhales, pressing her fingertips to her cheeks, and I see she's been crying. I reach over and take her hand. She squeezes back.

"I can't take care of that kid," she says. "I can hardly take care of myself."

We look at each other and I can almost see her as she used to be. Cartwheeling in the yard. Braiding my hair. Big sister. Lost girl. We will never know each other. Not really. I squeeze her hand and say, "Okay."

1987

Rewind and then fast-forward a few years. High school. A new world opened. I wore my uniform and blended into the sea of gray and green, where girls relied on hairstyles to express their group allegiances. Most wore it moussed into airborne configurations, bangs spiked and curled like rakes, and because many of those girls came from the town of Cooksey, this style became known, not affectionately, as the Cooksey Claw. With my asymmetrical style, I was embraced by a group of oddballs who chopped and shaved their hair into punk and goth arrangements, edgy confections sparked by shocks of color. They came from towns closer to the city and knew things I didn't, about bands like the Cure and the Smiths, and about films—that word, instead of *movies*—seen at places not the Shawmut Mall Cineplex. One girl played the bass guitar, another painted her nails black, and one was a poet who introduced me to the work of Sylvia Plath. I went to their houses after school and, on Saturdays, we met in the city to spend hours looking at books and records.

My vocabulary unfurled all at once, as if the words had always been inside, tied in a sack, waiting for someone to pull the string.

I remember the moment it happened. I was sitting in English class on a winter day, the snow-covered lawn outside casting its pristine brightness into the room. The teacher was talking about "liminal situations" and I said something haltingly about the liminal as a threshold between one thing and another, between awake and dreaming, conscious and unconscious. "It's the space in between," I said. One of the Cooksey Claws turned in her chair and called me a freak, but in a good way, explaining, "I just mean you're so deep and that's cool. You talk really deep." No one had ever called me deep before. The teacher asked what the liminal situation had to do with the phrase "The moment of change is the only poem," a line from Adrienne Rich. I answered, "When you write a poem, you write it while standing on that threshold, when you're about to change and you don't know if you should step one way or the other." After that, one girl sat on my lap in the cafeteria and told me she loved my mind. Another said, "You're like the ocean, you're so deep," and offered up her French homework for me to copy. I was a boy and those girls could smell it. All of this is written in my diary and if it wasn't, I might not believe it, how it happened so fast and in such sweet fashion, when a part of me, first ignited by Sylvia Marks, came fully to life among the girls of Sacred Heart.

My time in Swaffham got smaller. My bike sat under the porch and turned to rust. I almost never went to the Square or walked the streets, so my path did not cross Jules', except for one last time, during the spring of 1987. My mother had sent me to Coogan's for a gallon of milk and two packs of Salems. I was walking down the sidewalk, hefting the paper bag, when I heard someone call, "What's up, loser?" Jules sat behind the wheel of Ginny's El Camino, Old Brownie, a.k.a. the Shitmobile. She was grinning with a cigarette in her teeth, looking proud of herself as the car sidled up along the curb.

"Nice hat," she said teasingly. I was wearing a black derby I'd bought in Harvard Square and a pair of round metal-frame glasses, the lenses clear, no prescription. I thought the outfit made me look smart and British.

"Nice car," I said, using my sarcastic voice and hitting the *r* hard, something I'd picked up from my new friends, so it wasn't *cah*, but standard American, an absence of accent that I hoped made me seem educated and higher class.

"It's mine now," she said. "Want a lift?"

She said it so easily, as if nothing had happened, the years hadn't passed, and we were still friends. I was not about to forgive her, but she had a car, the gallon of milk was heavy, and I hated walking. I got in. Jules looked like herself only more so, blonder and thinner, more elongated and gamey, her eyes rimmed in red, cheekbones sharp as blades. Beside her, I felt dark and thick, as I always had. She flicked the cigarette out the window and banged a U-ey, turning the wheel hard, just missing a car going in the other direction.

"This is not the way to my house," I said. "In fact, this is the opposite way."

"Take a ride with me," she whined. "It's so friggin' nice out, it's like summah."

She gunned the engine through the Square, past the drugstore where we used to moon over teen magazines and drink Slush Puppies. She gave me a cigarette and punched the lighter. Everything she did had a sharpness, a certainty about what her body could do. When she lit her cigarette, pressing its tip to the red-hot coil, her fingers didn't fumble. When she propped her elbow in the window and made a one-handed left turn, cutting off another driver, she didn't hesitate. It was easy to imagine this Jules with a can of gasoline and a book of matches, ginned up on her own tough-girl swagger, the intoxication of youth and who-gives-a-fuck. Whatever the truth was, I wondered if I would ever know. The Cobbs were never arrested for the crime. No one was. People said it was an accident, but I didn't believe that.

When Jules hit the open farm road, she floored it and took us flying. I gripped the armrest, my stomach flopping as we bucked over dips, but when I saw her grinning with joyful confidence, I relaxed into it, the way you do on a roller coaster, submitting to the ride. She turned up the radio, the Who doing "Baba O'Riley," and we sang about being wasted teenagers, even though I was in the Honor Society and hadn't smoked pot since I couldn't remember when.

Jules pulled into a dusty turnout marked "Scenic Overlook" and shut off the engine. She took a pipe from the glove box and packed the bowl with fragrant weed, making me nostalgic for our afternoons in the underground house, the times we spent sitting in the cemetery grass, bare legs tickled by the yellow buds of hawkweed, and our moment on the culvert pipe, where we kissed, a memory so suppressed it felt as hazy as a dream. We took a few hits and Jules got out of the car. Through the dirty windshield I watched her climb onto a split-rail fence and stand up high, shielding her eyes to take in the scenic overlook. She looked heroic, I thought, a Viking girl surveying the field of battle.

"Big whoop," she said, gazing down a slope of meadow to a blue ribbon of water she called "some rivah."

"It's the Assabet," I said as I joined her, explaining how Nathaniel Hawthorne and Henry David Thoreau both went boating on it and how the name was an Algonquian word for "place where the river turns back." Jules gave me a look, screwing one eye closed, and I said no more, declining to mention that Thoreau's boat was named the *Musketaquid*. That would have been too much. At school, I was in Advanced English, and Sacred Heart taught me that showing off your intelligence made you more appealing, not less. It was hard to hold back.

"Assabet," Jules muttered. "Where does a queer like to get fucked? In the ass, I bet." This made her laugh so hard, she jumped off the fence and bounded into the meadow. I didn't think the joke was funny. I was a queer and sure of it now, though I was far from out.

I had my first girlfriend, a secret lover who bit her fingernails to the quick and wore a white slip that hung down below her plaid skirt, showing a bit of lace that caught my eye in theology class while we learned about the trials of Job. We would often skip lunch and meet in the chapel, a room next to the vice principal's office that was reserved for student prayer but never used. With pillows scattered on the floor, the lights off, and a romantic red glow from the Eternal Flame of Christ, it was the perfect place to make out. If my friends asked where I'd disappeared to, I told them I went to the library, and they called me a grind. Only Jules knew what I really was.

I followed her across the meadow to a spot where the grass was flattened, as if a pair of bodies had lain there, maybe kissing, or something more. We took their place, but did not touch, leaning back on our elbows to watch the Assabet. I plucked a stalk of plumed grass and stuck it in my teeth, giving myself a Huck Finn feeling. I took off my hat and glasses, lay back, and put my hands behind my head to look at the clouds and steal glances at the golden sheet of Jules' hair as it fell along her silhouette. We said nothing. The air was sweet and warm, rippling with river sounds. I considered asking the questions I'd been holding. Who wrote the graffiti? Who set the fire? Finally, I managed to ask, in a whisper, "Did you do it?"

"Do what?" She kept on gazing at the river.

"You know," I said stupidly. Sacred Heart had unlocked my words, but around Jules I could not form the ones I needed.

She turned, squinting at me over her shoulder, and the look on her face was amusement, like I was playing. "Have *you*?" she said, snatching the stalk of grass from my mouth.

"What?"

"Have you done it?"

She thought I meant sex. When I shrugged, she called me a virgin, swiveled to face me, and told me about a guy she was seeing, Mike from another town, like the boy I used to pretend to be on the telephone, good old Danny in his dungaree jacket and yellow work boots. She and this Mike guy did it all the time, every chance they got, she said, parking up Hooley's and going at it on the flatbed of the El Camino. They did it all over that car, on the seat, the hood, even the roof.

"One time," she said, "the cops came and put a flashlight on us and we freaked and fell off the roof. It was so fucking hilarious, we were howling our asses off."

Though I no longer loved her like I once had, I felt a prick of jealousy. I envied her boyfriend, of course, for having what I never would, and I envied Jules, for being a normal girl. Mostly, though, I envied the two of them for the freedom they enjoyed. They didn't have to worry about the things I worried about. For Jules and Mike, love and sex could be fun and open. The cops might hassle them, shine a flashlight and tell them to get moving, but they'd never be arrested for what they did or who they were. They'd never be publicly shamed. No one would tell them to die and burn their houses down. They had something I could not access. Back then we didn't have the words *cisgender heterosexual privilege*. The idea itself was not yet invented, so I had no way to think it. Without this and other related thoughts, I could not entirely exist, except in halftones, a bunch of dots separated by empty space. At a distance, I might appear continuous, but at close range, anyone could see I was built from clusters of bits and gaps. Over the years, as I've gained more words, those spaces have grown smaller, but they will never disappear. It doesn't work that way. That day in the meadow, above the Assabet River, I wanted to tell Jules about my girlfriend and the things we did by the red bordello glow of Christ's Eternal Flame. We might have laughed about it. But I did not trust her. I wish I had. I'm not sure what difference it would have made, only that it feels like a wound we never got to close.

On the ride back, Jules drove wild along that winding road, speeding through blind turns, crossing the double yellow and giving the finger to cars as she passed. She got me home safe and I watched her peel away, into the rest of her life, which would not last much longer. A few years later, she would flip the El Camino on one of those turns. I was in college then, in another state, and didn't think about her much. I still have the article my mother sent, clipped from the *Sentinel.* They used Jules' high school yearbook photo. She is outdoors, leaning against a tree. She is wearing a striped shirt with the collar pulled up high, and her hair is shorter than I ever saw it, fluffed into a dandelion cloud, shocked white with sunlight.

> Julie-Anne Cobb, 20, of Swaffham, died in a rollover crash on Oxbow Road early Saturday morning. Police say that Cobb, the driver of a two-door coupe utility, was ejected from the vehicle and pronounced dead at the scene. She was not wearing a seatbelt. Passenger Michael Voigt, 21, of Millbrook was hospitalized in critical condition. The accident occurred a little after 1:30 a.m. when the car hit a berm near Wampatuck Drive and flipped before coming to rest in an open field. It is not known if alcohol was a factor.

The field into which Jules was ejected was not the one from our last day together. I wish it were. I visited the accident site sometime after the crash and found it disappointing, a muddy patch at the edge of a cow pasture, hemmed in pokeweed and poison ivy, a place no body wants to rest. I regretted going to see it. I wanted to imagine my friend settling in a meadow full of fountain grass and flower, something that would have softened the impact, but Jules' death was as hard as her life, so maybe it's right just the way it is. You cannot change the endings of things.

What was left for me in that town? Its culverts and streams, fallen trees and dead ends, the woods quilted in rotting leaves, graveyards with their broken stones. The muddy bottom of the pond. My mind runs over it all. Trumpet creeper. Blackberry bush. Wasps breaking out of oak galls. And woven through every piece of it, the persistent residue of lost girls. Their names I will never forget. Brenda White. Jules Cobb. Donna, my sister. My mother, Irene. And Mel and Sylvia, too, the parts of us that did not survive that place and time, the skins we shed and left behind, like shreds of paper scattered after the firecracker's blast. Those fragments don't go anywhere. They sink into the earth and stay.

2019

When I go to meet Sylvia, it is already fall. My favorite season is not what it used to be. Global warming has drained color from the leaves; they no longer turn jewel bright. The air sits heavy, too warm and damp, so I am sweating in November under a light jacket. Harvard Square isn't what it used to be, either, ravaged by gentrification. The Tasty sandwich shop has been replaced by CVS. Uta's vintage store, where I got my suit and cowboy boots, sits shuttered. Nini's Corner, where I used to buy loosies, has turned into a trendy dessert chain. Everything looks cleaner, washed with bleach, all the rough edges smoothed away.

I am watching every woman who walks by, looking for Sylvia at the outdoor café that used to be Au Bon Pain, where I spent my high school Saturdays smoking clove cigarettes and reading the *New Yorker* magazine because I wanted to be sophisticated. The new tables are clean and white, but it's not so different. Except no one is smoking and everyone is looking at a smartphone. One addiction traded for another. I catch the bug of second-hand distraction and check my phone to see if Sylvia has texted. She hasn't. I wonder if she'll show.

After I found the Polaroid in my mother's closet, I searched for Sylvia Marks on the internet. I'd never before had the courage. To look would have been to risk the possibility that she wasn't there, vanished into the ether, or else passed away, killed like so many trans women. So it wasn't until after I found the Polaroid, after the sight of her brought her back to life, that I searched. I clicked on a few women with her name, but they were not Sylvia. One sells carpets in Saskatchewan, another works as a professor in New York, and one is a Twitter spam bot that tweets out nonsense phrases like "Pathogenic kindergarten cocky wsmnjq" and "Process-Oriented diascope bacterioidal." A few pages in, I found the right Sylvia. In her LinkedIn profile photo, she looks older, softer in the face, eyes crinkled behind a pair of round, rimless glasses, her black shag haircut gone silver and bobbed. Alive and well. I sent her a message.

While I waited for Sylvia's reply, my sister and I closed up our mother's house and handed it over to Jerry Logue. I don't know if the demolition has begun and I don't want to know. For now, the house remains standing, at least on Google Maps, where I went to look for it and found the current Street View image is from May of last year, before my mother's decline. Captured behind her screen door, in what she must have thought was a private moment, she wears a pink bathrobe and looks out to the street, cigarette in hand. Though her features are smeared by Google's privacy-protecting face-blurring technology, I feel that I am seeing something more of my mother, like she's an unobserved quantum particle in its natural state, expressing something of herself that could only be expressed when no one was looking. From this distance, she's not my mother, laden with all the meaning that goes with it; she's just a woman in a house, at the end of her life, watching the world go by.

Donna has gone back to New Hampshire, living free, but barred from driving into Massachusetts where she is on one-year probation for the DUI. She leaves next week for her Caribbean cruise; it's hurricane season and tickets were cheap. Dakota lives with me. They're trying out they/them pronouns, which comes as no surprise, and they've started seventh grade at Ampleforth, working with a tutor to catch up but doing well. I am also doing well. I have not been canceled. KT has graduated and no one mentions the scandal; they've moved on to other dramas. I am no longer teaching the course on LGBTQ literature, which is fine with me. Let someone else walk that minefield. I'm doing Literature and the Human Condition. "What does it mean to be a person," reads the description in the course catalog, "to make decisions, and live with the consequences?" We are studying *Paradise Lost*.

When Sylvia arrives, she spots me first, and she is smiling. I'm surprised by this graceful, silver-haired being, draped in a rust-colored shawl and sporting a pair of dangly earrings in the shape of maple leaves that seem so un-Sylvia. She puts her arms around me in a warm embrace and I hear her bracelets chime. She says my name, "Hello, Max," and we look at each other. She is thicker than she used to be, rounder in the face, and I wonder if she's had surgery to pare down her angles or if it's just the softening brush of time. She looks at me the way I looked at her years ago, the way people look at trans bodies, searching for traces of the past. I let her look, wondering what she sees and what she remembers, a girl with asymmetrical hair, a gawky amateur who didn't sit right in her body, now a man sitting before her, middle-aged with a thinning thatch of wavy salt-and-pepper hair, more salt drifting down into his once-black beard.

"You look wonderful," she says. I tell her she does, too, and when I start to ask about her life, Sylvia raises a hand, "No real talk until beverages," so we go inside and order two large iced oat matcha lattes. We both wear glasses now and when I take mine off to inspect the menu, a sheet of distressed paper full of trendy items like deconstructed cheesecake and sandwiches dosed with sriracha aioli, Sylvia tells me I should get progressive lenses. I tell her I won't adjust to them and she says I will, that everyone adjusts. She talks to me like she knows me, like she's always known me. We carry our green drinks to an outdoor table where she tells me about her marriage to a woman, their two children and recent divorce. I tell her about the scandal at school, and about Dakota and their pronouns. As a social worker at the local LGBTQ clinic, Sylvia says it's challenging to work with young people who are doing trans in a new way.

"I don't doubt the reality of their gender identities," she says. "It's just so different from my experience. They're not especially dysphoric. They want choices. I support them, absolutely, but in my uncharitable moments, I blame capitalism for everyone wanting their own special gender. It's like ordering at Starbucks, you know?"

"Of course," I say. "Remember those old Burger King commercials? Have it your way?" When I recite the jingle, "Hold the pickle, hold the lettuce, special orders don't upset us," Sylvia laughs, a light, crackling laugh that reminds me of her younger self, on the front porch of her vanished house, guitar in her lap.

"Oh my god," she says, grabbing my arm. "Have you been *they*'d yet? It happened to me last week. I was giving my Trans 101 talk to a group of social workers, and a cis woman, one of those super-woke white knights, you know the type, just assumed I go by they/them. My whole life I had to deal with getting *he*'d and now, after decades of difficult, not to mention expensive, gender work, I'm getting *they*'d? It's a new kind of mis-pronouning." She sits back with a sigh, exhausted from it all, but then laughs and says, "Do you know what we sound like? A couple of cranky old trannies."

"Careful," I whisper. "You're not allowed to say the T-word anymore. The kids will roast you on Twitter."

"Oh, for fuck's sake, I've been a tranny since these kids' parents were shitting their diapers. I'll call myself whatever I want."

Now I laugh. It's refreshing to talk this way, in the ease and safety of our shared experience.

"Can you imagine," I say, "if trans was cool when we were kids?"

"Who would I be today?" Sylvia wonders. "A lot less neurotic. But it isn't easy for young people. They're so critical of each other. Coming out in the age of social media is rough. Just think of all the stupid shit you did because you knew it would be temporary, not forever on the internet for everyone to rip to shreds. Would I have taken my clothes off for Robert Mapplethorpe? Well, probably. But you know what I mean."

The Polaroid hums in my jacket pocket. I almost forgot about it.

"Also," she continues, "I think we're at the beginning of what will be a massive anti-trans backlash from the Right. In our day, the politicians didn't notice us. We flew under their radar."

"True, it's not easy," I say. "But I do envy the kids for having more representation and acceptance. Dakota seems to be completely without shame. Maybe this is the generation that's finally going to topple, you know, capitalist-white-cis-hetero-patriarchal whatever. They're doing radical stuff. It gives me hope for our fucked-up world."

Sylvia lifts her matcha for cheers. We tap the plastic cups together and sip. If Dakota were here, they would scold me for using a straw. Sea turtles are suffering because of me. I am imperfect and casually criminal. A liar, a thief, a user of plastic straws. I slip my hand into my jacket pocket and touch the Polaroid.

"I have something that belongs to you," I say.

When I slide the photo across the table, Sylvia claps both hands over her mouth.

"Look at her," she says tenderly, gazing at the girl in the Chelsea Hotel, so many years ago. "Where did you get this?"

"I stole it from your bedroom. At your Fourth of July party."

I wait for her to react to my confession, but she only picks up the photo and looks closely at her younger self.

"That girl had no tits," she says, clicking her tongue. "Poor thing."

"Mapplethorpe Polaroids go for a couple grand, if you want to sell it."

"Never. I lost all the others. Left them in some girlfriend's apartment or somewhere. Who knows."

The fire, she means. She lost them in the fire. I don't say this. I don't want to remind her of something painful she'd rather forget.

"I was so young." She looks at me and says, fondly, "I can't believe you stole this."

"That's how it all started," I say. "That and the kiss."

"What kiss?"

I remind her of the day at Walden, when I kissed her in the warm sand and she told me not to. I tell her how ashamed I felt. She shakes her head, says she doesn't remember anything except a nice afternoon together. This seems impossible. For me, it was disaster, but for Sylvia? She takes a sip of matcha and rattles the ice.

"Was it a good kiss?" she asks flirtatiously, untroubled by the magnitude of the moment I am recounting, how it has reverberated through my life, a long-shuddering bell.

"It was awkward and quick," I say and saying this opens up the possibility that the kiss was not as momentous as I made it out to be. Maybe I was not such a terrible person. But there is more to confess.

"Do you remember my friend Jules?"

"Vaguely. Skinny blonde?"

"I told her about that kiss. I lied and said you kissed me back. I was bragging, I don't know, being stupid. And then Jules told her whole family. The Cobbs?" Sylvia shrugs like she doesn't remember them either. "Then my mother found that photo. That's when the shit hit the fan. Everyone went after you. Because of me."

"That's not right," she says, but I keep going. I can't stop now.

"The Cobbs burned your house down," I say, "because of me." I go on about that day, watching the fire, feeling powerless, how

I wanted to tell her I felt sorry for the whole thing, but never had the chance. What I don't say is that the fire, and all that led up to it, proved to me that my love was dangerous, too destructive to let loose on the world, and I have kept it buttoned up ever since.

"Max," Sylvia says, shaking her head. "You've got it all wrong. That fire was the best thing that happened to me. It saved my life. I got out of that town. I got enough insurance money to go to school. It was the best thing."

"You could've been killed," I say.

"I wasn't killed."

"I stole from you. I lied."

"You were what? Thirteen, fourteen years old? Kids do stupid things. Our brains don't finish developing until we're twenty-five. You didn't cause the fire. You weren't that powerful."

I feel small when she says this, like a kid, but it's okay. I'm the kid and Sylvia is Sylvia, the woman who leaped from a flaming car, bright and bold in her silver helmet. I shake my head. There are things she doesn't understand. About that town and its people. About Ray Cobb, god of fire. Ginny on the warpath. Dale and Jules with knives in their hands. I try to explain, forgetting that Sylvia comes from the same place, that she knows well its men, women, and children with their capacity for violence.

"Stop," she says, holding up a hand. "I'm going to tell you something I've never told anyone. If you ever repeat it, I will deny it. Understand?"

I nod but she makes me say it out loud. "I understand."

"I'm only telling you this now because you've got yourself tied in knots."

"Okay."

"Those people didn't set the fire," she says. "I did."

I let out a laugh of disbelief and ask if she's joking.

"That house was a disaster," she explains. "I couldn't sell it and I needed the money. I was broke. Nobody was hurt. Nobody went to jail. All that got destroyed was a place full of shitty memories."

The past buckles and warps into a new shape. My old picture of Jules wielding a can of gasoline fades and becomes Sylvia, splashing the accelerant on her mother's carpeted floor, lighting the match, watching the flocked wallpaper and the Jesuses and the bigmouth bass ignite and blossom into bonfire.

"How?" I ask.

"Doesn't matter. I knew nobody would question it. When a transsexual's house goes up in flames, everyone turns away."

She's right. After the fire, no one talked about Sylvia. My mother never again brought her up and I went on with the business of life and forgetting. It was as if she'd never existed. Now and then, over the years, I would ask myself if I'd imagined her. She had become translucent, a gauzy dream you can't quite grasp.

"Now do you understand?" she says, leaning in. "It wasn't your fault. Everything that happened, everything they did, led me to the fire. To freedom. They thought they beat me, ran me out of town, but they were wrong. I escaped."

Hearing this, I should feel free. Absolved at last. And I do, for a moment, but my thoughts turn to Jules. I discarded her for a crime she did not commit. It seems crazy now to think she could have set that fire, that my best friend, the girl who talked to me while I fell asleep and kissed me in the forest, could do such damage. My thoughts turn to Jules, dead in a field, unforgiven. While I was moving out into a wider world, she lay in the mud, grass touching her shuttered face, the engine of the overturned El Camino softly ticking. She made her choice, I know. But what if I'd tried harder to take her with me? I always thought I'd be the one to sink, that's how these stories always go—the Melanies get buried, the Sylvias are burned—but that is not the way it happened. I don't know if I'll ever stop feeling guilty for surviving the wreckage of that time and place, but at least I'm not the only one. Sylvia is here, as glorious as she ever was, with things she still has to teach me.

"We made it," she says, taking my hand. "We got away. That's enough."

Acknowledgments

I owe immense gratitude to Doug Stewart, a true champion whose insightful suggestions helped to shape this book; to Tom Mayer, who edited my work brilliantly, compassionately, and with great attentiveness; to Maria Bell for the enthusiastic support and advice; and to Nneoma Amadi-obi for the kind guidance and assistance.

To my readers Avgi Saketopoulou and Laurel Larson-Harsch, my deepest thanks for helping me work through the tricky parts with graciousness and sensitivity.

Endless gratefulness to Rebecca Levi, my first reader, who is always there through the best and worst parts of getting a book into the world, and who never fails to offer thoughtful, intelligent observations and loving support. And many thanks to my mother for teaching me early the value of storytelling and books.

One note on "the T-word": for a nuanced and detailed analysis, please read Julia Serano's essay "A Personal History of the 'T-word,'" at her blog *Whipping Girl*.